SCHOOLBOOKS & SORCERY

An Anthology of
Inclusive YA Urban Fantasy

edited by Michael M. Jones

For more information contact:
Riverdale Avenue Books/ Circlet Press
5676 Riverdale Avenue
Riverdale, NY 10471
www.riverdaleavebooks.com

Design by www.formatting4U.com
Cover by Scott Carpenter

Digital ISBN: 9781626016040
Print ISBN: 9781626016057

First edition September 2021

TABLE OF CONTENTS

Introduction

Welcome, my friends, to *Schoolbooks & Sorcery*. This anthology has been in the works for a long time, and I'm both thrilled and relieved that we've finally reached the end.

In many traditions, the number seven is considered lucky, or magical. It's not uncommon to see seven years as a term of service, or the duration of a spell or a curse. It's can also be seen as the length of an education; Harry Potter, after all, spent seven years at Hogwarts. So it's fitting, if entirely unintentional, that this project will have taken somewhere around seven years to reach fruition.

It all started when I saw a kerfluffle focused on a YA anthology, where one story had been sent back for editing because it featured "alternative sexuality." Needless to say, dear readers, there was indeed Outrage and there were Consequences because we deserve and demand better than that. Meanwhile, I, in a moment of hubris, decided we needed a YA anthology that encouraged, embraced, and supported queerness and diversity and "alternative sexualities."

Friends, I was young and foolish at the time, and I made a few mistakes. I miscalculated my own selling power as an anthologist. I miscalculated publishers' desire to invest in such a project. I assembled a tentative lineup and proceeded to lose almost all of the prospective authors by the time I finally found a publisher and issued the official invitation for submissions. And time marched on. I went looking for more authors, and more, until I finally had an actual Table of Contents. And time marched on. We ran a Kickstarter, and raised the funds for the anthology, and I issued yet another call for submissions because I realized we needed a few more stories to further flesh out our representation. And time marched on.

But here we are. And if this introduction feels a little self-indulgent, that's because I feel like I owe everyone a story worthy of the journey.

1

And of course I owe a heck of a lot of thanks and appreciation and gratitude to everyone who's stuck with us for the duration. The authors who never (openly) lost faith in *Schoolbooks & Sorcery* or its humble editor. The readers who backed us and trusted that we'd deliver our product. The friends and family who talked me down from my cat tree on bad days. Circlet Press, for giving us the chance we needed when no one else wanted to take the risk.

It's been seven years, give or take, since I started shopping this idea around and approaching authors at conventions. In that time, we've seen amazing progress in the field, with anthologies and magazines and novels and movies and TV shows all championing diversity. Representation is increasing at a steady, encouraging rate. The #ownvoices movement is producing some of the best material I've ever seen.

And *Schoolbooks & Sorcery's* mission statement remains the same as ever: to feature LGBTQ protagonists in magical stories of their very own. To showcase queer teens in stories where they can be the heroes, the love interests, the champions. And, to quote my initial call for submissions from all those years ago, "…to send the message that it's not *just* okay to be gay, it's okay to be gay and to have the same crazy, wicked, scary, seductive, exciting, magical, strange, funny, romantic, dark adventures as everyone else. To be all-inclusive, with the characters writers have been dying to write and readers clearly want to see, diverse and interesting, with an underlying current of tolerance and acceptance."

Younger me clearly had the stars in his eyes, but his heart was in the right place. I know now that no anthology, no matter how many stories it might contain, can truly be all of those things for all of its readers. In some ways, this may feel like a time-lapsed reflection of the past seven years, the project changing as the world changed and as my understanding of it changed, and hopefully that's okay as well.

So please, step inside. Come meet our protagonists as they encounter magic, struggle with entrance tests and final exams, first loves and bad roommates, identities and acceptance. Join them as they cast spells and break curses, brew potions and confront bullies. Find strength in their battles, and rejoice in their victories. And thank you for being here.

—Michael M. Jones
September 2021

Finals

By Seanan McGuire

Four girls running down a city street, dressed in the meticulously pressed uniforms of a private school: black skirts, orange ties, white shirts. Polished black shoes and tights in whatever color they choose, for the administration recognizes that some individuality is essential to a healthy student body. One wears striped black and orange, like something from a Halloween store. One wears bright pink, knees already ripped up from encounters with the pavement. Another wears staid gray, cool as concrete. The fourth wears no tights at all: she runs bare-legged and swifter than the others, reining herself in when she pulls too far ahead, her heels beating a staccato rhythm on the sidewalk, like she's wearing tap shoes.

She is not wearing tap shoes.

See them run, beautiful children of a beautiful age—for all ages, and all children, are beautiful if one looks closely enough, overlooks the things which do not seem beautiful on the surface, or better yet, learns to see those things as the most beautiful of all. See them run, each with her own gait, her own approach to the concrete, from our girl of the bare legs and phantom tap shoes to her sister in patient gray, who runs smoothly but with no hurry at all, at all, for her destination will wait until she gets there. See them run, and know them for the miracle they are. Now hurry, hurry. Class is about to start.

They run until they come to a rusty gate in a crumbling wall, sandwiched between a convenience store that boasts 15 big jackpot lottery winners in the last six years and an apartment building that has been thoroughly, utterly condemned, masked over with plywood boards and orange caution tape. Someone with canny eyes might see those girls slip through the gate, disappearing from the street, only for flickers of motion to show through the boarded-up windows, in the places where the light slips through.

Always the light slips through.

* * *

The students of Mrs. Pennington's School for Magical Beings slid, skidded, and charged into the hall just as the final bell was ringing. The echoes died, and their illusions went along for the ride, leaving them exposed in a way that would have gotten them substantially more than a detention, had it happened on the street.

"You almost made us late again," snapped their leader, the girl with the previously bare legs. She had two more legs than she had possessed a moment before, and they weren't bare anymore: they were covered with russet fur that matched the hair on her head, as well as the hair of her tail, which had been twisted into a multitude of tiny braids. She glared at the girl in the gray tights, who still had the same number of legs, but whose skin had taken on a pearlescent sheen. "We're going to stop walking to school with you if you don't stop making us almost late."

"Let's not fight in the hall," said the girl in the pink tights, her wings buzzing anxiously until her heels lifted off the ground and she was suspended in the air. "You know Mrs. Pennington hates it when she finds us fighting."

"'A good coterie is a happy coterie, and a happy coterie doesn't fight in front of others,'" chanted the centaur girl, and stomped her right forehoof in protest. "We're allowed to fight when somebody almost makes all the rest of us late! That's simple logic!"

"Is it now, Clementine?" asked a sweet, matronly voice from behind her. All four girls went still. It was too late: they had been noticed. Mrs. Pennington stepped out of the alcove that had been concealing her from the group, continuing, "It seems to me like that sort of logic would lead to infighting being perfectly reasonable if, say, someone should slip in the presence of non-magical creatures, and reveal the location of the community. It seems to me like that sort of logic would nullify the purpose of the coterie, for how could you ever trust that someone would be careful? Watch your words, my sweet girl, for speech is a form of serpent. Allow it to slither free, and there's no telling who it may bite."

"Sorry, Mrs. Pennington," murmured Clementine, pawing at the floor in shame as she looked down at her hooves. The other three girls shifted in uneasy sympathy.

"My forgiveness does not absolve you." Mrs. Pennington looked to the other girls, fixing them with her cool yellow gaze. "Well? Do you forgive her for her trespasses against you?"

"Yes, Mrs. Pennington," they chorused, in long-practiced unison. They might fight amongst themselves, but they were experts at the fine art of closing ranks against an outside enemy. Even when that enemy was their beloved, terrifying teacher.

Maybe especially when the enemy was their beloved, terrifying teacher.

Mrs. Pennington looked from face to face, searching for signs of weakness or dissent. She found none. Finally, satisfied, she smiled a thin reptilian smile. "Get to class," she said. "You're already late."

The four girls ran for the safety of their classroom faster than they had run to school. This time, the girl in the gray tights was at the head of the pack.

* * *

"Magic is…?" asked their teacher, a pretty dryad with birch-bark stripes on her skin and tent caterpillars slowly weaving a crown atop her head. One of them had fallen when she turned to face the class, and was now dangling, slowly twisting, on a silken thread.

Clementine put her hand up. The teacher nodded to her, and she recited, "Magic is the imposition of the will upon the world."

"Very good, Clementine. What is the centaur philosophy of magic?"

Clementine cleared her throat, cheeks flushing pink, and said, "That if it were easy, everyone would do it, and that means it must be hard."

"Excellent. Rosemary?"

"Ma'am?" The girl in the pink tights looked up from her desk, her wings buzzing a brief, frightened staccato against her back. A loop of rope held her to her seat, tied across her lap like a belt. Without it, she would have been bobbing against the ceiling, held aloft by her own constant, thoughtless flapping.

"What is the piskie philosophy of magic?"

"Um, ma'am, that it's easier than breathing, because some people

5

don't breathe, but they do magic anyway, so that means everything is magic, and the hardest thing is not doing magic. Ma'am."

"Very good, Rosemary. Now, who can tell me how we reconcile these two opposing schools of magical thought? Anyone?"

Maura, in her orange and black tights, hunched down a little further and tried to focus on her notes, which were a jumbled mess not helped by the fact that her calligraphy was still elementary at best, and a sloppy mess at worst. It was at worst a lot more often than it was at best. She liked Magical Theory class well enough—it was always interesting, and their teacher sometimes gave extra credit for bringing in particularly attractive caterpillars—but whenever it started down these paths of comparing and contrasting, someone would bring the human system into the conversation. The human system, which was twisty and confusing and why did they keep pretending that there was a system, anyway?

The centaurs had 100 different schools of magic, determined by which herd you were born into, whether it was wild or domestic or like Clementine's family, masquerading as human with complicated illusions and even more complicated cover stories. Piskies like Rosemary reached maturity in under a decade, and had 500 or so different schools of magical thought. The golems, like Suzie, were long-lived and only sculpted offspring once every two or three centuries, and even they had three distinct ways of approaching the magical world. It was in all the books, and those diverse ways of thinking inevitably came up in any deeper discussion.

So why did people keep pretending that humans had one school of magical thought, that there was one way of being a magical human being, and that that way was based on gender, and that there was no way around it? It was stupid. It was wrong. It was—

"Maura?"

"Yes, ma'am?" Maura raised her head, hoping against all common sense and prior experience that just this once, their Magical Theory teacher (who had never told them her name, believing, as all dryads did, that to share your name was to share your soul, and thus would not speak that precious thing aloud in the presence of anyone who was not already an important part of her life) would be kind.

"What can you tell us about the human approach to magical thought?"

"Um." Stall, Maura, stall, she thought frantically. But the whole class was looking at her, faces curious and expectant, and there was no way out of the question. She sat up a little straighter, cleared her throat, and said, "Humans have many conflicting schools of magical thought. We have never found a way to unify them into a single approach, which means that humans will probably continue to have arguments about how magic works until there aren't humans anymore." And arguments about whether magic was real, and whether magic-users should be put to death for the good of the species, and whether magic made perfectly normal people into freaks, made their daddies leave and their mommies cry at night when they thought no one was listening—

The nameless teacher sighed. It was a soft sound, like leaves rustling, and it stopped the frantic flow of words from Maura's mouth. She gulped, feeling the air move down her throat almost like a solid thing.

"Maura, you know that isn't the purpose of these discussions," she said. "We're here to talk about the dominant schools of magical thought amongst our respective species, so that we can have a better foundation of shared understanding as we go into our next unit. You do want a foundation of shared understanding, don't you?"

Not when we have to build it with someone else's tools, Maura thought. She knew better than to say that out loud. That sort of thing always led to a discussion she didn't want to be a part of. Not that her teacher meant her harm. Not that any of her teachers meant her any harm. It was just that sometimes they didn't think.

Another of the human students put her hand up. The teacher nodded toward her. The girl smiled brightly, directing it squarely and venomously at Maura, before she said, "Humans believe that there are two magical forces, male and female, and that all power flows from either one or the other. So girls do girl magic, and boys do boy magic, and even if someone from one force learns how to fake the other, it won't do them any good. Magic always knows."

"Very good, Jenny."

"Thank you, ma'am," said Jenny, but she wasn't looking at the teacher: she was looking at Maura, and still smiling that cruel, venomous smile. "I was glad to answer."

Maura hunched further down in her chair, and let the class go on without her.

* * *

After the bell, and after the other students had filed back out of the room—after their teacher had stepped back into her tree, effectively shutting herself off from the world—the rest of Maura's coterie swarmed around her. Literally, in Rosemary's case: she had unfastened her anchor belt, and now hovered with her feet easily three feet off of the floor.

"She's wrong and she's stupid and she probably smells bad," said Suzie, folding her arms like she had just conclusively resolved the situation.

"You have no sense of smell," said Clementine. "How would you know?"

"Because people who do have a sense of smell say that all the time, when people are wrong and stupid," said Suzie. "It stands to reason that it would apply to Jenny."

Maura laughed. She couldn't help it: the sound just came out. She clapped a hand over her mouth to prevent it from happening again, but still she felt the color creeping up her cheeks, along with her smile. But somewhere along the way, the wires got crossed, and her smile became an anguished scowl. To her shame, if not to her surprise, she began to sob, sliding her hand up so that it covered her right eye before clapping her other hand over her left eye.

"Aw, no," said Rosemary. "No, Maura, no, don't cry. This isn't crying time. This is getting ready for Alchemy time. Crying time is later."

Clementine glared at her as she moved to put her hands on Maura's shoulders. "She's not worth it, Maura, and she's wrong about you. Just because she's horrible, that doesn't mean she actually knows anything. If being horrible made you smarter, the forces of evil would have wiped us all out generations ago."

"Mom says the forces of evil are a stupid kind of smart," said Suzie. "Great at devising evil plans and wicked spells, really lousy at resource management and remembering not to install self-destruct clauses in everything. They invented golems, you know."

"I thought human mystics did that," said Rosemary, briefly distracted from fussing over Maura.

"Lots of people invented lots of kinds of golems, but it took the forces of evil to think that we needed to be self-aware and intelligent," said Suzie. "They forgot that self-aware, intelligent people sometimes ask 'why?' when you tell them to raze a village. We sort of wandered away. Our creators got defeated. And now we're an accepted part of the magical community, largely allied on the side of good. So see? I hate Jenny because she reminds me of the forces of evil. And she smells bad."

"I give up," said Clementine. "Maura, honey, please. You know she's wrong, and you know Suzie's weird, so stop crying, okay? It's going to be okay. You wouldn't be enrolled here if it wasn't going to be okay."

"I wouldn't be enrolled here at all if the administration knew about human hospitals," said Maura, uncovering her eyes and glaring at her friends. "This was the fourth magical school we tried. The first two were human-run, they took one look at my birth certificate and threw us out. The third was co-ed, but they wouldn't let me be in the classes for girls. I was six. I wasn't going to do anything that could hurt anybody. I just wanted to learn how to make my magic work, and I wanted to be in the right class."

"Wow," said Rosemary, eyes wide. "You were already a girl when you were six?"

Maura blinked at her, and then, in a very small voice, said, "I've always been a girl. From as far back as I can remember."

"That's amazing. I didn't become a girl until I was eleven." Rosemary flapped her wings a little harder, lifting her another foot above the ground. "We're all born boys, and then we have our second pupation right before puberty, and that's when we find out what we're going to be. It must be amazing to always know."

"...I should've been a piskie," said Maura. She shook her head. "Jenny still doesn't think I'm a girl, Rosemary, even though I am, even though I always have been. Her mom was in my mom's coven when they were both pregnant. We used to play together when we were really little. She was so mad when I started casting spells before she could. She got even madder when she realized they were the 'wrong kind' of spells. I don't she's ever going to forgive me."

"She can bite my hairy horse's ass," said Clementine, causing Rosemary to erupt into giggles. "Come on. We're going to be late, again, and Jenny's not worth that."

"Okay," said Maura, and rose, still drying her cheeks with the backs of her hands, to follow her friends out of the classroom.

* * *

Founded in 1821 by Mrs. Urania Pennington, of the Hyde Park Penningtons, Mrs. Pennington's School for Magical Beings was intended to patch what Urania—thus far the school's first and only headmistress—saw as a growing gap in cooperative education. The children of the wealthy and elite would always be schooled among their own kind, learning ancient wisdoms and how to brew wealth potions that required a pound of powdered diamonds to work properly. But what of the poor, the working class, those who had no peers among their own perishingly rare species? What of the children who needed to learn how to live in this new and changing modern world, rather than in the world of their ancestors? Urania Pennington wished to change all that.

Nearly two centuries later, she was still struggling to make the change stick.

She entered her Alchemy classroom one minute after the bell, as was her wont. The pause gave her students time to settle and reflect on the lessons to come. It also gave them time to remember that when your teacher was also your headmistress, in addition to being a manticore who had been cursed to live in a demi-human form, it was best to have your pencil in your hand and your mind ready to absorb as much knowledge as possible. Mrs. Pennington had never actually eaten a student, but the possibility was always there, lurking at the edges of their thoughts.

She liked to keep it that way.

"Good afternoon, class," she said genially, strolling over to the blackboard and picking up a stick of chalk. She liked chalk. She wasn't opposed to modern technology—Mrs. Pennington's had been the first magical school in North America to offer Computer Science and Computer Conjuring classes—but she liked the old, familiar feel of chalk against her fingers. She had it flown in from Scotland twice a year, and damn the expense. "Who's ready for this week's final exams? Anyone?"

Some hands went up. Not as many as she might have liked, and not as many as she would have feared—too many hands would mean that the class was overconfident; no hands at all would mean that none of them felt prepared to handle the material—but a decent number. Mrs. Pennington nodded. "Very good. Today, we're going to be isolating and purifying the humors. There will be a quiz at the end of the hour, and anyone who fails will be donating tears and urine for next week's classwork. Unless you want your fellow students knowing whether you've eaten asparagus recently, you will pay attention. Now…"

And she was off, drawing beautiful alchemical models across the board while her students hurried to keep up.

Each coterie had been designed according to the strengths and weaknesses of the students involved. Someone like Rosemary, whose attention span would never be more than a few minutes long, worked best when paired with someone like Suzie, who needed to be reminded that most people were made of meat, and were thus in what would seem, to her, like an unbearable hurry. The pairing of Clementine and Maura was similar. As a centaur, Clementine believed that almost any problem could be solved by kicking it until it went away, and was naturally inclined to see humans as beneath her. Maura didn't see anyone as beneath her, but she needed a strong protector, and her sweetness was just the thing to leaven some of Clementine's acidity.

At least usually. At the moment, she was sitting in the back of the class with her head bowed and her shoulders slumped, looking like the fight had been beaten out of her bones. Mrs. Pennington frowned, watching Maura out of the corner of her eye. The girl was purifying her humors, as she had been instructed, and there were no incidents involving Clementine's tail and the alembics this week, which should have seemed like a victory. Instead, it felt like a holding pattern of sorts, a brief pause before the truly difficult things began. It was wearying, and it put the spines on Mrs. Pennington's back up.

When the class period ended and the students streamed for the door, Mrs. Pennington approached Maura's desk. The rest of the girl's coterie stopped what they were doing and shifted slightly toward their friend, as if to protect her from their headmistress. It was a noble, if misguided gesture, and Mrs. Pennington smiled, just a little, to show them that they weren't in trouble as she said, "I need to speak to Maura. If you would be so kind as to wait in the hall, I promise the three of you that she will not be eaten, bled, or sentenced to unfair detention simply because you left her."

"But Mrs. Pennington—" began Clementine, before she was silenced with a mild glance and a raise of the headmistress's eyebrow. She gulped. "We'll be right outside, Maura, okay?"

"Okay," mumbled Maura. She remained in her desk as the rest of her coterie followed the other students outside, waiting to hear the door close before she raised her head and asked, in a perfectly calm tone, "Am I in trouble? Did Jenny's mother complain about me again?"

11

"No, child, and yes, every week. Like clockwork. I've considered asking her to pick up my dry cleaning on her way in, since I know I can count on her to be here for my office hours without fail." Mrs. Pennington sat gingerly on the edge of a nearby desk. "What troubles you?"

"Everything. Jenny. Finals."

"Ah." So much was now clear. "You're worried that you won't be able to complete your conjuring, aren't you?"

Maura nodded, very slightly. "Jenny says I'm not a proper witch, and only a proper witch can conjure the Autumn."

"And she says you're not a proper witch because...?"

Maura colored, her cheeks flaming red. "I'd rather not say, ma'am."

"Ah. You see, I thought it would have something to do with Jenny's mother and her remarkable fixation on your genitalia. I swear, I have never heard someone talk about something so irrelevant so much. It's like playing a broken record." Mrs. Pennington reached out and gently placed her fingers under Maura's chin, tilting the girl's head up until the two were eye to eye. "This is a girls' school, Maura. I opened it that way. I oversaw your admission personally, and I know that you belong here. I also know that you have never questioned who you are. Your sense of self is something which I quite frankly envy. So why are you letting her get to you now? What changed?"

"She brought a book to my house," said Maura, pulling back just a little, so that the headmistress's fingers lost contact with her skin. "It was about a man who was... like me. He'd studied men's magic his whole life, from the time he was a kid. He'd put up with people making fun of him for binding his breasts and refusing to pretend to be a woman. But when it came time to conjure the Spring, like he was supposed to, he couldn't. The leaves all turned dead and dropped off the trees, and the corn started growing. He conjured the Autumn. The whole thing. Because the magic didn't believe in who he really was."

"Ah," said Mrs. Pennington slowly. "And was Jenny there when this book was written? Or was her mother? Did either of them know this man, or know his heart, or witness this supposed botched summoning? The past is half truth and half fiction composed by people with a vested interest in keeping things as they have always been. Jenny's mother is a woman with a small mind and a smaller grasp of what is possible. If there were any justice in this world, she would have been born into a non-magical family, and we wouldn't have to deal with her. Sadly, we all have to pay our debts to the universe before we can receive our blessings, and for us, one of those debts seems to be the elder Ms. Sylvan."

"The book said it happened a long time ago," said Maura slowly. "Neither of them was there."

"Then you see? Maybe it never happened at all. Maybe the man was a woman who liked to wear men's clothing, but embraced her gender and was trying for the Autumn. Maybe he was one of those rare individuals who can summon both. We'll never know, because it was a long time ago. But I can tell you this, without hesitation: you are a gifted witch, Maura, and when the time comes for you to summon the Autumn, you will. It will come to you. Believe in yourself, the way all the rest of us believe in you, and," Mrs. Pennington paused dramatically, long enough for the sound of the bell ringing to cut through the silence, "get to class."

Maura got.

* * *

The rest of the week passed in quizzes and in questions and in increasingly dirty looks from Jenny and her coterie, all of whom seemed to agree with her belief that Maura was going to fail finals. They weren't foolish enough to blatantly attack her in front of her teachers, but they whispered and they implied, and by the time Friday rolled around, Maura and her entire coterie were nervous enough to chew nails.

"I still say we could entomb them in the gardens for 100 years, and make them into somebody's else's problem," said Suzie. She had already passed her finals at midnight the night before, when she had convinced the stones to rise up from the ground and sing her the songs of the long, long dead. She had been waiting for the rest of her coterie shaking and half blinded when they arrived at school. Her eyesight was returning slowly. When they did their senior projects, just before graduation, she would give up her sight completely, and would see through all the dust and gravel of the world. It was a fate she was almost looking forward to: blindness justified the fashion sense of older golems, after all.

"I wish," murmured Maura. "Who's testing now?"

"Dryads until lunch, piskies and pucas after lunch, leprechauns and luties during last period, and humans and centaurs at dusk," said Clementine. She pawed at the ground. "I won't be able to be there."

"Don't worry. We'll tell you all about how she failed," said Jenny.

13

The coterie turned. The other witch was standing in the doorway, with her own coterie—a wilted dryad, a faun, and a piskie whose wings were a bright creamsicle orange, who offered Rosemary a little wave—arrayed behind her. Jenny sneered.

"You shouldn't have come to school today," she said. "You could have failed privately in a makeup exam. I'll be there when you summon Spring all over the auditorium. And I'm gonna make sure everybody knows about it."

"Go away, Jenny," said Maura wearily.

"No," said Jenny. But she turned on her heel anyway, and stalked away, her coterie following her.

Rosemary shook her head slowly. "She really hates you. Why does she hate you so bad?"

"Do piskies do arranged marriages?" asked Maura.

"No," said Rosemary. "We don't do one-on-one the way you humans do. I mean, I know who probably laid my egg, 'cause I have wings just like our swarm-queen, but my nest-mother chose me out of the nursery, and she has three wives."

"Well, humans do," said Maura, in a gloomy tone. "Humans are really big into protecting magical lineages by making sure that every good little girl has a good little boy to marry, especially when they're born on the same day."

"Don't you and Jenny share a birthday?" asked Rosemary.

"Uh-huh."

"And didn't your parents think you were…?"

"Yes."

Rosemary fanned out her wings in sudden understanding. "Oh. I guess it makes sense that she doesn't like you very much."

"Yeah." Maura sighed. "I've been ruining everything since I was born."

Clementine whacked her on the shoulder so hard she nearly fell over.

"You haven't ruined anything," said the centaur sternly. "Shut your mouth. If you weren't you, we might've gotten stuck with Jenny in our coterie. You're the best thing that's ever happened to us."

"I think I can see colors again," announced Suzie.

Maura blinked once, and then joined the rest of her coterie in laughter.

* * *

Finals.

The gymnasium had been cleared for the human students, with four summoning circles drawn in the quarters of the room. Two were in use at any given time, at a diagonal from each other, while the other two were being cleaned and reset. Jenny had just finished summoning the Autumn into her circle, getting a few long stalks of corn to sprout from the floor while her pumpkin seed matured into a healthy fruit. She was in the bleachers, hugging her pumpkin and shooting smug looks at Maura, who was stepping up to her own circle.

"Begin when you are ready, Maura," said Mrs. Pennington.

"Yes, ma'am," said Maura, and opened her hand, revealing the pumpkin seed she had been clutching there for the last hour. It had left an imprint in her palm, so deep that it felt like it might never pop out again.

Boys got sunflower seeds. Boys got sharp little wounds, not deep flat ones. Maura looked at the seed in her palm, and bit her lip, and whispered, "Grow." The language she spoke was not English, or her grandmother's Gaelic; it was the old, slow language of witches, which has never been transcribed in this world or any other.

The seed shook as the floor around her feet burst into grass and violets. Springtime flowers. Maura looked down, her eyes going wide with shock and filling with quick tears. The violets continued to grow, becoming lush. Maura stood frozen, tears beginning to run down her cheeks. In a moment, she would turn and bolt; the motion was already beginning to manifest itself in little tremors of her legs and shoulders. Mrs. Pennington pressed her hands over her mouth, horrified.

Clementine kicked the gym door open, dragging Jenny's little brother, Jonathan, by the leg. His head knocked against the floor as she trotted toward Mrs. Pennington. Clementine either didn't notice or didn't care. She dropped the offending warlock at the headmistress's feet, pointed to Jenny, and declared, "She had him outside the window, summoning Spring into Maura's circle!"

"I see," said Mrs. Pennington. She turned to look at Jenny, who was suddenly pale. The girl's coterie inched away from her. For once, Mrs. Pennington had no harsh words about a coterie's duty to support one another. "Jenny Sylvan, we shall discuss this. At length. But first, finals must be finished." She turned back to Maura. The grass and

15

violets were dying around the young witch's ankles. "Maura? You may begin again."

"Yes, ma'am," whispered Maura. Still crying, she looked at the seed and whispered, "G-grow."

It burst into life, the pumpkin taking shape with such speed and ferocity that she almost dropped it in her effort to keep it from breaking her hand. All around her, corn began to sprout, maturing quickly into tall green stalks, which turned golden and put forth healthy ears. Maura laughed, and her coterie laughed with her, and the Autumn, the blessed Autumn, was incarnate and alive around them.

* * *

Four girls running down a city street, their arms laden with sacks of fresh-grown corn, heading home, heading home, heading home at last. The air around them tastes of autumn, of harvest and of loam, and the adults who watch them go can only smile. Oh, when they were that young and the world seemed that infinite; oh, when they believed in magic.

Four girls, running, bathed in light where it slips between the buildings. The sun is going down, but still the light finds them.

Always the light slips through.

The Delicate Work of Bees

By Emily Horner

The first time I saw Rosemary Zhou she was standing on my Aunt Violet's back porch, propping up a bulky camera in her hands, her nails glinting turquoise in the sun. She was wearing a sundress and purple leggings and new sneakers, like she'd flown straight from Brooklyn to my little corner of Ohio, and for a second I thought all these terrible things about hipsters who think they invented beekeeping and herb gardens. Then she put down the camera and let it dangle from the neck strap, and I could see her face, and even if she was a terrible hipster she was the most beautiful girl I'd ever seen.

I spent a solid minute just looking at her, thinking how beauty wasn't some supermodel thing, it was the curious light in this calm, almost plain face.

"Hey," she said. "I'm Rosemary. I'm doing a thing for the school paper and your aunt said I could take some pictures. You're Melinda, right? Do you go to Catholic school? I haven't seen you around here."

"Home-schooled," I said, and regretted it. It always led to way too many questions about my religion and my parents' religion and just how weird my family was, precisely. I suddenly felt awkward about the dirt under my fingernails, the mud caked on my boots, the basket of herbs and berries and mushrooms I was hauling back to Aunt Violet's place. But as soon as I put the basket down on the porch she took my hand and gave it a good shake despite the grime.

She started clicking her shutter button—at me, at the back yard, at the basket. "Did you bring back anything good?"

"The blueberries are just getting to where they're perfectly ripe. What is it you're here to photograph, anyway?"

"I'll take a bunch of pictures and see what kind of story I've got when

17

I'm done. That's usually how it goes. You know, to let the story develop organically. Your aunt said you might be able to show me the beehives?"

"Sure," I said, a little overwhelmed by her enthusiasm, how she said 10 words to every one of mine. "Let me go get a thing."

Inside, Aunt Violet was measuring something into a flask in the kitchen. I turned on the faucet and scoured my hands with hot water. "That girl doesn't know anything about us, does she?"

"She knows that I know more about keeping bees alive than anybody else in the county."

In other words, keep quiet about the whole witch thing.

It was a hard thing to measure out: you couldn't be so obscure that the people who needed you couldn't find you, but you didn't want to be showing up on the Weekly World News either.

I snagged a few pinches of herbs from the apothecary cabinet in the kitchen and ground them into a paste. The bruised leaves let out their oils, and the air filled with a sweet, green, medicinal smell. Just a small magic, friend-to-bees magic, and it didn't look like magic unless you knew.

"Put this behind your ears," I told Rosemary, passing her the little jar. "Bees are sweethearts normally, and there's no reason for us to be getting them mad as long as you don't act a fool, but it's better to be safe."

"Don't beekeepers have those smoke things?"

I nodded. "We've got one. But I like to leave them alone as much as I can."

She gave me a half-scandalized look, like I was some daring rebel.

We walked down into the meadow, past the rows of carefully tended cooking herbs and witch-herbs, into the patches of clover and alfalfa and locust trees.

"I've been studying Colony Collapse Disorder," Rosemary said. "You know? Hives suddenly all dying off, with no explanation, or too many explanations—pesticides and mites and fungi and everything else you can think of."

"So you want to know what Aunt Violet's doing right?"

"I don't really know anything about bees. But I'm curious if you have a theory."

"My theory is we worked hard and got lucky." I didn't say anything about the nights Aunt Violet stayed up until after midnight measuring one herb tincture or mushroom powder after another, looking up lore in half a dozen different languages, and once standing vigil while singing and cursing and gently lecturing the bees. Also in half a dozen different languages. "But I also think, if you insist on spraying everything with bug spray, don't be surprised when the bugs you like die too."

Rosemary stopped where the locust branches were hanging over us. For a second I thought she was going to take a picture—but then she just stood, straight and tall, and listened. To the hum of the bees, the chirp of the sparrow close by, the clear whistle of a wren further away. The air felt like it was wrapping you up in something gentle and fragrant, like it does at the beginning of summer.

"You get lonely out here?" she asked. "I mean—I know home-school kids aren't automatically isolated. It just doesn't strike me that your family's the type to spend all day driving you around to softball and youth orchestra."

I smiled at that, because they weren't, but I wasn't the type to want to go, either. How weird would it sound if I talked about being friends with the dogs and the bees and the goats?

"I like it," I said. "I don't need all that. But right about when I was 12, 13, all the neighbor kids decided I was too weird to be friends with. I could've done with somebody my age who had more sense than to tease me for being a dirty hippie."

She snapped a picture of me as I walked up to the beehive, talking my soft patter: "Hi there bees, don't mind us, just taking a look around." She snapped one as I used a hive tool to jimmy off the cover of the hive, no gloves, like I was used to doing. I took out the frames to show her the cells with the honey, and the pollen, and the larva. Bees were buzzing around us, squirming all around the frames, lighting on my hand and my face and then taking off again. I'm showing off for her, I thought; I'm showing off for her and it's a silly thing, it's nothing but pride. All right, then, why shouldn't I be proud of what I could do?

There was a yelp, and then, "Oh, crap!"—there was the thunk of the camera falling from her hands and getting caught by the neck strap. I looked up, and before I could even look over to Rosemary, I noticed the bees. They had become cautious, and focused, in the way they flew and circled. These weren't swarming, attacking bees. They were bees who had noticed a threat.

"Okay, babies. It's all right. It's all right, babies." Gently, slowly, I slid the frame I'd been holding back into the hive, and put on the cover, and backed away.

19

I turned back to Rosemary, once the bees had started to go back to their feeding and foraging. "You got stung?"

"Yeah. It's not bad or anything. But—yeah." Her voice snapped with resentment.

"Come back to the house. I've got something for it."

"Maybe you should've used the smoker."

"Sorry," I said, sulking. It felt reckless and stupid, now, that I hadn't. But my magics had betrayed me, too, and that was the floor falling out from under me.

"I wasn't acting a fool."

"I know," I said.

Back at the house we sat down across from each other on the bar stools in the kitchen. I brought tweezers, alcohol, home-made bee-sting paste—another small magic I'd learned from Aunt Violet.

"I'm fine doing it myself," she said, but she let me take her hand and pluck out the stinger from the flesh at the base of her thumb. It was a shockingly intimate moment, to be hovering my face so close to her hand that my nose got the full strength of her perfumed lotion. It made my heart freeze up. I couldn't even look her in the eye when I put on the bee-sting paste.

"Sorry. I should've used the smoker. I was being show-offy and... I thought we were safe, I really did."

"Well, art is pain," Rosemary said with a small smile. "This stuff is actually really good, though. You made it yourself?"

"Yeah."

"So what else have you solved, besides bee-stings? Homework? Siblings? Plucking your eyebrows?"

I laughed, because it meant I was forgiven, and because there wasn't any way to tell the truth.

Rosemary stayed past supper. She took another crack at photographing the bees, and later I took her to see the workshop, with its mortars and pestles, scales, cabinets, oils, notebooks. We had jars of apple butter, blackberry liqueur—and on the higher shelves, with their mysterious labels, tinctures and pastes for love and heartache, forgetting and remembering, salves for the skin and the heart. I got vague when she asked about those, and then she stopped asking.

"You're not really home-schooled," she said, out of nowhere. We were out on the back porch again, under the stars, under the smell of lilacs. "You're apprenticing in your folks' line of work."

"I do geometry. I do Latin. They make me do a big portfolio every year to prove to the authorities my folks aren't just letting me run wild. But this is my work, it was always going to be my work, and that's how it ought to be."

"I can't decide whether that's really sad or not." Rosemary rested her head on crossed arms and looked at me doubtfully.

"Maybe it would be really sad for somebody who isn't me, and they should be lucky I got this gig instead of them."

"Don't get me wrong, school's horrible, but there's people to go to the diner with, and go to the movies with, and—you've just got goats and bees and all these stars and nobody to dance under them with."

"Have you got somebody to dance under the stars with?"

"Well, you know how it is. This is Nowheresville and I'm pretty damn gay."

"I'm pretty damn bisexual," I said, giving her a daring-myself look, a going-in-the-beehive-without-the-smoker look. "Which should be easier, in theory."

She grinned. "Twice as many options for a date on a Saturday night doesn't actually help when there's nobody around but bees, huh?"

I was formulating plans for hauling the laptop and the Bluetooth speaker out to the front porch for dancing when a car horn honked. "That's my stepdad," Rosemary said. She threaded her way between the rows of plants to the front of the house. I caught her by the hand, and she turned around, and for a moment we just stared at each other, like we wanted to drink each other up with our eyes.

She turned away first. "I can find you on social networking places, right? So I can send you the pictures?"

"Yeah," I said. My mouth was dry. I combed through my brain to find the right spell to stretch this out just a little longer—and already she was in the passenger seat, swinging her legs in, tossing her camera down.

* * *

The first hint of real trouble came the next morning. I started staring out the window in the middle of going over Titus Andronicus; I forgot so many of my math tools that geometry class turned into a house-wide hunt for the compass and ruler and protractor; I stepped barefoot in the dog's water dish and went through the family room hopping on one foot and yelling all the worst words I knew.

21

"This isn't like you," Dad said after I had toweled off my foot and come back downstairs. "I'd hardly expect it from one of my middle schoolers, on their worst days."

Aunt Violet was only in charge of my witch education. My mother apprenticed as a witch, but now she did less of the day-to-day witching and more of the nitpicky money stuff the family business needed to survive; Dad taught middle school history, and I got the full dose of artificial school-like product (he insisted on calling it "academics") from him on weekends and during the summer. It was Saturday—hence Titus Andronicus.

"I had a concentration spell," I said. "And an organization spell. And a clumsiness spell. I refreshed them in the morning like always."

"Did you smell them?"

"Yes, I smelled them," I said, grouchily. Then I went upstairs and actually smelled them.

Witchcraft is as much about learning to smell as it is about learning to grow herbs and combine them in the right ways. A spell that turns out right has a different smell from one that turns out wrong—sometimes it's the wrong ingredients, sometimes it's the weather, or the witch, or the technique, or a million other things. Sometimes it's a sweeter scent when you get it right, and sometimes it's harsher, or more bitter, or sometimes you get a strange note out of nowhere, like the licorice smell from a concentration charm that doesn't use any fennel or anise in it. Aunt Violet knew her spells so well that she could brush past my shoulder and say, "Your concentration's off, do it over," but I usually had to take a few deep sniffs to get anything.

So I stood there in the bathroom, sucking in air and feeling ridiculous and trying to deny that I'd gotten everything wrong this morning. Then I remembered the friend-to-bees spell. Did I get that wrong, too? Was that why Rosemary got stung? I tried to remember the smell, and all I could remember were the lilacs, and her hand lotion.

"I need to go over to Aunt Violet's house," I said.

"And so you will," Dad said, "After we finish this play. It shouldn't be as boring as all that. It's certainly bloody enough."

I didn't argue, but I didn't stop wondering, either. I wondered about Shakespeare's tragedies, where people who abuse their power always die violently. People who are too weak to use their power well die violently. It's very medieval—it's not quite a sad ending. In a way it's God doing the scut work of setting the world to rights again.

One day I could work spells, and the next day I couldn't. And all that changed in between was me falling for Rosemary.

When you think about it rationally it's hard to believe that the force of divine power that inhabits the earth and the trees and the grass cares awfully much about whether a person likes girls or boys or both or people who are neither girls nor boys or whether they like nobody at all. And while somewhere out there witches might exist who would go all Focus on the Family on you, I had never met one in all my years of witch summer camp and witch family potlucks. But when you read the old books, and you get to the passages on raising children in a witch family and you read "The daughters with an off-kilter balance of masculine and feminine energy may never be destined to take up the family trade," or "Young ladies may well be skeptical of marriage, but to be skeptical of boys altogether is a worrying sign"—how do you read something like that without your heart skipping a beat? You laugh about how silly folks were in the old days, and then your heart clenches up around the idea that it could be true.

When I finally got to Aunt Violet's, I hurried up with my usual chores while she finished some potion she was working on over the gas stove. After I was done I stood over her shoulder, watching like I did sometimes, trying to find the right moment to say anything.

"Melinda, Lavinia Taylor still needs 25 wedding charms. It's a big task to handle by yourself, I know, but it's a rush job and I think you're up to it."

"Um," I said, suddenly embarrassed to bring my worries to my aunt who never had any patience for nonsense. "I don't know if I can."

"It's nothing you haven't practiced a dozen times before."

"Yeah, but—I don't know if I can. Something's going wrong with my spells."

"Hmm." Aunt Violet frowned. The potion turned subtly from purple-gray to gray-purple—I ran to get the clean flasks from the pantry, and we worked as a team, her pouring out the liquid, me corking the flasks and wiping off any liquid that poured down the edges. It was only when we were done, with the saucepan soaking in the sink and all the flasks lined up in the cupboard, that she spoke to me. "This isn't a simple crisis of confidence. You're too fast, and too good, out there."

I wanted to argue—that wasn't magic, that was just work. But Aunt Violet hated it when people argued with compliments.

23

"Let me watch you," she said. "On the wedding charms."

We sat down at the bench in the workshop. Aunt Violet would take a small round stone and twist loops of wire around it until it was held firm in the wire; and then I would thread bits of leaves and stems and flowers through the wire. I didn't like Aunt Violet looking over me. It was hard, precise work, choosing the right herbs, and choosing the right way to place them into the design. Part of the magic is beauty, and part of it is the complex formulas I spent years studying, balancing different kinds of energy with each other. But I knew this so well. I finished the charm, and to my eyes everything seemed right.

To my nose it was wrong.

"I see what you mean." Aunt Violet held up my eyelids and looked into my eyes, and she put her hand on my forehead, and she sniffed my wrist. "Well," she said at last. "These things happen, especially when you're young. Trade places with me. You'll do the wire bits, I'll do the herbs."

She was so practical with it, and so gentle, that I got to work and didn't say anything, but as the charms piled up on the corner of the table, I felt sadder and sadder. More and more like I was being punished for something that wasn't my fault. There were all these questions in my head that would sound foolish if I said them out loud, questions I didn't even want answers to.

When all of the charms were finally done, she sent me back inside to watch cartoons. She brought me a potion mixed with blueberry iced tea from the pitcher in the fridge. After laying the
tray on the coffee table, she knelt by me and gave me two taps on the forehead like she did when I used to work myself in knots studying some little point of magic.

"Rest for a while. This doesn't last, for witches who are faithful to themselves and faithful to their craft."

How could I even know for sure if I could be both?

I didn't want to think about it. I didn't.

* * *

Sometime later, the doorbell rang, and Aunt Violet called out without opening the door, "That's Rosemary. She's looking for you, not me."

I sat up, with a jolt of terror that she was going to find me lounging in front of the TV watching Spongebob. "Tell her I'm not here."

And yet, God, for a second I was so happy that she was here, here to see me.

"Don't," I said.

If I could fix this by giving her up, then—I would. She was just a pretty girl. She wasn't my family, my career, my whole life's work. But if I had to renounce her forever, I could do it after I went to the door and saw what she wanted.

"Can we talk in private?" she said as soon as I opened the door. She wasn't put together like she was the day before. No makeup, no jewelry, chipped nail polish and her mouth set in a worried line. I still more or less wanted to just stare at her.

I poured her an iced tea and took her up to the guest room. We both sat on the bed, because there wasn't anywhere else to sit, and maybe she felt as awkward about it in the back of her mind as I did, but it didn't matter.

"Back in Sunset Park I used to know a witch. Winnie Lang. She used to babysit for me," she said. "I thought I shouldn't bring it up, because it's none of my business, but—I know what the deal is."

"Okay."

"I have this friend at school. Okay? It's not me, and it's not a girl I'm into. Just for the record. She really is a friend."

She waited for me to nod that I understood before she went on.

"She had this boyfriend, and he's a major creep, and she broke up with him once and he did all this romantic-stalkery stuff until he convinced her to get back together with him, and now they're broken up again, and he's putting her through this wringer again. So I was thinking maybe you had something that could make him leave her the hell alone."

"You better go see my Aunt Violet about that. I'm not really —"

Rosemary shook her head, with real fear in her eyes. "If she thought she could trust adults with this, she would've already gone to her parents, or the school counselor. They're just—but don't you think it's partly your fault? But don't you feel sorry for him? But he's so sweet and harmless?"

I dropped my head, stared at my hands. I didn't want to say no to her. I didn't want to try, and fail.

But God, if I tried it and it worked, and I didn't have to admit being scared and being a failure and having lost the only thing that made me halfway interesting. Maybe there wasn't one chance in 100 that I'd succeed, but if the alternative was just to say I couldn't do it, I was in a gambling mood.

I went down to the kitchen. I measured herbs (and Rosemary thought it was hilarious that I had to borrow my aunt's "drug-dealer scale.") Half a dozen ingredients, dried herbs and dried flowers and bark fresh-stripped from a tree in the back yard, all went into the pot with a pint of goat milk, and I turned the heat on as low as it would go and watched for it to start to bubble.

Through it all, Rosemary had her head over my shoulder, smelling when I smelled, swiping her finger through the hot milk when I did.

"Hey, you better not accidentally have any going-away spell," I said.

She laughed. "Oh yeah? You trying to keep me around?"

I didn't mean it that way—really, any magic not meant for you is sure to be a bad idea, accidentally ingested—but having said it, I just said "Well," and kept stirring.

She leaned her head, just barely, on my shoulder.

Fifteen minutes. Nothing happened. I was thinking about what it was to have her head on my shoulder like that, and it felt like happening on a wild animal in the woods and knowing that you'd only be able to keep watching it if you stayed totally still and silent.

I was weirdly happy and almost able to ignore that knot of fear in my head about what if this didn't work.

"Is it done?" Rosemary asked after a while, shifting away from me.

"Not yet," I said.

"Did you do everything right?"

"You saw how carefully I measured all that."

"Once I made muffins with half a cup of salt instead of half a cup of sugar."

I turned and looked at her, one eyebrow raised. "You want me to name every ingredient I put in there and how I know I used the right one instead of something that just looks similar?"

She shut up, and I shut up, afraid that I was scared enough and mad enough to say something awful.

"Can you do me a favor though?"

She nodded.

"Down in the basement, there's some racks of wine bottles and things. Can you go look for a bottle of homemade peach mead?"

"Mead?"

"Honey wine. It's in a wine bottle but sort of the color of apple juice."

I felt bad for asking her to rummage around in somebody else's basement, but then she went off down the stairs. I put my head against the wall and let out a long breath, then opened the door to the workshop. "Can you fix this?"

Aunt Violet pushed the wooden spoon around the sides of the pot and lifted the un-potion up to her nose. "I can't. Thought I told you to give this a rest for a while."

"She asked me for help," I said. "Anybody else, I'd just have said no, I'd have told them to come ask you. I don't even know her that well and I'm trying to impress her, I can't figure out how to back down from anything, I can't figure out how to be nice, even. I don't have any idea how I'm going to shake this thing off, and if it's not her, it's just going to be somebody else, and is this why the books say queer girls can't be witches?"

Aunt Violet's eyes widened. She turned the heat off and walked me away from the stove.

"Do you think it's possible to be a good witch while you're fighting yourself? While you're tied up in knots between the person you are and the person you're trying to be, or trying to pretend to be?"

"It's not really ideal," I admitted.

"Then consider, perhaps, how many girls over the centuries have ended up locked in wars with themselves for one reason or another."

She smelled my goat's milk mixture again. "You haven't gone wrong here," she said, and she swept out of the room and shut the door behind her.

I stood there a few moments, leaning on the kitchen counter, feeling like the air had been blown out of my lungs. Only when I heard footsteps on the stairs did I light the stove again and start lazily stirring the pot.

Rosemary put the mead on the counter and inspected what I was doing. "Was I being a jerk, before?"

"No," I said. "Maybe I was. Maybe you're just scared for your friend and I'm just scared I'm not a good witch like I thought."

"I'm okay with you being an evil witch." She shrugged. "Was the mead just to get rid of me?"

"Half. Um—are you allowed to drink?"

"A little. If there are adults around, and I stay off the roads."

"The truth is, I don't know if I can do this. I don't even know if I can be a witch anymore. But I would like to sit out on the porch with you

27

and have some fresh blueberries and some mead, because I think I like you."

Even as I was saying that I felt like I was prying the words out of my mouth, and I had to keep my eyes on the potion and not look at her at all, but then I was done, and the inside of my head felt like I'd put down something heavy.

"Sounds like a plan," Rosemary said, and even if I could tell she was disappointed that the go-away spell hadn't turned out she was back to being cheerfully sarcastic as she helped me wash the blueberries and toss them with sugar, and pour out the mead into plastic house-party cups.

And then, as I started for the door, she turned back.

"Hey, we better not abandon this on the stove, because it's starting to smell weird. I don't know if it's burning or something."

I came over and I stuck my face in the pot because I wanted to be sure, I wanted to breathe in the full smell of it, and the heat and the fumes were almost enough to choke me but I was so happy, I could hardly keep calm well enough to get the flasks out of the pantry and pour out little servings of the potion. Rosemary kept asking me, "Wait, really?" and "What happened?" and I didn't know what to say.

I just took her hand and squeezed it tight and kept breathing in all the sweetness and all the bitterness of the air.

All that Matters

By Elizabeth Shack

Jason's sneakers squeaked on the gym floor as he fidgeted on the hard folding chair. He watched the current competitor go through his spell sequence in fluid gestures. Inside the protective dome, colors burst into being like fireworks. No sound escaped.

"You'll do fine," Kevin said. His voice shook a little.

Jason elbowed him gently. "Relax! You did great. It's over."

"It's not over until I find out if I'm in. You're lucky you're going last."

Jason grimaced. "Yeah, it gives me plenty of time to imagine disasters." Sure, he wouldn't have to wait long to find out if he'd been accepted to the Chicago College of Magic's summer program. Or to predict how angry his parents would be when he told them he couldn't help on the farm this summer. He shoved that thought away and focused on the student in the dome.

The boy's left foot skidded on the polished gym floor, and his spell faltered. Fire slammed into the inside of the dome. The boy dodged out of the way, and the audience in the bleachers gasped. Jason dug his fingers into his legs until the other boy scrambled up and calmed the flames, panting.

Someone snickered. It was a familiar snicker. Zeke never missed a chance to laugh at someone else's misfortune. Jason reached out for Kevin's hand and laced their fingers together. Kevin's shoulders drooped, but by unspoken agreement, they ignored Zeke.

"You can't do worse than I did," Kevin said, all the spirit gone out of his voice. "I couldn't even hold a class three illusion for 30 seconds. My dad's going to be so disappointed."

They both looked up into the bleachers, packed with the parents of

29

the high school juniors and sophomores trying out for a spot in the prestigious summer program. Some of them had brought younger siblings to watch. Kevin's dad sat halfway up the left side. He'd come down from his job at one of the federal research labs in Chicago to watch his son compete. Jason felt like everyone's parents were here, except for his.

"No, he won't," Jason said. "He'll take you out to dinner anyway. Besides, you did better than most of the others." Kevin had probably made it. That just made Jason more nervous. If Kevin made it and he didn't, they'd be apart for eight weeks.

"I guess." A smile flew across Kevin's face. "Don't you wish you'd told your parents about this?"

Jason shrugged, keeping his face a mask that Kevin could surely see straight through. His parents cared about his education, that was obvious. His mom had moved to Urbana with Jason and his little brother so Jason could attend the Magic Academy of Central Illinois, while his dad stayed downstate on the organic vegetable farm. He wasn't sure they thought the split was worth it. It was hard to explain to them how much he loved magic, how he didn't want to do anything else with his life except develop new spells. Even if he got into the Chicago program, they might not let him go. They wanted him to get a good education, but not at the cost of losing him as a weekend laborer.

"They saw the announcement months ago," he said. "But the farmer's market's tomorrow, and my mom's gone down to help Dad harvest the greens."

A teacher opened the protective dome to let the boy out. He stopped, eyes wide. Kevin whispered, "It was weird, coming out of the circle where there's no sound or light except your own magic. Suddenly you're back to the gym, and it's so bright and loud." He gave the boy a thumbs up, and he stumbled toward the waiting students.

The head judge called the next candidate, a girl from Springfield. She walked forward with her head high, but her hands trembled at her sides. Zeke snickered again. Jason couldn't stop himself from shooting him a dirty look. The girl reminded him of himself. Most of the students here were dressed to impress: creased khakis, ironed dress shirts, polished shoes. Jason was wearing his newest jeans and the sneakers he kept in Urbana for school. The girl wore a new dress, but it didn't fit quite right, and her shoes were scuffed. He bet that like him, she didn't have the years of private tutoring and summer lessons most of the others did. Even Kevin, who spent all his free time working at the bike shop, took weekend lessons. Jason spent his Saturdays and Sundays weeding gardens.

Kevin seemed to read his mind. "I bet she's worked hard," he said as the teachers closed the dome around the girl.

"Must have," Jason agreed. "I hope she makes it."

Zeke laughed, close by, and Jason looked up, startled. Zeke loomed over him. "Hey, farm boy," he said. "Shouldn't you be picking cabbages or something?"

"The judges aren't scoring us on insults," Jason said. "Shouldn't you be trying to learn a spell or two?"

Zeke laughed again, and Jason felt his cheeks burn. "If you were nicer I'd teach you one," the other boy said. "Too bad for you I don't feel like it." He strode back to his friends, who'd been watching the conversation with smirks.

"Jerk," Kevin muttered. "You all right?"

"A-hole," Jason agreed. "I just hope he screws up." He wanted Zeke to lose almost as badly as he wanted to win. Losing and watching Zeke win.... He wrapped his arms around himself.

"You'll feel better when it's over," Kevin said, patting his leg.

Jason wasn't so sure. Zeke's dig about teaching him a spell had stung. Zeke was arrogant, but he really was good at doing magic. Jason was better at the theory than at performing spells. And Zeke's parents didn't need his help on a farm, so if he got into the program, he'd get to go. Jason glanced at the bleachers, wishing his parents were there to cheer him on. He'd left the competition schedule sticking out of his backpack, half-hoping his mom would see it. He hadn't wanted to ask outright. They might have told him there was no point to competing when they needed him to work.

The judge announced Zeke's name, and the bleachers erupted in chants of "Go Zeke!" like he'd brought his own cheering section.

The longer he watched Zeke's amazing performance, the further Jason's stomach sank. The judges were scribbling notes and didn't look impressed. But they hadn't looked impressed at any time during the competition, even when one kid had done a class four transmutation and a metal chair melted into water.

Zeke's spell sequence had a higher base score than Jason's. Jason told himself that a lower-scoring program executed well would be better

31

than a high-scoring program done badly, but he wasn't convincing himself—and Zeke's execution was flawless as far as Jason could tell. He tried to keep his breathing deep, to focus on his magic, not the competition.

Finally it was his turn.

"Jason Yoder."

The speaker system made his name sound tinny, and for a moment he didn't move. This was it. Then Kevin poked him in the knee. "Go on. You'll do great."

Jason stood and forced his legs to carry him forward without tripping. The gym seemed to disappear until there was only him and the judges and a teacher holding the dome open with widespread arms. She nodded at Jason as he passed by, and let the dome close behind him.

In the black silence there was no sound but his beating heart and ragged breathing, no light but what he imagined.

He smiled at its familiarity, and raised his left hand before him in a class two Olsen's Strike. Flame arced to the top of the dome and stretched to the other side, vanishing where it hit the boundary. Jason tied off the magic, dropped his hand and stepped to the right, ready for his next move.

The flames lit the inside of the dome with flickering orange. Flames from a class three Strike would have held steady, but Jason couldn't spare the concentration required to hold it.

His second move was an illusion. The tree that sprouted from the basketball court's center circle in the middle of the dome was a little pale. Jason bit his lip. He'd meant to perform a class two illusion, but had pulled back on his power too early and achieved only a class one. Not good enough.

He paused an extra moment to regain his concentration. The opening moves were supposed to set the stage for what was coming next, not stump him. Any more mistakes like that and he might as well just quit. At least he couldn't hear Zeke laughing.

He launched into his next three moves, a rapid sequence in which the flames spread, the illusory tree morphed into a real fountain to contain the fire and then, in a piece of his own innovation, a class three version of Chen's First Summoning, aiming for a bobcat.

Then disaster struck. The bobcat was supposed to be easy to fight, but in Jason's excitement he overpowered the spell and found himself face-to-face with a cougar.

The cougar crouched, leaped, and Jason panicked. He banished it without even trying any of the required martial spells.

"Shit," he muttered. He imagined Kevin learning forward, saying *Come on, Jason, you can do this*. But it was over. Even if he did the end of his program perfectly, he hadn't earned enough points. Zeke was going to gloat.

And Kevin would go to the summer program without him. He'd meet smarter, richer, better boys.

No.

There was nothing Jason could do to earn enough points in the time remaining except one thing. One thing that he'd never successfully done before. One thing that no one had done before.

He let the dome clear, knowing the audience would see him standing there and think he'd given up. Then he raised both his arms out to his sides. Magic thrummed through his muscles as he performed the first steps in Getu's Maneuver. It was a common enough beginning for class two and three spells, but as the power built, Jason twisted, pulling the magic into a funnel cloud in the center of the dome. Then he Summoned again—they were allowed two—and produced a mockingbird.

He paused a moment, imagining Zeke's guffaw at Jason's supposed opponent, and Kevin's anticipation. Jason's heart thudded faster than the bird's wings as it circled the dome, searching for an escape. He closed his eyes and took a deep breath. He had one chance.

With a snap of his fingers, Jason sent the mockingbird into the funnel cloud. Then he held his arms out to his sides, palms down, and slowly lowered them. The funnel slowed its spin, spitting out the mockingbird. Then another. Then another. By the time the wind vanished, a dozen gray and white birds whirled through the air.

Jason whooped. No one had used Getu's Maneuver for Replication before. He'd wanted to prove he deserved a place in the summer program, and surely this had done it.

Now was not the time to celebrate. He had less than a minute left to run through his martial spells, and the birds were not happy at being cooped up in the dome with him. Two dove at his head, and he banished them with flicks of his wrists. He took out the next three birds with Feinstein's Cant, the following four with a fire spell, and the last three with Jacob's Gust.

The magic faded, and the dome became dark and silent once more.

Then it opened and he stepped out, knees shaking. He stumbled away and collapsed into his chair next to Kevin, who flung an arm around his shoulders. After the silence inside the dome, the cheers were deafening. It took him a moment to realize Kevin was talking. "... Amazing. Just brilliant!"

Jason started to relax. Then he heard his name being shouted, and he turned toward the bleachers.

His parents were standing in the crowd, applauding. They'd come to see him, they looked proud—and his mom was holding a sign, handwritten in black marker: *Chicago-bound.*

Warmth spread through him. For the first time, he was sure that his parents understood how important magic was to him. And he was sure that he was important enough to them that they'd let him pursue it.

He grinned and waved at them. For that moment, it didn't matter to him whether he'd won a spot or not. All that mattered was that his parents were there cheering him on.

Dirty Deeds

By Kelly Swails

The sun warmed my back as I prodded the slug with my finger. It didn't recoil from my touch. Dead. Mom had refreshed her salt traps in the garden yesterday and this morning they were full of the slimy creatures. This one must have fallen in not long ago. I hardened my resolve, reached into the coffee can buried in the ground, and pulled out my specimen.

A soft bark sounded from a few yards away. Our dog Boomer watched me as he lay under the shade of an old maple tree. He'd seen a squirrel bouncing across the yard and out the gate at the side of our yard, and he really wanted to go after it. He knew he wasn't allowed out of the yard, though, and he also knew he wasn't fast enough to get past me.

"Attaboy," I said. "You have to go after the ones that stay here." He whined and put his head on his front paws as if to say that squirrels only existed to taunt him.

I shivered as I lay the slug gently on the dark earth and wiped the resulting muck on my jeans. If I had walked around the neighborhood I could have found a dead bird or maybe even a squirrel, but out there it'd be harder to hide my actions. I could work in peace in the relative seclusion of Mom's flower-and-vegetable garden.

I pushed my will toward the slug. Nothing. I grimaced and scooted a little closer. Still nothing. I sighed and held my fingers over the slug. Tingles instantly traveled down my arm and through my fingers. Once I touched the slug, the tingles turned the corner to pain. It felt like 1,000 needles pricked me at random, much like when an arm or a leg falls asleep, but more intense. I pressed my lips into a line and touched the slug. Agony exploded in my finger for a split-second and I reflexively jerked my hand away. My heart pounded as I brushed the salt from my hand. The slug crawled away, leaving a silvery trail behind it.

"Isabella? What are you doing out here?" Mom said as the porch door swung closed behind her. She wore a big, floppy hat and ratty-for-her jeans. The clothes were old and suitable for working in dirt and mud, but she could have gone to the grocery store without anyone looking twice. Not that she would dare do such a thing. One didn't go outside the perimeter of their property in their gardening clothes.

"Checking the peppers," I said. I peered under a few leaves. "I think they have a few more days yet." I stood up and brushed the dirt from my butt.

"I could have told you that," she said as she walked to the little shed in the corner of the yard that housed her tools.

I gently pushed the slug beneath a squash plant with the toe of my sneaker. The big leaves might hide it from Mom's sharp eyes. Probably not. She really had no patience for anything less than perfect in her garden.

She joined me, a trowel in one hand, a hoe in the other. "How'd it fare?"

"How'd what fare?"

"Isabella."

I rolled my eyes. "I brought a slug back from the brink."

Mom continued to look at me.

"Okay. It was dead. There. Are you happy?"

She smiled for a split-second. "You're getting stronger."

I took a deep breath. "Maybe."

Her eyes turned hard. "Which is why it's so important for you to hide it. If people find out— "

"Yeah, yeah, everyone will want me to fix everything and I'll never have a moment's peace. I get it."

"No, I don't think you do." She tossed the trowel to the ground and began hoeing the few weeds that had dared to grow in her garden into submission. "But you will if you're not careful." As I moved to walk away, she said "Latch the gate on your way inside, would you?"

I sighed, walked across the yard, and wiggled the latch on the white wooden door until it caught. It had been loose for as long as I could remember but in the past few years it had gotten worse. I gave the doors a few shakes to be sure the latch held before I went in the house.

* * *

"Let's have an adventure."

I rolled over onto my side and gazed at Madeline. We were at her house, sharing her double bed. Her parents were gone—her mom antique shopping, her dad puttering with his boat—and so we had just spent the last 10 minutes exploring each other's bodies. As much as a body could be explored with clothes on, anyway.

"I thought we just did," I said.

"No, silly." She swatted my arm. "You know what I mean."

"Like this?" I leaned over and kissed her, pressing her soft lips to mine. At first she tensed, but then she let herself fall into it, a small moan escaping her. I pulled back and gazed at her flushed cheeks and brown eyes, her pupils so dilated they almost looked black.

"No," she said again, this time the words catching in her throat. She swallowed and continued. "As tempting as that is, let's go do something. Go to the art store and buy supplies and paint a picture. Go to a museum. We could find a pawn shop and buy you a guitar and I could teach you how to play. Or we could just start walking and do whatever inspires us."

I smiled. Madeline oozed creativity. She couldn't keep track of her bank account, but she could write a song in the morning, paint a canvas in the afternoon, and then spend the evening reading Cormac McCarthy. She bought thrift shop clothes and made them look expensive just by putting them on. She wore the same pair of Doc Martens her dad had worn as a kid. She was the yin to my yang and I loved her.

"That all sounds like stuff you'd like to do," I said.

"We could go for a bike ride or find a volleyball game to join at the lake," she said. "We went to the pottery place last Saturday, so it's your turn to pick. Whatever you want to do." She meant it. She'd rather touch a snake with her bare hands than hang out in the sun or run around getting sweaty but she'd do it for me. She loved me back.

"How about we just lie here all day?" I said as I ran my fingers up her arm. Her skin prickled beneath my touch.

"My parents will be home at some point," she said as she rolled off the bed.

My smile faltered. I sighed as I rolled off the other way and helped her straighten the bedspread. We'd done this so many times muscle memory took over: fluff, pull, smooth. I punched the pillow on my side and replaced her childhood teddy bear in the middle. She'd sewn the outfit he wore—a vest, bow tie, and felt sheriff badge—when she was six. Her parents knew Maddie and I hung out a lot but they thought we were nothing more than best friends.

"When are you coming out?" I said.

Her face darkened. "When you do."

"I already have."

"You know what I mean." This time the phrase didn't hold any playfulness.

I gave the pillow on my side one last punch, maybe a little harder than I needed to. "Point to Maddie."

"I'm not keeping score," she said.

"I know you're not," I said even though a small part of me thought otherwise. Everyone kept score a little. "Let's go play volleyball."

She kissed me on the check—a small apology—before we left her bedroom. I accepted it by bumping her shoulder with mine.

* * *

We made it to the beach before the heat of the day and the resulting crowds had materialized and found a game about to begin. We kicked off our shoes and joined in, Maddie on one side, me on the other. The warm sand squished between my toes and I giggled. Since I'm almost five-ten, I asked to start in the front. I jumped and spiked and blocked and tried not to hit the ball to Maddie. Not because she couldn't play—she was better than she would admit—but because I knew she didn't really like it and was only there because I wanted her to be. My teammates didn't hesitate to hit the ball to her, though, and before we'd finished the first game Maddie took a spiked ball to the face. She hit the sand like a bag of rocks.

"Time out," I said as I ducked under the net and rushed to her. "Are you okay?"

"I'm fine," she said, clearly anything but. She sounded like she had a head cold, her eyes had already started to swell, and blood rushed out of her nose. The other players crowded around us.

"Give us some room." Everyone took a few steps back as I peered at the damage. "That's going to leave a mark," I said.

She tried to snort but only succeed in making a wet, bubbly noise. "Can't wait to see it."

I looked over my shoulder. The other players hid us from the rest of the beach. The only people that would see me were strangers. I bit my lip and hesitated for a moment before touching my fingers to Maddie's nose. She had cracked cartilage and the beginnings of two black eyes. She flinched but I didn't take my hand away. Instead I pushed my will through my fingers and into her injury. Instantly pain rushed through my hand and up my arm. I cried out a bit as the swelling in her eyes went down and the blood stopped flowing from her nose. Once it was done I pulled my hand away and shook it out. My entire arm throbbed and I felt dizzy and a little sick. I hadn't ever healed anything that big before.

Maddie blinked. "Thanks," she said. She sounded normal.

I looked around. The vibe of the other players had turned from concerned curiosity to astonished eagerness. Of course they'd heard about people like me. They probably even knew other people that could do what I had just done. But they hadn't ever watched it happen.

"We should go," I said.

Maddie glanced at the onlookers. "Why? You didn't do anything wrong."

"It's not that. Please."

She consented, but too late.

"Can you erase my freckles?" A redhead asked.

"That's stupid, Heather. I can't believe you'd ask that," A girl almost as tall as me said. "If she fixes anything it should be my shin splints."

"My dad has heart problems," another said so quietly I almost missed it.

I hurried off the sand and grabbed my shoes. Maddie did the same and ran to catch up with me. We walked several blocks before she spoke.

"I'm sorry," she said.

"Why? You didn't do anything wrong."

"You didn't either."

My throat tightened. "I shouldn't have let people see that. I should have waited until we left."

"You didn't want to see me in pain."

"Yeah, but— "

"Don't worry about it. No one there knew you." She grabbed the hand I had used on her and squeezed. I fought past the residual pain and squeezed back.

* * *

Mom knocked on my bedroom door. "Isabella? We need to talk."

My stomach dropped as I closed my laptop. She had that tone that meant I was in deep shit.

"Sure," I said.

She walked in and my legs went a little watery. I had never seen her so angry, not even when I had put a bunch of dirt in the bathtub and added water so I could take a mud bath when I was four.

"Mrs. Brookmire called me," she said. Ice hung from her words.

"Oh, yeah?" I said, trying my best to pretend I had no idea what came next.

"She called to thank you for helping Madeline." Mom took a step toward me and I involuntarily scooted back in my seat. "With her broken nose."

"Her nose wasn't broken. Just cracked. It looked worse than it was." As soon as I said it I knew I had made a colossal mistake.

"How many times, Isabella. How many times have we talked about this?"

"Mom, my girlfriend took a volleyball to the nose. Of course I'm going to help her."

"That's not the issue and you know it. It's not the fact that you chose to heal her. You know I don't have a problem with that. But on the beach? In front of a dozen other people?"

"You're making a bigger deal out of this than it is. There were maybe eight people there."

Mom crossed her arms. "And how many asked you to heal something on them?" When I didn't answer she shook her head. "This morning. We just talked about it this morning." A few tears streamed down her cheeks. "I'm sorry, Isabella, but you've forced me to do this."

"Do what?"

"You need to leave."

I blinked. I had to have heard her wrong. "What?"

She cried harder but her voice stayed strong. "You need to leave. If you refuse to keep your powers secret, then you can't be here."

"You don't mean that."

"I do. Sooner or later people will know your name and where you live and what you can do. They'll come from all over and sleep on our lawn until you help them. They'll threaten to hurt you if you don't."

"It doesn't—"

"Don't you think there's a reason that not every single healer goes to medical school? Don't you think there's a reason that most healers who chose to out themselves are hidden away enclaves that only allow a few dozen people a day in to be healed? It's because humanity will take and take and take from them until they're used up. And people will still want more." She wiped her face. "If you want that for yourself, I can't stop you. But I don't have to witness it. I don't have to experience it."

At some point during her speech my entire body had gone numb. My only thought at the beach had been taking care of Maddie. I hadn't thought about Mom finding out. And I hadn't thought about how my powers affected her.

"If that's the way you want it," I said, trying to keep an "I don't care" tone to my voice. I opened my closet door, pulled a duffle from the top shelf, and started shoving clothes into it. She left, closing the door behind her. I threw underwear and socks and jeans and T-shirts into the bag until I couldn't fit anymore in. I tossed my laptop and a few books into my backpack before thumping down the hallway. I found Mom sitting at the kitchen table, an untouched mug of tea in front of her.

"Just something to think about," I said. "I didn't force you to do anything. You're choosing to do this." I let those words hang in the air as I walked out of the only home I'd ever known.

* * *

"My mom is such a bitch," Maddie said as yanked the sheets off the guest bed and dropped them to the floor.

"Because she's making you make a bed?" I said.

"No. Because she wants you sleep in here."

I grabbed the clean sheets off the wooden chair in the corner and tossed the fitted one to Maddie. "You didn't really expect her to let me sleep in your room, did you?"

"You spend the night all the time," she said. "How is that any different?"

"We don't know how long I'm going to be here, for one thing."

Maddie rolled her eyes. "So?"

"She thinks I sleep on the floor when I spend the night. She doesn't want me to do that for weeks."

"Quit defending her."

41

"Quit being unreasonable and I will." I pulled the last corner of the sheet into place before helping with the top sheet. I watched her from the corner of my eye for a few moments. "That's not what's really bothering you."

She swallowed a few times. "I don't know what you're talking about."

"You never get this angry about anything."

She tossed the comforter on the bed and straightened it before mumbling a response.

"What?"

"Hypocrisy pisses me off." She took a few deep breaths. "She's all 'her mom will come around' and 'her mom will realize that she loves Isabella more than she hates that she's a Healer,'" Maddie wiped angry tears from her face. "But she'd have the same fucking reaction as your mom if she learned I date girls." She sniffled and coughed. "It's all bullshit."

I blinked. I'd never seen Maddie cry and it unnerved me a little. I wanted to comfort her even though I was the one who should be upset.

"Parents suck," I said. "Even the ones who let me crash in their guest room."

"Especially the ones that make you use the guest room."

I grabbed a tissue from the box on the bedside table and handed it to Maddie. She accepted it and blew her nose.

"You sound like a linebacker."

"Fuck you," she said even as she smirked. She blew her nose again, somehow making it even louder. She tossed the tissue into the garbage after she finished. She scrubbed her face with her hands. "Come on," she said. "Let's go have an adventure."

* * *

Mom volunteered at the library on Sunday afternoons, so instead of having an adventure, we snuck into my house to pick up a few things. In yesterday's anger and betrayal I had forgotten essentials like deodorant and lip gloss and my iPod. I scratched Boomer on the head before using the key hidden under a pot of petunias—she hadn't thought to move that—to let ourselves into the house.

"I like your house," Maddie said as she ran her hand along the kitchen counter and took a fresh cookie from the cookie jar. I shrugged. "Yeah, I like my house too. Too bad I don't get to live in it anymore." My words caught on my sarcasm and I cleared my throat.

"I mean your mom is so domestic but not in an ironic way. Or a 'don't get dirt on the carpet' way."

"She is as long as you don't live here," I said. "She likes to have everything in its place." I swallowed. "A healer in the family pretty much fucks that all up." I shrugged, trying to pretend it didn't bother me. "Let's get my stuff and get out of here."

I grabbed my other duffle from the closet—I had used it for basketball in middle school and it still smelled like a gym, despite being washed several times—and filled it with makeup and toiletries and electronics. I had just zipped it when I heard the screech of tires, a thump, and a yelp.

My stomach dropped to the floor. "Boomer." I ran through the house. "Did you close the gate?" I yelled to Maddie.

"I thought I did," she said from right behind me. The tension in her voice increased my own.

I slammed the back door open and ran through the open gate at the side of the yard. Boomer lay at the side of the street, his back legs lifeless, his front ones pulling him into the grass. The car that had hit him was nowhere around. Bastards.

"Oh God," Maddie's voices cracked and I knew she was about to lose it.

I didn't think about what came next or if anyone saw me; I had to fix Boomer. I dropped to my knees beside him and placed both hands on his sides. Instantly pain washed through me as I psychically examined his injuries. His legs weren't broken, but his spine had been shattered in several places, severing his spinal cord. A few ribs had been broken and punctured some internal organs, making them bleed. His insides were a mess. He was dying.

Boomer reached back and licked my hand, whimpering as he did so. I rubbed his head and bent down so he could lick my face. Instead he nuzzled me before lying back down. I wiped my nose on my sleeve. This couldn't be happening. Not my dog, not today. Not something I couldn't fix.

"How bad is it?" Maddie whispered. She was crying as hard as me.

"Bad," I said. I couldn't bring myself to list everything I'd felt.

43

"You can it make it better, though. Right?"

I shook my head. "This is way beyond me. In a few years I might be strong enough, but now…" I took a deep breath. I forced myself to say my next words. "All I can do is make it so he doesn't suffer." I rubbed his ears before moving my hands down his body and closing my eyes. The world fell away as I concentrated on siphoning his pain into me. My ribs ached and my back hurt and my legs went numb as Boomer's chest rose and fell beneath my fingers. Hot, sick energy poured into me, and I tried to replace it with as much love as I could. At one point I felt someone touch my shoulder and heard far-off words, but I was in so deep it might have happened to someone else. After some time—I don't know how long—Boomer took his last shuddering breath. As his body released it the pain flowed from me. I slumped over and sat on the ground, the feeling returning to my legs. Gravel from the edge of the road dug into the side of my thighs.

"Is he gone?" Mom said from behind me.

I turned and looked. Her bag and a few library books were spread on the ground several yards away as though she had dropped them while running. Tears streamed down her face, her only expression panicked grief.

I didn't trust myself to speak so I nodded.

"I saw him get hit," she said. "Bastard just kept on going." She wiped her face. "Why didn't you…" She made a vague gesture in the air.

"He had too much damage. I took his pain away so he could go in peace."

"You felt everything he did?"

"Yes."

"I wondered by the way you cried out. I told you to stop… did you hear me?"

I shook my head.

She knelt beside me and hugged me. "I'm glad you were here for him. I'm sorry you had to see him like this, but I glad you could help him."

Relief flooded over me. Part of me thought Mom hated me because of my powers. But maybe Maddie's mom was right. Mom just hated what the power could do to my life. She didn't hate me.

Mom released me and looked at the bag sitting next to the gate. I must have brought it out with me without realizing it. She stared at it for a moment before speaking. "I judged you harshly and I'm sorry. I'm your mother and I'm supposed to love all of you, even if it's inconvenient or messy to do so." She turned her gaze to me. "Maybe especially if it's inconvenient. You don't have to go. I understand you might still want to."

The tears I had been fighting fell on their own accord. I nodded and strived for a casual tone. "I'll be leaving for college next year anyway," I said. "Why move twice?"

A shadow of a smile crossed her face. "I'm glad." She stood, and brushed the dirt from her knees. Her next words were all business. "I'll get a box and take Boomer to the vet. You girls will have a few days to pick out a spot in the yard for his ashes. Madeline, I assume you'll be staying for dinner?" She walked away without waiting for an answer.

Maddie squeezed my hand. "Looks like she's back to normal."

I put my free hand on Boomer. He still felt warm. Fresh tears threatened to fall but I blinked them away. "At least she is."

"I know," Maddie said. "Life sucks sometimes."

"Yeah. It does." I squeezed her hand back. "Your turn."

"You know what? Maybe you're right. Maybe it is time."

* * *

That night, after Boomer had been taken for cremation and dinner had been eaten and I'd retrieved my clothes from Maddie's house and left her there to have her big discussion, I lay in bed and listened to the wind rustle the leaves outside my window. Familiarity surrounded me—the bedspread, the shadows on the wall, the creaky floor in the hallway— even as everything had an invisible tarnish on it. My life had turned a corner I hadn't known existed, and nothing would be the same again. But maybe in a good way.

Man of the Mist

By Evelyn Deshane

Adrian held up his wrists which were, in spite of his best efforts, shackled.

"Oh. Wait." With his brow furrowed, he glanced between himself and his best friend Charlie, where he'd set the magic trick book before beginning his latest endeavor. "I don't think this is quite right."

"What gave it away, Houdini?" Charlie's soft laugh was soon replaced by concern as Adrian struggled against his bindings. He looped his wrists around one another in an attempt to strike the cuffs and free himself like the book had instructed, but to no avail. No matter how many slaps and nicks, combined with the bumps from the school bus, the cuffs were not coming off.

And Adrian was becoming more frazzled.

"Hey, calm down little man." Charlie ignored the shiny magic book entirely to dig through Adrian's bag underneath the bus's seat. She pulled out a set of metal keys and held them up with a smile. "Seems like the real trick here is simple mechanics. Come on. I'll let you out."

Begrudgingly, Adrian extended his wrists and allowed Charlie to unshackle him. His heart fell as he watched the cuffs slip easily off. He'd been practicing as an escape artist for the past two weeks, determined to get everything right before the talent show at the end of their senior year of Junior High. Sure, Portside's Junior High Talent Show was a small event—everything in their Ontario hometown was a small event—but it was important to Adrian. On stage, he could become the magician he always wanted to be. He could disappear and reappear at a moment's notice, folding himself in and out of tight spaces like his role model Harry Houdini. He'd already gotten his costume for the big event: a suit with a bright purple tie across the neck, which matched the purple gloves that

Charlie had agreed to wear as his assistant. Now his outfit felt too much like another illusion. He wasn't Adrian Li, master of himself through magic; he was still Rose Li, a girl to everyone else's eyes because that was how he'd been born.

At least, he was a girl to everyone but Charlie. She smiled as she handed him his handcuffs and the magic trick book. "There's still time for practice. You'll get it right, Adrian."

Instead of a response, the bus jostled them once more. Mrs. Potter, the chaperone for the four day long Senior Trip to Niagara Falls, Ontario, stood in the bus's aisles in spite of the bus's turbulence. "Class of 2018," she called out in her strong, boorish voice. "I think it's about time for lunch. In another 15 minutes, we will be halfway to our destination in Guelph. I expect everyone here to behave as we embark on lunch. You will have full reign to go where you wish—but please, remember your same-sex buddies and to report back minutes 15 before departure. Any questions?"

Adrian huffed, but nodded to his former math teacher's instructions. He and Charlie had always been buddies on field trips like this, back to first grade when they were seated next to one another through their surnames Leigh and Li. They'd remained best friends through so many different grades and boring trips to conservation areas, but the end of year Junior High trip was something else. Not only was it four-days long and filled with many different tourist destinations (not just educational ones)—but everything was sex segregated, and yet another reminder to Adrian's lost power. He would never remove the handcuffs by himself, and he would never be anyone but Rose to the administration.

"Oh, cheer up," Charlie said, nudging his shoulder. "I'm pretty sure we're going to find a good lunch spot. And you'll get the hang of the tricks."

"I know. It's just..."

Charlie nodded, understanding Adrian's awkwardness around the school staff. Adrian's trans status had been confessed during a sleepover two years ago as the two played with a Ouija board. He'd spelled out his new name with the sensor, pretending to be a ghost. When Charlie had assessed his confession through a round of Truth or Dare, she was bound to secrecy and promised to use his name whenever she could. If anyone overheard Charlie calling Adrian Adrian, then they defaulted to the magician storyline. They were practicing. It was a game. Except that,

47

over time, it had become more and more real, and even Charlie could see Adrian's stories coming apart.

"You know..." She began, but soon stopped as the bus pulled into the parking lot. The dull chatter of the fourteen-year-olds on the bus soon became a roar. Adrian already knew how Charlie's sentence would end, anyway: You could tell them now. You could be trans in Junior High rather than waiting until High School when guidance counsellors were surely prepared and could support you. You could just be who you are now, instead of treating it like a fantasy.

Adrian could do a lot of things, he knew. But he still didn't think he had the power yet.

"Hey, Charlie?" Adrian slapped one handcuff on her wrist as she turned around.

"Oh, you're mean, Mr. Magician," she said, barely hiding laughter. A wide smile crossed her face as she worked through the kinks in the cuffs before the sliver bracelet slid right off. "But it's just a simple trick."

* * *

After a large Coke from the 7-11 and two prepackaged sandwiches, Charlie and Adrian were done their lunch with a half an hour still to spare. Most of the other junior high students had gone into the mall close by the parking lot, while the two of them had wandered closer to the city centre of Guelph. They bypassed the gas station and convenience store first visible from the highway, before turning down a side street filled with local bars and establishments.

"I'm bored," Charlie said. "Put the cuffs on me again. I bet I can get out. Then I can teach you how easy it is."

Adrian handed over the cuffs with a shrug. "I think you should just be the magician."

"And you be the beefy male assistant? Hmm. I like it. Mix up those gender roles."

Adrian chuckled. While Charlie tinkered, he pulled out a cutting rope trick that was also part of his act, followed up with a deck of cards. Their walking pace slowed considerably as they were consumed by their trinkets. They were about to take a seat on the curb by the gas station when a wind gust cut right through them, scattering Adrian's cards like a flock of butterflies.

"Oh, crap!" Both Adrian and Charlie darted off in opposing directions to help grab the deck. Adrian desperately grabbed fistfuls of Jacks and club cards before realizing he was at a loss. His deck was gone and now belonged to Guelph.

"We can fix this," Charlie said. She held the Queen of Hearts in her hand, along with a dozen others. "There's gotta be a store around here that sells this stuff."

The two turned down a side street and found another handful of Kings and the Two of Diamonds. A feeling started to churn in Adrian's stomach, familiar yet strange. It was like the first time he'd gone on YouTube and realized that there were people just like him who updated their vlogs about something called gender dysphoria. Hearing that term was like being given a magic key to unlock a door and explore an entire new terrain, once unimaginable, but now in front of him and realer than ever. Because he'd found his trans identity by wanting to look up magic tricks online, the utterance of gender dysphoria seemed like a magic word in and of itself. And that magic feeling permeated Adrian as he continued to look for cards down the side street with Charlie. Something was familiar here, but utterly different. If he could find the right words to express himself, maybe Adrian could become something better than what he was right now, too.

"Here!" Charlie said. She gestured to the door of a quaint, small building that was half-covered in a leafy moss. The Jack of Clubs was caught between the vines. The sign above the door read The Black Cat Occult Shoppe.

"No way," Adrian said under his breath. There was nothing like this in their small town. The tingly feeling from before spread out from his fast-beating heart to his hands as he stepped forward.

"I bet they have more cards, and possibly more magic tricks. Maybe the handcuffs don't work because you're far, far too advanced." Charlie winked before peeling back the Jack of Club card from the vine. She grasped the doorknob and gestured him inside. "You coming, Mr. Magician?"

Adrian nodded. There was only a split second of weightlessness before he set his foot down again. The world in front of him became Technicolor, vivid like the Italian film *Suspiria* he and Charlie had watched late one night. The film had been about witches; though they were evil witches in the movie, he and Charlie had gone online and

Googled a dozen other videos about modern day witchcraft and Wicca. They were real things, not make-believe, and like his surfacing of gender dysphoria, the discovery of the occult in the everyday was earth shattering and amazing. The strange feeling from before now spread through his entire body, radiating around him like an aura.

The bell behind him clanged to alert the store owners of their presence. Adrian snapped out of his daydream and became struck by the quiet beauty of the curiosities on the shelves. There were dragon figurines, candelabras with pentacles on the front, incense and herbs hanging from the ceiling, and a dozen of jars filled with many coloured liquids. He struggled to find the words he'd remembered from YouTube tutorials, but it was all too overwhelming. Adrian knew all about these types of stores, but his old-school Christian mother and his live-in grandmother would have nothing to do with it, much like trans identity. Adrian had to survey around the corners of the store, behind him, and through the small front windows next to wind chimes to be sure no one was following him, and no one could see. He and Charlie were seemingly alone in the occult shop, and it was the first time in a long time that Adrian truly felt safe.

"Can I help you?" A woman appeared from a back room. A thick black choker was around her neck and her hair was clipped in a short bob with prominent bangs. She wore dark make-up. In spite of her shadowy appearance, she smiled when she noticed Adrian's shoulder bag and the top of the gold-gilded book sticking out.

"*New Tricks for the New Magician?*" she asked, her smile growing wider as Adrian nodded. "Oh my Goodness. I haven't seen that book in decades. Can I?"

Adrian stepped closer and handed over the book he'd been studying for the talent show. Outside the gold edges and titling, the cover contained an image of Harry Houdini bound up in ropes and chains, hanging from his feet. The woman touched the cover as if it was an old friend before looking inside.

"I'm Becca, by the way," she said as she skimmed the first few entries.

"Adrian." His voice was quiet, so much that Becca glanced up from the pages and cocked a brow. Adrian was highly aware that, in spite of his baggy clothing which covered any type of feminine form, he didn't look that much like a guy. His hair was cut short, but it also grew fast and his mother would only take him so often. His voice was high-pitch and not cracked by testosterone. Saying his name was Adrian without a deep baritone behind it seemed like a lie, and he knew it. Yet he still didn't want to tell this woman that he was Rose, like he did almost every other time. In the magic shop, he wanted to feel safe.

Becca, for all the scurrility in her gaze, didn't linger in judgment. She closed the book and considered Adrian with a considerate gaze. "What can I do for you today?"

"Um. I need..." Out of the corner of his vision, Charlie appeared and held up a deck of cards triumphantly. She was on the other side of the store, dealing with another employee who bore the same dark choker Becca had on. "Oh. Well," Adrian continued. "I needed cards but my friend has it."

Becca nodded. "Are you interested in more books?"

"Like New Tricks? I suppose so. I've been trying to learn them, but it doesn't always work."

"Illusions are hard to master. You have to believe they can be so, even while knowing the trick. And that requires someone of two minds."

"Two minds?"

"Knowing the truth and knowing the lie. And knowing that, at certain points, the truth and the lie cross paths—and that is where the real magic lies."

"Real magic?" Adrian asked. His throat was suddenly dry. His head spun with Becca's cryptic words. He thought back to the YouTube videos. "Like in Wicca?"

"Sure. We can call it that, but magic is magic is magic. All real and all fake." Her darkly painted lips formed a smile. "And I think you want something specific, right? That's why you're here?"

"Maybe."

"You know, if you say what you want aloud, it might just appear."

"A glamour," Adrian said, surprising himself with his boldness. He'd heard of this particular type of spell that cast doubt on someone's appearance. A glamour disguised someone so they could elude detection. Or maybe even become someone else entirely. "Do you know how to get a glamour?"

"I do. But what does a kid like you need a glamour for?"

"Nothing. Never mind."

"No, no," Becca said. "Tell me what you want. You were so close. So... a glamour for crime?"

51

"No, nothing like that. I just... I want a glamour because. Um. Or a body swapping spell would work. Or something. I just... want to be someone else for a while. A famous magician. You know, like Houdini." Adrian gestured to the book again, tapping at the image on the cover, as a way to steady himself. "I want to be an escape artist, and if I can just get enough magic to use, then maybe I can... "

Becca held up a hand to cease Adrian's babbling. Though disquieted, he was relieved. He didn't know how far he'd keep going; knowing how much was inside of him, an entire Tower of Babel was ready to spill out.

"I think you're going about this the wrong way," Becca said after some careful consideration. "Houdini was an escape artist, but he never escaped who he was. He never actually bound his identity, only his physical body. And he never tried to escape using a glamour or switching to someone else. Those spells never really work."

"Then what did he do?"

"He didn't change himself. He changed the world." Becca gestured to the cover and the upside-down magician, turning him so that the world was reversed. "When you use a glamour, you damage the face underneath. It's an extreme act of magic that must only be temporary. To damage yourself means that you've given up on the world; that you don't trust the world. And for someone doing magic, well, that means you don't trust the audience. You think they'll see the sleight of hand and the trick becomes a lie rather than a playful fun illusion. You have to trust the world. You have to trust the audience. Everything else is bad magic."

"Well, okay. But then what good is magic?"

"Magic is there for changing perceptions. It's a veil beneath the mundane world, a place where knowing the lie and knowing the truth intersect. In that place, you understand that the world doesn't change you—you must change the world."

Adrian repeated her words in his mind. He turned Houdini on the book upside down and then right side up. "I... still don't understand. None of this makes sense. I..."

"It does make sense. Just give it some time."

"I don't exactly have time." Adrian could feel himself grow frustrated. His chest hurt. His hands hurt. His entire body hurt and he wanted to leave, to go home, and hide in his room. He wanted to be Adrian in secret because he didn't know if he could trust the world so

52

easily. To open his mouth and say that he wanted to be called Adrian and then have someone not do it hurt worse than keeping it bottled up inside.

"Here." Becca produced a new book from under the counter, sliding it over Houdini entirely. The title read *The Phenomenology of Magic*. The meaning of the word evaded him, but it filled him with the familiar sense of discovery. Maybe like gender dysphoria, phenomenology had a way to unlock another part of himself. The thought was both elating and terrifying. Becca stuck a few more pamphlets inside the cover of the book. "Take these back. Read them. And see what you can come away with."

When Charlie appeared at Adrian side, a bag in hand with the store's logo of a cat on it, Adrian let out a breath. The interaction was over. Their 15 minutes before the bus count was inching closer, and they still had to get to Niagara Falls and get this stupid senior trip over with.

"Thank you," Adrian said, speaking more to Charlie for the cards than to Becca. But she, too, nodded. Under her breath, she added, "Good luck Adrian" that only he seemed to hear.

* * *

At the hotel room in Niagara Falls, long after Charlie had gone to bed, Adrian opened up *The Phenomenology of Magic* and the pamphlets inside. An image of the Leonardo's Vitruvian man caught his attention on one of the pamphlets; the body was bisected with lines in full colors of the rainbow spectrum. *New Ways of Being* was written underneath the body, followed by a table of contents on the next page. There was only enough room for three spells, plus a book advertisement for more on the back page, but the second spell was all Adrian needed.

"Over Water, Under Soul" was an incantation for a change in perception, followed by a ritual in water in order to bring forward a "new sense of being, and a new world to exist it." Everything that Becca had told him in the store—about truth and lies, about changing the world, and about being in charge—was repeated almost verbatim. Change your perception, change your world, the pamphlet indicated. And once you have a self to seek, go under water for the rebirth. Bury a royal sign. And spin three times in a circle, and three times back. Now you have become your own world.

Adrian scoffed. This couldn't be real. This had to be some mumbo jumbo, like horoscopes in the newspaper, that were only there to fool people into buying something. But while Charlie slept in their shared hotel room, Adrian stayed awake. He reviewed their itinerary for the Niagara Falls trip and realized that the next day was the Maid of the Mist ride, where the class would get on a boat, go under the falls, and get covered in water. Soon, he found the Jack of Clubs card from his old deck that had become tangled in the vines of the occult shop and buried it in a plant by the hotel front desk. He spun around three times, and then spun around again.

The rest would have to wait.

* * *

"Hey. Are you ready?"

Charlie nudged Adrian in his ribs through the large rain coats they both wore.

His heart fluttered with how close the boat was to the falls. The entire day had seemed like a drag as Mrs. Potter took the kids through the military bases, a park, and the wax museum before it was finally time to step aboard the Maid of The Mist. Adrian had kept the magic pamphlet in his cargo shorts pocket all day, fingering it when he needed encouragement. The strange enchantment from the occult shop, that tingling ready feeling, coursed through his veins each time he touched it. He rubbed his fingers over the edges now, somewhat damp, and then along the metal handcuffs in the other pocket. The clanging of the metal against the edge of the boat made Charlie roll her eyes.

"I still can't believe you brought those," Charlie said, teasing. "Magic knows know break, I suppose. Are you planning on disappearing over the falls in a barrel like Annie Edson Taylor?"

"Who?"

Again, Charlie rolled her eyes. "You gotta listen more, Adrian. Especially about badass women daredevils. She was at the wax museum!"

"Oh, well. I'm not quite like her."

"No, I suppose not."

When Adrian held out his hand out for Charlie to grab it, she did so without question. The spark that Adrian felt inside his body passed to her. She glowed, he was sure of it, under the oncoming mist. Was this another moment of discovery and exhilaration? Of love moving the world? He didn't quite know, but the answer was coming to him. This time, he wasn't afraid to find out.

The instructor's voice drowned out as the roar of the water came closer and closer. He chanted the words of the spell and Becca's cryptic lines as they passed under the falls. The class screeched with delight as they all became drenched. The raincoats did little to keep them dry. The water was cold and sharp, hitting against Adrian's face and making him close his eyes. When Adrian shivered, so did Charlie; an electric current passing between them through their still-entwined hands. By the time the boat moved through the falls, no more than a couple splashes had gotten on board, but it felt so much stronger than that.

And so much more powerful.

Adrian wasn't sure what was different as he opened his eyes. The rest of the world seemed the same. Mrs. Potter was still droning on, echoing the instructor on board. Bobby, a kid in his science class, was still a bully and made inappropriate comments as the boat moved closer towards land. Charlie was still there, still smiling, and still holding his hand.

As they reached the shore, Adrian pulled out the handcuffs. He slapped them on both of his wrists and took a deep breath. He imagined himself as Houdini on the cover of his book, hanging upside down and then hanging right side around with the world inverted instead. He imagined himself going over the falls in a barrel and, through some kind of magic, surviving and becoming a daredevil. Finally, he saw himself as himself—a man, not Rose Li—and a magician all at once.

The cuffs slid off.

"Ah-hah!" Charlie said, excited. "The magic works."

"Yeah," Adrian said, smiling. "I guess so."

"Everyone," Mrs. Potter's voice cut in on the celebration. "Straight lines as we disembark the boat. Remember to stay together as we go towards the bus. And that means you two, Charlie and Adrian."

"Sorry, sorry," Charlie mumbled as she gathered her stuff. It was another moment before Charlie realized that Mrs. Potter had said Adrian, and not Rose. She cast another glance to Adrian, who only smiled.

"Huh. Impressive," Charlie said. She linked her hands with Adrian's. "But do we still get to share a room?"

Puppies and Piglets and Tricksters Oh My

By Chelsea Smith

No shit, there I was, minding my own business. Well. Not minding my own business so much as running for my life from a mermaid-haired track star who stole my English paper. I didn't mean for anything to happen to her. You see, when I was born, the hospital didn't exactly hand out instruction manuals titled "So the Sperm Bank Donor Was Really a Trickster God." My folks had no idea, so they couldn't warn me about what could happen. And whoever my real father was, he had decided not to. Nice as it would have been to know a little more about who I was.

Frankly, it's a miracle all I did was blow Elissa into a tree. Seeing her long, stupid mermaid hair tangled in those branches, I almost felt bad. Almost. Except for the part where she screamed "Kesi!" and names that sounded suspiciously like "witch." Well, it was her fault for stealing my English paper. Cheater.

It was a hell of an introduction to magic powers. I'd had six months since then to get used to my powers. So, when I heard my girlfriend's trembling voice on the phone, I knew my time had come.

"They, um," Ann sniffed, barely squeaking out each horrible word. *"They recognized me in weight training today. And I thought they were going to leave me alone because they didn't say anything at first, but then they caught up with me in the locker room… They… they said I should leave the class. That even if I lost a ton of weight that… Kesi, they said that with my face and my nose I'd still look like a p-pig, so there was no point in me trying to lose weight…"*

Evil she-demons from the depths of hell.

Magic from my unknown father prickled under my skin, egging me on as I stormed back and forth across my room. Dimly, I heard faint *pops* as my possessions transformed around me, feeding off the excess energy.

Pop! Paperclips turned into matchboxes. *Pop!* Pictures of my parents turned into fluffy, spotted rabbits. *Whoosh!* A treacherous wind gusted around me, rustling through my books and homework, threatening to storm across the whole house if I didn't rein it in. If I wasn't trying to keep this thing under wraps, I'd let it.

Sweet, pink-faced Ann. *My* Ann. The best person on this planet. Six months ago, when I was still new to magic and mayhem, I might have responded the normal way: grab a pint of ice cream, watch *Legally Blonde* on repeat, and hold her. Maybe even curled up in her bed with her if her parents weren't watching.

That was then. I could do better for her now. Besides, I'd been looking for an excuse to show off. If I was going to join the ranks of the world's tricksters, I needed to pull off a serious trick. Why not a trick for Ann?

I sucked in a sharp breath. The wind and the *popping* stopped, leaving my room in its usual state of disarray. Gritting my teeth, I threw a heap of dirty clothes onto my bed and closed my eyes. Heat flooded my fingers, seeping into the dirty tank tops and old underwear until they shifted into something to keep my parents off my trail in case they decided to poke their heads in. The mannequin looked sort of like me. Short, red curls, a few freckles… hmmm. The skin was a little waxy, but as long as the lights were out it would pass.

"Well, aren't you a cheeky one?"

The familiar voice echoed through my head, unexpected and unwelcome. I glanced over my shoulder, but there was nobody there. Or, at least, it looked that way. Was it my imagination, or did that rocking chair look a little smug? No, it always looked like that.

"Come or don't. Just stay out of my way," I growled, sliding the window open. How dare he spy like that? *He* was the one who'd slammed the door on *me*. *He* was the one who'd stood in this room and said I wasn't worth teaching, who kept secrets when he was the one who'd told me I was a trickster in the first place. As if he was in any position to give me crap. Well, if he wanted to watch, I hoped he'd enjoy the show. I'd make it a good one—just as soon as I figured out what to do.

* * *

Jackie Blair, by virtue of living about 10 minutes away, was first on my list. I paused outside her house, and peered through her first-floor window. Garish, neon, animal print burned my eyes. It looked like Lisa Frank had puked all over her walls. That eyesore alone would make this a pleasure.

I crept around the outside of her house, nimbly dodging branches and dead leaves as I sniffed out an entrance. There! Just past her bedroom, a vent no bigger than a jar of peanuts spewed out warm steam that smelled like dryer lint. No alarm systems here. I crouched down in front of it and squeezed my eyes shut, picturing myself as small as Jackie's shriveled little heart.

Static crackled over my skin, seeping through muscle into bone. Then, like a net, it tightened around me and *squeezed*. I clenched my jaw and struggled not to fight it. If I did, the magic wouldn't work. This was just energy displacement. Every trickster in every storybook could pull it off. Why shouldn't I?

The static turned to lightning, burning through my gut. I doubled over, pressing my forehead into the grass as I clenched my jaw. Just a few more seconds...

"My dear, it looks as though you're having a little trouble. Are you sure you know what you're doing?"

My eyes flew open. Blades of grass stretched up to my ears, smelling stronger and sweeter than a freshly cut lawn in July. The vent towered above me. Holy crap on a cracker, it worked. I reached for it with a hand that wasn't a hand but... a paw. I sniffed, and something on my nose twitched, something I hadn't had before. Whiskers?

Dear Lord, I'd imagined myself tiny as a mouse, hadn't I? My heart skipped a beat, and the grass began to recede. No! No, this was fine, really...

The prickling returned, and after a few seconds, I let out a slow breath. The magic held. For now. Lord, if I made it through tonight, I was going to go home and practice shifting until it knocked me out.

I stretched my nimble new legs for a few seconds before I scrambled into the vent. Steamy air washed over me until my thin fur was soaked with sweat or humidity. Warm metal clacked under my tiny claws. I padded forward, shivering at the sensation of my long, naked tail brushing up against the sides of the tube until I reached a small, slatted barrier. Of course there was a barrier; otherwise it would have been too easy. I sat back and observed. Every couple of seconds, the slats fluttered open, sending out more warm air through the vent. I could probably fit. I waited for the next gust before I hopped up, catching the slats with my tiny paws. Then, sucking in a sharp breath, I wriggled through. Even with my new, tinier form, it was difficult. This clearly wasn't mouse size. Next time I'd have to go for beetle or something. Just as my hind legs scraped the edges, my treacherous mind began to wander. Suppose the disguise wore off? Suppose I got stuck here?

That was all it took. The vent began to shrink all around me. My hands stretched out in front of me, my hind legs pinching sharply. I caught my breath and squeezed my eyes shut. I was a mouse, I was a tiny, nimble mouse.

No dice. I could feel my tail receding as my natural form took over.

"Nngh!" I grunted and jerked. My legs came free as I stumbled forward into the thin, foil tube linking the vent to the dryer. The foil ripped and the ground dropped out beneath me. There was a low screech of metal on tile. My elbow banged against the backside of the dryer, sending pins and needles prickling up my arm as my butt hit the floor.

I lay on the linoleum for a moment, dusted with lint and holding my breath as I waited for someone to come investigate the noise. The seconds ticked by without so much as a sniffle from the household. These people would sleep through an armed robbery.

Swallowing my well-earned groan of pain, I climbed to my feet and stretched. My sore back screamed in protest, but I could feel a couple of loose vertebrae pop back into place. I definitely couldn't go out that way, but that was a problem for later. For now, I had to find Jackie's room.

I took a step forward and wobbled. I couldn't quite touch on what was wrong, but it was something. Had something gone wrong with my shift? Ugh, clothes. I frowned, reaching up to adjust my bra. Which wasn't fitting. It wasn't even full. I blinked and glanced down.

It was one of those surreal, phantom limb type moments. I could feel the way my body had always been. It was still right there in the front of my mind... but that wasn't the body I had now. Same height, but my shoulders stretched my shirt, I had no breasts to speak of, and that wasn't even going into the underwear situation. I shifted, tugging at the killer wedgie. Suddenly, I understood boxers a lot more. Geez, how off could I be? Girl to mouse to what I assumed had to be a devastatingly attractive guy. No mirror yet to say otherwise.

I sighed and closed my eyes, preparing to change back. Except I didn't. Each second I spent in this body, it felt a little less weird. A little more natural. I couldn't exactly walk around in my day-to-day life like this. Why not try it out? Could be fun. The thought made my heart flutter perhaps a little more than I'd have expected.

Adjusting my shirt again, I sniffed, trying to clear my nose of all the lint and dust. That was when I smelled it—something like bacon and old leather. I glanced down. There, like a gift left just for me, sat a bag of roasted, pig ears. I grinned.

Call my Ann a pig, will you?

I grabbed the bag and slipped into the hallway, feeling the strange way my clothes moved on this new body. I tried out a few different ways of walking until I found the rhythm that worked for these legs.

Jackie's door stood ajar, practically welcoming me. I didn't even have to sneak. By the sounds of her snores, I could bring in a full brass band and she still wouldn't hear me. I crept inside, clutching the bag of pig ears to my chest. Shoes and dirty clothes littered the floor. If it wasn't for the neon paint job this might have been my room, right down to the pile of old schoolwork in the corner. For an infinitesimal moment, my gut twisted. We weren't so different. Was this really justice, or was I just petty? God, I could make this girl's life hell. Thankfully, the moment passed and I remembered how much fun hell could be. Back to work.

Jackie slept on her back, a large, white teddy bear clutched in one arm while the other dangled off the edge of her bed. Her dark, curly hair fanned out on her pillow like a crown, her face the very picture of angelic peace. Only the low rumble of her snores shattered the illusion. Nice to know she had the nose of a 50-year-old man with sleep apnea.

I bit my cheek as I pulled two greasy pig ears out of the bag and leaned over her. My hands grew warm as I positioned them on either side of her head, just over her real ears.

Jackie grunted in her sleep, and I froze, waiting for her to wake. After a couple of seconds the snores resumed. My stomach flipped. The pig ears grew warmer and warmer until, after a few agonizing seconds, they grew soft. The grease dried up and the brown, leathery color faded into fleshy, pink tone of Jackie's skin.

I had to bite my lip to suppress a happy squeal. Delicately, I released the ears and took a step back. The magic held. The pig ears poked out from under her dark curls. God, they were absolutely beautiful! Now to pray they lasted until morning.

I returned the half-empty bag of dog treats to the laundry room and turned to leave when I found my way barred. A sandy little corgi whined, licking its lips.

"Shoo!" I hissed in a voice that was almost but not quite the pitch I was used to. Huh. Guess I'd never be a baritone.

The corgi whined, hopping back and forth like a preschooler who had to pee. Its dark eyes flicked to the bag of pig ears. Of course.

"Fine, if that's what it takes."

I pulled one of the greasy treats out of the bag and dropped it on the ground. With a happy, doggish grin, the corgi took its prize and waddled off to gorge itself. I heaved a sigh of relief and smiled. I sure hoped *he* was paying attention.

I positively danced to the back door. One down, one to go.

* * *

Astrid Wilmes's house wasn't such a trial to enter. Really, they were practically begging for a break-in. A large, inviting doggie door lead straight into the kitchen. It took only a little twisting and squeezing to slide through, no transformation necessary. That was where a lack of boobs really came in handy. I was actually really getting to feel okay in this body. There would be time to explore that later. The job came first.

After locating the fat old tabby cat draped over the back of the couch—no doubt the intended owner of the doggie door—I swung by the laundry room. Unfortunately, no dog meant no pig ears. No problem. I'd improvise.

I snuck into the spotless kitchen and frowned. The counters gleamed, the stove was spotless, and even the garbage can looked like it had been scrubbed with bleach. This was creepy. In the faint shine of the stove, I could just make out my features. And paused. It felt right. Just as right as my normal… my other body. I touched my cheekbones, frowning at the masculine face that stared back at me. For the first time, I had to wonder about Ann. What would she think if she saw me like this? A not-so-small part of me really, really wanted her to be okay with it.

An awful, niggling feeling gnawed at my insides. Later. I'd deal with it later. Hell, she didn't even know about the trickster stuff. No reason to talk about this any time soon.

I opened the first drawer. Silverware. Fun, but too malicious for this prank. Scowling, I switched some of the forks and knives, just to

61

introduce some much-needed chaos. On to the next drawer. Rags. I could do better. In the drawer next to the fridge was the Wilmes junk drawer. Even they had one. I rummaged as softly as I could through the rubber bands, alligator clips, and dusty old tea lights before... Jackpot! Beautiful, bright red Christmas ribbon! A snip and a curl later, I had six inches of lovely, spiraling revenge.

I think it showed considerable restraint that I didn't trash the too-tidy house as I searched for Astrid's room. I was here for Astrid, and even my admittedly fuzzy relationship with right and wrong had to respect that.

Astrid's room was almost too easy to find. There, right in the middle of the door, hung a blue plaque, covered with sparkly, white butterflies and her name in flowing letters. Soul of a demon, room of a nine-year-old. I nudged the door open, heart in my throat.

Astrid's room was cleaner than Jackie's and mine, but here and there the tell-tale clutter of a lived-in space. It served as a relief from the sterility of the rest of the house. Her backpack and drill team uniform hung off the back of her desk chair. An expensive-looking umbrella and a pair of heels had been discarded at the foot of her bed. There was a personality fighting for freedom beneath the cookie cutter exterior. I almost felt sorry for her. Almost.

Astrid slept on her side, facing the window. As I eased off her blanket, she mumbled and flopped onto her stomach, eyes dancing under her lids. I froze.

"I've had enough cookies, Mom..."

Crap. She wasn't the heavy sleeper Jackie was. It could have been just as much fun to wake her up, let her scream at the sight of some random guy leaning over her bed. I probably could have whispered something menacing, given her nightmares for months. Even better if her parents caught her. Still, it just wouldn't be poetic enough. This was for Ann.

With the precision of a surgeon, I lifted the back of her nightdress, exposing her back. I couldn't reach her actual tailbone, but I could get close enough. I touched the ribbon to the skin just atop her underwear and closed my eyes. The ribbon grew warm in my hands, thickening as it sprouted short, wiry hairs and latched on to her exposed skin. Astrid mumbled in her sleep again and rolled onto her back, completely oblivious. I had to jump out of the way before she rolled on top of my hand. Time to go.

I felt a warm, pleasant glow deep in my belly as I turned to leave. I'd done a good thing here. All I had to do was wait a couple of days, long enough for Jackie and Astrid to stew, then I could release them. If I felt like it. Hell, I felt so good I deserved an ice cream. The mini-mart by my house was probably open. Could even be fun to take this new body for a spin in public.

The sight of the red-haired man leaning against Astrid's doorframe drove all thought of ice cream from my mind. There he was, the original devil in disguise. *Loki.*

"Impressive." His voice sounded so much more mocking outside of my head. "But too easy if you ask me. No good story ever came of a trickster who had it easy. Though I must say, I am impressed. You're holding this transformation very well." He leaned forward, his smile sharp enough to cut. Then, *her* smile. The shift was so fact that I hadn't even seen him do it. "I remember my first shift to female. It was quite fun. Less fun when I mothered a horse, but it seems you're going in the opposite direction. Tell me, Kesi. Are you having fun?"

My cheeks burned, and I had to fight the urge to cover up.

"Get out of here!" I hissed. "We can talk later."

She grinned, the pocked scars around her lips twisting grotesquely. "So you can pump me for information I'm disinclined to give? But then I'd miss the show. I haven't been this entertained since you first caught my attention, Kesi dear." She brought up one slender hand, fingers dancing on the air. Teasing me. Testing me. Oh *crap*.

"Loki—"

But it was too late. Loki winked at me and snapped her fingers. Heat washed over my body, smoother and stronger than any of my own spells, then it began to press inward. Sweat beaded on my forehead as the too-hot, too-foreign magic began to compress my insides. I gasped and blinked, but all I could see was the heel of Loki's expensive leather shoe. I tried to clench my fists, but my tiny paws couldn't quite manage it. Loki smirked down at me. From this angle, she looked positively monstrous, his sharp, white teeth gleaming in the darkness.

"I'll see you later, Kesi dear."

I tried to scream, but all I could manage was a faint *squeak*. With another snap of her fingers, Loki faded like smoke on the breeze. That evil Norse son of a—

"Nngh!" Astrid moaned, pushing herself up from the bed. I whirled around, eyes wide. No! Not while I was still here. She yawned and ran her fingers through her hair. "God, it's almost mid-augh!" Her eyes widened. "Crap! Oh crap, holy crap, mom! *Mom!*"

Astrid leapt to her feet, teetering on top of her bed, arms windmilling as the springs squeaked. Just under her nightdress, I could see the outline of a curly, pink tail, but Astrid didn't seem to notice.

Footsteps pounded down the hall.

"Astrid? Honey, what is it?"

I squeaked and scampered under the bed, right into a growing family of dust bunnies spilling out of a pair of forgotten sneakers. Lucky for me, the thundering of two pairs of bare feet covered my sneezing fit.

"Sweetheart, what is it?" a clipped, feminine voice asked. No doubt Mrs. Wilmes.

"There's a mouse in here somewhere!"

"There can't be, I just sprayed the house." The gruff grumble had to come from Astrid's father.

The mattress creaked overhead as Astrid scrambled onto the floor.

"I swear, I just—"

"Oh my God! Sweetie, what is that under your pajamas?"

That sounded like my cue. I inched close to the edge of the bed, waiting for my opening, but Astrid must have glanced back at the tail. She let out an ear-splitting screech and bounced from foot to foot. Damn! I retreated back a couple of steps, kneading my tiny paws against the carpet. I could positively feel the dust bunnies rolling over my tail. I suppressed a shiver.

"Astrid, where did this come from?"

"I don't know, Mom. Maybe the tail fairy dropped it off!"

"Don't you take that tone with your mother!"

"What's going on?" A new pair of feet joined the others. I wrinkled my new, sensitive nose. These smelled like cheese.

"Get out of here, you little toe-face!"

"What crawled up your butt and—" the newest voice broke off in a howl of glee. "Jesus, Astrid! This is great."

"Rich!"

"I'm getting my phone."

"Don't you *dare!*"

Rich's cheese-feet took off, followed by the furious pounding of a pig-girl in pursuit.

"I will kill you, Rich!"

"Rich, do not take a picture of your sister like this!" There went Mom...

"I'll call the emergency room!" And Dad.

I held my breath and counted to 20. The shouting continued, a door slammed and, outside, an engine turned. The family was probably headed either to the emergency room or to the church for a quick and clean exorcism. Idly, I wondered if the pig tail would revert back to ribbon if it was cut off. Pity I wouldn't find out.

I crept out from under the bed, prepared to bite a couple of toes if I needed to. Lucky for me, it looked like I could go another day without knowing what cheese-feet tasted like. The house was devoid of any arguing or evil, pig-assed queen bees. Not one member of the Wilmes family had stayed behind. I crept into the hall and sniffed. The tidy house was as empty as it felt. I picked up the pace, heading straight for the doggy door. And here Loki thought—

"*Mrow.*"

My heart plummeted right into my tiny stomach. Heavy footsteps shook the floor. Right. There was one member of the Wilmes family that wouldn't go to the hospital. I turned slowly to see the fat, tabby cat prowling toward me, his orange ears perked. As soon as he knew I'd seen him, he froze. Or, at least, he tried to. It took a couple of seconds for all of him to come to a stop.

I drummed by claws against the stainless tile and tried to focus on being big—on being *me* sized again. It was hard to focus with those yellow eyes staring at me like, well, like their next meal. The familiar, prickly feeling began to wash over my body...

Only to stop abruptly as the searing heat of Loki's spell pushed it back. That Norse son of a bitch!

The tabby tried to leap for me, but all it really managed to do was flop forward like an animate pumpkin. It might have been funny if said pumpkin wasn't aiming for me.

I turned and scurried as fast as my little rodent legs would carry me, which apparently wasn't fast enough. The cat swiped, catching my tail. I yelped—well, squeaked—and squirmed around. The tabby opened its mouth wide, revealing rows of pearly white daggers, each the size of my arm.

"*Hisssss!*"

The cat's tuna breath washed over me and, for just a second, I swear my heart stopped. Before it had the chance to use those horrible teeth on me, I lurched forward, burying my teeth in its soft paw.

"*Nrrreagh!*"

The tabby shrieked and jerked back, flinging me across the floor. That probably would have killed a real mouse. Gotta love magic. I slid like a hockey puck, the world spinning around me, but I just managed to find my feet a second before my pal Garfield. I charged through the doggie door as fast as my little legs could carry me. Once I hit the grass, I knew I'd lost him, but I didn't stop running until I was home.

* * *

Loki's spell wore off just as I rounded the corner to my street. Like the flick of a switch, I was back to two legs. It came so suddenly I stumbled forward, face-planting straight into the concrete. Yet another ego-bruise that I could blame on my least favorite trickster.

My clothes were twisted, but they fit again. Probably a good thing, but it came with a certain level of melancholy. It had been strangely nice to be in another skin. Maybe another day, when Loki wasn't likely to be watching, I could try again. Definitely. So long as Loki didn't try to make me feel weird about it.

After double checking that my parents' light was out, I scaled the old live oak that twisted up to my window, padded across the porch roof, and slipped back into my bedroom.

Loki leaned against my desk, male again, using a pair of scissors to clean out his fingernails. Show-off. I shot him a filthy glare as I shut the window.

"Get out," I snarled.

Loki chuckled. "Oh, don't pout at me, it wasn't all that exciting. Though you really ought to practice more. That enchantment should have been easy to drop."

"Garfield tried to turn me into lasagna!"

Loki rolled his eyes. "Only at the end. You hid under the bed for most of it. But you are getting better. And I'm proud of you for learning that a true trickster is not strictly one thing or another. Tell me, do you think that girlfriend of yours would appreciate the male you as much as the female?"

My stomach squirmed. But no. Loki didn't get to scare me out of this. "I don't remember inviting you on this particular trick." I crossed my arms. "In fact, I remember you told me you'd rather teach ice to melt."

"Yes, well, opinions can change. However grudgingly." Loki tossed the scissors back on the desk and shrugged. "You showed more promise tonight than you have since I told you about your parentage in the first place."

"Gee, thanks, I'll add that to my wall of special things."

"Don't use sarcasm against me, Kesi. I quite literally invented it." Loki pushed himself up off the desk and, with an air of practiced nonchalance, he stretched and yawned. "I've reconsidered my position and I'd like to take you on as my student after all."

"Oh?" With an equal nonchalance, I made to plop on the bed. I missed. My breath wheezed out from between my teeth as my butt hit the floor. Undeterred, I toed off my filthy sneakers, trying to maintain my cool. "Maybe I don't want lessons. In case you weren't paying attention, I did a pretty good job on my own."

"Yes, but you couldn't break my spell." Loki grinned, stretching the scars around his mouth as he leaned forward. He looked like an evil scarecrow as he draped himself across the foot of my bedframe. "Think of what else my friends and I could show you. Mimicking. Dreamwalking. Would you like to dreamwalk? I can talk to Anansi for you. He's got this tea you drink and, once the visions of flying elephants go away it's lovely. We could maybe even teach you about that new form you like so much."

He was so damned smug. I shot Loki a blank look as I pulled off my socks.

"I want information. Right here. Right now."

Loki rolled his eyes and rolled back on his heels. "Really, Kesi, you need to—"

"Which trickster is my father? My parents don't know. As far as they're concerned, the donor was perfectly Joe Schmoe, dude-next-door human. But you know better."

Loki sighed and ran his hand through his mane of fiery curls. "He'll be cross with me."

"I'll be your student."

Loki's lip twitched. He shrugged and reached past me to tug the curtains away from the window. I glanced out, seeing only the night sky through the twisted branches of the live oak.

"Your father is said to be responsible for the stars in the sky and the waxing and waning of the moon," Loki mused. "He is the perfect mimic, and walks the very line between hero and villain. He's one of the big names, you know."

"Then cut the crap and give me a name."

Loki straightened and let the curtains fall back into place.

"Coyote."

I tested the word in my mind. Coyote. *The* Coyote—hero and harlequin for the Apache and the Navajo. For the first time, I had a name. I had a father other than the man who'd raised me, taken me on vacations, snuck me extra cookies even when I was grounded. Could Coyote even compare to the man sleeping downstairs? Could he compare to the woman who'd taught me to ride a bike but wouldn't let me have a car? Who exactly was Coyote to me? He was a shifter, too. The stories said he loved men and women alike. Was he just like me, then?

I needed to know.

"Can you help me find him?" I demanded.

Loki gasped and pressed a hand to his chest. "Kesi, dear, what would your parents think?"

"Yeah, because you're one to talk about healthy parental relationships, Frosty. They don't know about any of this, and they won't." I sat up and scowled. "*Please*." The platitude tasted like chalk in my mouth and I almost gagged, but Loki perked up.

"Since you asked so nicely, little pup, I'll lead you to him," he offered. "In the meantime, you play *my* game. Tomorrow. Gray Branch Park. Four o'clock. You will not be late. Do we have a deal?"

He held out his slender hand. I stared at it and felt my stomach twist. I knew better than to make a deal with the likes of him, but I was a trickster by blood. Only a trickster could help me. I could play his game. I took a deep breath and took his hand. A jolt of electricity sparked against my palm, shooting up my arm and right into my chest. I started and yanked my hand back.

"What—"

Loki straightened and smirked.

"Goodnight, Kesi. I'll see you tomorrow." Then, like smoke on the breeze, he was gone. I stared at the empty spot for a moment, waiting for him to come back. He didn't.

Good. I thought he'd never leave.

I slumped back against my bedframe and sighed, letting the lingering rush of adrenaline buzz through me. That had been risky, but I'd killed four birds with one stone. This time yesterday, I didn't know who my father was, I had no means of contacting him, no means of learning more about what I was, and Astrid and Jackie were making Ann miserable. A small, sensible part of me felt guilty that I'd used justice for Ann to get Loki. I shouldn't have had ulterior motives. I squashed that small, sensible part with the ever-pleasant delusion that I knew exactly what I was doing. It wasn't like Ann would know what I'd done, anyway. Not until I decided she was ready for all of this. Besides, I hadn't exactly invited Loki. I'd just let him be nosey.

Still, my conscience was relentless. Fine. I'd buy Ann a card on my way to school. And maybe a teddy bear. That should be enough to get Jiminy Cricket off my back.

When the adrenaline wore off, I rose and tugged back the curtains from my window. Through the spindly branches of the oak, I could see the full moon shining. My stomach flipped. As the story went, each month Coyote tried to eat the moon one massive bite at a time, but he could never keep it down. So he put it all back by the end of the month. Only to try it again and again, as he always had and always would. My father, the Moon-Eater.

My *absent* father.

I let go of the curtain and closed my eyes, trying to imagine the taste of the moon. Sugary, sweet, and powdery, or maybe sandy and gritty. Maybe little moon beams would fly out of my fingertips the way Jimmy Stewart described it in *It's a Wonderful Life.* Maybe nothing would happen at all. The thought made me feel at once horribly powerful and painfully small.

Things were easier when my only father was an eccentric, sterile college professor and my mother was a clever doctor who couldn't be tricked by anyone. This time a year ago, I couldn't be bothered with the identity of my benevolent sperm donor. Hard to say if it was better back then, but it was definitely easier.

"I know what I'm doing," I said out loud. I wasn't sure if I was trying to convince myself or the world at large. It didn't matter. This was my trick. If it went wrong, it was my fault and nobody else's. I'd just have to figure it out.

Protection

By Cheryl Rainfield

Janelle's presentation on depression is so good that I lean forward in my chair and smile at her before I remember that I shouldn't. From the front of the class, Janelle narrows her eyes at me. Her friends all turn around in their seats to see who she's glaring at. As if they had any doubt.

"Ewww, did you see that? Kennedy came on to Janelle!" Layla says, shuddering dramatically.

"Keep your lesbo self away from her!" Zhi hisses at me, her shining black hair swinging like a curtain over her face.

I roll my eyes. Like I'd ever want to be with a straight, two-faced homophobe. Just because I'm out, just because my hair is so short the hairdresser always asks me why I want my hair cut like a man, just because I don't wear makeup or giggle about boys, Janelle and her gang think I'm coming on to them if I even look at them.

"Janelle, anything else?" Mrs. Medina asks crisply.

Janelle sorts through her note cards. Someone coughs; someone else scrapes their chair along the floor. The classroom lights flicker and buzz discordantly, and even with the air conditioning, the room feels hot.

I sigh and shift on my hard seat. I don't understand how someone like Janelle, with her mean streak and her constant need to be admired could talk so compassionately about people who suffer from depression. Could talk about it like she really gets it. It's as if she shadowed my mom around for a month. Not that she'd have to go anywhere but Mom's bedroom.

Janelle's eyes flick up to mine for a moment. Zhi turns around again to glare at me.

"No, I'm all done," Janelle says.

Mrs. Medina claps her hands briskly. "Very good, Janelle. You can go back to your seat, now. Gino, Ebba, be ready with your presentations on Monday."

Janelle stalks to her seat, her gaze on mine the entire time. I shift uneasily. I should never have let myself smile at her. It was like prodding a lion.

The last bell rings, and before Mrs. Medina can say anything more we're all up out of our seats and racing for the door, backpacks on backs and books in hand. Janelle and her gang exit before me.

I breathe easier.

I walk out into the hall—and Janelle thumps her shoulder into mine, slamming me against the shiny brick wall so hard my teeth jar together. My shoulder aches but I try not to let it show.

Her friends surround me in a half circle, backing me up against the wall, blocking off my exit. Students rush past us in the usual frenzied escape for the weekend, some looking over curiously, others ignoring the tight knot of humans closing me in. Shouts and catcalls sound out, but not for me, sneakers squeak against the floor, boys throw half-finished lunches or sweaty socks at each other.

"Don't think you can make a pass at me, dyke," Janelle says, pushing her face up close to mine, her lips a snarl, her normally pretty face transforming into an ugly mask that I'm sure none of the teachers have seen. This close, her sickly-sweet perfume is overwhelming.

I push my breath out. "I wasn't coming on to you! I just liked your presentation. I thought you made depression real. I've never heard anyone put it like that before—that it's like a happiness-eating virus, eating up all the happiness before the person can taste it. It was... real."

Janelle's eyes soften a little, and for a second I almost think she wants to ask me something, or maybe tell me something. Then one of the girls snickers. Janelle's gaze darts sideways at the girl who laughed, and when she looks back at me, her face is hard again, like a mask. "Don't kiss up to me."

"I'm not. Besides," I say, "you're not my type."

"Not your type?" Janelle stiffens, tossing her head. Her hair whips my cheek. "What's that supposed to mean?"

I don't understand this whole straight-girl fear that I'm coming on to them, then offense when they realize I'm not. "I don't like straight girls. Think about it; why would I? Rejection, aggravation, and there's no attraction."

"Maybe you like to suffer," Zhi says.

"Seriously? Get real," I say. "No one does."

"Yeah? Then why are you always trying to flaunt it?" Janelle says.

Flaunt it? "I'm just trying to be me." Trying to be comfortable in my body and who I am, which is more I can say for any of them, with their faces all made up, the fake girly-girl way they laugh and talk, their designer clothes bought to show off their bodies to boys instead of, god forbid, being liked for who they are.

"So you were just born that way? A big fat dyke?"

Janelle says the words like they're an insult. Good thing I've gone to Pride for the last three years, even taken part in the Dyke March. I've reclaimed the word "dyke". "Lesbo" and "queer," too. Not that they don't still have a slight swampish quality coming from the mouths of homophobes, but they don't hurt the way they used to.

I force myself to laugh. "Were you born straight?"

Mrs. Medina comes out of the classroom carrying her leather briefcase, her high-heeled shoes clicking along the floor. She stops when she sees us. "What's going on here, girls?" she asks sternly, looking at us over the tops of her wire-rimmed glasses.

"Nothing, Mrs. Medina," Janelle says sweetly.

Mrs. Medina locks her door, her keys jangling, then looks right at me. "Everything all right, Kennedy?"

I blink, surprised. Usually teachers get duped by Janelle. "Uh—yeah. We were just having a talk," I say, shouldering my backpack. "But we're done now."

I push out of the circle of girls, and they part for me, giving me cold stares. I hurry down the emptying hall, feeling their gazes prick my back. I stop at my locker, spinning the dial on my lock with sweat-slick fingers. I grab my books without sorting them, then rush off down the hall again. I don't want to be left alone with Janelle and her gang. They make my life miserable enough already.

I ram open the school door and escape into the heavy, humid heat of the afternoon, the sun biting into my skin. I sigh. I'm glad school's over until Monday, though it's not like I want to go home. But I have to make sure Mom got out of bed, and Rod didn't hurt her again. Happy times.

I start through the parking lot and pull out my cell.

When r u getting here? I text Aisha.

I've only walked a few steps when my cell beeps. Pick u up 5-ish. Love u, girl.

I grin. The air around me grows lighter. Even the sun doesn't seem to burn any more. Aisha's coming! I'll see her tonight. Maybe even the whole weekend, if I can sneak her up into my room again. I never went to Pride looking for a girlfriend—I went for the community, and to feel less alone—but last year I found Aisha. She lives in the next town over. She's beautiful and smart and talented, wants to become a dancer or act in theatre. I'm the most bookish, geeky person I know, can't dance with any sort of rhythm, and she still loves me. I miss her so much the days I don't see her, but everything feels better when she's here.

I feel so high it takes me a moment to register the figures standing at the gate. Janelle and her gang—and their boyfriends. Watching me as I get closer.

My heart pounds harder. Do I turn around and go the other way? Or pretend I don't see them? Will they leave me alone?

I lick my lips. There are other students still about, the odd teacher walking to their car. Surely Janelle and her gang won't do anything here, in such a public place?

But when I take a closer look, I realize no one's paying any attention. Everyone's too busy getting on with their lives.

"That the girl who came on to you?" Dylan says, squaring his thick shoulders. Janelle would date a football player.

I lock gazes with Janelle, refusing to show any fear. *Don't do it*, I tell her in my mind.

Janelle hesitates, tugging at her hoop earring.

"That's her!" Layla cries, stabbing her manicured finger toward me in case he somehow missed me.

Dylan starts toward me, his face dark as a thunderstorm, the others following close behind.

I swallow hard. I might not like to show fear, but I know when the odds are against me.

I spin around and run back through the parking lot.

Dylan roars. Heavy footsteps pound along the asphalt behind me. It sounds like they're all after me.

I zigzag around the cars that are left, then make a sharp right through the side entrance onto the street, my shoes slapping the pavement, my heart pounding so hard I can hear the echo in my ears.

I peek over my shoulder.

Dylan is gaining on me, his head thrust forward, his thick arms pumping, his hands clenched in fists. The others are close behind him.

I push myself faster, past the Pizza 'N Wings and Roasted Beanery that students often go to. I've been shoved and hit and tripped and slapped before, had slurs spray-painted on my locker, my belongings destroyed, had other kids ignore me and taunt me and act mean—but I've never had a whole hoard of them come after me like this, ready to hurt me. So full of hate. It must be mob mentality—we learned about it in class. People do horrible things in mobs, things that they might not do on their own. And I watch the news. I know that hatred can make people do crazy things, like the 10 men who attacked the lesbian couple in Chicago, or the man who shot and killed a gay man in Greenwich Village.

I don't want to die, please don't let me die. I keep running past Smith's Variety, then a XXX store.

My breath burns in my throat, sweat pouring down my sides. I don't think I can run any faster, but I do. And still their footsteps pound behind me, sounding closer.

How do I get rid of them? Where can I go? Home is too far away, and a store owner might turn a blind eye, or might just shove me back out with the others, thinking we're just being rowdy teens.

I turn the corner, running faster than I ever have in my life, and almost bump into Mrs. Medina.

"Kennedy, slow down!"

"Sorry, Mrs. M!" I yell, surprised to see her here, but I can't stop. I pass Green Papaya Thai, the scent of garlic, fish, and grease strong.

And there to my left is an alleyway, with a row of battered green dumpsters lined up along one wall, the closest one turned on its side, garbage spilling out. I swerve into the alley before I can even decide if it's the right thing to do.

An orange cat screeches at me from the top of a dumpster before it leaps down and runs past my legs, into the street.

I dive between the first dumpster and the second, something cold and hard lodging onto my finger. I wriggle on my stomach until I'm all the way behind the dumpster, against the wall, hidden from the sidewalk. I lie there, trying to quiet my breathing and still my heaving chest.

Don't let them find me. Please don't let them find me.

Footsteps pound past the alleyway—one heavy set, then a bunch more, voices calling to each other. "Where did she go?"

I lie there rigidly.

The cold metal slides further down my finger. It's a large brass ring, dull and tarnished, like a ring from an old curtain rod. I think about shaking it off, but I want to keep as still and as quiet as I can. And then I realize it's not loose at all; it's tight around my finger. I shift uneasily.

Something hard digs into my chest, and the stink of old fish, rotting vegetables, piss, and beer fills my every breath, making me nauseous. What looks like years of food stains and grease and guck cling to the bottom edges of the dumpster, the wheels grimy and rusty. There is litter all around me—crushed soda cans, used napkins, greasy take-out containers spilling moldy Thai food along the ground. Flies crawl over the food and buzz near my face.

I shudder. But I'd rather go home smelling like a dump than let those guys hurt me. The brass ring seems tighter than before, like there's no way it could slide off. I must have misjudged how big it was when I first looked.

"Damn it, where is she?" Dylan cries out angrily, his voice as loud as if he's standing right in front of my dumpster

I jump. My foot hits a soda bottle, and it rattles and clanks along the concrete.

Damn!

"Hey—I think she's in here!" Dylan yells, his heavy footsteps echoing in the alley.

I flatten back against the wall. *No, no, no!*

The ring on my finger tightens harder against my skin, growing warm, then hot, so hot it feels like it's burning. I bite down on my lip. *Please go away! Don't find me.*

Hands appear on one side of the dumpster, and a head appears around the corner. Dylan. "Got you," he says, grinning tightly.

I try to shrink back further, but there's nowhere to go.

His head disappears from view. "I found her!" he roars.

I should run. Run while I can. I get to my feet, trembling, the wall behind me.

The dumpster shakes. Hands appear on either side, and then Dylan and Otto drag the dumpster away from the wall, soda cans and fast-food containers tumbling to the ground. Dylan's friends, and Janelle and all her friends, crowd around me like a human pen, closing me in. They leer at me, pressing too close, their eyes excited, their bodies tight with suppressed tension.

I back up a step until my heels hit the wall, and raise my fists in front of my chest. I feel light-headed, almost woozy, my breath coming in tight, short pants.

"Ha! Look at the trash we found in with all the garbage!" Dylan says, grinning like he's said something witty.

Strands of pasta cling to my shirt. I can feel a wet stain on my thigh. I probably stink now, too. "*I'm* not the garbage here," I say, looking at Dylan pointedly.

"Yeah you are, you faggy freak," he says, jabbing his pointer finger so close it almost touches my nose.

"She can't be a fag, you dumbard," Janelle says, slapping him. "She's a girl."

"Lesbo freak," Dylan says to Janelle. "Whatever." He turns to face me. "That'll teach you to come on to my girlfriend." They're not going to believe me; I know they're not. But I try any way. "I *didn't* come on to her."

"Then why did you run?" Dylan asks, as if I've said something stupid.

I stare at him. "It's 10 of you to one of me! And you didn't look like you'd listen to anything I said, anyway.

"Damn right," he says. He pulls back his fist to punch me.

I stiffen, anticipating the pain, and raise my arms higher.

Dylan's fist slams into the air a millimeter away from my cheek, then bounces off again, as if he hit something hard.

I don't understand what's going on.

Dylan's lips go white. "What the—?" he says, his eyes wide. He pulls back his fist and gazes at the raw skin, his knuckles bleeding.

I stare at his raw knuckles. He definitely hit something. But it sure wasn't me.

I stand there, laughter building in my chest. It's just so crazy.

"Dylan, quit playing around," Janelle says, propping her hand on her hip.

"You trying to fake her out?" Otto asks, scratching his chest.

"No, damn it!" Dylan shakes his head, his eyes desperate. He pulls back for another punch, his mouth gritted in a tight line, his arm muscles flexing, and swings hard.

I press myself back against the wall, the brick pricking into my scalp, his bloody fist whizzing towards me.

His fist rushes toward my nose and mouth, so close I can feel the heat of his skin—then bounces back with a crunching sound.

I wince.

Dylan howls in pain.

"What're you playing at, man?" one of the guys says.

Dylan stares at his bleeding fist, then back at me, his face twisted in pain. "Witch," he whispers.

I shake my head. This is crazy. I'm not doing anything. But something or someone is.

Dylan cradles his fist to his chest. "*You* hit her," Dylan says hoarsely to the other guys.

"Sure!" Otto says, grinning. He lunges at me, one fist, then the other, going for my face.

I cringe.

Both fists smash hard into the air right before my face, then bounce away without touching me at all.

"Shit!" Otto says, jerking backward, his fists bleeding.

I stare at him, then at Dylan. That's three times now. It can't be a coincidence. And judging from their faces and their bleeding fists, it's not an act either. It's something, though. Something amazing. Something impossible.

I take a deeper breath, feeling almost dizzy with relief.

"Why are you dicking around?" Janelle asks Dylan, her eyes narrowed. "I thought you were going to make sure she never came on to me again with her skeevy lesbo smile."

Dylan turns to Janelle, his face flushed. "I tried, babe. Otto did, too. You saw that. But we can't get her. It's like she's a witch, or got some freaky voodoo protection going on."

It's just so crazy he might be right. I think of the way the ring tightened around my finger and grew so hot just before Dylan tried to hit me. Maybe it creates an invisible force field. Or maybe there really is a witch around, protecting me. I crane my neck, but I don't see anyone. And then I think of how I almost ran into Mrs. Medina. I've never seen her in this neighborhood before. But it couldn't be her—could it?

"*You're* the freak," Janelle says, spitting at Dylan.

Diego lets out a high-pitched, uneasy laugh.

They're starting to get freaked out. Not just Dylan, but the others are too, because they can't hurt me. A small smile creeps onto my face. I bite my lip to make it go away.

"Shut up," Dylan snaps, and Diego stops laughing.

"Look, Janelle," Dylan says, turning to Janelle. "I'm pretty sure I busted my finger. I'll have to tape it to play. This girl isn't worth it."

"You mean *I'm* not worth it," Janelle says. "Fine, then—we're through! Just watch me, dickwad. I'll show you how it's done."

She shoulders him aside and steps right up to me, her eyes dark and glittering, her mouth compressed.

I pray that whoever or whatever is protecting me keeps on protecting me. But just in case, I shift my feet so I stand steadier, and raise my arms higher.

Janelle opens her hand and swings it hard at my cheek.

I raise my hands to protect my face.

There's a loud cracking sound as her hand reaches the air in front of my cheek, and then her hand bounces back, punching Diego so hard in the nose that he stumbles back, howling.

Janelle clutches her hand between her thighs. "Fuck! That hurt."

"I told you so," Dylan says, sounding like he's enjoying her pain.

Janelle stares at me, her eyes wide. "How'd you do that?"

"Do what?" I say innocently.

"Come on, let's get out of here before she does another spell on us!" Diego says.

"This isn't over," Janelle says, so close to my face her spittle flicks my cheeks.

I don't move away, just stare back at her.

"Come on," Dylan says.

They turn like a pack, and run down the alleyway and back out onto the street.

I watch them go, my legs weak and trembly. I lean my head back against the brick. I can't believe what just happened. Can't believe that the others came out of this bruised or hurt, while I don't have a scratch on me.

I look down at my hand, at the yellow ring softly gleaming there. It looks more like gold now, not brass, and it isn't tarnished anymore. There are tiny words printed on the surface, but I can't read what they say, not even when I bring the ring right up to my face.

* * *

I push open the apartment door. The smell of unwashed body and sweat hits me, even through the garbage-smell clinging to my clothes.

I sigh. She didn't shower. Again.

I walk to Mom's bedroom door and look in. She's closed the drapes after I opened them all this morning, and the room is dark and dank. Mom's a huddled, unmoving shape on her bed.

I march in and wrench open her curtains, letting the light stream in. Piles of dirty dishes sit on the dresser next to the bed, the milk in the top bowl curdled into clumps. I was hoping if I left them there that they'd make her get up, but it's clear I was wrong. I trip over a twisted knot of dirty clothes on the floor, then catch myself.

"Time to get up," I say, forcing cheerfulness into my voice.

Mom stirs and shields her eyes. "That you, honey?"

"Yeah, Mom, it's me." I sigh. "Did you take your meds today?"

Mom shakes her head, her stringy, unwashed hair like worn shoelaces. "You know I don't like how they make me feel. Like there's a glass wall between me and the rest of the world."

"I know, Mom," I say, trying to keep my voice gentle and patient. I don't want her bursting into tears or lying back down and blotting out the world again. "But it's got to be better than the way you're feeling now, doesn't it? So depressed you can't even get out of bed."

"I got out of bed," Mom says hesitantly.

Right. To go to the washroom when she couldn't hold it any more, then crawling back into bed under her cocoon of blankets.

I go into her bathroom, find her pills, and shake two out onto my palm, then bring them back with a glass of water.

I hold them out to Mom. "Swallow," I say, mock sternly. But I mean it. It's hard to see her like a robot, going through the motions of the day, her emotion all one level, never rising or falling. But it's harder still to see her like this.

I miss the mom who used to sit on the living-room floor with me and draw pictures of lollypop trees and starlit skies, laughing. Miss the mom who would read me *Harold And the Purple Crayon* over and over so many times she must have been sick of it but never complained, who would have freshly baked chocolate-chip cookies waiting for me after school, and a warm supper before bed. But she hasn't been that mom since I was five. Not since the memories came back of her dad raping her when she was my age.

I watched her slip farther and deeper into the depression until she wasn't the same person any more. Until my dad left us. Until there was only her and me, and then Rod, Mom, and me—and her depression.

Mom squints up at me. "What's wrong with your shirt?"

I glance down. Grease and food splatters and bits of pasta stain my shirt. "Nothing. I had an accident with a dumpster." I thrust the pills closer to her. "Swallow."

Mom looks up at me with puppy-dog eyes, pleading with me not to make her, like I'm the parent and she's the daughter. I close my heart to her plea. I have to. I need some semblance of a parent. Some ghost of a reasonable, rational adult around here. Because Rod sure isn't it. I hand her the water.

Mom's lips squinch up, but she sits up and takes the pills, tossing them back into her mouth, then swallows, her throat moving up and down. She sticks her tongue out so I can see that she really swallowed them.

"Good," I say, taking the glass from her. I rinse it out in her bathroom and set it next to her sink, then walk back to the bed. "I'll make supper now, and you can come out and eat with us. Then I'll be going out with Aisha for a while."

"You're a good daughter," Mom says, sadly reaching out her warm, dry hand and cupping my cheek. "A kind daughter. I'm sorry I've been such a failure to you." Her other hand plucks at the yellow cotton sheets. Yellow because I'd hoped they'd cheer her up.

"You're not a failure," I say, squeezing her hand. "But have a shower and get dressed before you come out for supper, okay? You know Aisha's coming over."

Mom nods obediently, like a little child.

I turn and go to my room, stripping off my dirty clothes and putting them in the tub to soak, then tugging on clean, dry ones. I go into the kitchen, pull vegetables out of the fridge, open the pack of pre-seasoned ground tofu, and drop it into a pan with butter. I put water in a pot on the stove to heat, and start chopping up the vegetables, scraping garlic and onion into the pan, then spinach, stirring it.

The door shudders open, and my stepfather, Rod, stalks in. He throws his briefcase onto the floor, then crowds up behind me at the stove, so close I can smell his male body odor, feel the heat from his body.

"Aw, not that freaking tofu crap again!" Rod says, leaning over my shoulder. "Can't you cook anything good? You're just like your mother—a useless waste of human space."

"My mother is not a waste." And neither am I. Though I know he's made us both feel like one. I slide away from him along the counter toward the sink, then turn around to face him, the spatula in my hand. "You want something different? You cook it," I say, my mouth dry.

Rod's face reddens. "You little shit." He lunges for me, making a backhanded swing with his meaty hand.

I press back against the counter, waiting, hoping the ring will protect me. Hoping I wasn't hallucinating it all.

Rod's hand snaps back from my face and hits his own head.

"Wha—?" Rod says, stumbling.

It's happening again! I almost laugh aloud. I can't believe it.

Rod clenches his reddened hand, his eyes stretched wide. "How'd you do that?"

I stand taller. "Don't ever try to hit me again. Next time you hit me, I'll report you."

"You little—!" Rod lunges for my throat, both thick hands outstretched.

I don't move. His hands bounce back as if they've hit an invisible wall.

Rod yells and holds his hand to his chest, cradling his thumb. He looks at me out of the corner of his eyes, then licks his lips. "What are you?"

"The same girl you beat for years."

I take a step forward, and he takes a step back. It's a weird reversal of our roles. "I mean it. Touch me or my mom again, and the cops will be here. Understand?"

Rod nods and backs away even more.

For a second I almost get why he beats us. The feeling of power. But it's not a clean feeling, making someone do what you want out of fear. It feels heavy and ugly.

Mom appears in the doorway, her hair wet, her tattered bathrobe wrapped tightly around her scrawny body. "What's happening in here? It sounds like a stampede."

"Rod was just telling me how he's never going to hit you or me again," I say.

Mom's mouth makes a soundless oh.

"Isn't that right, Rodney?" I say.

Rod glares at me, but he nods.

I can hardly believe it. I almost want to cheer.

Mom looks back and forth between the two of us. "That's... lovely," she says uncertainly.

Rod snorts. "I'm going out to get some real food to eat. Something with meat that I can dig my teeth into!" he yells, his belly hanging over his belt. "None of this gay tofu crap."

"Right. Like a Big Mac is real food," I say. "Or tofu makes you gay." I shake my head. That's a new one to me.

"It's better than this pussy shit!" he yells, slamming the door behind him.

I almost hope that his diet—heavy in processed foods, empty carbs, and additives and preservatives—makes him sick. Almost.

Mom wraps her arms around herself and shivers. "Kennedy, I don't think you should bait him like that. He'll get in an awful temper, and you know what he's like..." Her voice trails off.

I straighten up. "No, Mom—he promised he'd never hurt us again, and this time, I think he'll keep his promise."

Mom shakes her head. "You know what he's like, honey."

"But this time is different. He can't push me around anymore, Mom, and he knows it. And I won't let him hurt you again, either."

Mom smiles sadly at me, like she doesn't quite believe it, but she stands taller, and her eyes grow brighter. I wish I'd been able to stop Rod years ago. The one time I called the cops he beat Mom so badly in retaliation that I'd been afraid to ever try again. But now, with Rod not being able to touch me, I feel braver. If he tries anything again, I can just stand in front of her and he won't dare hit her.

Mom shuffles into the kitchen. "Something smells good."

I smile at her. This is more life than she's shown in a long time. "Good. Dinner's ready. Will you get the plates and forks out?"

I hold my breath, wondering if I've pushed her too fast, too hard. But she just nods and slowly reaches for them, her hands shaky.

I dish out the food onto two plates, and sit down at the kitchen table across from Mom. It's nice to have her eat with me, just the two of us. I can't remember the last time we did this.

Mom leans across the table. "What a lovely ring." She stops mid-chew to stare at my finger. "Is it new? Did Aisha give it to you?"

We only talk about Aisha when Rod isn't here.

"No," I say, looking down at the ring. "I... found it."

Mom reaches for my hand. "It looks valuable. Maybe you should put an ad up that you found it. Let me see."

She's actually acting like a mom again—more than she has in years. I blink away hot tears, and tug at the ring.

The ring tightens around my finger. I tug harder, and it tightens so much it feels like an outgrowth of my finger, like a knuckle or a nail. "I— I can't get it off," I say. "It's stuck."

Mom smiles a half-smile at me. "Maybe it's meant to be yours, then."

"Maybe it is," I say slowly. I sure hope she's right.

* * *

Alone in my room, I sit down at my particle-board desk, turn on my desk lamp, and peer at the ring on my finger through the magnifying glass. I can just make out the words etched into the gold:

You are granted 3 uses of protection

Three uses. I've already used up two.

I blow out my breath, trying to ignore the heavy feeling in my chest. I need to protect my mom. But after today, I don't think Rod will try anything. I'm not so sure about Janelle, though.

I turn my hand over to see the rest of the text.

Once completed, you must pass on to a new owner

I sit back. So the ring can be used again, just not by me. I can give it to my Mom. It doesn't say it has to be a stranger.

I wonder if someone left it in the alleyway for me, if they somehow knew I needed it and would end up there, or if it was all by chance. I prefer to think someone was watching over me; it's a comforting thought. But if they were, why didn't they give me this ring years ago? Mom and I could have been spared so much abuse.

I shake my head. I'll never know. And it doesn't really matter. I'm grateful I have it now.

Just in case it's somehow a living entity—I have no idea how magical items work except what I've read in books—I whisper, "Thank you." The ring seems to glow even brighter, before fading back to its golden shine.

A quick, repeated knock sounds at the door. Aisha! I leap up, knocking my chair over, and rush for the door, opening it.

It's a relief to see Aisha's face, her wide lips curved in an easy smile.

"Hey, you," she says softly, her brown eyes warm and happy.

"Hey," I say back. "Just give me a minute to get my stuff."

"Why don't you invite Aisha in?" Mom says from behind me.

My face heats. *I will not be embarrassed Mom's wearing a bathrobe,* I tell myself firmly. *At least she had a shower. And Aisha's seen her worse than this.* I hesitate, then open the door wider and turn around.

I blink. Mom's dressed in a pair of old jeans and a green silk blouse that I haven't seen on her since I was little. It's so different than her usual uniform of grey sweatpants and T-shirts or her ratty bathrobe. Tears prick my eyes.

Aisha steps in. "Nice to see you again, Mrs. Robinson," she says.

"Sepherina," Mom says. "You can call me Sepherina." She smiles at Aisha. "Where are you two girls going tonight?"

Oh my god—she's acting like a protective father whose daughter is going out on a first date! I don't know what's going on with her.

I stare at her. Her hair has been brushed, and she has just a touch of lipstick on. Her eyes are more focused than they've been in years. Can all this be just because I stood up to Rod—and he backed down?

Aisha clears her throat. "Well, uh, I thought I'd take Kennedy to the bookstore, treat her to a book there. You know she loves books almost as much as she loves people."

I laugh and swat at her playfully, but she's right. I'm not sure I could have survived all the years of Rod's beatings and put-downs if I hadn't had a way to escape.

"That's very thoughtful of you, Aisha," Mom says. "I'm glad you're seeing Kennedy. I think you're good for my daughter." She smiles at Aisha, her lips trembling.

Don't cry. Please don't cry, I silently will her.

Mom fumbles in her pocket, then pulls out a few bills. She stuffs them into my hand. "Get Aisha something nice, too. Or treat both of you," she whispers.

I shove the bills back at her. We don't have much money; Rod keeps tight control over the bank account, and watches every penny. I don't know how she managed to save even this much.

A fragment of memory expands in my head.

I'm nine. Mom's crouching on the floor, lifting up a corner of the bedroom carpet, her bloodied hand shaking. "This is our emergency fund, baby. You have to know where it is in case you ever need it."

"What do you mean, Mommy?" I say, moving closer to her.

"If you need to get away, or anything happens to me, you take it and run."

"I'm not going anywhere without you!" I say, and burst into tears.

"No, no, of course not," Mom says, pulling me close and rocking me in a hug. "Shhh, it's all right now. Mommy's got you." She pulls away to look at me. "But I want you to remember this, Kennedy. Promise me you'll remember where it is."

"I promise," I say, and press my face into her neck.

"You keep it," I tell Mom.

Mom shakes her head and presses the bills back into my hand. "I've been saving it for something special. Something good! And this is good."

I hesitate.

"It's not everything. There's something left. And you work so hard, Kennedy. You're such a good girl. Now go have yourself some fun." She pats my cheek.

"Yeah!" Aisha says, grinning. "You said it, Mrs. Robin—Sepherina."

"All right." I kiss Mom's cheek. "Thank you."

"Be back by eleven," she says.

"Nice seeing you again, Mrs.—Sepherina," Aisha says.

Aisha takes my hand, and we walk down the hall together. Her hand is warm and soft, and our skin pressed together makes me shiver inside. I relax, my body loosening for the first time today. I feel so good with Aisha. So right. Aisha is my home, my heart. The person I feel most me around.

"Your mom is sweet," Aisha says. She darts a look at me. "I mean, when she's not all depressed and stuff."

I grunt. I know she's right. I should be grateful I even have a mom. Aisha's mom died when she was six, and she misses her every day. I know it hurts her sometimes when she sees my mom, or when I talk about how depressed my mom is, how hard it is to have her that way. Or how I wish my mom had been able to protect me, and herself too. Aisha would do anything to have her mom back, even if she laid in bed all day.

"So what happened?" Aisha says. "Why is she so... normal today?"

I tell her, starting from when I found the ring in the alley. We've walked three blocks, past pizza and roti takeouts, gift shops and clothing stores, before I've finished.

Aisha stops walking and lets go of my hand, staring at me. "You're kidding me, right?"

I shake my head. "It's true. I swear."

Aisha runs her hands through her nubbly braids. "And your mom believes you?"

"She doesn't know. Not about the ring or Janelle. Only that Rod backed off."

Aisha shakes her head. "You sure you didn't read this in one of those books of yours?"

"I'm not making it up!"

Aisha holds up her hands. "You have to admit it's a lot to believe. This kind of stuff doesn't happen in the real world. Or I didn't think it did." She looks wistful, and I know she's thinking about her mom, wishing she could bring her back to life. She tilts her head. "Unless... you let me test it out?" She raises one eyebrow, her mouth quirked in a silly smile. "I could kiss you till you couldn't breathe! Or tackle you to the ground, our bodies pressed together. Or..."

I laugh. "I know what's on your mind! But don't test it for real, Aisha. I'm serious. I only have one use left."

"You sure?" Aisha leans in closer, our noses touching, then kisses me. Her lips move softly against mine, lighting up my body. I breathe in her sweet cocoa-butter scent, kissing her harder. I forget that we're standing in the middle of the sidewalk, forget what happened today. Nothing else matters but the soft warmth of her body pressed up against mine, her kisses getting stronger and more urgent, matching mine...

"Dykes!" A shrill voice screams. "Lesbo pervs!"

Aisha and I jerk apart.

I turn to see Janelle running across the street toward us, her face twisted with hate. Dylan stands on the sidewalk behind her, calling her back, white tape on two of his fingers.

To my right, a red car races to beat the lights, the driver talking animatedly on his cell.

"Look out!" I yell, pointing to the car.

Janelle just laughs and keeps coming.

I pray that I still have one more use left, pray that the ring counts the uses the way I do. I leap off the sidewalk and run toward her, dodging cars coming the other way.

"Oh my god, what are you doing?" Aisha yells.

I reach Janelle and grab her, twisting to turn my back to the oncoming car. Something nudges me, like a gentle shove. There's a screech of tires, then a loud crunching sound, like metal impacting on cement, and then a horn blares drunkenly.

"Get off me!" Janelle says, pushing me away. "What are you doing?"

"Saving your life," I say.

Dylan runs up to Janelle. "Holy shit, you almost got killed! That car would've run you over if Kennedy hadn't—" His voice trails off.

He stares at me. "How did you—?"

Janelle turns to look over my shoulder. Her eyes widen, and she gasps. "Holy freaking mother of god."

I slowly turn and look.

The front end of the car is folded in on itself like an accordion, the hood rising upward in a tented V, as if it hit another car at high speed. The bumper hangs crookedly, one end drooping along the road. Glass from the windshield is strewn over the asphalt like broken stars.

The driver rams his shoulder against the door, trying to escape the growing airbag. Some bystanders run over to help.

"What the hell?" the driver says dazedly as he staggers along the road, bleeding from a small cut on his forehead. "Will you look at my car!"

Someone squeezes my arm.

I whirl around.

Aisha stares at me, her eyes wet with tears. "You weren't kidding."

I shake my head.

"Are you all right? You hurt anywhere?"

I mentally feel my body, my limbs. "Nope. It just felt like someone shoved me. Lightly."

"Crazy. Damn, I'm glad you're alive, girl." Aisha pulls me to her hard, cupping the back of my shaved head, stroking me.

I hug her back. "Me, too."

Around us people are talking, their voices rising and falling. All the attention seems to be on the driver loudly talking about how some girl stepped in front of his car and smashed it. The others look at him pityingly, like they think he's crazy or the bump on his head made him hallucinate. One man tries to make the driver sit down on the curb. The driver shakes him off and grows even louder, pointing an accusing finger at me.

I chew on my lip. I don't think anyone will believe him. His car doesn't look like it hit a person.

Cars on the other side of the road slow down as they pass us, drivers and passengers staring. Crowds of people line the sidewalk, coming out from stores and restaurants.

A few people are examining the front of his car, shaking their heads and asking if anyone saw the car that got away. Someone's called the police, another an ambulance though it doesn't look like anyone really needs it. I don't want to be around when they get here.

"Come on," I say, tugging Aisha's hand.

"Hang on." Aisha turns to Janelle, who is standing there, her face gray, her arms wrapped tightly around herself, Dylan rubbing circles against her back.

"I think you owe us an apology," Aisha says. "And you sure owe Kennedy a lot more than that. She saved your life. After what you did, I wouldn't have blamed her if she'd let you get hit."

Janelle flinches. She slowly raises her head to look at me. "How did you—? *Why* did you save me? After what I did?"

Janelle and Dylan lean closer, waiting. Even Aisha looks like she wants to know.

My face heats up. I shrug. "Just because you're a homophobe doesn't mean you deserve to die. I couldn't just stand there and watch you get killed. I never could've lived with myself if I had."

Janelle swallows, then straightens her shoulders. "I—thank you. You talk the way my dad talked. Before he served his last tour, I mean. Before he got all..." She hesitates, looking at me, then at Dylan. "Depressed. Angry. They say he has PTSD." She swallows again. "He was my hero. Now he's just a guy who sits all day in his chair, drinking and yelling and watching TV." She swipes her mouth, like maybe she said too much.

I get it now. Why she's so angry. It doesn't excuse her behavior— but I get it.

I know it was hard for her to tell me. Judging from the look on Dylan's face, she never told him any of that. I want to give her something back. Let her know I understand.

"It's hard when someone you love is depressed," I say softly. "My mom has been for a really long time."

Janelle nods sharply, her eyes watering up. "Look—I'm real sorry about before," she says in a strangled voice.

I nod. I'm not sure it's enough, but it's so much more than I ever thought I'd get. "Thank you."

Janelle blinks, looking relieved.

Aisha squeezes my hand.

Somehow I don't think Janelle will be my enemy anymore. But with the ring all used up, I want to be sure. "You'll leave me alone now?" I ask Janelle. "You'll stop bullying me?"

"I—yeah, of course," Janelle says. "I owe you."

That's a strange twist of fate. I suppress a grin. Janelle owes me. Maybe even respects me now. I look over at Dylan, and he bobs his head up and down.

"Good. Because we come in peace," I say.

Dylan's mouth drops open.

I don't know why I said that. But maybe it'll keep them guessing. At least keep them away from Aisha and me.

Sirens wail in the distance, growing louder and louder.

"Come on." I tug Aisha's hand. "Let's go."

This time she doesn't resist.

"Hey!" a man calls out. "If you saw anything, you need to stay and tell the police. You're a witness!"

But I keep walking, Aisha's hand in mine, faster and faster until we leave all the noise and chaos behind.

"We come in peace?" Aisha says, bumping me gently. She giggles. "What is that?"

I shrug. "It seemed like a superhero thing to say."

"You *were* a superhero! You're my superhero!" Aisha stops and kisses me. Then she pulls back, her face serious. "I don't know if I could have done what you did. Risk my life like that."

"I wasn't risking my life. I still had one use left."

"But you said Dylan tried to hit you, then Janelle. Then your stepfather. So how did you know?"

I almost tell her the truth: that I didn't. I shake my head. "I just did."

Aisha raises her eyebrow, but doesn't say anything more, just takes my hand again. We start walking toward home.

"It would have been crazy to try that without the ring," I say. "That really would be risking your life." I hesitate, looking down at the golden band. It's not so shiny anymore; it looks more like tarnished brass, and it feels loose on my finger, like it might fall off. I slide it down my finger carefully and tuck it into my pocket. "I want to give it to you, want you to have it next—but my mom... I think she needs it more."

"I know," Aisha says quietly. "She does. Maybe it'll stop your stepdad for good."

"I sure hope so," I say fervently. Then I grin. "I bet he'll think he's gone crazy, not being able to hit me *or* my mom! Either that or that we're witches or secretly practicing magic. He'll leave so fast we'll never see his sorry backside again! But maybe afterwards my mom'll give it to you...."

Aisha squeezes my hand. "I'd love to have some real magic, even for just a little while," she says wistfully. "But I don't need protection. Especially not since you showed that homophobe!" She laughs. "Let's just get it to your mom. If it helps heal her—makes her feel strong again—that'll be enough for me."

I squeeze her hand back. "I love you. I love who you are."

"I love you, too."

I breathe deeply, feeling strong and light and happy. "Let's go home."

* * *

Aisha and I sit at the kitchen table across from Mom, the magnifying glass next to me.

I take the ring out of my pocket and hold it in my outstretched palm. "Mom, I have something to give you...."

Mom looks at me quizzically. "A curtain ring?"

I shake my head. "No, something way, way better. But you have to try to keep an open mind when Aisha and I tell you. Promise me you will?"

Mom hesitates, then nods. "I promise."

I slip the ring over Mom's finger. It shrinks almost immediately, tightening around her finger, growing a glossy, rich gold.

Mom gasps.

I smile, and wait for her to ask me about it.

The Two Cities

By Rajan Khanna

The air raid siren released us, and we ran through the streets to its roar. While families huddled in their Anderson shelters and in Tube stations, me and the boys shot free, like ghosts loosed from the world of the dead.

I wasn't fearless—I knew a German shell might find me one day—but some primal joy infused me while laughing in the face of safety and propriety.

Spider yanked open the door and we tore into the house. Unlocked or locked seemed to make no never mind to him. Then we buzzed through the house, a swarm of insects, a multi-limbed beast liberating the possessions of the people huddled in their hidey holes.

While the others looked for silver, for jewelry and food, I gathered saltshakers and matchbooks, a pocket watch and a small silver figurine of a knight on horseback, stuffing them into my pockets.

Then I saw the bookshelf.

I sidled up to it, my naked fingers running along the spines. They were yellowed and dog-eared, mostly paperbacks, but the easier for carrying. I selected three—a copy of Hamlet with a torn cover, a book of poems by Alfred, Lord Tennyson, and a translation of the Arabian Nights.

The other boys piled their booty in bags around me, then Duff announced it was time to move on.

Never too much time in any one house. It wasn't safe. To have four walls around you, I told myself, could only ever be temporary.

We moved to the next house, then another. The boys had discovered an art to it. You could only carry so much and remain nimble. And you always wanted to be light enough to bugger off if the coppers came.

As we prepared to leave the third house, Duff stopped me, one broad

91

hand clapping against my chest. Without asking, he grabbed for my satchel and rooted through it, through my treasures.

"Shite again," he said. He pushed me with the flat of his hand, shaking his head. "The golden boy who never nicks no gold. Bloody useless, you are."

My size was nothing against his strength and I stumbled backward, a battered paperback spilling from the bag.

Paris stepped forward, his tweed cap low on his head. He came only to Duff's chin, but he stood straight, unwavering. His face seemed to shine despite the darkness of the house, an angel's face, beautiful and strong, as if he'd just stepped out of a painting.

"Back off," Paris said. "He's doing what Pross wants."

Duff grunted and bared his teeth, but then backed away. "Out. Now," he said.

I nodded at Paris, then ran out behind him. The smoky night air was cool and bracing and we pumped our legs hard.

The All Clear sang us home.

* * *

Prospero laughed like a barking seal, often at the comedy of injury. He coughed like scissors closing after he'd smoked too many cigarettes. He ate each meal like he'd starved for days.

I'd heard of him shortly after I'd run away from the orphanage. Prospero's boys knew the safe places to sleep, the warm vents to huddle around in winter, the rubbish bins that were likely to have scraps.

It was Paris who'd spoken on my behalf. He'd always been quick to chat or just to smile. A long week passed, a cold and hungry week where my finest meal was a hard, moldy loaf of bread and I warmed myself on the hoods of just-parked cars. Winter approached, howling and hungry as a pack of wolves, and I feared it would devour me.

Paris returned with welcome words. "Meet Prospero in Whitechapel." I met him in an empty warehouse, a large, empty space that smelled like petrol and rust. My excitement began to turn to fear.

Prospero sat on a lone stool and chewed on a chicken bone. He was old, thin, with a long white beard and a threadbare wool cap on his head. He looked me up and down. Crossed his legs. "What can you do?" he asked.

The question gave me pause. What could I do? "What do you need me to do?"

He shook his head, impatient. "That's not what I asked." His voice was a Londoner's, touch of Cockney. "What can you do?"

Nervous, I filled the space with words. "I can see well by moonlight. I can read two good-sized books in one day. I can find and catch slugs better than anyone. I can build miniature castles and forts. I can fit into small spaces."

He pulled the chicken bone from his mouth, flinging a spray of spit into the air. "Do you know this is where Jack the Ripper killed one of his victims?"

I shook my head.

"Just outside," he said. "Slit her from groin to gullet."

I suppressed a shiver.

He popped the chicken bone back into his mouth with a wet sound. "Report to Liverpool Station tomorrow for your assignment."

* * *

The sirens had already cut out by the time we poured back into our quarters inside the closed down York Road tube station. The other boys went to deliver their spoils to the room we called the counting house.

I went to see Prospero.

Duff was right in that my relationship with Prospero differed from the other boys'. The others had been catalogued as I had, assessed for their skills, but they mostly stole the items we could sell.

I, however, had other duties. Prospero smiled one of his thin smiles when I walked into the room. "What did you bring me?"

I pulled the paperbacks from my satchel and fanned them out to show him. He reached for the Arabian Nights with one long-fingered hand. "Ah. Yes. This will do nicely."

I smiled and placed the other two books on the rickety bookcase that, together with two of its mates, stood against one stone wall in Prospero's sanctum.

"Let us have a story," he said, leaning back on his threadworn divan, placing his scuffed boots upon a pile of old newspapers.

"Which one?" I asked. "There are 1001, after all."

"I was born in March of 1898. Read me number 398."

93

So I read him of The Caliph al-Maamun and the Pyramids of Egypt. He dropped his head back the way he always did, his eyes closed, a look almost like ecstasy on his face. When I was done, he looked at me pointedly.

"Another?" I asked.

He shook his head. "No. No time. Go tend to the city."

I placed the book on the bookshelf, then ran into the adjoining room where the city awaited.

I had begun building cities back at the orphanage. I used whatever I could find for my building materials, assembling fortresses from matchbooks and discarded dice, using the cardboard tubes from toilet paper rolls, cigarette boxes, salt shakers and even, once, some cubes of Stilton, admiring the way the cracks and bumps resembled stone.

The glue to hold it all together I had harvested from slugs, collecting them by the light of the silvered moon, storing them in jars until I could remove their slime and use it as mortar.

These edifices I filled with whole societies, creating imaginary kingdoms to populate them. Each person had a name and a function and I knew every one. They were so real that in the morning I would see the captain of the guard upon the battlements, and at bedtime he would be patrolling the halls. The bakers baked fresh bread in the hours before dawn. Alchemists toiled by the lights of flickering candles.

I kept my patchwork creations in one corner of the dormitory until, once a month, one of the orphanage attendants would come in and remove them all, burying them in the back garden as if consumed by the desert's sands.

Prospero had me describe this to him one day after I read to him from *The Tempest*, learning then where his name came from, of Ariel, Caliban, Miranda and the tempest for which the play was named. He sat up, alert, hearing of my lost, but not forgotten, kingdoms. I recalled them for him in detail, the memories, once ghostlike, becoming sharper and solidifying in my mind. Soon he asked me to build one for him.

He supplied me with bricks and blocks and an assortment of materials and bid me take more from our house raids. I thought he was indulging me, but I wasn't one to look a gift horse in the mouth. I built him a city, a small one, and presented it to him. I wasn't prepared for the rapturous look that lit his face. He looked at me intently. "There is power here. Now you must build me London."

"London?"

"It must be as close to the city around us as possible. It will take time, but you must build it as we go."

"I don't understand," I said.

"Symbols," he said. "Symbols are everything. There are arts, ways to establish connections between things. So a small city might stand in for the larger one."

"I still don't see," I said.

"You will." He smiled.

And so Prospero mapped out my days and nights. In daylight I would roam the city, looking, sometimes sketching. Absorbing the details around me. It wasn't all about architecture—sometimes it was about the feel—the particular color of a door, or the faded texture of a wall. These things helped give life to my London.

My companion during all of this was Paris, my sponsor into Prospero's band. He was a year older than me and much wiser about the streets. He became my escort, guiding me to the appropriate neighborhoods, guarding me while I watched or sketched, whisking me away if danger threatened.

He captivated me. His confidence, his surety. He reminded me of a cat, the way he traveled London. Each step exactly where it needed to be, no wasted movement. All grace.

It made it hard to talk to him, though.

Then one day, as I sketched a cathedral in the stained pages of a notebook, I became uncomfortably aware of him leaning over my shoulder. I could smell the peppermint on his breath from the lollies he was always sucking on. "That's brill, that is," he said.

"Thanks," I murmured.

"How do you manage it?"

I shrugged. "I just see it in my mind and it comes out of my fingers." I flushed as I realized how stupid that sounded.

He reached for my hand, and gently stroked my fingers. "Must be magic," he said with a smile.

* * *

The next night the sirens sounded again and we tumbled onto the street like tossed dice. Our target that night was farther out so we had more distance to cover.

This is where my London came into play. Prospero used it to determine where we should strike. I still remember the first time I saw him, hovering over it, rubbing his long hands together, one side of his mouth curling upward. He claimed to be able to see what was happening in the city that way, to use it as a character in a book might use a scrying pool or a crystal ball. I'd looked intently at my city, often when Prospero had, and had never seen anything. But we were each of us dependent on the other, me to build the city, Prospero to divine from it. He claimed its power grew as I filled it in.

Paris grinned at me as we ran through the streets. Butcher, the lookout, ran ahead, checking for trouble, signaling us that the way was clear. Duff gave the signal to start entering homes.

Once more I searched for books and materials for the city. The first house yielded little of the former—just Mills and Boons romances which Prospero didn't care for. In the second, however, I found a copy of a recent book—The Sword in the Stone. I smiled as I tucked it into my satchel.

The boys around me stuffed candlesticks into their bags and sacks, grabbed for silver serving trays and fancy-looking vases.

Then the hum began, a kind of thrumming whine that you could feel in your teeth. The house shook with the firing of guns. We heard a boom, then *crump, crump, crump* as the bombs fell.

I moved to the window and saw the orange glow of a fire some blocks away. I turned to see Paris, also transfixed by the scene, his full lips slightly parted. He looked back at me and our eyes met, and I was suddenly breathless. The fire and the bombs forgotten, all I felt was the pounding of my pulse, the rush of my blood.

He walked to me.

My breath stuttered in my chest.

Then his lips were on mine. Warm and wet and with the faintest smell of peppermint on his breath. I grabbed onto him, my fingers gripping his jacket, and he pushed me back hard against the wall and we kissed hungrily.

In that moment, London could have burned around me. The house could have fallen, come crashing down in fire and debris and I would not have moved.

All the world, all time, was forgotten.

Then a voice broke us from our embrace. One of the others. "Oi," he said. A face appeared a moment later around the door. My face flushed. "It's gettin' bad out there. We better leg it."

Paris nodded, grabbed at my sleeve and pulled me after him.

No one had seen us, it seemed. Had they, it might not have gone well for us. We were a boy's tribe, a bloke-ish brigade, and such things weren't tolerated.

I still tasted Paris on my mouth as we entered the chaos of bombed London. The fire was near enough for us to hear it crackling and the smell of smoke filled the air. The voices of firemen carried through the night air. In the distance I could make out incendiaries falling in quick succession like diving fireflies.

Duff signaled us back. Butcher ranged out ahead again, skirting the firemen and the Boy Scouts who guided them.

On the way I could see down over the hill to St. Pancras Old Church, the roof collapsed and smoking, the firemen tackling the myriad fires with water and sand. The church that I had sketched and sat beside so many times. Where I once found a whole loaf of bread, left by some kind soul. Now broken.

In that moment, the Blitz became my personal enemy, a thief stealing something from me.

I wanted to reach for Paris's hand, to hold it tight, but I dared not. Not with the boys around us. I thought instead of late nights spent by the Thames.

After coming to London from the orphanage I had searched in vain for slugs to milk. Paris had suggested fish.

"Fish?"

Paris loved to fish. He brought dinner to Prospero often. "There's this eel I often catch by accident. It coats my nets with a kind of slime. Sticky, see? Maybe you can use that?"

"I've never fished before," I'd said.

"It's easy peasy." Paris had risen and brushed off his pants. "I'll show you." He'd held out his hand, pale, almost silver in the moonlight.

I'd taken it.

* * *

Back at Prospero's I placed *The Sword in the Stone* on the bookshelf, but I didn't stop to peruse its pages. Instead I headed for the next room

97

where my London stood. My hands shook at my sides. The destruction of the church had unnerved me, the tearing down of London, my London. The London of my hopes and my fears.

I looked at the model of St. Pancras Old Church, one of the features I had added in detail, and tears blurred my eyes. I would have to break the roof.

I fought that destruction with the only means available to me—creation. I worked well into the night, until my eyes burned and my fingers cramped.

I needed to have a London that was inviolate, that the bombs couldn't reach.

I built the carriage house in Marylebone, the Natural History Museum, even the estate agent near Portobello Road with the green paint and the carving of a Gryphon. And, of course, the Tower of London.

I worked long into the night—Prospero was not around—until at some point I fell asleep next to my new creation and dreamt of London rising like a phoenix.

* * *

I awoke to Prospero bending over me, his face mottled with dark stains and what looked like a bruise high on one cheek. I scrambled up—I was supposed to return to my bunk at night. The stone floor was cold beneath my weary fingers.

"Working late, eh?" He looked over my newest additions.

I nodded.

He bent down to me and cupped my face in his large hands, tilting it up to his. "I want you to build me another city." His breath reeked of cigarettes and wine.

"Another?"

"A new creation." He paused. "Creation is the ultimate power. Any fool can destroy. Hitler may burn books, but the ideas in those books, their effect on those who read them remains. He may bomb London but England, her strength, her character… they live on."

I felt alarm rising through me. "But what of my London?"

"You can still build it," he said. "But do this as well." He released my face and turned away. "Build me a city somewhere in the realm of the forgotten and the dreamt."

He bent down over the model city, waved a hand over it. "I am not for this world. I should have been alive in older times. A court alchemist, or a sorcerer, poking at the boundaries of the world." He turned his face back to me. "I am made for castles and kings."

He walked toward his room, his long, shabby dressing gown trailing behind him like a cloak. "You can go now," he said. "Get some rest. I expect there'll be another raid tonight."

I nodded and climbed the stairs that led to the boys' bunks. They were quieter than usual and I found Paris waiting for me in my bed.

"Where is everyone?" I asked.

"Duff took them out," he said. "They went to see the damage."

I frowned. Something about that image, the boys hovering over shelled buildings, leering and fascinated, disturbed me.

Paris moved over, giving me space to lie down, but he didn't leave the bed. I stretched out next to him. I was taller than him, but painfully thin in comparison. My black hair was long and lank and my features sallow. I thought of the contrast between his cherubic face and mine and it twisted something inside of me.

I caught the scent of his sweat, of the peppermint lollies, the faint trace of fish that always clung to his small and slender hands.

He turned his head toward me and the warm peppermint wash of his breath tickled my face. Then his lips pressed against mine, and mine against his. Soft lips, the hungry nibble of his teeth. The faint scratch of the hair above his lip. Our movements, at first clumsy, soon melted together. I let the wave wash me away until at some point sleep took me again.

I awoke some time later to the voices of the other boys and sat up, startled, afraid they'd caught us together. But Paris was gone as if he'd never been there.

I returned to the two cities—my London and the foundation of Prospero's city. I sat down to the latter, the Arabian Nights swirling in my head alongside T. H. White's vision of Arthur and Merlin. Together they birthed something entirely new. I made a tower made out of shiny black Backgammon pieces. Then I placed a small sugar bowl as a mosaicked dome atop what would become a temple to a non-Christian god.

Later, flush with a feeling of satisfaction and success, I joined the others for our nightly excursion. The other boys hovered close to one another, and it seemed only Paris and I stood apart. I wondered if that was some effect of the recent change in our relationship or if there was something else at work. But then the sirens called and we spilled out into the London streets.

The smell of smoke hung in the air as we headed to our next target, near Bond Street. Even before we reached the first house, we heard the buzz of the airplanes above us, like a grinding of celestial gears.

Duff and the others quickened their pace and we entered the first house. As usual, I went to search for books and construction materials. I didn't have a good feeling about the house. It smelled sour, like old people, and the furnishings were poor and uncared for.

I pushed into the bedroom and froze. On the bed, lying still, was an old man, his face wrinkled and covered in liver spots. Below, I could hear the noise of the others as they rummaged through the meager pickings of the house, yelling to one another.

I knew I should alert the boys, perhaps even sound the alarm that would send us all out of the house, but I drew closer to the bed, wondering at the figure there. I couldn't tell in the dim light if any breath moved his thin form or if his eyes were open or closed.

About halfway to the bed, I felt a hand on my shoulder and almost shrieked. I turned to find Paris there. "Something's happening," he said.

I nodded toward the bed, but he didn't pick up on my message.

"Duff and the others... there's something dodgy there. I think they're brassed off at Prospero."

"For what?" I asked, the old man momentarily forgotten.

"Dunno."

"Can they do anything?"

Paris shrugged. "Duff has the others behind him." He took off his cap and ran a hand through his unruly brown hair. "I—bloody hell! That's a man there, that is."

"I know," I said, lowering my voice. "I was going to see if... you know."

"Okay." Paris grabbed my hand and together we inched toward the bed. I knew that the man had to be dead and that's why he was there with the air raid sirens all around us. But I had never seen a dead body before, and it both attracted and repulsed me.

Paris's grip tightened as we neared until it was a steady, almost crushing pressure as we stood over the old man. Wispy white hair clung to his scalp, which seemed dry and thin like paper. Even in the dim light I could see the blue veins spidering below his skin.

His eyes were indeed open, pupils large and dark inside bloodshot orbs.

Then they moved.

The eyes flashed to us and back again, as if trapped, and I leapt back pulling Paris with me. Together we scrabbled out of the room and down the stairs and out into the night.

* * *

We sat by the Thames together, hidden among some stacked up crates, and breathed in the smoky air, finally recovered from the shock of the old man.

"There were other bedrooms in that house," Paris said, skipping a stone into the water. "He didn't live alone."

"You think someone left him behind? While they went to the air raid shelter?"

He raised his eyebrows. "Maybe they couldn't move him. And they thought he's almost dead anyway."

"That's horrible," I said. To be abandoned by those who loved you. Left to die alone…" I trailed off. I had been abandoned, too. As a child. Left at the orphanage.

Paris moved closer to me and pulled me against him. "You're not alone now." I felt his heart beating through his chest. Felt my own breath stutter.

"What should we do?" We weren't supposed to leave our companions during a raid.

Paris pulled me to him and kissed me hard on the mouth. I melted against him, heat rising inside of me until it felt like my skin was on fire. I grabbed at him as if he were the only stable thing in the world. His tongue flicked across mine and I ran my fingers down the front of his shirt. Then, I tucked my trembling hand down the front of Paris's loose, corduroy pants. He gasped, his eyes wide momentarily. My breath shuddering in my chest, I thrust my hand down.

I wondered if his cock would feel like mine, if it would respond like mine. My fingers pressed through the damp tangle of his pubic hair and found the hardness there. The angle was strange—not quite the same as

101

doing it to myself—but I managed to move my hand until he moaned and shuddered against me. "Oh god," he said in a breathy whisper. We sat there, tangled together, both breathing hard. I ran my fingers through his hair.

Around us the world was coming apart in violent explosions. But we clung to each other as if we could fuse into one being, as if that act could counter everything else.

"I love you," I said, and he said the same.

* * *

Back at the tube station, I returned to my London. It seemed that every time I saw the city suffer, I needed to minister to its miniature, as if somehow that would help. Only I had Prospero's city as well, and Pross kept demanding more progress. I tried to move twice as fast and cut myself, my blood mixing in with the dwindling eel slime.

I still had one building left to go for the evening, though—the stately bank on Tottenham Court Road, the one with the columns. I had spent hours on the columns alone. So I wrapped my hand as best as I could and pressed on.

The next morning, as I walked with Paris, fishing rods and nets in hand, we passed Tottenham Court Road where a row of buildings stood smoking, the victims of incendiary bombs. I almost couldn't look, couldn't bear to see the bank, which I had just reproduced, a charred ruin.

Yet it wasn't. The buildings on either side were crumpled and black, but the bank seemed untouched. "It's the damnedest thing," a volunteer fireman was saying. "There were bombs all over the place, but none hit the bank."

Paris looked at me curiously as I stared at it. The thoughts in my head were strange. They coiled inside of my mind as we pulled more eels from the water and milked them into a glass jar. If Paris thought I was unusually distant, he didn't say so.

That night, I cut myself again, scoring my arm with the pocketknife I used to smooth edges, bleeding into the slime and mixing the two well enough together so that some of my blood went into all of my new constructions. Some of it even went into Prospero's city. As I built, I prayed that my suspicion was correct.

Excursions over the next few days confirmed one fact to me—none of the new buildings I had constructed had been damaged in the bombings since I had started mixing in my blood. I couldn't prove that anything was happening, but it seemed a strange coincidence.

I poured myself, literally, into both model cities, spending every moment I wasn't on the raids or with Paris on expanding the buildings, adding as much as I could from memory, using the nightly excursions to help remind me of what I needed to build next. I felt as if I were in a race, racing the Germans, racing the Blitz itself. Every night I returned to my bed pale and woozy. Scars lined both of my arms, hidden beneath the ratty shirts and sweaters that I wore.

London was so vast, so endlessly complex, but Prospero's city neared completion. All that I needed to do was to place the final spire on the Presidential Palace. And I had all the ingredients I would need.

Prospero came in that night to check on my progress and stopped with a gasp when looking at his city. He sniffed, then bent down and pressed his head down close to it. "What have you used here?"

I knew that Prospero had strange senses. "My blood," I said. Then, because I feared his response I added, "I cut myself by accident. Some of it mixed into the mortar."

He rose and nodded, his eyes gazing somewhere else. "Yes. Of course." Then his eyes seemed to find me once more. "You must finish it now. Quickly."

"Why?"

He waved a hand. "All great men have their rivals. I have built something special here. There are those who wish to tear it down." He frowned. "I am not certain I can withstand them."

As I moved to his city I heard shouts coming from the door to the room. We both looked up as Paris entered and hastily dropped the bar into place.

"What is going on?" Prospero demanded.

"It's bad business, guv," Paris said. "The other boys are in revolt."

Prospero swallowed and looked down at his feet. "I see. Are they coming for me?"

Paris, eyes wide, nodded. Prospero nodded back.

The shouts without grew louder and someone banged on the door.

"Quickly, lad," Prospero said to me. "You have to finish the city now."

I reached for the spire, for my knife and other tools, and, using my

103

adhesive, I glued it into place. Then it was done. The city lay before us, one of my most beautiful creations. The minarets of the palace glittered from the shards of glass embedded within them. The streets leading up to it were lined with columns of biros and tin whistles. And above all, the great clocktower stood, the working timepiece, assembled from a wristwatch, counting down the seconds.

"It's finished," I said to Prospero. He hovered over it, eyes wide. He inspected it all very carefully, without touching it, bending to get the best light from the lantern that lit the room. When he looked back at me again, tears streamed down from his dark eyes, leaving tracks on his grimy face.

"Thank you," he said, his voice breathy.

The banging on the door had continued through much of my work, but was now strangely silent. Paris stood by me and with Prospero distracted by the city, he held my hand.

The next strike on the door shook it in its frame and strained the metal hinges. I looked at Paris and he ran to the door. "Piss off!" he yelled.

The door shook again and I heard the wood splintering.

I pushed Paris to one side just before it came crashing in, falling hard against the floor. It only just missed Little London, though the buildings shook and it seemed that all around us the floor shook as well.

Duff's band pushed into the room, Duff at the front, red-faced and snarling. "Where is he?" he yelled.

I turned and Prospero was nowhere to be seen. I looked at Paris and he shook his head. The old man was gone. And there were no exits to the room. No other doors or windows. Just plain brick walls.

"He's not here," Paris said.

"Some of the boys saw him come this way," Duff growled.

"Do you see him here?" I said. "Look for yourself."

Duff stalked into the room. He could see that Prospero wasn't there. Still trembling with rage, he looked down at Prospero's city and began to kick it, trampling it with his boots, knocking apart the buildings and structures I had spent so long to create. In a moment the other boys had joined him and began doing the same until Prospero's city was nothing but scrap.

But Duff still wasn't satisfied. His blood was up. He moved toward Little London.

I stepped forward but Paris beat me there. Duff backhanded him and

Paris fell to the ground. I let out a strangled cry and took another step, holding up a thin hand. "No," I growled. I swayed on my feet. Week from lack of sleep and the food I had forgotten to eat.

Duff pulled back his hand and it seemed to move so slowly. I could see Paris on the ground to my side. Behind me I felt my London, felt its weight, its strength, it's power. Suddenly, I could feel him. He was in front of me, yes, but I could feel him, in the space. I could feel all the boys behind him. Felt men outside, waiting to be let in. I felt something vast and large and strong all around and inside of me.

I met Duff's eyes. "No." That's all I said. One word.

I tensed, waiting for the blow, waiting for the explosion that led to all of Duff's boys falling on me and Paris.

But it never came. Instead Duff looked at me, then at the city, his face twisted into a look of hatred. "We're taking over," he said. "We've got new mates. You boys leg it by morning or there'll be trouble."

I nodded, then Duff and the boys filed out, most of them giving us hateful looks.

When they were gone, I exhaled and helped Paris to his feet, holding him close. His face was bruised, but he was otherwise okay.

"Where do you think Pross went?" Paris asked.

"I don't know," I said. But a voice in my head said otherwise. It could have been that he knew a secret passage in the room, some hidden means of escape that none of us knew about. But when I felt Duff and the others, I hadn't felt him. Not nearby. No, what made more sense to me in that moment, as mad as it sounds, is that he found his way into his city. That it became real for him. I found some dried blood in its wreckage, though whether it was mine, Duff's or Prospero's, I didn't know. I hope if it were mine that it somehow protected him.

"What do we do now?" Paris asked.

"I have an idea," I said.

I wasn't sure it would work, but I knew I had to try. I cut myself again, this time using only my blood. Paris almost stopped me, asked me what I was doing, but I explained. Then he did something that made me love him all the more—he offered his own arm. "No," I said. "As much as I love you, I don't know that it would work the same way."

So I worked through the next few hours, adding to my London, particularly the green estate agent's building, which didn't have a flat underneath but which I added one to, complete with its own garden and concealed entrance. I sealed all of these with my blood as well, ignoring the dizziness that came upon me, knowing that our time was running out.

Then, in the wee hours of the morning, Paris helped me carefully move all of the buildings I'd so far constructed into a large wheelbarrow, and gathering what little we had (and the copy of The Sword in the Stone), we pushed it out into the London morning.

The smoky streets were filled with the aftermath of the bombing the night before, but they were also filled with every day people, going about their lives, going to work and plying their trades. Simply living.

I led Paris to the small flat beneath the estate agent's and stopped.

"What's this?" he asked.

"Our castle," I said. And opened the door.

Where We Came From

By David Sklar

Ocean's sister was born with white hair. Not platinum blonde, not towhead—white like ice. Or rice. Or white mice. He showed me a picture once.

Of course, then Jimmy DiNardo grabbed the picture out of my hand and said, "Dude, that baby's *old.*"

"Give it back!" I said.

"What happened?" Jimmy asked Ocean. "She just didn't want to leave your mama's cunt?"

Ocean glared at him but didn't say anything.

"Bet she was comfy, there," Jimmy said, "with all that space to move arou—"

"Is that why your head's so flat?" I blurted.

"Whaddayou mean?"

"Well, 'cause your mom was so sick of you she shot you out too fast for the doctor to catch."

Jimmy slammed me against a locker. "You're a dyke. You're a dyke like your drag queen mom."

"My mom's not a drag queen," I said.

"You mean she's a dyke?"

"What—I didn't say—"

"Didn't say she isn't."

"I—" I tried to answer, but I couldn't remember her with a man— not for a very long time.

"Leave her alone!" Ocean said, pulling uselessly at Jimmy's arm.

"Why?" said Jimmy. "Whatcha gonna do?"

"It's not what he will do," I said, in my witchy voice. "Two weeks from now, you will be walking home when a—"

Jimmy let me go. "I ain't afraid of you."

"Of course not," I answered.

"That witch stuff's bullshit," he said.

"Of course it is," I said as he sulked away.

Of course, it is. Bullshit, I mean. I don't like to use the witch voice. It isn't real. But when I was little I learned how to scare people with my voice, just telling them stuff. Then one time I got "lucky," and Jenna Greenberg fell off her high heels, the way I said she would, and got six stitches in her face and three in her hand. After that, people thought I really could put a hex on them, like some sort of freak.

I think that's why me and Ocean became friends—the freak factor—even though we don't have to be. Freaks, I mean. I learned some kickass tricks with makeup from my mom, and Ocean's dad is a pop star. Not a big one, but he opens for Things That Go Bump in the Night. Plus, Ocean could be on the swim team if he cared about being on teams. Hell, he could *be* the swim team if he wanted. But—well, I don't know. People think I can do magic. And sometimes I think Ocean *is* magic. Not like he can do magic, but like he *is*. Like that's how I feel when he's around.

We'd know each other anyway, because his mom works for my mom. Or the other way 'round. I mean, his parents own the Ocean Diner, but my mom makes the business decisions and his waits tables. And his dad plays music there when he's not on the road.

* * *

It's summer now, and people like Jimmy DiNardo or Jenna Greenberg—all the non-freaks—could be miles away, unless we run into them on the beach. So I'm sitting with Ocean in the diner his folks named for him, and I ask, "Was your mom a groupie?"

He says "What?"

"I mean, your dad is this big rock star, right? Or not BIG big, but big enough. Is that how they met? Did she follow his band?"

Ocean looks down at his fish and chips, like he doesn't want to tell me, but he's smiling like he kind of really does. I like how his face looks when there's something up.

"Spill," I say.

He looks at me. He's wearing the necklace I gave him—the one that used to be my mom's. A shiny blue stone on a silver chain. "Actually, I think he was *her* groupie in the beginning."

"Was she in a band?"

"I don't think so. She has a beautiful voice—have you ever heard her sing? But I don't think she's ever sung on stage. The thing is, when they started out... I think he needed her more than she ever needed him, even now that she's raising two kids."

"Really?"

"He wasn't famous then anyway; I think they got... married because of me."

"You mean..."

"They have a picture of their wedding in a drawer. She was out to here." He holds a hand out in front of his belly—which is kind of brave for a guy, I mean—being a woman, just for a moment, that's really something.

"Oh."

"It's a great picture. They're sitting on the grass in Central Park, and she has flowers in her hair. And everyone's sitting in a circle, including them."

"How come it's not on a wall?"

"I don't know. It's in a drawer."

"Do you think it's in a drawer *because* she was pregnant?"

"Maybe." He *doesn't* think so.

This place has a pretty good view for a diner, but we're at the back wall. To look out the window he has to look past the paying customers.

"Stop it," I say. "People will think you're staring at them."

He looks back at me. His face kind of squirms.

I want to change the subject, but that isn't who I am. I mean, I know he doesn't like it, but I have all the stupid questions kind of wiggling in my head, and my mouth is their only way out. "So if she was pregnant, doesn't that mean she needed him more?"

Ocean kicks me under the table.

"What was that for?"

Just then his mom comes up behind me with the coffeepot. "How are you doing, Grace? Do you want some more?"

* * *

When I get home I'm wondering if my mom has a picture somewhere, and if I open the right drawer I might find out what my father looked like.

109

I start wandering through the basement to see what I find packed up down there. Is there a picture of them together, in a drawer or in a box? It's an idle thought at first, kind of like twiddling my thumbs, but it gets twiddlier and twiddlier, like the more I look the more I need to find something to justify all the looking. So, like, I *could've* walked away back when I started, but by the end I have to find it however I can.

Of course I don't. I find three mismatched buttons, a couple of keys that don't know *what* they open, some pictures of my mom singing under bright lights—I wonder if that was how she met Ocean's parents—and a clipping from *Weird NJ* about a dome-shaped hut put together from scrap wood and traffic signs, with pine trees around it and moss growing on the roof.

I hear tires in the driveway. I dump a hamper out into the washer so I'll have a reason for being downstairs. My head almost hits the lamp when I hear Mom's voice at the top of the stairs. "Grace, honey?"

Oh shit. "Yah?"

"What are you doing?"

Shit. "Nothing." I turn on the washing machine.

"Cold? Hot? Dark? Light?"

Oh. Oh shit. "Cold light." I click the dial on the washer to where it belongs.

"Can I give you something?"

"Sure."

A white blouse that smells of restaurant sweat comes billowing down the stairs. "Thanks hon. I'll be in the shower."

I breathe until my heart isn't quite so jumpy-thumpy, then I start to put the boxes away. Well—and to look through the pictures, which I do first.

First off, she wasn't a pop star like Ocean's dad. The pictures are karaoke. But there are a *lot* of them, in different outfits, at different stages of pregnant. I pocket one where she looks like a Volkswagen in a blue sequined dress. Maybe when school starts again in the fall I can take it in, to prove she's not a guy in a dress. It's not like she looks like a guy, she's just really... tall. But what kind of nut-job puts a preggo picture of their mom in their locker?

When Mom comes down from the shower, I'm on the living room sofa, with the pregnant karaoke pics spread on the table.

"You used to sing a lot," I say.

She thumbs through the pictures. "Where did you find these?"

"A box in the basement."

"Did you find anything else there?" She pulls her robe tighter with one hand, like she's afraid someone might be watching.

"Some buttons," I answer. "A couple of keys."

"You didn't find a... never mind."

"Were you a regular?"

"I was the hostess. The flamboyant lady who could almost sing, so that the customers would keep coming. Before we moved here."

"Is that my father?" I point to a good-looking guy in the background of one picture.

"No, that's..." She picks up the picture and looks at it. "I don't know who that is."

"Do you have any pictures of my father?"

"Are you sure you didn't find anything else?"

I cross my heart with my finger. "Does that mean there *are* pictures of him downstairs?"

"No, just... Grace, honey. Your father was a very bad man. I don't have any pictures of him, and I don't want any pictures of him. That chapter is closed."

"Were... were you with him long?"

"No... just once."

That's the freak factor again. I mean, I think it's cool that she can put it out there. But the kids who really *are* cool—there's no way their moms would admit to something like that.

"Do you regret it?"

She sits down next to me on the couch. "Sweetie, he gave me you. How could I regret that?"

I sneer. "You've gotta say that, right? It's in the *Moms' Handbook* or something?"

She gets me straight in the eye with a very serious look. "Do you know why I named you Grace?"

I've heard this before. "Because I'm your *mir*acle child."

"Do you know what that means?"

I shake my head. "It *means* something?"

"Sweetie, it means I didn't think I *could* get pregnant. I was born without... I was born *wrong,* you know? And the doctors tried to fix me, but there were things they couldn't do. Your father... he was a bad man,

111

but he knew how to fix me. And without him you wouldn't have been born."

"How could he fix you, if the doctors couldn't?"

"I don't know. There are... there are things I can't really explain." She has this *gone* look, like she's somewhere else.

"Uh-huh."

"But it's... it's not what they make it out to be."

"What's not?"

"Listen, honey, if you ever..." she seems for a moment like she's going to choke up. "If you ever get close to magic, turn and run the other way, unless it's for something you want more than anything else in the world. Any less than that and it just... isn't worth the cost." She puts her arm around my shoulder and squeezes.

"Magic?" I ask.

She nods.

"For real?"

She nods again. She's crying now.

"You mean..."

"You're my miracle child."

"Your magical child."

"My totally... totally... *worth it* magical child."

And we sit there on the couch and I hug her, and I feel stunned and confused and really really bad about the *Weird NJ* clipping in my back pocket.

* * *

After Mom's in bed, I dig out the clipping and read the letters from *Weird NJ* readers. One guy spotted the Jersey Devil near the hut in the woods. Another decided to look inside but had a seizure the moment his hand touched the plastic door flap. And a breeze blows in from the ocean as I read.

* * *

I'm at the beach with Ocean, telling him about all of this—we're in regular clothes, it's not warm enough for bathing suits yet—when he says, out of nowhere, "What does the picture mean to you?"

112

"To *me?*"

"Do you long for it? Does this cabin feel like home?"

I shrug. "Like home? I've never been there."

Ocean's face gets kinda wistful, and he looks across the sea. "You can long for a place you've never been, if it's enough a part of you."

"It's my mom's picture."

"Well what does it mean to her?"

"I don't know. I haven't asked."

"Are you going to?"

"She doesn't know I have it."

"Why not?"

"She got weird when I mentioned the Karaoke pics, like there's something in the basement that she doesn't want me to find."

"And you think this is it?"

"I don't know…. Maybe."

His eyes are kind of vacant, like his mind's hanging somewhere in the air above the water.

"Ocean?"

I look at the curvature of his cheek as he stares out to sea. But I want to know.

"Ocean!"

"Huh?" He startles slowly, so that even his turning to look at me is a fluid, streamlined motion.

"What are you thinking about?"

He turns a rock very slowly in his hand. I don't remember him picking it up.

"Ocean?"

"A yellow suitcase."

"What?"

"Nothing."

"It's always nothing, and it never is."

"What?"

"Spill."

Ocean looks at a place further down the beach. "My father was sitting down there, with a guitar in his lap and a small yellow suitcase beside him."

"Bright yellow, like a lemon?"

"Pale yellow, like lemon ice cream. With a big gray stain on the side." He moves his hand vaguely in a space about the size of a lopsided pizza.

"When?"

"The year before my sister was born. I was having a really bad day."

"Was he going on the road?"

"He'd just come home. I'd asked him to, and it was the first time he ever came home because of me."

"And he stopped there first?"

"No, he went to the attic and brought the suitcase down. It wasn't his suitcase, it was… mine."

My shoulders tense. "Oh my God—your dad threw you out?"

"What? No. It wasn't like that, it was…"

Maybe you've noticed by now Ocean has a habit of trailing off in the middle of sentences.

"Spill."

Ocean skips the rock across the surface of the sea. "It was something he needed to show me. He didn't want to, but he had to."

"Why?"

"Because I found out."

"Found out what?"

"He isn't my father."

"What?"

"See, I'd called him when he was on the road, and I asked him to come home, because I'd seen my mother kissing another guy. And he came home right away, and he told me, 'That guy's your real father.'"

"No way."

"Way."

"And he didn't punch him out?"

"Well, yeah, but that was later."

"Good, because I would've *totally* punched him out."

"It wasn't for kissing my mom, it was for trying to take me when he left."

"He *what?*"

"When my real father left, he wanted me to come with him, but my dad punched him out."

"Good for him."

"It was kind of scary. I thought it was going to storm."

"At the same time?"

Ocean shakes his head. "Be*cause* my dad punched him. Like my real father was bringing it on."

"Bullshit."

"That's what it felt like."

"Like for real?"

"Yeah."

"Weird."

A very long silence comes next, and I touch him on the back, between his shoulders. It makes me nervous, touching Ocean. I mean, I *want* to touch him, but I don't have a lot of friends, and I don't want to screw up the friendship that matters most.

"The thing is," Ocean finally says, "ever since then I've *wanted* to go. Not to *be* with my father, but to see where I came from, to live in the world where I belong."

I feel like he's stabbed me in the chest. I'm sure he feels the shudder in my hand. I put on a brave face: "There's a place where *you* belong?"

He smiles. "Yeah. There maybe is."

"Can you take me with you? Maybe I belong there too." I wink.

"Well, *you,* Grace—you might be a harder case."

I look into his eyes for real. "Don't go."

He looks into my eyes too, those big, sad eyes of his that are brown almost all the way through. And I think if I kiss him he might kiss me back. But if I'm wrong I don't want to be what drives him away. So I wait for him to kiss me first, and when he hugs me it's too late.

And his arms feel so right around me, and he smells so right beside the sea, but still I want more from him, and I do not dare.

* * *

It's not until the next day I'm parking the pickup at the diner when I realize I never asked what was in the suitcase. But then I walk into the restaurant and my mom's on the warpath—which doesn't happen often, but when it does you know to watch out. So I step in the front door and I'm barely past the Please Wait to Be Seated sign when she looks at me the way the headlights on a 4 x 4 look at a deer, and she says, "Grace. Office. Now."

Now when she gets like this you know for sure you *damn* well better not mess with her, so I do my best, without running or looking rushed, to get to the office behind the kitchen 10 minutes before she told me.

"You said the karaoke photos were the only thing you found."

"Uh, yeah."

"Did you take a magazine clipping out of a box?" Her fist is on her hip. This is serious.

"No."

"I'm not kidding. There are some things you're just not ready for."

"Mom, it's just a clipping from *Weird New Jersey.*"

And that's when she goes quiet, and the silence hits like a wave, and I feel a bit of oxygen leave the room. At the distant end of that silence, she reaches out and touches my hand, and I was not expecting the softness in her voice. "Grace. Darling. I wish I could… I wish I could protect you. I know you want… I wish you could have a father. I haven't spoken to my father *or* my mother since long before you were born, and I wish I could give you two parents who love you for who you are, but… there's just me." I watch her face. It's fucked up, to see a grownup look so lost. "Your father… your father is not a good man. I met him when I needed something nobody else could give. If he knows about you… if he takes you back… then it's just me alone."

"Huh?"

"I don't know what will happen to you." She squeezes my hand. "Please don't go looking for this. Please?"

"OK," I say, but I'm not sure I mean it. Not even sure *what* I'm not sure I mean.

"Thank you." And she brings me close and clings to me like the wind might pull me away. And the air that was sucked from the room she squeezes out of my lungs, so I guess that puts everything right, although I feel like I'm just piling up more and more questions—like whether I can get through a day without being hugged.

"Mom, I gotta start my shift."

"Huh? OK." But she doesn't let go.

"Uh… Mom?"

"It's all right. I'm the manager."

"Right."

* * *

When I go to see Ocean after my shift, I see the tour bus in front of the house before I hear Elijah's sweet soprano saxophone, and Tofie's crazed violin. I park the pickup behind the bus and listen a while. You won't hear this on any album—Tofie's in Things, with Lem and Galen, while Elijah opens for them with Ocean's dad. But now they're at home, just jamming. She's teasing him, her rapid fiddle dancing around his mellow jazz, egging him on to go faster, but the old man takes the notes at his own pace, blowing a smooth counterbalance to Tofie's frenetic chaos. I don't know which is more astounding—that Elijah can play with such discipline and such feeling both at once or that Tofie can play so fast without flubbing a note. Either way, I'm sweaty from work and not really dressed to hang out with the band. And Ocean's reunion with his dad will be full of too many extra people already. I turn the ignition back on and drive away.

* * *

That night I dream I'm standing among the pines, and that mound-shaped hut is whispering to me. I try to think where I might run to through the woods, but I have no idea where I am, and still the secrets inside the hovel softly call. As I approach, I know that *anything* could be behind me, anything at all, and I walk with quiet caution, afraid of the snap of a single twig. I don't know which frightens me more—what might stalk behind me or what waits ahead—but I must have crossed the distance somehow, because I pull back the plastic tarp where a door should be, and beyond it, inside of the building, I'm in the diner again, but it's empty except for a blond man in an old flannel shirt who hasn't washed his hair in at least a week. I approach him with my pad to take his order, and he says—I'm not sure what he says, but I feel a droning terror at the sound of his patient and merciless voice.

"We don't serve that here," I tell him.

"Are you sure?"

"Why don't you try the moussaka? Or a lobster roll? The owner's a vegetarian, but we do serve fish. Our salmon is very good, and the halibut just came off the boat."

He rests his hands on the table in front of him. "I think you will take the order the way I gave it."

"We make a great rice pudding," I say. "We have fresh soft-shell crabs. You should try the clam chowder."

117

And in that patient and terrifying voice of his, he repeats, "It may take a while, but you are going to take the order as I gave it, without substitutions."

"Have you tried one of our omelettes?" I ask. "Or the spinach pie? I think there's some monkfish with lemon butter that's supposed to be next week's special, but we have the ingredients in the back, and I can ask them to make it for you. Or potato pancakes? We have brownies shaped like mice. Have you seen the size of our cheesecakes or tried our fries?" I'm fidgeting with my pen, fidgeting with my hair.

But he just sits there dispassionately, as I run through tilapia, falafel, calamari, baba ghanoush. In the end he's right: I take down the order the way he described it and the words are a gash on the page, an emptiness that rips through any comfort in my mind.

By the pass-through to the kitchen I tear the order off my pad and clip it on the carousel. My mom's behind the counter in a black veil, and she cries as I give her the order, but she has it already prepared. She puts the food on the pass-through: a plate of meat on the bone the size and shape of a woman's thigh, with the thin blood pooling under it on the white plate, and a crystal decanter filled with a wine the exact same color.

I carry it to the table, my heart full of fear. The fear that something is behind me comes again, and the fear that what lies ahead of me is worse.

And my steps seem to bring me no closer, the way they sometimes don't in dreams, and the distance to the table is like the distance to my grave. But I cross it somehow, with trembling legs, and the tray almost ready to drop, and between dropping the order and bringing it to him, I don't know which is worse. I approach the table, too afraid to do anything else, and as he slowly turns to face me, before I get to see his face, I wake up tangled in the sheet, and sweaty although the blankets are all kicked off.

* * *

It's dark outside, but the first bit of pink is suffusing the edge of the sky. I try to remember the face of the man at the table, but all I remember is how he limps.

I throw on clothes without a shower and I drive to Ocean's house. The tour bus is still parked in front, and as I get out of the pickup I see

Galen walking down the steps from the porch, carrying Tofie in his arms like a sleeping baby.

Tofie's not quite five feet tall, and Galen's probably over seven—I haven't asked, but he makes the upright bass look small when he's on stage. Tofie's fast asleep, her spiked blond hair poking haphazardly this way and that, so I whisper when I ask Galen, "Is Lemuel here?"

Galen points his chin toward the beach.

I grab a side-view mirror and climb on the tire to see Lemuel and Elijah, silhouetted against the sunrise, in morning prayers, bobbing on their prayer mats on the sand.

My heart sinks a little. I thought he was lapsed. I don't know if practicing Muslims are allowed to interpret dreams.

"Can I wait on the bus?"

Galen nods.

Their tour bus is a repurposed tour bus. I mean, before it took the band to shows, it drove the tourists around Manhattan to see tall buildings. They still have the observation deck on top, though they've taken out some of the seats, so while Galen sets Tofie gently into her sleeping berth, I go upstairs to watch the sun rise on the Atlantic.

The sky is pink and orange right around the rising sun, and the ocean isn't still, but you can't really call it waves—more like an undulating surface, like a waterbed, the reflected sunrise-orange alternating with cool ocean blue. Elijah and Lemuel are two nodding silhouettes in the shadowy part of the sand. They should be too far away to hear, but Lemuel's haunting baritone just carries. Even in prayer, he can't help showing off. I watch the morning advance as the two men bob in time with the sea, and a moment passes before I realize someone is standing behind me. "Galen?" I ask.

He steps forward to the rail. His fair skin and pale blond make a perfect canvas for the pink morning light, which creeps into the creases between his muscles.

"You look good in this light," I say.

He doesn't comment.

By this time Lem has finished and is sitting on his mat staring out at the sea, while Elijah still has some bowing left to do.

"I thought he was lapsed," I say.

Galen cocks an eyebrow.

"Lem. How long has it been since he last set foot in a mosque?"

Galen shrugs.

"Is he going back?"

Galen shakes his head.

"So what's this about?" I gesture toward the two men on the beach. Lem is standing now, with his rug in a yoga bag over his shoulder, while Elijah is just beginning to roll his up.

Galen smiles. "Hangin' with God on the beach."

I laugh. For Galen, this is talkative—but I can imagine Lemuel saying it, and once you put it that way, who *wouldn't* want to be out on the beach with them? I watch the two of them walk up the beach, the old black Muslim with his rug tucked under his arm and the young Arab poet carrying his slung over his back. Galen taps my shoulder and points just as my eyes alight on Ocean, further down the beach, sleeping on the sand. "Oh shit," I say, and run for the stairs down off the deck.

I'm dashing out the door down to the street just as Elijah and Lemuel cross back to us.

"Grace!" Lemuel shouts as I almost crash into him, and he picks me up with a smile and spins me around—which allays my fears a bit; I mean, they're not even supposed to touch a girl, right? At least that's what I've heard.

"You're gonna be here a while, right?" I ask, not letting go of his hand even as my feet try to take me away.

"Sorry, can't," he answers. "Have to get Elijah to NYC before lunch."

That's an ambitious drive for anyone, but Lem has some kind of inside track to the traffic gods.

I look at Elijah, hoping for some sort of mercy. "Sorry, Grace," he says. "Bahseera is giving a lunch talk today, and I don't want to miss it."

I know better than trying to get in the way of anything to do with his daughter. "OK, look," I say to Lemuel, "I had this dream and it's bugging me—I mean, it's *really* bugging me—and I wanted to get your take on it, but when I was sitting up top on the deck I noticed—actually Galen noticed—Ocean is down there sleeping on the beach, and I want to find out what that's about and make sure he's alright and besides there's this yellow suitcase he told me about was it yesterday—maybe the day before—but he's asleep so he ought to be fine for a while and stay in one place while I tell you—*quickly*—about the dream. OK?"

Lemuel calls up toward the deck, "Y'up there, Galen?"

Galen looks down at us over the rail.

"Keep an eye on this one's boyfriend, OK? Let us know if he wakes up?"

My insides do a somersault when Lem calls Ocean my boyfriend. I mean, yeah, I want him to be, but... hoo-yeah. Galen nods.

"You used to posting lookouts for women's boyfriends?" Elijah asks.

Lemuel mock-slaps him across the back of the head, knocking the lace skullcap forward so it slants across his forehead. "Come aboard," Lemuel says as he steps up onto the bus.

So I'm, like, still freaked out about Ocean being out there asleep on the beach, but I follow Lem in. Even as Lemuel and Elijah are closing compartments and tucking things down, I'm like, "So I was walking in the woods and there was this cabin in front of me, really scary, I saw it in *Weird New Jersey* in an article in my basement, and I was going there and I wasn't, but inside it was like the diner, but there was this man there who wanted meat and wine, but the meat could've been a woman's leg-bone and I think the wine was blood."

Lem's packing a stuff sack, but his hand is still. When I stop to breathe he starts tying off the strings. "So this cannibal at the diner—what did he look like?"

"I don't know—I can't remember his face."

"Did you see his face?"

"No, umh—I don't know. I kind of remember talking to him. But all I remember is his limp, like he has a club foot."

"Where was he walking to?"

My jaw drops open. "He wasn't. He sat at the table the whole time I saw him. But I swear I remember the limp. Is that messed up?"

Lemuel smiles. "Not really. When you dream, your mind is editing things before the story unfolds. So you have access to information that you don't always get to see."

"But not his face?"

"It might not be important. The stuff that isn't important, you might not fill in, so you don't get distracted from the parts that matter."

I breathe. "My subconscious does that?"

"Yeah."

"Kewl."

"Or he could just be hiding it from you," a breathy whisper suggests from a lower berth, as a pale thin arm emerges from behind the curtain.

121

"What?"

And like the Bride of Dracula rising from the crypt, Lemuel's girlfriend crawls out from Lemuel's sleeping berth, in a tattered nightgown that barely covers her bone-thin frame. "If someone is sending these dreams," she softly exhales, "then he might be hiding his face to protect him from you."

I roll my eyes. I'm about to say something, but Lemuel nods and Elijah says, "That's true."

"I…. *Sending* me *dreams?*" I ask.

Zombie-girl nods her pale, gaunt face.

"But how—?" I stammer.

"If he can alter a person on a chromosomal level, sending a dream would be no problem for him." She has this breathy-soft Marilyn voice, but dammit, Marilyn had some meat on her. She's just bone.

"If he could *what?* Who said *anything* about chromosomes?"

Dead-girl shrugs. "You said it was your father, right?"

"No, I di—what does *that* have to do with *any*thing?"

She opens her mouth to answer, then Galen pounds the roof three times to tell me Ocean is on the move.

"Crap," I say, and bolt out the door.

"Good luck, Grace," Lemuel shouts as I run out.

"Thank—um, have a safe trip," I say, and I take the moment to really mean it and turn to face him with a smile, because Lemuel says that matters—that it's important to wish others well and always to form your thoughts completely. Then I turn and run.

* * *

I don't know who decided flip-flops are beachwear—they suck for running on sand. And for running across the street and clambering over the roadside levee to get to the sand. Really, they suck for running at all, so I ditch them halfway down the beach before I get to where I saw him, but it doesn't matter an awful lot because he's walking very slowly, and when I catch up with him he's already on his way home.

"Hi," I say, trying to sound relaxed, but my breathing hasn't slowed from running yet, and the effort to fake control tosses my voice into the stratosphere halfway through.

"Hi," Ocean answers, though he seems to be somewhere else.

"Are you OK?"

"Yeah, I… yeah, I guess I am."

"What happened? Did you—did your dad throw you out?"

"What? No, I—Why do you keep asking that? It was too crowded there, last night, just too many people around. I wanted the stars."

I look up at the sky. It's in that grayish pale it gets to when the night just can't hold on. But I know what he means, and I imagine the stars in the places they belong, because I've looked up from this beach so many times. A light wave whispers against the sand.

Looking up toward the stars I cannot see, I say, "Morticia thinks a wizard is sending me dreams."

"Morticia?"

"Lemuel's girlfriend."

"Liane."

"Whatever. What does he see in her?"

"I used to wonder. But another time the band took over the house, I was sitting out here wishing for some quiet, and Liane came out and sat next to me and told me everything on my mind. She stopped short of saying what was in the suitcase, but I think she knew."

He looks so kissable, right now. But we're not there yet. I say, "Weird."

"Yeah."

"So, um…" I need to keep talking, because if I don't, I'll try to kiss him, and I'm not ready for that rejection, not just yet. "Do you think she's a junkie?"

"No way." He shakes his head. "She's way too lucid."

"Maybe you caught her in a sober moment?"

"Nah. Lemuel wouldn't go for that. Galen wouldn't allow that stuff on the bus. And my dad would never ride with them if that was going on."

"Your dad gets worked up about other people's stuff?"

"Not usually. Not for most things. But…" His voice trails off.

"But what?"

"That stuff's different."

"Oh."

And there's silence, for a moment, and I hear my body breathe. Did Ocean's dad lose someone to drugs? I want to ask, but I also want to ask what's in the suitcase, and before I can make up my mind, Ocean says,

"Thanks for coming to find me." And he reaches over and takes my hand, interlacing his fingers between mine. I squeeze it once, and I'm dying to kiss him, but I'm afraid if I do he might pull his hand back. My heart's going ba-bump, ba-bump, ba-bump, but I try to be nonchalant, and the two of us stand there together holding hands as the rising sun suffuses the sky with pink.

And that's it. At least for now. I mean, there are things I want to know, but the summer has a way of getting between them, and when I remember to ask what's in the suitcase I don't want to, because I don't want to make him think of it. He's finally *touching* me—holding my hand, putting his arm around my shoulders, once even slipping off our flip-flops and playing footsies in the diner—and I'm finally happy. I don't want to probe too deep. Which is really weird. I mean, normally I can't shut up, but now I have this question burning a hole in my head and I just *can't* ask.

And one day, at Alden's Cove, we're sunning ourselves side by side, and I realize I'm ready to kiss him. I mean, I feel brave enough at last, but there's that question still between us, and I don't want it in the way. So that's it. The question will have to go. But right now it feels so good to simply lie on the beach beside him. And you know, the thought that I'm ready, finally *ready*—that feels good. I savor it.

* * *

The next day I'm just showing up for my shift and the sun is setting behind the restaurant, so all that chrome is surrounded by pink but reflects the cold and dusky blue of the eastern sky behind me as I walk up the ramp. My reflection cuts the blue dusk with my hair tied back.

My mom is in the office in the back, on the phone with a worried look. I come in to change into my work clothes. "Now, sweetie," my mom says into the phone, "snooping in basements and attics is something that teenagers do. Why, just recently Grace was... oh, no, you can't assume that. Just because he dug out an old suitcase doesn't mean he's planning to leave. He might just be wondering what's in it.... Uh-huh..."

"Is that Ocean's mom?" I ask, pointing to the phone.

She puts her hand over the mouthpiece and nods.

"And Ocean took a suitcase from the attic?"

She nods again.

"A *yellow* suitcase?"

She takes her hand off the mouthpiece and says, "Hang on, sweetie" into the phone, then she covers it and talks to me again. "Why, Grace? What is this abou—"

"And he's not home now?"

"No. Grace, honey, what's going—"

"I gotta go. See if Gloria can cover my shift." And I drop my work clothes on the desk and run outside in my white henley and coveralls.

He's not on the beach by his house, or by where he slept when I had that dream. I try up and down every place I can think of, and finally I spot him after dusk at Alden's cove. The moon is full, and Ocean is standing on the rocks with the suitcase in his hand, like he's waiting to board a train but the platform is somewhere beneath the waves.

"Ocean," I call, "what's going on?" I'm stumbling over the rocks in my jagged rush, boots slipping on the stone although I know these outcroppings by heart.

He turns and looks up at me but doesn't say anything, just stares at me with those big brown irises as I scamper across to him.

"Ocean?"

He puts the suitcase down on the rocks. "Grace?"

"What's happening?"

"I'm sorry. I—"

"No—what—don't apologize, you don't have to be sorry for anything, just stay."

"Grace, I—"

"Don't be sorry; please don't be sorry; just stay with me, stay here."

"Grace, I—"

"Please!"

"I have to go."

"Please don't."

"I'm sorry, Grace."

"Please… take me with you?"

He stops and stares at me. "I can't."

"You're what matters to me, you're the only thing that matters."

"Grace, I—"

"If you're going to go away, then I'm coming with you. Take me with you."

"Grace, I can't."

"Don't you leave me here without you, Ocean, please! Don't go!"

"I don't think it's possible, Grace. I don't think I can."

"We'll find a way."

"It's not possible."

"Anything's possible, Ocean!"

"Grace..." And he kneels down on the stone and flips up the fasteners on the suitcase. He opens it and takes out the weirdest thing I've ever seen, like a wetsuit made of rubber made of fur.

"What is that?" I ask.

"My skin," he says.

I pinch his arm, right above his wrist.

"My *other* skin."

"What do you mean?"

He looks down, as if he's dropped the right word in the spaces between the rocks. "This is what I am. This is what my father—my real father—was. Is."

"What? What are you talking about? What is it?"

He starts unbuttoning his shirt.

"Ocean, what—?"

"This is where I come from," he says. He keeps unbuttoning his clothes, taking off his shirt, his shoes, his pants.

I want so badly to touch him, but I don't know what he's doing. I think about maybe being bold and taking my clothes off too, but I know I'd be reading the moment wrong. When he's absolutely naked, I have the thought that I could walk over to him and kiss him and just take him in my hand—he isn't hard, but I don't care; I've never actually seen one before, and this one is *his*. Maybe if I had he'd still be here—I don't think it's likely but I don't know—and while I'm paralyzed in the moment he steps into that rubberskin suit before I can get past the jumbled thoughts, and he slips it on over his shoulders, *becoming* a *seal* as the skin closes around him, but I don't know what's going on except that I'm *running out of time,* so I step forward and reach down before he's totally changed, and I stick my hand in there and touch his chest, my fingers between skin and skin, and I'm lightheaded with the impossibleness of the moment. "Don't go," I say.

"I have to." And the moonlight seems to well up around my hand.

"Please stay," I plead as the moonlight slips through my fingers into the suit.

"I can't," he answers, and the sealskin closes around his throat, his face. I try to hang on, but it runs through my fingers like time, and I'm holding his necklace in my hand with the shiny blue stone, and Ocean is walking on his flippers to the sea. He looks back at me with those sad, unmistakably human animal eyes.

I don't know when I fell to my knees—if I slipped as he pulled away, or when he turned his head to look forward, or if I just dropped in that dizzy impossible moment when I interrupted his change—but I feel the rocks on my knees and watch the moonlight on his fur as he paddles away. He isn't wet, not the way you might imagine a seal, and when the wave comes in and soaks me through my overalls it wets him too, but his head and the middle of his back stay above the water as the moonlight glistens off his flippers and his sides. When the second wave comes, he dives under and is the glistening seal you always picture swimming to sea, breaking the surface for a moment, and then gone.

I hang the necklace around my neck to keep it safe.

* * *

After that I just kind of drive around. I don't want to go back to the diner, and I can't think of where else to go, and it's around 2:00 a.m. I realize I must be on autopilot, because I look up and I'm at his house.

It's backwards, though: all the windows are lit and his is the only one that's dark. I'm on the beach side, across the street, looking up at that empty window. I feel the empty place inside me where he should be. And I'm alone, so I let myself cry, big, wet sobs that shake the insides of my lungs.

I look at the other windows around his. They shine like starlight through the water in my eyes. It warms me inside and I don't want to leave, to be alone. Not now.

Ocean's mom is already at the door, looking wispy, like a woman on the rocks in some Irish ballad, waiting for her fisherman to come home. In my memory of this moment the wind blows her skirt, even though the screen door is closed. I don't know what's real. Even through the screen, the hope leaves her face when she sees me on the steps, and she opens the door and clings to me like I'm all she has left of him. The stone in his necklace presses against my breastbone under my shirt.

"He's gone?" she asks, without letting go, but with nothing in her voice, 'cause she already knows.

And I want to answer, but I can't, so I just cry into her neck.

And we stand there in the night, and cry on each other, and I bury my face in her hair. The breeze blows gently against my back, and it moves her skirt against my legs, and we cling to each other like children who don't know where we are.

And, when we know we can't get the comfort we need, she lets me inside and, without saying anything, goes to the closet for pillows, sheets, and blankets for the couch. I fold it out with her, and I help put the sheets on the sofa bed.

Ocean's dad comes out from the next room and watches us there, until I look at him. "So it's happened?" he asks cautiously.

I nod.

"Is there anything I can—"

Something made of glass hits the wall beside his head and shatters before I can figure out what it is. "Dammit," Ocean's mother says, "you let him go! Why did you let him go?"

"He couldn't have—" I start, but stop myself.

Ocean's dad stands there a moment, his eyes watchful and cautious and not entirely surprised, then retreats into the kitchen.

Ocean's mom stands with trembling hands, and she cries in place a moment, then grabs me and clings, and I have to support her because her legs aren't holding her weight.

Ocean's dad comes back with a teapot and three cups on a little tray. He pours a cup and is ready to pour a second when Wave shows up at the top of the stairs and says, "Daddy?"

It's scary to see a child that small at the top of a staircase. Ocean's dad puts the teapot back on the tray and goes to her. I pour the second cup and give it to Ocean's mom.

She sits on the edge of the sofa bed mattress and clings to the teacup with both hands like it's the only warmth in the world. "What's the point of loving people?" she asks. "They just go away."

And—this is kind of petty, but—I resent her for crowding my moment. I mean, Ocean is her son and all, but *I* love him. I'm sup*posed* to be with him. *Her* husband's still here. But... then I look into her face and realize... *she* isn't. Even sitting on this sofa bed and facing the other direction, she's still staring out to sea. And I wonder what's worse, losing someone all at once or living with someone and losing them day by day.

Ocean's dad is upstairs, serenading Wave. I hear the guitar very softly from where I am. For a moment I feel Ocean. I mean, I *feel* him, in the form of a seal, ducking under a wave, with a long way to travel to a home he's never seen. I give him a little of the strength I have left, to help him and keep him safe. I try to trace his wake back to me, to know where he is, so I can feel some connection between us, but then he's gone. I lost the signal. Or whatever the hell it was. If Mom was right and magic is real, then it sure isn't easy. But I guess she said that too.

Ocean's mom is asleep on the sofa bed, sitting up against the back, her half-full teacup perched on the arm of the couch. I move the cup to the tray on the end table and put a blanket over her. Then I go up to Ocean's room.

Ocean's dad is in the next room, singing Wave that song about gamblers and trains—not the Kenny Rogers song about knowing what to keep, the Leonard Cohen song about always going away.

The necklace used to be my mother's. She gave it to me. She was mad when I gave it to Ocean, but I wasn't going to ask for it back. I kick off my boots and lie back on his bed and wish him well.

And Ocean's dad is finishing up the lullaby in the next room. The gambler seems like he might stay, but then he pulls an old train schedule out of his pocket and says, "I'm a stranger. Didn't I tell you that when we met?"

And I think about strange and I think about weird and how they're not really the same, because weird is the opposite of normal, but familiar is the opposite of strange. People make fun of you if you're weird even though it's really who you are, but if you're strange they think it's cool, even though it's an act. And it gets harder to keep up the act the better you know them, because normal is an act, no one really is, but a Familiar is a rat who drinks the blood from a witch's breast...

* * *

I wake up not remembering where I am. The sun is shining through the curtains and I'm the only one awake. The knives in the kitchen call to me, the way they sometimes do. I step out of the front door onto the porch, where the sun has not yet risen over the sea.

My story doesn't end the way it's supposed to. If this was a story, I'd walk barefoot on the beach and look at the sky and think about how he was never really mine, and if you love someone set him free, and all

129

that stuff, and while I was mulling it over I'd get a glimpse of some inscrutable understanding of the way the universe works.

Me, I go inside and grab my boots, and I toss them through the open window into the passenger seat, next to the yellow suitcase with Ocean's clothes that I forgot to bring back to his mom. I reach into my hip pocket and pull out the clipping about that dome-shaped hut in the woods. The directions aren't fantastic, but I'm sure I can figure it out. I get in behind the wheel and slide the seat forward for barefoot driving.

Honest Tea

By Sara Fox

"This isn't right at all, is it?" Mrs. Gromek asked kindly, tilting the teacup this way and that. The tea was rosy and clear, nothing like the mud Eloise had produced last exam, but even as it developed rose petals on the inside: it was still wrong. Eloise sniveled once, then tried to swallow it down as Mrs. Gromek smiled and waited for a half-credit answer. *Better to at least get the verbal*, she had told Eloise when she failed the first time but—but Eloise wanted to succeed. It was only tea.

She would have preferred a good chastising. She could have withstood a lecture with not so much as a lip quiver. A teaspoon of kindness, however, and her eyes were already filling. "I'm doing it exactly as the book says, honest!"

Mrs. Gromek's office was set up for exams today. Normally awash with books and papers, she had whittled it all down to two hot pads, two kettles, and a cutting board placed on top of a wide, flat desk that could be twisted upright and turned into a chalkboard. Even with the threat of exams, the office rarely felt ominous. Most days she left her windows open, allowing sunlight or a spring shower to brighten her room and titter on the sill. Today, however, the sky was full of storm clouds and the window had clipped itself shut as soon as heavy rain began knocking against the roof. Eloise was trying not to take it personally.

"Look here." Mrs. Gromek took off the lid of her own teapot, allowing the scent of oranges and earl gray to waft across the desk.

Eloise sighed through her pointed nose, leaning forward with her head in her hands until she was almost in the pot. As she watched, white steam chased itself into shapes of orange slices and the silhouette of a young woman swinging an umbrella over her head. Mrs. Gromek replaced the lid and began pouring tea into two cups; it bubbled with bits of stones and ghostly images of seagrass. *It's easier for you,* Eloise wanted to complain, but didn't dare. *You can see all that by walking down the street. Your memories are at the local chop shop and among the dunes. This isn't my home.*

"As you can see things develop, yes? But they don't appear until I release the steam or pour it." Maybe Eloise had released the steam too early. While she didn't remember touching the lid before presenting it to her teacher, maybe she had. Maybe she had been over-eager and tipped the lid? Eloise netted her fingers together, watching the tea go from brown to a rich ocean turquoise studded with clouds made of cream.

"Drink up." Mrs. Gromek placed the cup in front of her nose. "I think you could use it."

The tea was supposed to make her feel better, but as Eloise finished and tumbled out of the office she just felt flushed, strangely eager, and seasick. Maybe Mrs. Gromek's tea had been a little off that day, too.

* * *

By the time Eloise got back to her dorm, the rain had quieted into a mist better suited to twilight. Drowsy raindrops slumped out of tree branches to fill her metal-tipped boots in fractions and weigh down her hair.

"How did it go, Eloise?" Ulysses called from a slouch at the dormitory front desk. Ulysses was the most responsible student receptionist at the school and the only time they weren't in residence seemed to be when they had their own exams. Sometimes Eloise thought Ulysses must sleep at the desk, it was so rare for them not to be there.

She waved, still sleepwalking through failure, towards Ulysses' bright green fingernails and camouflage pants. "I don't want to talk about it," she lied as Ulysses buzzed the inner door open for her.

Eloise didn't see the stairs as she climbed them, ignored the doors propped invitingly open along the hall. She put one foot in front of the other until she was able to slump inside her room. Outside, an oak tree two windows down groaned against the wind and a streetlight began to flicker. The weather was going to get worse before it got better.

Since there wasn't enough green or gravel for Eloise to pretend she was home, she decided to call them. Her phone was dropped unceremoniously on a stack of books in a futile attempt to find the best angle to video chat with. She tried to wring her hair out but no matter what she did it was thick and dripping. By the time she hit *Video Chat: Sister Dearest* Eloise wasn't sure if she was aiming for *most pitiful* or *paradigm of awesome—but still a failure.*

She probably shouldn't have worried so much about presentation. When Esther answered it was mostly with her nose and chin in the frame. "Ella—Ella, how'd it go?"

"Failed again, Ester." Eloise folded her arms and knocked her forehead against her wrists two times. "I don't even know what I'm doing wrong."

"Well, obviously, selling your soul to the factory model..." The answer was easy for Esther, though this time it came out more of a tease then her normal waspish annoyance. They would never see eye to eye over Eloise's decision to trade homeschooling for the posh over-intellectualism of a northern magic school. It didn't matter why Eloise was calling; Ester always had that specific answer on the tip of her tongue.

To Esther's thinking, Eloise' interest in Kinetic Magical Philosophy would ruin her ability to problem-solve magical problems in a more practical manner. How could Eloise feel what was right with her head stuck in book rules? Eloise, on the other hand, didn't know how to explain to Esther that books and rules allowed her to create scaffolding so that she could do more than just figure out how to wash away a curse or a ghost.

Each step Eloise made in academia was one more away from home. Eloise normally liked it. Esther did not and she blamed everything on that change from potholes to spilled coffee to a ruined hex. "But I don't know, Ella. You've, like, done tea magic since forever. We all have."

"This is different."

"Yeah, yeah, *hot* tea. Such a difference."

Eloise pursed her lips in frustration and Ester mirrored her perfectly save for the fact that her curls came in blond instead of mousy brown and her blouse was buttoned two places higher. She was wearing makeup, though, which was new. Eloise opened her mouth to comment, to needle her about what she had on her lips, when Esther's eyes suddenly warmed with mischief.

"Hey—you know, why don't you just spit in it?"

"That's so gross!" Eloise laughed, shaking hard enough that water from her hair dotted the screen. She picked up the phone and tried to dab the water off as it bulged her sister's cheeks and bloomed her teeth into half her face. "Besides, no one does it that way anymore. Not unless they're desperate."

Esther sniffed. "Aren't you?"

And they might have started fighting right then if their mother hadn't swooped into the background with, "Is that your sister?" And although Esther said, "She's just calling to complain again!" their mother plucked the phone away and held it so that only her eyes and forehead were really visible.

"Hush your mouth, Esther, and let me talk to her." There was a bit of mud from the garden on her mother's brow and it looked for all the world like a witch's wart. "Eloise, is this about a boy?"

Like Esther, their mother didn't understand going away for school but she did understand anything being about a boy. 'About a boy' was how their grandmother had explained the sisters' existence when they were knee high, even though neither of them had ever seen 'a boy' so much as stay the night. Eloise had never understood the explanation, even when her sister snickered: *just wait 'til you get kissed!*

Eloise had already been kissed—but no matter if she kissed Jessica or Justin, kissing just felt like lips and saying so always led to sad, unsettled eyes. Kissing begged to the question: *Why don't you like me?* Eloise wanted to contend that the two were unrelated but didn't know how. It was just another way that she didn't seem to belong.

So she said, "No!" for the 100th time. "Just school. It's just school. I still can't brew the damn tea right."

Her mother sighed but resisted the urge to chastise or threaten soap as she swung the phone around. "That is ridiculous. You have Nanna's recipe don't you?" Her smile meant that she had already forgotten that Nanna's was a sun brew and therefore somehow *wrong*. It was good enough for their hometown contests, utterly useless in a bricked-up school stacked with desks in perfectly straight rows. "Have you asked to brew in better weather? It's all rain there. I can taste it."

Next her mother would suggest yoga, or finding someone to go mudding with while conjuring. Eloise sighed into a shiver as the air conditioning clicked on.

"Come on, ma, we have to get going. Gimmie my phone." Esther snatched it back before their mother could protest and stared seriously into the camera. "Remember, dummy, *spit*."

"A lady doesn't spit," her mother declared from out of the frame. "Hair," she suggested instead. "Or blood if you're really looking to give it to someone."

Eloise did not want to "give it" to Mrs. Gromek. She just wanted to pass.

* * *

While ingredients (a stone charged in moonlight, the ashes of intention carefully measured and blended with tea leaves) are of paramount importance, perhaps even more so is the preparation of the tea. It is easy to sour a pot with bitterness, over sweeten it with jealousy, and so on. Brewing must commence with a strong memory base, but one that is unhindered by superfluous emotion. Without a strong memory both the mood-influencing properties and the image reflection are unable to render and, at best, the result is simply a normal cup of tea.

Reflection Tea p. 226

* * *

None of the tea tasted right.

Eloise settled in the dormitory lab and refused to leave for the three days between her last failure and what she was certain would be her next failure. Each day she produced at least two batches that were bitter, that were salty, that were just altogether *wrong*. Once, the tea clotted the color of blood and was just as viscous—as though the pot had been cut straight from the vein and then started to dry. Another time her tea was indistinguishable from water, smelling faintly of magnolias with steam reflections that hazily appeared and then melted back into the ether. Each pot, Eloise was certain, tasted worse than the last and each memory reflection rendered increasingly fragmented.

When friends turned up on the third day with cling-wrapped food and words of encouragement she demanded: "Show me yours."

For breakfast she had a cup of bubblegum tea, tempered by leather and mint. Justin smiled sheepishly as the steam swirled wild horses around the currents of his cup. Eloise's own brew was black, with no proper scent, and she threw it out before anyone else could see the fingers made out of sugar which peeped over the rim of the cup and waved at her. Her mother would say it was just her grandpop playing a prank. Eloise wasn't sure why she kept thinking of graveyards—but it didn't matter since the tea was still wrong and, worse, unsettling.

At lunch, she tried Hannah's cup of fresh cut grass, matcha, and a hint of lemonade. The water balloons dizzied themselves in the glass, then burst tartly on their tongues. Eloise's attempt turned her breakfast blend so salty even the evaporating reflections cried.

"Why is it so important that you get this final correct? You won't fail the class," Parker asked that evening, handing Eloise a cup of her sweet saltwater taffy tea.

Eloise stared at the summer fair that bubbled and twirled under the surface. "It's not like I haven't done it before." She grimaced a little. "At home—it's all cold brew tea, you know? I just... "

"I don't like sweet tea," Parker interrupted, "But if it's kind of the same and you know how to do it, who cares if you don't brew the same as everyone else?"

The books did, Eloise didn't say. Brewing on the windowsill was country magic. She didn't want to admit she was embarrassed. Embarrassed felt an awful lot like *shame* and Eloise didn't want to be ashamed of her mother or sister and the little magics that made them.

* * *

As penance Eloise brewed sun tea the morning of her final attempt at the tea practicum. She filled a clear glass jug with fresh water, a stone charged by moonlight, and all the good summer memories she could think of: the slip and slide with her sister, barbeque and pineapple upside-down cake, the pond that served as a swimming hole on the hottest days. She packed four tea infusers full of her breakfast blend, tied them together so the infusers couldn't get lost, and then let them dangle in a chain above the stone that nested in a cup of white sugar.

That morning sun poured in through her dormitory window and with that light, it only took two hours for memory reflections to form inside the glass. By noon her jug was the color of caramel and the memory of Esther caught itself in the sunlight, reflected like liquid gold on Eloise's desk. She wanted to be bitter about it but, in her exhaustion, all Eloise could do was watch the image dance while it licked it ghostly her fingers clean of imaginary cool whip. Her entire room smelled of honeysuckle.

Eloise almost poured the entire pot out her window as she left for her test. The reflection of her sister waving and blowing kisses stopped her.

* * *

Eloise trudged down the stairs, stomped through the front room, and would have made her way irritably to Mrs. Gromek's office 40 minutes early if Ulysses hadn't stopped her.

"You have time, right?" Ulysses seemed to already know she did. "I want to show you something."

They enlisted Hannah to man the front desk and then Ulysses nudged Eloise into the lab again. She pulled one knee up on the stool and leaned into it as she watched Ulysses take out a hotplate and all the ingredients for a pot of reflection tea. "I don't need a primer before the exam," she said. It came out as a whine.

"Of course you don't." Ulysses pulled out some sweet and condensed milk and two tall cups. "This isn't a 'don't forget to boil your water' lesson."

Eloise felt her face heat a little, and she distracted herself from the tea preparation by picking at a loose thread in her skirt until Ulysses commanded her attention again with a, "Look here."

She wanted to tell them 'no'. That she didn't care if they used a different kind of creamer: it wasn't going to help. She could only brew sun tea correctly. "I don't—"

"Just watch." Ulysses clicked their tongue and Eloise knew this time she was truly flushed, much to her chagrin. The tea went into one cup and the condensed milk followed, drowning the first reflective images. Eloise opened her mouth again, to warn Ulysses that the images might not form again, when Ulysses began to pour the tea between the two cups they had put out—destroying those first scenes for good.

"Lean away a little," Ulysses warned as Eloise leaned forward. "It's very hot."

Eloise had never seen anyone pass tea between cups before. The mixture gurgled a little, splattered when Ulysses was a little too cavalier with it, and then eventually the drink settled half in one cup and half in the other with a thick layer of froth making up the difference.

"It's called Teh Tarik." In the foam three children, no bigger than a

137

fingerprint, rose to build a castle from the froth. When Eloise cupped one glass between her hands, she smelled cardamom and something she couldn't place. "My uncles make it all the time. Other tea—it's not the same, right?"

Eloise nodded; she felt slightly breathless and a little like she might start crying again. She sucked on the feeling with pinched eyes and a bowed head and then tried to dismiss it. "Thank you."

"Don't be so worried about being different," Ulysses smiled. "Get results."

Eloise nearly knocked over the carton of heavy cream in her haste to retrieve the glass jar from her room. When she returned to the lab to apologize, there was nothing but a few foam footsteps left on the counter. She stood there for a long moment, then got a plastic bag and filled it with ice. It was nearly time for her exam.

* * *

"I want to make it a different way." Eloise put her finished jug of tea right in the middle of Mrs. Gromek's desk. "It takes too long to brew in the exam time. Can I show you how it's done and you can see the results in... in. When it's done?" She had never been so direct with a teacher in her life and couldn't stop trembling over the impertinence of it.

"I think that would be just fine." Mrs. Gromek reached over to run a finger across the glass. Her pale blue eyes chased Esther's outline, then rose to meet Eloise's. "It's good the storms have stopped, isn't it?"

"Really?" It came out as a breath Eloise didn't even realize she was holding in. She hurriedly ripped open the bag of ice, twisted the jar's top off, and began dropping the ice cubes in. The single reflection shattered and reformed into a swirl of women laughing and talking together. The brew still smelled of honeysuckle but Eloise thought she might have sensed a hint of the woods after a spring rain when she swirled it with a spoon. She wanted to say *thank you*. Instead she reached for a glass on the table so she could pour her morning brew for a taste test.

"If your brew this afternoon is like this I suppose we won't have to do the verbal portion." Eloise thought Mrs. Gromek was just being nice—but she drank the tea without a grimace and helped Eloise find what she needed to brew another pot. It took an extra half an hour to find a clear jar big enough, then an extra 10 minutes to find two more infusers.

Sometimes, as Eloise measured and poured, her hands started to shake. The jangle of nerves caught in lungs and almost forced her to stop. They only settled when she looked up at her finished, half empty jar of tea. The ice had finished melting in the sun, causing the women's silhouettes to become loose and elongated, like giants or afternoon shadows. Even still, they reminded her: she'd done this 100 times.

"The images develop differently, without steam." The warning clattered against her teeth over and over as she worked.

Mrs. Gormek nodded every time, then patted her hand. "They develop as they are supposed to."

Awaken

By Rain Fletcher

As always, Mr. B managed to time the last run-through of the song in such a way that he could conduct the final cutoff within 15 seconds of the bell heralding the end of third period. "Good work today," he nodded to his class. "That one's really coming together. Tomorrow we'll start on the Tallis piece, so any of you who feel so inclined, take a look at it in preparation..." The bell sounded, and the rest of his message was lost in the noise of 45 choir members getting up from their seats, gathering their things and heading off to their next classes.

As always, Aerie Kersulis was one of the last to leave, waiting for the press of bodies to subside before coming down off the risers and placing her folder of sheet music into its numbered slot on the rack. As always, Mr. B gave her a nod and a friendly smile as she left, and as always, Su Nakajima was waiting for her just outside the rehearsal room, looking up at her with an expectant smile, as if to say: "And..?"

Aerie shook her head at the shorter girl. "Still nothing," she said softly.

"All things in time, my dearling," Su assured her as they fell in step together. "It'll come; I know it will."

"I wish I had your confidence."

"I'm your mentor," Su reminded her. "It's my job to have confidence in, you, remember?" She gave Aerie a sidelong grin to show that she was teasing, but it quickly faded as she noticed the look on the other girl's face. "So serious, poor thing."

"Su, what if you're wrong about me?" Aerie asked, not for the first time. "What if they're all wrong about me? What if they brought me to this school for nothing?"

A small hand slipped into her own, and Aerie felt her pulse quicken as a liquid warmth spread from Su's fingers to her own, quickly flowing through her and making her gasp at the sensation of it.

"This right here?" Su smiled. "This is why they weren't wrong. This is why you belong here, and *this* is why I know it'll come for you in time." She laced her fingers around Aerie's and gave her hand a gentle squeeze, sending a wave of tingling energy shooting up her arm. "So relax and let it happen."

Aerie nodded wordlessly, as she did not trust herself to speak at that moment over the combined sensation of Su's hand holding hers, and Su's energy flooding her entire being and lighting her up inside. How much of it was magic, though, and how much was... something else?

They parted ways about halfway across the school grounds, as Su's next class was French and Aerie's was Calculus. "See you at lunch?" Su asked, giving Aerie that effortless smile of hers.

"Of course," said Aerie with a nod and a reluctant smile. "Thanks, Su."

Su gave a tiny wave and disappeared into the crowd of passing students, leaving Aerie to take a deep breath and let it out in a sigh.

"I love you," she said under her breath, as always.

* * *

"You worry too much," Su assured her over lunch. Mr. B generally left the choir room open for his students during the lunch period, and Aerie and Su often ate here, preferring the relative safety of this haven to the bustle of the lunch quad, particularly for having this sort of talk. Most of the student body was unaware of the subculture of magical education happening around them, and Aerie had had it drummed into her since day one that it was vital to keep it that way.

"Are there ever Sensitives who never Awaken?" Aerie asked her point-blank.

"It's possible," Su said patiently, "that singing might not be what triggers it in you, though the Administrators seemed pretty convinced of it. You're in Calculus, right? All those formulae are just another form of arcanery, when you come right down to it. The practitioners on the math team always like to joke that once you master triple integral, you're ready to unlock all the secrets of the universe."

"I don't know," said Aerie. "I mean, I'm *good* at math, but..."

141

The room was beginning to fill up a bit as some of the boys from the choir came in for an impromptu rehearsal of some *a capella* doo-wop. Su smiled in their direction for a moment, then hummed a soft tune that only Aerie could hear. There was a tingle that she now recognized as Su's magic taking effect: a simple spell to disguise their conversation. As Su had once described it to her, people on the outside would hear what they expected to hear two girls talking about, which would probably be boys. The merry roll of the eyes as Su had said this had been cute and a little heartbreaking at the same time.

"It doesn't resonate with you?" Su asked in the here and now. "Hasn't music always called to you? Mr. B says you were the alto section leader at your old school."

"I don't know if 'called to me' is the right way of putting it," said Aerie, frowning as the memories threatened to break through again. "Choir was... really the only place where I felt... I don't know, like *myself*. Like I didn't have to hide. I was a voice in a crowd, so I could be..." She paused for a moment and tried to find the words. "It was like I could be both anonymous and... fearless."

When Aerie looked up, she saw that Su had fixed her with a studious gaze. "You don't talk about your old school much," Su noted. "Bad memories?"

"I didn't exactly have a lot of friends." Or indeed any, for that matter.

"Were people unkind to you?"

Aerie forced back the images of accusing eyes and disdainful faces and instead told a smaller truth. "Ehh, you know how people are," she said with a dismissive wave. "Anyone who's got a weird name is doomed. I was Airy, Air-head, Eerie, Lake Erie, Irie Mon..." She shrugged. "I figure with only my senior year here, there won't be time for that to catch on."

"I think Aerie is a lovely name," Su smiled. "A beautiful place high in the mountains where birds can make their nests."

"A lonely place," Aerie said without thinking, and immediately felt her cheeks heat up.

Su laid her hand over Aerie's, which did nothing to diminish the blush. "Well, then," she said softly, "perhaps a sparrow can come and keep that lonely place company?"

A sparrow. Rather than Susan, as most people presumed, the

nickname Su was actually short for *Suzume*, the Japanese word for "sparrow." Aerie found it a very fitting name for her, given that she was little, terrifyingly cute, and could trill like a bird.

"I don't know how a sparrow would fare," Aerie said carefully, treading around the edges of the metaphor. "Lots of birds of prey up there, you know."

"Ever seen a sparrow drive off a hawk?" said Su in an amused voice. "Sparrows are tough little birds when they're fighting for something important."

Su, you have to stop doing this to me, Aerie said in the privacy of her own head. If Su knew the reasons for that lonely place, would she be so willing to visit?

The doo-wop boys continued their rehearsal, blending their voices around love songs from generations ago. "You know, you never answered my question," said Aerie. "Is it possible that a Sensitive will never Awaken?"

After a long pause, Su nodded. "It happens that way sometimes. It's rare, though."

"Then... what if it does?" Aerie asked, feeling her throat clench. "Would they... send me back?"

"Absolutely not," said Su. "You'll finish high school here, whatever happens. If you Awaken, you're guaranteed admission at one of the most prestigious universities in the state, where you can study whatever you want on a full scholarship, and you'll get to continue your training with others like us. If you don't..." Su made a vague gesture with her free hand. "You'll be guaranteed admission at *another* of the most prestigious universities in the state, and you'll *still* get to study whatever you want on a full scholarship. You don't ever have to go back there, Aerie. Your education is taken care of. Our patrons will make sure of that, whether you become a practitioner or not."

As relieving as it was that she would never have to go back to the toxic atmosphere of her former high school, another dread quickly took the place of this long-standing fear. She now recalled hearing something like this during the whirlwind of her transfer to this school, but only when Su explained it did she realize the implications: Unless she Awakened, she would not be able to go to college with Su, and this year together might be all they would have.

"I don't want to fail you," Aerie heard herself whisper.

Su stared into her eyes for a long time, then put her empty bento box away in her bag, stood up, and again offered her hand. "Join me outside for a bit? Let's let the boys have their fun."

"Sure," Aerie nodded, having long since finished her own lunch. She gingerly took the offered hand, and they exited the choir room together, emerging into the early afternoon sunshine. It had taken Aerie a few weeks to get used to Su's tendency toward hand-holding: not that she didn't enjoy it, certainly, but how long would it be before Su was found guilty by association and ostracized for being even this level of affectionate with the freak?

Su hummed another tune under her breath, and Aerie felt the now-familiar warm tingle of a spell that would hide them from sight. It was not invisibility, as such: like the earlier magic to hide their conversation, it simply ensured that no one would bother to notice them, even in plain sight.

Another tune followed, and with a gasp, Aerie felt herself being pulled into the air. Within seconds, they were soaring over the campus with the wind whipping through their hair, hands now clasped tightly between them.

Only once before had Su taken her flying, more to demonstrate the reality of her magic than anything else, and it was as breathtaking this time as it had been then.

"Forgive my presumptuousness," said Su with a warm smile as she brought them to a hover, "but you looked like you needed this."

"No, you were right," Aerie replied, feeling a wide, genuine smile light up her face.

* * *

They continued their conversation on the deserted soccer field, lying on their backs in the grass, hands still held between them. "Su, after you go to college... what will you *do* with your magic?"

"What do you mean?"

"Well... it sounds like the patrons are investing a lot in us. Is there something specific we're being trained for?"

Su gave a ripple of laughter. "Ah, yes, this is the part where I tell you about the shadowy organization using us for their hidden agenda, or about the ongoing war in which we must take arms against those who would use the world's magic for evil purposes."

Aerie blinked a few times. "Seriously?"

"Not even a little," Su giggled. "No, I'm afraid it's not nearly as interesting as all that. We're free to do whatever we want after graduation."

"But... isn't that dangerous?" Aerie asked. "Aren't there people who would use this power for... I don't want to say *evil*, but... maybe in a controlling way?"

"Taking over the world, no doubt," Su nodded along with her. "I think you'll find it doesn't work that way."

"How so?"

"Our magic," Su explained, sending another pulse of it through their joined hands, "comes from the world, and... you could say it's self-selecting. If you were the sort of person who would use it selfishly, it would never have come to you in the first place. So no, I'm afraid fighting evil sorcerers is not in our future, dearling, and our patrons are nothing more than a self-sustaining philanthropic organization whose purpose is to keep this flame alive in a world that desperately needs it."

Aerie's head was beginning to spin. What Su was saying made a certain idealistic sense, but was that how the world really worked? "Then what will you do?"

Su rolled her head to the side to give Aerie another of her effortless smiles. "I'll sing."

"You'll... sing?"

"Exactly," Su whispered, her voice suddenly hushed. "This magic that has been gifted to me, I will return to the world in the form of song, and if in so doing I may inspire others to sing and thereby find their own magic, then I will have done *my* part to keep that fire burning ever brighter."

She waved her free hand absently toward the school. "The others there are the same way. The alchemists and numerologists will devote themselves to making discoveries in the sciences for the benefit of all. The wordsmiths will tell stories to enrich our lives. The shifters will play their roles on stage and screen, holding a mirror up to the lives of those who would watch them. Some of us will become teachers for the next generation, like Mr. B. Whatever path we choose, though, if we can continue to pay this gift forward, then... perhaps one day everyone in the world will find their own magic, and my goodness, what a world that would be."

"You don't think small, do you?" Aerie whispered.

"I think it's a fine goal," Su giggled again. "I certainly hope you and I can sing a few duets along the way."

"I'd... like that a lot," said Aerie, understating the matter hugely.

They lay in peaceful silence for a few minutes more, then in the distance a bell rang. Su rose gracefully, brushed the grass from her dress, then offered her hand yet again, this time to help Aerie stand. "We probably don't want to be late for class."

* * *

As promised, the next day's rehearsal saw the introduction of *If Ye Love Me*, a piece by the 16th-century composer Thomas Tallis. As he often did, Mr. B opened the period with a brief, quietly enthusiastic lecture about the history of the work and the artist, calling Tallis one of the most influential composers of English church music, writing and performing for two kings and two queens during the tumultuous period of the English Reformation. His repertoire thus included works for both the Roman Catholic and Anglican churches, and this piece, written under the rule of Elizabeth I, was one of the latter. The brief text was two-and-a-bit verses from the Book of John:

If ye love me, keep my commandments

And I will pray the Father, and he shall give you another comforter
That He may bide with you forever, e'en the Spirit of Truth

After the introduction, the choir was split into sections to work on their parts individually, sequestering themselves in some of the smaller rehearsal rooms scattered about the music buildings. Sectional rehearsals were generally Aerie's least favorite part of the process, partly because it meant being away from Su, but largely because she was convinced that half the girls in the alto section just didn't care, and had only joined the choir to tick off a box for their college applications.

At least the staff accompanist was there to keep them on track as they "woodshedded" their way through the work over the course of endless starts and stops. Aerie, being a decent sight-reader by this time, was quick to catch on, and steeled herself to not get bored over the course of the endless repetitions. Nonetheless, by the time the bell rang, she was about ready to climb the walls.

One class period later, she and Su met for lunch in the choir room again. "So what do you think of the new song?" Su asked.

Aerie considered this. "It's pretty, I guess. It just seems a little... weird to be singing something so blatantly church-y in school, what with political correctness and all."

"Ah, let me guess," Su nodded. "Your old choir did mostly show tunes and popular music? Maybe a madrigal or two if you wanted to stretch things out?"

"Pretty much. I mean, we did Christmas music for the winter concerts, but never anything quite like this."

Su put her head to one side. "Well, regardless of your personal beliefs, if you remove sacred music, you're taking out a huge chunk of the choral repertoire. Like Mr. B said, these songs aren't just worship and praise: they're an integral part of the history of Western music." She then gave a half-shrug and a merry smile. "Plus, it keeps the Jesus moms and the born-agains happy while the rest of us can enjoy the pretty harmonies."

"Uh huh," Aerie snorted.

"More importantly, at least to *me*, is that this might be just the sort of song to help you out of your current predicament."

Aerie furrowed her brow in confusion. "What do you mean?"

Su paused, looked over at the doo-wop boys crowded around the piano, then hummed the spell to disguise their conversation. "Sacred music tends to be... powerful," she explained, choosing her words carefully. "It lends itself well to helping people like us channel our magic, because it hits upon a lot of the same energies."

"You lost me somewhere back there," said Aerie, skeptically.

"I'll back up a little," Su nodded. "You've been singing for a few years now, right?"

"Right."

"How much training in music theory have you had? Intervals, chord progressions, that sort of thing?"

"Not a lot in choir," Aerie admitted. "Mostly we did everything by rote. I had a really good piano teacher when I was younger, though, so I know a little bit from that."

"We'll start with that, then," said Su with another quick nod. "I'll stick with Western theory for now. There's plenty I could tell you about Eastern music and how it relates to magic, but I should save that for later in your training."

"Thank you," Aerie deadpanned, trying not to let on that she was melting inside. An excited Su was an adorable Su.

"Okay, you start with half-steps and whole-steps. Those intervals are a minor second and a major second, respectively. Add another whole step, and you have.. " She waved her hand in a small circle, indicating that she was asking a question.

"A major third," Aerie answered her.

"Very good. And then another half-step makes...?"

"A perfect fourth."

"Exactly!" Su grinned, holding up one finger in an "Ah-ha!" pose. "Now, add another whole step for..."

"A perfect fifth."

"A perfect fifth," Su repeated. "Then if you continue up the major scale you have a major sixth, a major seventh, and a perfect octave."

"Okay," said Aerie, uncertain of where Su was leading them.

Su again cocked her head, this time in the other direction. "Have you ever wondered why the fourth, fifth and octave are called 'perfect' intervals?"

Aerie blinked. "Um... no?"

"In the tradition of sacred music," said Su, smiling as though imparting a secret, "those were considered 'holy' intervals, if you will. You'll find perfect fourths, fifths and octaves all over church music, because they literally considered those changes of pitch to be pleasing to God. Thus, they came to be called 'perfect' for their inherent holiness."

"Huh," said Aerie, as she could not think of anything else.

"Now, it just so happens," Su went on, "that those very same intervals are some of the most basic and most powerful ways for you and I and others like us to channel magic." Her smile deepened. "Once you're ready, you'll find that a lot of the first spells I teach you will be loaded with fourths and fifths. The relation between pitches is the very basis of our form of magic, and different intervals build different energies. Now, whenever he wants us to sing an ascending perfect fourth, what's the phrase that Mr. B always tells us to remember?"

"*Here comes the bride,*" Aerie replied.

"Or as we opera geeks know it, the *Bridal Chorus* from Wagner's *Lohengrin.* Beginning that piece with a perfect fourth was no accident: whether Wagner knew it consciously or not, that's an *invocation*, and it channels *tremendous* energy: the very thing for a ceremony of that importance."

"Really?"

Su nodded fervently. "The same goes for chord progressions and cadences. The most fundamentally basic cadence in Western music is going from the dominant to the tonic, or the V chord to the I chord. In hymns you'll hear a lot of what they call *plagal* cadences, which go from the IV to the I, usually as a final 'Amen.' None of this is by accident either! In our magic, a V-I cadence is the single most common way to close the loop and dismiss the energies you've invoked, and a IV-I is close behind in terms of common use." Her smile deepened yet again. "And lest you think that musically inclined practitioners adapted their spells to something that was already there, let me remind you that these harmonics and resonances are as old as the world itself."

Here, Su leaned closer, her eyes shining. "The magic you'll be learning didn't grow out of the Western musical tradition, Aerie: The Western musical tradition grew out of the magic that was there all along."

By this time, Aerie's head was once more beginning to spin. "But... what does that mean about these composers who used this in their church music? Were they... practitioners?"

"Probably not," said Su, shaking her head and relaxing her shoulders a little after her earlier semi-manic explanation. "There are plenty of people on our side who think that a lot of them were at least Sensitives, though. On some level, they felt the energies they were invoking when they composed their songs, and they probably thought it was bringing them closer to God." She gave a small laugh. "And who knows? Maybe it was. Maybe the source of all our magic is some sort of divinity after all. That's not for me to say, though."

"How is it that you know all of this?" Aerie asked wonderingly. "No, how is it that you know *everything?*"

Su actually blushed a little at the compliment, and momentarily got a faraway look in her eyes. "I... had a good mentor," she said quietly, but then her smile returned to its normal brilliance. "Besides, I have to do my part to keep up the Overly Studious Asian stereotype, don't I?"

"I'm... pretty happy with my mentor too," Aerie said quietly, feeling a clench of something very much like jealousy at whoever Su's had been.

"Thank you," said Su, her earlier blush briefly intensifying.

"I'm not just talking about the magical end of things, though," Aerie went on. "You know so much about music already, and you've got this *gorgeous* voice that I'm *totally* jealous of... and we're still in high school."

149

"Why did you first join a choir, Aerie?" Su asked suddenly.

Blindsided by the abruptness of the question, it took Aerie a while to answer. "I don't know, really. I just... like to sing, I guess."

Su nodded, and her normally expressive face became unusually guarded as she spoke. "I started getting voice lessons when I was six. My teacher was a mostly retired opera singer, and she held me to a very high standard. I had to re-learn vowels and consonants to the point where I completely lost my accent and even started to have trouble speaking my native language. It was a lot of hard work, and a lot of pressure, and there were plenty of times that I hated it." A soft smile broke through. "That changed a lot when I Awakened, but... there are still some bad memories. So for you to be a singer just because it's something you love? I'm a little jealous of you, too."

Then, to Aerie's shock, Su actually winked at her. "Plus, you've got that super-sexy alto voice, and you can't go wrong with that."

"My voice is not... *sexy!*" Aerie gasped, feeling the blood rushing to her face.

"Matter of opinion, my dearling. Matter of opinion."

* * *

Aerie came to third-period rehearsal the next day in a dour mood, with not the slightest notion of what was about to hit her.

After warm-ups, Mr. B asked them to take out the new Tallis piece, to see if their sectional work had paid off. The accompanist gave their opening pitches, and the choir waited as Mr. B prepared to conduct their entrance. A quick raise of the hands indicating a breath, and then the downbeat.

If ye love me, keep my commandments

The first words were sung together in a lush four-part harmony, and considering that this was the first time all 45 of them had sung it together, Aerie was amazed at how well and how quickly their voices were blending together. Just like that, they were already making a beautiful sound.

The mildly euphoric feeling did not last long, though. The next lines were to be sung in sequence: first the sopranos led them in, followed by the basses two beats later, and next up were the altos. Aerie watched Mr. B's hands carefully, took her breath, and when he pointed to the alto section, she came in with their line.

Unfortunately, of the fourteen altos, she was one of maybe six who actually did so.

Mr. B cut them off, and the moment was lost, sending them back to the familiarity of woodshedding. The accompanist gave the altos their pitch, and Mr. B had her play along as they reviewed the line they'd just blown. Their tone was anemic at best, and Aerie felt frustration setting in. The altos were always the ones who needed the extra help. At first Aerie had assumed that it was because they just happened to have some of the weaker singers, but lately she was growing more certain that they just didn't give a damn. Either way, it was embarrassing.

She chanced a look over to the sopranos and saw Su staring across the crowd at her, giving her a sympathetic smile, as though reading her mind.

They went over the line several times, and Aerie's mood darkened. The sopranos, the basses, the tenors... none of them ever had this kind of trouble working together. Was she in the only section that didn't care?

Didn't they know that there was an incredible beauty to be found here, if they would only open themselves to it and let it sweep them along?

Aerie blinked rapidly, wondering where that last thought had come from, but there was no time to think further on it, as Mr. B was preparing to bring them in again from the beginning.

As the director raised his hands to give the upbeat, time momentarily slowed to a crawl, and Aerie swore the motions of those hands were leaving a trail of shimmering gold in the air behind them. Next came the downbeat, and it was all Aerie could do to come in on her pitch.

The room was beginning to glow. It started with Mr. B, but Aerie then noticed it across the rows of students as well, from a pair of the doo-wop boys in the tenors' section, to a bass whose name she still had not retained...

... to Su, who was shining like the sun.

They continued to the next section, and again, the altos more or less biffed their entrance, but this time Aerie was one of the ones who didn't come in. She was too busy staring slack-jawed at Su, and barely heard as Mr. B cut them off and patiently reminded the altos of their starting pitch and how they could get it from what the tenors sang a measure before. Su looked over at her as well, and her brow furrowed with concern. "Are you okay?" she mouthed across the distance.

"Aerie?"

Aerie tore her eyes from a quizzical Su and looked down at Mr. B. "Ah! Uh, yes?"

"Are you okay?" the director asked, repeating Su's unspoken words of concern.

"Yes! Yes, fine, sorry," she stammered. The glow was gone now, but the sense of surreality had not faded one bit.

"Again, then," Mr. B smiled, raising his hands to conduct the entrance.

The downbeat followed, and this time it was more than a glow. As Aerie watched, amazed, Mr. B, the two tenors, the bass and Su once again began to emit a soft, golden radiance, which spread from each of them in a web of energy, touching each of the members of their section as well as one another, reaching across the distance between to bring them into what could only be called *harmony*. It grew more and more faint as it tried to reach into the alto section, though, and Aerie felt her heart racing as she tried to reach out to it. All she knew was that she wanted this connection, the same way that she wanted Su's energy inside her always.

Then, faintly at first but quickly growing stronger, a light spread through the altos as well, first connecting each of them, and then reaching out to join the combined energy flowing through the other sections.

It took the seeming eternity of the opening words for Aerie to realize that the light was coming from her.

As they moved into the next section, Aerie could see the interaction between the sopranos and the tenors along the lines of energy, and then, where Mr. B had indicated the pitch sung by the tenors from which the altos could find their own, she saw as much as heard the note travel from their section to hers, allowing her to not only sing it, but to give it to everyone around her. For possibly the first time all year, she heard all fourteen altos absolutely nail their entrance with strength and confidence.

They sang the song flawlessly, and Aerie felt it all: all the energy invoked by the intervals, all the resonance and harmony, and all the interaction between the parts as they continued to give the words and notes to one another, taking turns with themes and phrases. The energy flowed between the singers and the conductor, amplified and shared by those who held the source of this golden glow, allowing all to partake of the beauty of this centuries-old work.

From the corner of her eye, Aerie saw the two doo-wop tenors look over their shoulders at her and smile, and a glance toward the basses earned her a knowing nod from the one there. They knew. They could feel this happening.

She looked over at Su, whose eyes were shining as brightly as the rest of her as she sang, and while she continued to face the conductor like the good little singer she was, it was obvious that her smile, more brilliant than ever, was for Aerie and Aerie alone.

At last, with the very V-I cadence Su had told her about, the song came to an end, and for a few seconds afterward the room was silent. Mr. B then dropped his hands, and the choir began to breathe again. Aerie took a dazed look around at her fellow altos and barely recognized the amazed expressions on some of their faces. She knew somehow that all of them, even the least invested, had been touched by what they had just helped to create, and she knew that she had helped to show them the way.

The glow, by now, had once more faded, but this time Aerie knew that part of it had stayed with her, blazing away like a small sun inside her and filling her body with warmth.

Su's earlier words came back to her, and Aerie found that she could not blame Tallis at all for feeling like music was bringing him closer to God.

"Aerie?" Mr. B called again. "You look a little pale. Are you feeling okay?"

"Um, sorry," Aerie managed, trying to smile. "Um... just a little... light-headed, I guess?"

Mr. B nodded, but there was a hint of a smile there, as though he knew exactly what had just happened. "Well, no sense taking chances. Su, would you walk Aerie down to the nurse's office, please?"

"Of course," Su smiled, setting down her sheet music and coming down from the risers. Aerie joined her a moment later, though her knees felt wobbly as the two girls crossed the room and exited into the late-morning sun.

As soon as they were outside, Su took her hand, and they walked in silence until they were clear of the music buildings, at which time Su stopped, took her other hand as well, and smiled up at her with eyebrows raised, just as she had done every day before. "And?" she said, aloud this time.

"Was that...?" Aerie managed. "Did I...?"

"Shall we find out?" Su grinned. Aerie again felt a wave of Su's energy passing through her hand and along her arm, but this time, when it reached that new spark inside her, she felt herself amplify it and channel it back, sending it through her other hand and into Su's, until with a knee-buckling rush of sensation, their joined energy became a loop: an endless river of warmth and light that filled Aerie's *soul*, for lack of a better word. She stared into Su's eyes, mouth hanging agape in wonder, feeling the indescribable sensation of being joined with her mentor at a level she could never have imagined.

"Good morning, Aerie," Su whispered. "I do believe you've Awakened."

Aerie nodded mutely, too overwhelmed to speak.

"I'm so proud of you," said Su. "This is just the beginning, my dearling. There's so much I can't wait to show you now. So many things to teach you."

Of course. Now that she had Awakened, they still had a chance at a future together. But... what sort of future? "Su," said Aerie, almost choking on the name. "Can you... can you do the spell so that no one sees us?"

"Class is in session, silly," Su giggled. "No one's here to see us."

"I know, but... someone else might... " She broke off, remembering her old school, and how she had thought *then* that no one would see her, to her regret. "Just... can you do it? Please?"

Su nodded and hummed the spell. "There we are, but... why?"

Aerie felt tears coming to her eyes as every ounce of good sense screamed at her to stop, but she was well beyond that at this point. "It's just... Su... I just feel like I really want to kiss you right now, and..."

For perhaps the first time since they had met, Aerie saw a look of naked shock cross Su's face, mixed with something else she could not identify, but it quickly faded to an understanding smile. "You're feeling a new connection for the first time," her mentor said softly. "It's bound to be confusing at first, but give it time to settle, and..."

"It's not the magic!" Aerie insisted, the clenching in her chest intensifying at Su's words. "I've been wanting to kiss you for *weeks* now, and it's *not* just the magic, Su, it's *you*, and it's *always* been you! I—"

At that moment, Aerie could not say anything more, because Su had thrown her arms around the taller girl and was kissing *her*.

For a time, she was too shocked to do anything at all, but then Aerie felt herself melt against Su as the flowing energy washed through her.

154

Every worry, every anxiety that she had faced in the weeks leading up to this embrace simply evaporated in the wake of that warmth. She felt her feet leave the ground as Su took them once more into the sky, their lips still joined in a kiss that had gone from frantic to tender, and for a perfect moment, the world was truly a magical place.

* * *

Several breathless minutes later, Aerie again found herself lying on the soccer field (thankfully not in use this class period), but this time, Su was cuddled against her, lying her head on Aerie's shoulder.

"So, tell me..." Aerie ventured, still somewhat afraid to shatter the moment with words, "does this mean that you... um..."

"Have been crushing on you since the day we met?" Su said into her shirt. "Yes, I'm afraid it does."

"Really...?"

"Don't tell me you haven't noticed the way I have to constantly *stop* myself from flirting with you?"

"I... thought you were just being friendly."

"Oh, I was, but... I also made the classic blunder of a teacher falling for her student," Su chuckled. "Of course, the fact that we're the same age changes the dynamic a little, doesn't it?"

"You could have spared me a lot of aggravation and told me," Aerie grumbled, but she was smiling as she said it.

"You could have made it irrelevant and told me sooner," Su countered.

"Yeah, but... I guess I didn't want to risk making things awkward if you didn't feel the same way."

"Understandable," Su nodded against her, and her voice darkened slightly. "To be honest, it's for the best that you waited until now. I think I've known all along... hoped, really... that you might have feelings for me, but I didn't dare let you know that I felt the same."

"Why not? If you suspected it, then... why not tell me?"

"I didn't want to put any more pressure on you," Su said with a sigh. "If I was wrong, then the awkwardness between us might disturb your Awakening, and you'd probably be given another mentor. On the other hand, if something *did* spark between us..." She sighed again, more heavily this time. "You were already stressing yourself enough trying to find your source. How much worse would it have been had we been... involved?"

Su was right, as usual. Aerie would have pressed even more, feeling that she had something to prove not only to her mentor, but to the girl she was in love with.

In love with...

"There's... something more, as well," Su said, sitting up beside Aerie and gazing down at her. Her face was clouded with darker emotions, miles away from her normal smile. "And I'm afraid it was a completely selfish reason."

"Tell me," Aerie whispered, reaching up to lay her hand against Su's cheek.

Su kissed the hand, then took it in her own and lowered it to her lap. "If you hadn't Awakened by the end of the school year," she said quietly, "we would have been sent to separate colleges."

"I know that."

"Yes, but what you *don't* know is that... you would have had your memories altered first."

Aerie felt her heart skip. "My memories?"

"Everything I've taught you about our world," Su nodded. "Every moment we've spent together, really. To preserve our secret, you would have been sent off to college with no inkling of this secret world existing alongside your own. Yours has been a very late Awakening, Aerie, and there was more doubt than I let on that it would ever happen. They would have kept an eye on you while you were in college just to be sure, but... the chances of Awakening drop precipitously after age 18, so they don't take chances."

Of all the surprises of the day, seeing tears in Su's eyes was perhaps the largest yet. "Forgive me, my dearling, for not having more faith in you, but... if we had fallen in love only to have those memories taken away from you... and to have *you* taken away from *me*... it would have broken my heart more than I dare imagine."

Aerie sat up next to Su, gently wiped the tears away from her cheeks, then leaned in and kissed her again, and it felt natural and right and wonderful. "Then I guess it's a good thing I got my head together, huh?"

"A very good thing," Su agreed, lying her head against Aerie's shoulder and holding her. "I'm so sorry, Aerie-chan..."

156

It was the first time Su had called her by that Japanese diminutive, and Aerie could not help but smile. "It's okay, Su. It didn't happen. That doesn't have to come between us now."

"True," Su nodded. "Now we just have to navigate the normal perils of high-school romance. Easy peasy."

A dark thought briefly eclipsed the warmth between them. "Are we always going to have to hide what we are, Su?" Aerie asked.

Su broke slightly from her and gazed into her eyes. "As practitioners?"

"You know what I mean."

There was a long silence between them, then Su smiled. "I have high hopes, my dearling. Times are changing more quickly than you may think. Perhaps one day we'll be able to share *all* of what we are with the world. Meanwhile, though... I would gladly share all of what *I* am with *you*... if you're willing to open that lonely mountaintop to an adventurous sparrow, that is."

"Will we get to sing those duets, then?" Aerie grinned, her heart filled to overflowing.

"All that and more, I hope."

"Sounds wonderful...

Bad Roommates

By Nina Kiriki Hoffman

It was my second year at Melampus High Boarding School, and this year, I lost the roommate lottery. Sometimes the administrators would let you room with a friend if you got your request in early enough. I'd roomed with a couple of different girls last year, but I wouldn't call them friends, exactly. Making friends was not among my skills. They were okay roommates, though. We respected each other's space and possessions, went to bed around the same time, and didn't play loud music, cast gratuitous spells or curses on each other, or put up irritating posters.

People were allowed to change roommates after a two-week trial at the beginning of the term. That meant I still had a week and a half to go with Kari, and I wasn't sure I would survive.

I came back to my room when classes were done for the day to discover big dirty splotches on my bed. "Why are there muddy footprints on my bedspread?" I asked. I used the quiet voice, the one anyone who knew me would understand presaged a bad spell or other backlash in the offing.

"Gods and devils, Thora, you're such a whiner!" Kari said. "My boyfriend was climbing to the upper bunk to visit me, and he didn't know there was a ladder at the end of the bed."

The upper bed was actually built into the wall, like a queen-bed-sized shelf or giant freestanding drawer, five feet above my mattress on the floor. (Our room had a very high ceiling.) I'd tacked an Indian bedspread around the bottom edge of it so I had my own private little cave under Kari's bed. There was room in my cave for my twin-sized mattress and a wooden fruit crate on its side that served as my bedside table, with my goose-necked lamp on top and my books inside. I had cut out paper stars with drawings of fae and mermaids and elementals on them, touched them with different colors of soft glow, and hung them on

158

threads from the underside of Kari's bed. I looked up at them while I lay on the verge of sleep, plotting the next day's magical mayhem or just thinking about homework.

I said, "Are you going to wash my bedspread, or is he?"

"It's *your* bedspread," Kari said. I heard the skritch of a match, and then noxious clouds of patchouli incense smoke puffed out from the crack in her curtains (she'd created her own cave with flower-patterned sheets tacked to the ceiling around the upper bunk, the really ugly ones that looked like cheap shower curtains).

I sneezed loudly three times, but of course she didn't take the hint. I wasn't actually allergic; I just hated that scent. Kari was the first room-mate I'd had who paid absolutely no attention to social cues and never asked before she did something potentially offensive, like turning on the Psychic Blisters really loud on her iPod. Her dad was rich, so she had the good speakers, the ones that could surround you with sound whether you want to be wrapped in it or not. Psychic Blisters. Wall of noise. Pchu. Pchu, pchu, I spat.

I'd like to say I wasn't usually so sour grapey, but that would be untrue. I didn't usually have such good reasons.

"So neither of you is going to take care of a mess you made," I said, just to be clear.

"Not my problem," said Kari.

I didn't want to admit it, but her boyfriend scared me. There was something off about him; he tingled my Spidey sense. I suspected he was more and worse than he appeared—he looked like a shaggy, overgrown idiot—lots of unbrushed hair, clothes ragged and crusty, and he smelled like goats and dirt. His expression usually looked imbecilic —mouth half-open, eyes dull—and his voice had a surfer drawl. I'd heard a lot more from him than I ever wanted to, because Kari didn't care whether I was in the room when he came over and they got frisky in the upper bunk. "Say it, babe. Say I give you the best O's ever. Uh huh huh."

I usually left, because I wasn't sure the upper bed's binding spells would hold with all the bumping around they did, and I didn't want to be pancaked under a fallen bed.

So I didn't have any plans to get after Bram to clean my bedspread. Everyone at Melampus was supposed to be gifted and talented in the magical arts. Just because Bram had never demonstrated competence at anything didn't mean he wasn't hiding boatloads of skill.

159

I forsaw laundry in my near future.

I undid the complicated wards on my grimoire and opened it to the clean air spell. Unfortunately, it called for powdered lemon zest, and I hadn't been able to replenish my compartmented spellstock box since I arrived. I'd used up too many of my ingredients trying to deal with Kari secretly already. She must be mega-warded. Everything I tried bounced off, pretty much, or rebounded.

I had to get into the wizard supplies here, or at least the kitchen pantry. Of course, all supply cabinets were locked five different ways, four of them intangible, which made them much harder to break into.

The patchouli smoke was giving me such a headache I couldn't think of a reasonable workaround, so I decided to lock up and leave. I put my grimoire and spellstock box in my pack, on top of my other most precious possessions—a spell stone my grandmother had given me that I hadn't been able to work with yet, one of the practice dolls I had made when I was younger, an heirloom locket with a compartment full of angel feathers, a picture of my parents, things like that. I tried to take everything I really cherished with me all the time. Most of the other students at Melampus were sneaky rather than direct, and beating me up to get my backpack wasn't sneaky enough for them. Plus, administrators did keep an eye on us in all the more public places.

I laid wards on my bed and bookshelf to protect them from anybody but me. I thought about packing my bedspread in my laundry bag and heading to the laundry room under the dining hall (kind of far away!), but what if Bram came back and stepped on my actual blanket this time? Despite the wards. I hadn't warded the bed before, but I didn't trust any of my wards, anyway. I was hot shit at home, where, as an only child, I had no direct competition, but I had learned the hard way last year that I was nowhere near the top of the talent pack here at Melampus.

My pack was so heavy I was building lots of upper body strength.

If I could find the right ingredients, I might be able to do a cleaning spell on the bedspread, and maybe set up my own bubble of atmosphere in my cave. I decided that would be my current quest.

I slipped out of the room, gasping in deep breaths of clean air in the hallway outside. I so needed to find out what Kari's spell specialties were so I could figure out what to counter and what to avoid. She seemed to have some air capabilities, because even though I had opened the window in the room, none of the smoke moved out. So far, she hadn't attacked me directly, nor had I attacked her. The smoke might be one of her indirect tools, though.

"Hey, Thora," said Sharada from the next door down the hall. She had been one of my roommates last year, as close to a friend as I had ever had. She was a tall, thin, gold-skinned girl with long, thick, black hair and dark brows and eyes. She was wearing a red shirt with gold paisley patterns on it, and black jeans, and she had a fat black messenger bag decorated with gold vévés across her shoulder. She smelled faintly of amber, another thing I liked about her.

"Hey, Sharada," I said.

"What's that stench?"

"My roommate's incense."

"Gaah!" She pulled her door shut and joined me on my way out of the dorm. I wondered where she was heading. "Okay if I do a cancel scent spell?"

"I wish you would! My best spells don't work on it. I hate the stuff! I think maybe she burns it to get rid of me. No idea what she's doing in our room now that I'm out of it."

She formed quick shapes with her fingers and spoke two words, and the stink lifted from my clothes and hair and drifted to the floor like feathers of putrid green ash.

"Thank you. I *need* that spell. Would you teach me?"

She frowned. "It's a family secret."

"Oh." Maybe I could get her to cast it a few more times in my presence, and I'd be able to figure it out for myself. "Could I ask you to help me with it once in a while, in case this continues to be a problem?"

"Sure." She smiled. She had a deep dimple in her left cheek when she smiled, and I liked seeing it again. "Two hours until dinner. Where are you going?"

"Anywhere away from this stink. Wanna come?"

"Yeah, sure," she said, surprising me.

"I need to collect herbs."

"Even better. I ran out of lavender and cursewort yesterday."

Melampus School was on a huge farm in the foothills of the Sierra Nevada Mountains in California. None of our magic was supposed to leave school grounds while we were training. Mr. Green, our boundaries teacher, who knew all the ways to contain a working and establish walls of any sort between one thing and another, had worked complicated wards

161

into the earth around the acres of school ground to keep us and our workings inside, and many other things, including wandering hikers, tourists, and reporters out. Useful plants grew all over, and magical objects were sometimes hidden in the forests and meadows. A small lake with a raft in the middle, Lake Janvier, was up in the hills, a half mile from campus proper where all our buildings, including classrooms, main office, dining hall, teacher residences, dorm, cabins, library, and art barn were. The seniors got to spellcast at the lake. It was a safe place to work with the fire magic we weren't supposed to even try until we were seniors.

I'd heard rumors of caves and tunnels and invisible buildings scattered around campus, but I hadn't figured out detect spells for them yet.

A creek cut through campus, with most of the buildings on the north side, but many footpaths to the south. We also had pastures where sheep gamboled, or, more likely, grumped, others with milking goats in them, an orchard of many different kinds of fruit trees, a warded herb garden we were only supposed to harvest under teacher supervision, and a barn where farm witches practiced skills on long-suffering cattle and pigs.

The day was bright with September sunshine. "There are some really good herbs near the south meadow," I said.

"Really? I usually go to the fields by the oxidation ponds."

"Everybody goes there. I found some wild patches in the shadow of the forest. The herbs are stronger."

"Excellent."

We took the dirt road around the teacher houses in the center of campus, past one of the sheep pastures, past the A-frame cabins where the boys would spend the first term—we got to switch with them for second term—and down to one of the creek crossings, this one a set of flat-topped stones.

"Who'd you end up with as a roommate?" I asked Sharada.

"Kristyl," she said.

We both sighed. Kristyl was a teacher's darling, a paragon. We were secretly jealous of her skills. Nobody could sneak up on her or prank her. Her wards were like Kevlar.

Sharada said, "She's the perfect roommate, too, so I can't even complain. Respects my space, never makes noises I don't like. She's irritatingly nice."

"I wish I had your problems," I said.

162

"Not trading."

"Yeah, I wouldn't, either."

We walked through the trees bordering the creek and crossed the meadow to the forest proper, pines with lots of underbrush. Birds fluttered and chirped on Ponderosa branches, and higher in the sky, an invisible watch-dragon bugled. A family of dragons nested above Janvier Lake. They'd accepted a contract with the school administration to guard the boundaries of the school in exchange for baby sheep and goats.

"I think it's this way." I found the deer path into the forest I had discovered last year, narrower than a human path, but usable if you placed one foot in front of the other instead of clomping along normally.

"What's that noise?" Sharada said.

I listened. A whirring, fluttering noise, like the buzz of locust wings during a plague, but fainter. I looked up.

A girl in a flying chair came toward us across the meadow, about 10 feet above the ground. The chair looked like an armchair without any feet, and the girl didn't have feet, either, or legs below the knee. She wore a short-sleeved teal dress, with black shorts underneath that closed over the stumps of her legs. Her skin was glue white, and her hair was ink black, cut in a short bob. Her hands gripped the arms of the chair.

"Oh," said Sharada, "Dushu."

"Dushu?" I hadn't seen her before.

"She just got in today. Kristyl was her first-day sister. Of course."

The chair came closer and lowered to hover beside us. The noise of 1,000 small wings throttled down to just a few hundred.

"Hatchings," said the girl. Her voice had a faint accent, but I couldn't place it.

Also, I didn't know what she was talking about.

"Hi, Dushu," Sharada said, and bobbed her head. "Dushu, this is Thora. Thora, Dushu."

"Greetings," I said.

"Archival," said Dushu with a nod.

"Uh. What?"

Dushu's lips thinned, pressed together. "Adjacent."

"Somebody put a spell on you?" Sharada asked.

Dushu nodded.

"Well, that sucks," said Sharada. "And on your first day. We're not supposed to spell each other on the first day."

"Pitified time zone," said Dushu.

"It's not the first day of school anymore," I said. "She came late. Might be a loophole."

Sharada frowned. "Thora, you know anything about communication spells? You studied them last year."

I slipped out of my backpack and lowered it, got out my grimoire and unlocked it. Last year, one of the boys had spelled me repeatedly so all I could say was cuss words. I never figured out why he was so mean to me. I had only corrected his grammar three or four times in front of teachers.

I found the page with the spell that had finally succeeded in protecting me from his attentions. Fortunately, the ingredients it required weren't the ones I'd used up on Kari. I still had dictionary dust and a few drops of fairy spit left.

"Are you warded?" I asked Dushu.

She pinched her lips together and nodded.

"I have a useful spell. I don't want to waste it on your wards. Will you let me cast it?"

She looked from me to Sharada and nodded again. Her hands flickered through a series of mudras, and she made three shaped hisses. Air flickered around her as her wards lowered.

She had strong wards. How had she gotten hit by a speech spell?

I got out my ingredients and spoke my spell in orb language, a private language my mother and I had developed when I was three. I touched my fingertips to Dushu's throat. Red light and a glittering skim of dust jumped away from her throat. She gasped and coughed. The coughing took a while. Then she pulled a water bottle out of a compartment in her chair's arm and sipped it. Finally she looked up at us. "Thanks," she said.

"How'd you get hit?" Sharada asked.

"I neglected to ward until after." Her voice was husky, maybe an after-effect of coughing, and her accent sounded British colonial—not U.K., but someplace they used to empire over. She tapped the other arm of the chair and another compartment opened. She fished something out, held it in a closed hand. "I believed there were more rules here than there are. I thought I would be safer. Will you friend-bond with me?"

Sharada and I took several steps away from her. I looked down and realized I had stepped into a clump of poison oak. I did a skin-clean spell and a ward skin spell right away, but I could feel the itch under my skin already. All the plants at Melampus had extra virtues and dangers.

"We don't even know you," Sharada said for both of us.

"I can be a useful friend. I am proficient in the Miscus Magic System, the Three Mutable Laws, the Fourteen Pleasing Misconceptions, and the Five Useful Truths. I can teach you things."

I had heard of the Miscus system, but the other things were new to me. It would be useful to have a skilled teacher with new systems, especially ones other Melampus students didn't know. But how skilled could she be, if she let someone lay a word curse on her? Then again, when I first got to Melampus, I'd endured four or five nasty and embarrassing attacks before I wised up. Only child syndrome. Not expecting it. Maybe Dushu was an only child, too. "What kind of bonding do you want?" I wondered if any of her skills would be useful against Kari's atmospheric messes.

Dushu lifted her hand and opened it. A blue, twisted, glowing root lay there, like a skinny yam. I blinked. It was oddly fascinating. "Only touch this, and we will know where each other is and whether each other is in danger, even when we're distant from each other, and can send help without being present."

"How long does the bond last?" Sharada asked. She turned to look toward the stream, away from the blue thing, which pulsed slowly. I blinked, trying to break the fascination it had trapped me in. I managed to close my eyes.

"It's lifelong, but it can fade, especially if we don't keep in touch with each other. Also we can end it with intent."

"Any one of us?" I asked. No way did I want to make a lifelong decision without some way to reverse it.

"It would take all of us to end it."

That could get messy. What if we hated each other later? Well, heck, then we'd all have a reason to end it.

I was terrible at making friends, and had no experience with keeping them. This was one way to do it, I guessed. How strange it would be to start the school year with allies, after my solitary life.

I opened my eyes and looked at Sharada. She looked at me. We turned to Dushu. I sighed. "Let's do it."

Dushu smiled. "All you need do is touch it while I speak the spell."

I laid two fingers on the glowing root. It buzzed under my fingertips, and I felt energy flow up my arm under the skin.

165

Sharada touched the root as well, and then Dushu spoke what sounded like French, but not any words I'd learned in French class.

It hurt.

Freeze and fire alternated in ripples through me, and music flowed through my brain. Throbbing and hypnotic, it pounded in my head, drums and flutes and strange stringed instruments. A blue light and an orange one came toward me through a gray darkness that was all I could see. The blue light entered my right eye, and the orange my left eye.

I blinked my way back to consciousness and found myself lying in the poison oak patch, my hand still burning from contact with the glowing root. I rolled my head. Sharada sprawled nearby, and Dushu's chair had sunk to the ground. She was torsioned, her pale face twisted in pain, both her hands spread wide. The root in her left hand had shriveled to a dry, twisted stick, and no longer glowed. Too late, I wondered what it had been.

"Your legs itch." Sharada groaned and sat up. "And you're dehydrated."

I got to my feet. My legs were starting to itch, all right, and I was thirsty. My throat felt tight, but it wasn't really my throat; my left hand burned, but it looked normal. My big toe—"Did you stub your toe?" I asked Sharada.

"Yeah. I forgot."

We both turned to Dushu, and we both put our hands on our throats.

Her hands twitched. The dried stick fell out. She closed her mouth and twisted her neck. Sharada and I gasped matching gasps at the pain. Dushu got the bottle out of her chair arm and drank again, and we both sighed. So much better. Whatever she was drinking tasted faintly of cinnamon.

"Stand still, Thora," Sharada said.

"Huh?"

She fished a chunky piece of turquoise out of her pack and muttered to it, then handed it to me. "Hold this."

I took it in my right hand, wary but feeling like I might as well do whatever she said. She spoke something that rhymed, then said, "Itch out now!"

My legs stopped itching. I let out a long breath. I hoped the spell had worked on all of me, because I'd been rolling around in poison oak. "Thanks. Much better!" I gave her back the turquoise lump.

"You're welcome. Dushu, is it always going to be like this? I don't know if I want to feel what you two are feeling all the time. Got enough going on with my own feelings."

"We can tune it. There are skills we can acquire."

"I need those skills," said Sharada. "As soon as possible."

Dushu looked in one of her armchair compartments. She was tired, I could tell—or someone was; fatigue weighted my shoulders, and it wasn't my own. She pulled out a small gray book wrapped in bubble wrap and silver string.

Now that I wasn't consumed with itching, I felt some other new-to-me things, including the sensation of what it was like to have legs that ended before they got to feet. I focused there, and got muscle memories, how strong Dushu's arms were, and a faint ghost sense of walking across the floor on stumps, an angular movement that involved knuckles to the floor, a hunched-forward stature. But doable.

Also I got the sense that she tried never to do this when anybody could see her. The chair was her nest and her shield and her refuge, her transportation, a large part of her public persona.

I also felt belly rumblings from Sharada, and tasted acid. I couldn't tell whether she was hungry or had eaten something her body didn't like. Either way, I wanted a Tums.

Brow furrowed, Dushu carefully unwrapped her book. She licked her forefinger and touched it to the final layer of bubble wrap before she opened it all the way. The book was silver, not gray, and it glowed. She frowned down at it in its nest of wrappings on her lap. Then she looked at us.

"What are you doing out here in the meadow, anyway, Dushu?" Sharada asked.

"Looking for a safe place," said Dushu. "My roommate is terrible."

"You, too?" I said.

"She brought her whole lifetime collection of magical supplies, and all her clothes, and she has different clothes for everything. She filled both dressers and desks with her things before I even arrived. There is no space for me in my room." Her hands clenched on the arms of her chair. "Not even enough floor space for my chair."

"They have to change that," I said. "It's not fair."

I felt a knot in my stomach, and knew it wasn't my own feeling. Sharada pressed a hand to her stomach, too, and frowned.

167

"You're used to not taking up room," Sharada said.

Dushu blinked. A tear streaked down her cheek. She lifted a handkerchief and blotted it, then tucked the handkerchief into a compartment. Tears could be used so many ways. You never wanted to let yours fall into someone else's hands or spell kits.

"Not making problems, not complaining. Containing yourself," Sharada continued.

I wondered what she felt from me. I wasn't getting these kinds of psychic hits from Dushu, just physical stuff.

"Time to change that," I said. In a way, I felt like Sharada might be talking to me. But I could tell Dushu's response was different from mine. I was nastier, and pushier, and maybe not so quiet.

Maybe we could use that. I knew a spell for influencing people's minds, and had been contemplating using it on my advisor to help me change rooms. It was the kind of thing that could get me expelled if they found out I used it, though, and Melampus was so much better than being at home with my overinvested and overprotective parents.

"Can we change?" Dushu asked.

I wasn't sure whether she was talking about rooms or characters.

"Teach us the skill, 'Shu," Sharada said. "Let's get out of each other's heads and bodies and figure out what to do next."

"This is a quieting spell," Dushu said.

"That sounds disturbing," I said.

"It's not a good solution for this, but it will work for now. The real controls are too complicated to manage in this moment. They take days of preparation and practice, and three days to cast. This spell quiets your sense of things outside yourself. So you'll stop feeling our feelings as strongly. You'll also stop being sensitive to a whole range of magic and occult things. You'll be able to dial your awareness up and down."

"So every time I want to check out something beyond my normal senses, I'll know what you're feeling, too?" Sharada asked.

"That's it," said Dushu. "This might dull your normal senses as well."

Sharada made a face. "Maybe I don't want this spell."

"I don't want it, either," I said. It was weird knowing about Sharada's empty stomach and stubbed toe, and maybe the beginnings of menstrual cramps, Dushu's fatigue and melancholy—and I was getting inklings of other discomforts she suffered. But maybe I could get used to it. I didn't want to be deaf and blind to other magic, especially when it was so often aimed at me, and not from a benevolent place.

The dinner bell rang from the dining hall, summoning all students and staff to the evening meal. It was enhanced so we could hear it everywhere on campus. We had about 10 minutes to get there, and it was a hike from where we were.

"Shucks," I said. "All I've collected is poison oak." I glanced at the undergrowth.

"Is that useful for spells?" asked Dushu.

"Huh. It ought to be," I said. "I don't know how to harvest it safely, though."

"Tongs," said Sharada.

"There's cursewort." I pointed. Sharada and I headed for it. We did the ritual permission, the honoring of the two plants we would leave to propagate, and then we each collected several other plants and tucked them into our spell kits. I looked at Dushu.

"I don't know its uses," she said.

I picked one plant for her anyway, and she placed it in the arm of her chair. "We better scoot."

Dushu tapped a pattern onto her chair's arm. A shelf pushed out from the back at the bottom. "Climb on," she said.

Whoa! Cool! Sharada and I stood on the shelf and gripped the chairback. We rose, the noise of locust wings rising with us, and kept rising, higher than the trees, until I felt dizzy and a little sick with the height and the thought of falling so far.

"Close your eyes, Thora. What a wuss!" Sharada said.

I closed my eyes. The wind of our passage whipped my hair and sleeves.

"We're there," said Sharada. The chair lowered amid a chaos of conversation, and I opened my eyes to see students and staff collecting on the dining hall porch. Most of them stared at us as the chair hovered a foot above the grassy ground near the hall.

"Thanks, 'Shu." I hopped off.

"That was fun," said Sharada. She smiled, her dimple showing.

We lined up with other people for the buffet that was dinner. We each picked different foods for dinner, and sat together. So strange to taste everything all of us ate, and feel the comfort of full stomachs times three.

* * *

169

After dinner, I went back to my room, hoping Kari would be elsewhere so I could focus on homework, of which I had a ton. But she was there, and so was mud-footed Bram. Kari parted the curtains around the upper bed and announced, "Bram's spending the night. We'd like you to go somewhere else."

I turned and grabbed the doorknob again. "I'm going to the dorm mother." It was totally against the rules for boyfriends or girlfriends to spend the night, and also to kick your roommate out of her own room.

Bram pushed the curtain back farther, laughed like a donkey braying, and said, "No, you're not." A spell spilled out of him, singsong words, but mostly hand movements. Sticky white strands flowed from his hands and wrapped around me, all of me but my nose and eyes, until pretty soon I was in a cocoon, barely breathing, stuck to the floor.

Bram snapped his fingers and the last strand cut off and wrapped itself around me. "Change of plans, babe. She can stay. She won't be making any trouble. Or if she does, you know about my stinger."

Kari giggled.

I had warded myself, of course I had, but this stuff just wrapped right around my wards and everything else I had on me, clothes and backpack. My spine hurt from the kink in it of lying half on my pack and half on the floor, and the silk that filled my mouth tasted like moldy bread. I was so mad my eyes leaked tears, and a sun ignited in my chest. My hands were wrapped tight against my hips. I tried wiggling my fingers, to see if I could cast anything, but no luck. I had no magic skills I could use without words or hands.

I wanted to kill Bram, spray him with human bug spray. And strangle Kari. Or pour a vial of patchouli smoke down her throat and drown her in it.

Nothing I could do but lie there and seethe, planning different ways to kill my roommate and her boyfriend. It looked like a long, disgusting, uncomfortable night. Or longer? Depending on how long these bonds lasted, I could be there a while.

Five minutes later, someone pounded on the door. "What's going on in there?" asked the dorm mother, Agree Solitude, a wiry, wizened practitioner of knot magic, one of the more powerful wizards on the staff. She was usually grumpy, and she sounded severely pissed off now.

"Nothing," said Kari.

"I have a report to the contrary. Open this door, or I'll open it for you, and there will be consequences," said Agree.

Bram jumped down from the upper bunk and went out the window, never mind it was on the second floor. Kari sighed, climbed down, and opened the door.

"Karina Megaera Sullivan, what have you done to your roommate?" Agree yelled. She pushed Kari into the room and came in to stare down at me. She worked her fingers against each other and threw the resulting red ectoplasmic lash at Kari. It wrapped around her waist, trapping her hands. Kari squirmed and settled. Her face got stupid and her mouth dropped open.

Agree nodded. "That should hold her until we sort this out. Okay, Thora, I'll get you out of there presently. I need to call Professor Driscoll do some detection first. This technique does not match Kari's skill set."

"Mmf," I said.

"You can wait, can't you? Kids are resilient." She pulled a cell phone from her pocket and hit somebody on speed dial. "Got a puzzle for you, Ian," she said. "Girls' dorm, room 5B. Student-on-student magic attack. No, you can't be in bed this early. Come on. This is your job."

I closed my eyes. At least I didn't have to find out what Bram could do with his stinger, whatever that was.

Now that I wasn't fuming anymore, I noticed I wasn't exactly alone in my head. Sharada and Dushu were there, a warm blue light and a cool orange one. "You okay?" Sharada said somehow.

"You got Agree to come?" I asked somehow. It wasn't words, more like a wave of feeling, somehow tilted into question.

"Dushu did it." Blue light sent a tiny arrow toward the orange light.

"Thank you, thank you, thank you!" A gush of gratitude from me to both of them, a pink and golden burst of sweetness, which I tried to stem as soon as I saw it. Who knew if they liked that kind of thing?

Professor Driscoll, who handled campus security, shuffled into the room in his slippers and a nubby blue bathrobe. He was short and shrimpy, his features grouped just above his chin, with a bald forehead rising above his face, and only feathers of black hair on the top of his head.

He stopped when he saw me. His gaze met mine. His eyes were soft brown, and for the first time I realized there were amber and gold flecks in them. The flecks were shining now. I couldn't blink.

"In-ter-est-ing," he said. "Nothing human did this." He brought out his wand, gestured with it as though he were conducting music, spoke something that sounded freezing cold and spiky, and then red glow showed on Kari's bed and on the windowsill and all over my cocoon. And all over Kari, including inside her still-open mouth. Yuck.

"Young lady, have you been consorting with demons?" asked Professor Driscoll.

Kari blinked stupidly.

"Just a moment, Ian." Agree adjusted the red snare around Kari's waist, and she came alive behind her eyes. Her mouth closed.

Driscoll asked the question again.

"He's not a demon. That's so racist. He's just a student here," Kari said.

"Who is it?"

"I'm not telling," she said. Agree adjusted the snare again, and Kari said, "Bram Romilly."

"Hmm," said Driscoll. "We'll have to conduct some tests. I thought we had wards against this kind of infiltration."

"Could you unwrap Thora, already?" Sharada asked from the hallway.

"What? Oh." Driscoll took out a tiny ceramic pot of something, dipped the tip of his wand in it, and gestured crosswise above me. The strands of Bram's web melted. I sat up, spat the web remnants out of my mouth, and pulled in some deep, though stinky, breaths. My mouth still tasted terrible. "I can't room with this woman anymore!" I yelled.

"The guilt is on someone else," said Driscoll, waving his wand toward the red traces that still glowed everywhere Bram hand set hand, foot, or butt.

"Her *boyfriend*! Even without him, she's a plague and a boil!"

Head cocked, Agree looked at Kari and pursed her lips. "You're requesting a roommate change?"

"I don't think I can wait the whole two weeks! Can I room with Dushu?" I didn't even know Dushu's last name.

Agree frowned. "I'll consult with the other admins," she said. "For tonight, you'll just have to bear each other—and no shenanigans! Or I'll bind both of you to sleep myself."

* * *

The next day, Dushu, Sharada, and I moved into the tower room. It took three flights of stairs to get up there, though it didn't bother Dushu, who could use her chair to fly in through the window, once we unwarded it

172

for her. The tower room had been empty for several years. The last kids who'd lived there had formed a secret society, practiced forbidden arts, and nearly killed three people. The room had been undergoing long-term purification, with special wards woven into the walls to stop people from having evil thoughts while they lived there. We had to get special dispensation from our parents to live there, since we'd be subject to mind control.

I'm pretty sure those kinds of controls don't work on the three of us. I still have a lot of evil thoughts about Kari and Bram, though Bram has been expelled to his home dimension, and Kari's being monitored more closely.

We can't get much going in our room, but sometimes we ride Dushu's chair up to the roof, where we can plot and plan and scheme all we like.

This is going to be the best year yet.

Aura of the Phoenix

By Cecilia Tan

Auntie Elena got a quaver in her voice whenever she was upset. Since the accident the quaver was almost permanent, but it would get worse sometimes. Like now. She stood in the doorway of my room with her hands clasped in front of her chest like a statue and quavered at me: "Bebe, the Harvard people are here."

I couldn't tell if it was something about me upsetting her or if it was them... but it was probably me. She stared at me extra hard, like she was trying to will me out of T-shirt and jeans and into a dress and Mary-Janes with the sheer power of her mind. "It's a new scholarship administrator and a... a counselor we haven't met before."

Great. Last thing I needed was another counselor. Between my guidance counselor at school, the youth counselor at church, the bereavement counselor from the hospital, et cetera, my life since the accident had become one counseling session after another.

I wished they'd all just leave me alone. But part of the Harvard deal was regular check-ins.

At least, I hoped this was just a regular check-in. "Do they seem upset or anything?"

"I don't know, Bebe." Her eyes were guarded behind the thick lenses of her eyeglasses.

I got up from the floor where my algebra homework was spread around me like an archipelago of aggravation. "Auntie, don't call me Bebe." It was a childhood nickname and I was not a child anymore.

"I'm sorry, Bebe," she said with a little duck of her head. In other words sorry, but I'm going to keep doing it. "Fix your hair, please. Just because these people are... a bit different does not mean you should not look your best."

Oh honestly. As if uncombed hair would be why they took the scholarship away and not my tanking grades.

But what did she mean... a bit different? That was an odd thing for her to say. I was suddenly curious about who was downstairs. I stuck a baseball cap on my head and she glared at me, but said nothing more, just turned on her heel and left.

Everything was a battle between us. I guess her retreat meant I won this round?

It's not like I didn't know how much was at stake. Auntie thought this ultra-special Harvard scholarship for bereaved orphans would be my only chance to have a future. I know she was terrified I'd blow it. She couldn't provide much for me. I didn't blame her for that. But since the accident I'd been struggling in school. Think about it: if the one thing I needed to do to secure my post-accident future was get good grades, I was stuck in a Catch-22 straight out of effing Kafka or something.

Grief isn't good for grades.

Neither is guilt.

My high-tops squeaked on the polished wooden stairs to the living room and stopped in my tracks before I reached the bottom. So that's why Auntie disapproved. "A bit different" was a good way to put it, because there wasn't anything glaringly obvious and yet... Two of the most androgynous people I'd ever seen were standing in the foyer.

A tall, willowy woman in a sharply tailored pantsuit, her dark hair shaved-short around the sides but wavy on top, was saying something in a hushed tone to her smaller companion. I suddenly wished I was better dressed. He was in crisp slacks and a spotlessly white Oxford shirt looking both tense and intense, if you know what I mean. I couldn't nail down what about him seemed feminine—his posture, maybe? —but definitely something.

He was about as tall as the trans guys who had come to speak at my school last year, which was to say not very. I thought I could pick out a trans guy from a mile away, but he didn't have any of the things I usually looked for. He had black hair, blue eyes, ghost-white skin, and a piercing gaze.

I'd never realized a so-called piercing gaze could actually feel like someone was skewering you—pinning me in place like a butterfly on a specimen card.

Then he looked away, dismissing me with a sullen huff. Jerk.

175

The woman stepped forward, offering her hand. "Bonita? I'm Master Brandish."

Did she say master? They say wishful thinking will make you mishear things. I came down the last two steps to shake her hand and discovered an iron grip. "P-Pleased to meet you, Madame Brandish."

"Master," she corrected, and I felt my stomach drop at my mistake. Here I was meeting people who I was suddenly desperate to impress or connect with or whatever and I had already effed it up. Before I could apologize, Master Brandish smoothly added, "It's the ceremonial title held by all heads of house regardless of gender presentation. And this is one of my resident fellows, Timothy Frost."

"I prefer just Frost," he said in a prickly tone, and didn't offer his hand. "In case you were wondering."

I was, in fact, wondering, and I felt exposed. How did he know? Was my urgency to know more about him obvious? "You're here to help me?"

They looked at each other as if trying to decide which of them should speak first. Frost's eyebrow seemed to insist that Master Brandish be the one.

"Bonita—" she began.

"Don't call me that," I blurted, and it came out much ruder than I intended. My blush deepened. Me and my big mouth. I was effing this up bad. "Please. I mean, I, um, I prefer not to be called that. Either."

"And what would you prefer to be called?" she asked, each word coming out light and distinct as if she were tiptoeing around the issue.

Around me.

I clenched my fists, and the sinking feeling that had begun when I'd used the wrong title for her was now swallowing me whole. Except I didn't actually disappear into the earth, which would have been a convenient escape. "I don't know!" I tried not to shout, but when I got like this something as hot as anger rushed out of my mouth every time I opened it. "I'm working on it!"

Frost touched her on the back of the hand and spoke to her in a low voice as if I couldn't hear it, but I could hear it plain as day. People were always making that mistake around me. "I think I see why you picked me and it isn't my math skills."

She ignored both his side comment and my outburst, and addressed me in a formal voice. "Student Reyes, as the administrator of your scholarship, it's contingent on me to see that your grades remain within an acceptable range. Officially, Frost is a tutor. To help you—"

"With my dive-bombing grades." My fists hurt. "Thanks for the reminder." You want to help? Bring my family back. Bring my mother and father back.

"Unofficially, though—"

Auntie Elena chose that moment to come back in from the kitchen. She had been preparing tea and crackers. She carried a tray into the dining room. "Please, Madame Brandish, young sir, please join us. In our country we call this merienda."

She got Master Brandish's title wrong, too, but that wasn't what I couldn't stop myself from correcting. "Auntie, it's not our country, it's your country."

She put the tray down on the table so hard the cups rattled. "You listen to me, Bebe. I'm your guardian now and if I say we're going back, we're going back."

I gasped. She'd threatened before, but always in an idle way. Now she sounded dead serious. Her fists were still clenching the silver handles as she spoke and the crackers vibrated on their plate. She let go abruptly, adding an angry sentence in one of the Filipino languages I'd been forbidden to learn. "I told your father he'd regret raising you here!"

"He didn't regret it!" I shouted. She was terrifying me with this talk of taking me out of the country and that made it even harder to control myself. "You! You are the only one who regrets it. I'm an American and I'm staying here!"

My Aunt Elena was four-foot-eleven but as she turned to face me, it was like she grew terrifyingly large, like a shadow looming. "Then you had better straighten up," she said matter-of-factly. "Sit and talk with the Harvard people like a nice young lady."

There it was. Her demand, same as my parents', spoken aloud at last. Be a lady or else. Or I'll take you to a country where you'll have no options at all.

I expected to see looks of horror or judgment on Master Brandish and Frost's faces. But they were unreadable. Then Master Brandish gave me a wink so slight maybe I imagined it, and Frost gave Aunt Elena a sharp side-eye.

They were on my side. These cool, mysterious paragons of androgyny and higher education were on my side. Okay. That helped me calm myself a lot. No more outbursts. I sat down to tea and rice crackers and played at being polite while they negotiated a schedule for my tutoring sessions and Auntie Elena grilled them about Harvard, as if the tables had turned, as if it were contingent on them to impress her now— as if she didn't know that Harvard was the top university in the world. They played along, saying all the right things to her. But they knew full well that I was no "nice young lady," even if my aunt didn't. And that was how I got through it without blowing up again.

* * *

Frost showed up a few minutes before the end of my last class and knocked lightly on the door. Mr. Glazer, the history teacher, looked him up and down in the open doorway, skepticism making his salt and pepper eyebrows huddle. They stepped out into the hall and shut the door. I could still hear them, though.

"You're a what? A Harvard tutor? For Miss Reyes?"

"Yes. Didn't the administration let you know? I'll wait out here. I just didn't want you to worry about a stranger lurking."

Mr. Glazer gave a wry chuckle. "Indeed. Can't be too careful."

Mr. Glazer had a good poker face. He came back in without giving me a glance and went right back to what he had been saying, which was a rundown of next week's quiz on the Roman political system. He was just finished when the bell rang.

Frost walked with me to my locker. He drew looks from several of the popular girls as well as some of the track team boys who passed by in their running shorts. I'm not sure which group looked at him more thirstily. If he noticed, he didn't show it. Maybe he was used to turning heads with his fey good looks.

I could hear Kathleen Randolph saying, "Don't tell me Bunny Reyes bagged herself such a fox." And Pietra Dumont replying, "She looks like she's about to puke. Loser."

Yeah, sure. A normal girl would have been glowing to get so much attention from a hot older guy. Just another thing that proved I wasn't a normal girl.

With the blessing of Mrs. Tettlebaum, the head librarian, we went to one of the study rooms off the library. We had to leave the door open— I guess so he wouldn't molest me or something—but otherwise we had the place to ourselves. We sat along one corner of the big worktable.

"Let me see your Algebra text," he said, pulling out his own notebook.

I'd gotten very blunt since the accident and my nerves only made me blunter. "Aren't we going to talk about... something else?" In my mind I had replayed the meeting at my house 100 times. Master Brandish had said that officially Frost was my tutor, but unofficially... ? She had never finished the sentence but there could only be one thing he was there to talk to me about, right? Gender stuff. It had to be.

"After algebra." He took the book from me and flipped through it. "Okay. It's a newer edition of the same book I used. I should be able to remember this."

"Oh, God, you're serious."

"Pardon?"

"We're really going to study math?"

He looked me in the eye. "Were you under the impression we weren't?"

I lowered my voice. "Wasn't Master Brandish hinting at exactly that?"

His gaze darted to the open door. "Look. There are things that technically I'm not supposed to talk to you about. Things that would... freak out your aunt. Things you know, deep down."

My heart was starting to thump and it wasn't because he was cute.

"But we have to be careful. You heard what your aunt said. You're still a minor and if she wants to yank you out of the country, we can't stop her. I'll be blunt: relocating you at this delicate point could be disastrous."

Disastrous sounded a bit dramatic, but I nodded. This was like being part of a spy movie, except the secret message wasn't locked in a briefcase, it was inside of me. "Okay. But... seriously... algebra?"

He was all pragmatism rather than sympathy. "If I bring your grades up, your aunt and teachers will trust me. Besides, the best cover story is the truth."

"Okay, but I have qu—"

"I'll answer your questions after we work on Algebra for at least 45 minutes."

"Did you learn to be such a hard ass from Master Brandish?"

"As a matter of fact, yes. Now, where are you in this?"

"Parabolas. Something about parabolas."

"Parabolas I can handle."

We dove in. Maybe the secret to understanding math was having someone drop-dead gorgeous explain it to you. Or maybe he was actually a better teacher than Ms. Linden, which I could believe. The woman seemed incapable of finishing a sentence.

My eye kept drifting to the clock above the door, though. The second 45 minutes was up, I tapped my nonexistent wristwatch. "A deal's a deal."

"Indeed." He closed the textbook and slid it over to me. "First thing. A question."

"Okay."

"Same one as before. What do you want me to call you?"

Oh, that. Yeah. I had read a million blogs about people transitioning picking new names. Some of them wrote about how they always knew what name they wanted.

I didn't. "I hate the name Bonita. You know what it means?"

"Pretty?"

"Ugh. Yeah. I'm not fucking pretty. It doesn't fit in the slightest. Never has. And all the nicknames people try to make out of it! Like Bunny. God, no. Like I'm the fucking Easter Bunny or something." I was ranting but he didn't seem to mind. "And it's such a prissy, weird name. I mean, if my parents were going to pick a Filipino-type name, why that? Why not something cool like Flor or Liezel? I hate it. Hate it hate it hate it."

He had an amused look in his slitted eyes. "What if you masculinized it?"

"A bonito is a fish," I said vehemently.

"No, then." He crossed through something he'd written in his notebook while I was ranting. "Is Flor gender neutral?"

"I'm not sure." I knew a girl named that through church, but no boys. "But at least it doesn't *sound* girly, you know?"

"It means flower? I'm guessing from my high school Spanish."

"Yeah, it means flower. I didn't say it *fit*, just... it would be an improvement over what I've got."

"Then let's find something that fits." He sat back, a small smirk on his face, trying to act casual, but I got the feeling Frost was never really relaxed. He was always a little bit on edge. "Brad."

I had to stifle a sudden laugh. "Like Brad Pitt? Do I look like a Brad?"

"I take that as a no, then. It's like trying on clothes. You can keep trying until you find something that fits. Samson."

I laughed again. "No. Definitely not."

"Peter? Pete?"

"Ugh, not Peter. Nothing that could be construed as a, you know, reference."

"A phallic reference, you mean."

"Yeah." I was blushing hard all of a sudden.

"So no Dick, no Johnson." His little smirk widened and I saw where his teeth gripped his bottom lip for a sec. "Probably should avoid names like Randy, too, then?"

He was making me laugh on purpose and I felt a little giddy. When was the last time I laughed? Seeing him holding tight to his smile only made me laugh even harder. It took a minute to get my breath back. "Is this really going to help?"

He nodded slowly. "Sometimes it takes a while to find out who we are, what our strength is. I mean, that's true for mundane people as well as us. It's just more complicated for us."

Us. The word reverberated in my head like a bell ringing. Had I ever been an "us" before, other than belonging to my nuclear family? I wasn't Filipinx, I wasn't white. I was the only child of Isidro and Dora Reyes.

And they were gone. I realized my hands were shaking and I sat on them, tucking my fingers under my thighs. "What does it mean that I don't have a name in mind?"

"Names are important. They're like a..." He hesitated, before going on: "A magic word. Presto! They carry power and meaning. More importantly, they telegraph intention. So—"

Telegraph intention? I really wasn't sure what he meant by that. "So it's bad that I can't think of one. Am I... like... effed up?"

I was afraid he would laugh at me, but he was deadly serious. Both his eyes and his voice dropped and he seemed to shrink in his chair. "I used to think that. That I was... crazy."

"My aunt thinks I am."

"She's not like us." There was that word again, *us*. His fingers were gripping his pen so tightly I could see the bluish veins standing out on the back of his hand and I was afraid he was going to snap the pen in half. He had gone from being poised and jocular to shaken and distant in a heartbeat. "I was afraid that things I felt inside were just some fantasy. Some daydream I had that would... save me, somehow."

My pounding heart stuck in my throat for a second, until I said, "Yes."

It took him a moment to realize I'd spoken, and I wondered what memory he was lost in. "Yes, what?" he asked.

"That's what I'm afraid of, too," I said. "My aunt believes I'm trying to escape the accident somehow." By wanting to become a new person. "Did you?"

"Did I what?" He looked angry now.

"S-save yourself? From whate—"

"No," he snapped. "I mean, let's not talk about me." He took one deep breath and let it out slowly. As he blew the air through a tiny hole between his lips, his eyes seemed to clear and he focused on me again. "Can you tell me about the accident?"

I didn't remember much. When I tried to think about it, my mind shied away from it, sliding away the way your eyes avoid a light that's too bright. And what I did remember, I wanted to forget. Then no one would know. "I mostly remember waking up in the hospital."

"Were you hurt?"

"Um, no. I guess I was... really lucky." If you can consider losing both your parents at the same time "lucky." A lump was starting to form in my throat.

I didn't want Frost to see me cry, and he clearly didn't want to see me cry, either. He was looking away, like the posters of quotes from Oscar Wilde and John Steinbeck on the wall were suddenly fascinating. He shifted uncomfortably, folding his arms as if he were chilly. He pressed on with a reluctant tone. "Do you... can you remember... anything? Any... details?"

The doctors said I probably took a blow to the head even though they didn't find a bruise or anything like that. I tried to say that to him, but the words wouldn't come. I started to breathe faster, as if my tight throat were starting to choke me. My eyes went hot with tears and my chest tightened with panic. I suddenly didn't want to be there in that room with him.

Both of us jumped, startled by a loud buzz from the speaker grille attached to the clock over the door. All the emergency strobes began to flash. He put a hand over his heart. "Ugh. I'd forgotten how unpleasant that noise was."

I began shoving my books into my bag as quickly as I could. "It's been happening a lot lately." I had to half-shout over the noise of the alarm. My heavy emotional flash was gone, replaced by the real need to vacate the premises. "Something is flaking out in the alarm system, I swear. Or maybe someone's been pranking the school and they just haven't been caught yet? That's like the third one this week."

He held one hand over his ear. "We're out of time, anyway. See you tomorrow?" He held out his hand somewhat awkwardly.

"Tomorrow," I said, and shook his hand, and then we both fled.

* * *

I thought about Frost a lot that evening. I was pushing rice and chicken adobo around my plate trying to figure out his deal and I was so distracted that I didn't realize Aunt Elena was trying to ask me about him. He'd been through something traumatic, too, obviously. I had overheard one of my trauma counselors telling Auntie that certain behaviors were normal for a traumatized person. Mood swings. Sudden anger, prickliness, or sullenness. Distraction. That described both me and him.

"Bebe! Are you even listening?"

"What, Auntie? Sorry, just, I learned a lot today." Truth.

"Well, that is something, I suppose." She reached for the ladle to spoon more onto my plate.

"No, no, Auntie, I've had enough."

"Did it taste all right?"

"It was fine, I've just eaten a ton of it."

She settled back into her chair, her voice vibrating as she said, "It's just, you know, I used your mother's recipe this time."

"Oh." She and my mother used to have epic arguments over the right way to make it. My mother browned the chicken first and then simmered it in the vinegar and soy sauce, while Aunt Elena simmered it first and then browned it. Honestly, they came out tasting so similar to me I couldn't tell the difference. I wondered what it meant that she had decided to try it the other way.

"I thought you would like it better." She stirred the pieces of chicken in the pot and pulled up a drumstick and put it on her own plate. She pulled up a second one and looked at me.

I finally got that it was a peace offering of sorts. "I guess I could eat one more."

She actually smiled as she ladled it onto my plate. She waited until I had started eating again to say, "I was going through your mother's things today."

My mouth was full so I just nodded.

"I found a few things you might want. I didn't want to give them away until you saw them."

"Okay, let's look after dinner." We had settled into a kind of routine where she would cook dinner and I would do the dishes. When the loss had been fresh, it had felt awkward and strange. My mother had always done the cooking and Auntie had cleaned. But it was starting to feel normal.

We carried our dishes into the kitchen from the dining room and I turned on the water.

"Don't wipe down the stove yet," she told me as she peeked into the oven. "I'm baking a flan."

"Oh, nice." Leche flan was one of my favorite desserts. My mother's version was coated in caramelized sugar and packed with sweetened condensed milk from a can. I used to help her make it. She'd flip the mold over and let the sugar drip, and when it hardened we'd eat the drippings like candy.

Auntie packed the leftovers of the adobo and rice away while I loaded the dishwasher and set the pot to soak. Then I followed her up to my parents' bedroom. The house we lived in was old, from the 1800s, and the wooden stairs creaked.

I was expecting some photo albums or diaries or something. I should have known better.

Laid out on the wide bed was a frothy creation of white lace. My mother's wedding dress.

"You've got to be kidding me." The last argument my mother and I had was over a dress.

"Bebe! She didn't want you to be alone. She wanted you to have it, to wear it—"

"Are you kidding me?" I was shouting now. "I'm 15! I'm not getting married! I'm not even going to the fucking prom!"

"Language, Bebe!"

"Don't call me that!" Mine wasn't the loudest screech in the house, though. The smoke alarm in the kitchen began to go off. We both rushed back down to the kitchen in a panic.

Fortunately the whole kitchen was not on fire, just the liquid sugar that had escaped the flan mold and ignited in the oven. I'd never seen it do that before. The flan was ruined, which was just as well, since I didn't want to eat it anymore.

* * *

The next day at school was rough. I wore my secondhand engineer boots and ripped jeans to school, slipping out of the house without breakfast before Auntie saw me. In her eyes the tears in the jeans weren't art, they were a sign of poverty. There was really no explaining to her that they were supposed to be like that. No one at school seemed to care or notice, though.

At least there was one person in my life who wanted to see the real me.

Frost came into the classroom at last bell and charmed Mr. Glazer with some comment about the Austro-Hungarian empire. I'm not kidding. When we got into the hallway, though, he turned back into his serious, moody self, which suited me just fine.

We settled in the library in the same spot as before. The study room had two ancient computers sitting in carrells along one wall, while the center of the room was dominated by a large table. We took the corner farthest from the door and Frost sat where he could see it.

As he opened his book bag he said, "So how are you today, Russell?"

I just shook my head.

"Too English?"

"I don't mind English, but I don't want a jerky guy name, if that makes sense?"

"Why don't you explain it and maybe that will help us find something?"

I'd been doing a lot of reading and so often the guys I read about would pick a name that was super-masculine like Nick or Billy or Hank. "You know how we were talking about Flor? I think I want something gender neutral, but I'm afraid that means I'm not... committed enough."

"Committed enough to what?"

"What if they're right and this is just a phase I'm going through?"

"Then you'll need another new name when you get to the next phase, whatever that is," he said. "Did a therapist actually say that to you? That this is just a phase?"

"Um, the grief counselor from my church. Not to me, but to my aunt. I overheard."

His mouth twitched like he was suppressing a snarl, and then he schooled his expression back to neutral. He rubbed his chin, which

185

seemed quite smooth, much smoother than I'd expect from either a guy his age or even a trans man if he was on T, which stoked my curiosity about him again. His voice was as neutral as his face as he asked, "Is your church important to you?"

"Not really," I said. "I had friends through there when I was younger, other Filipino American kids, but most of them go to private schools in the burbs and have their own friends. Plus, you know, priests can be pretty, um..."

"Judgmental?"

"Stupid. Like last week the sermon was about God sending us misfortunes to give us opportunities for growth. Seriously? The... things that happened to me were so I could grow? It's like they don't even really think through what they say." I laughed a little at the memory, though. "But, get this, the priest caught his sleeve on fire by accident while up there at the altar and I couldn't help but think, hey padre, what lesson were you supposed to learn from that? Maybe God didn't like your message so much after all."

He gave a weak laugh. "Churches can be... problematic for people like us."

"Yeah, I know." I was suddenly eager to get off the subject of churches. "Um, let's do some algebra before we get in trouble?"

"Unless there's another school subject you need more?"

"There's a chemistry test tomorrow, actually." I felt slightly embarrassed to admit I needed help. I'd always been good at science before. I'd loved biology. But I was struggling with chemistry. "If you wouldn't mind."

"I don't mind. I almost went into alchemy." He shook himself like a cat being startled. "I mean chemistry. I meant to say chemistry." He let out a skittish laugh, checking the door as if someone might be eavesdropping on us. "My brain is funny sometimes."

"Yeah, mine, too." I couldn't miss the feeling he was hiding something, but what? I opened the chemistry textbook and tried to find the most recent chapter.

The chemistry teacher, Mr. Cranford, had sniffed too many questionable chemicals in his day, and it was often difficult for me to figure out what he was saying, even with the help of the book. He didn't teach things in a logical order. Science was supposed to be logical, wasn't it?

Frost, for his part, tried to make sense of things for me, digging into ions and protons and electrons. He made balancing equations feel like a vital part of maintaining the universe. I'm pretty sure the universe would balance itself without any help from us, but it made it a lot more interesting to study.

Finally he closed the book. "I can tell you're nearly bursting with wanting to ask a question, and it isn't a question about the periodic table."

Was he psychic? That wasn't the first time it felt like he was reading my thoughts. "The questions I want to ask you are rude, though. Things you're not supposed to ask." Like hey, were you born female? Did you used to be like me? You just didn't say those things. You didn't ask those things. And not because your Auntie disapproved of the topic. People got roasted alive on Tumblr for stuff like that.

He swallowed and narrowed his eyes. "That's right. So how about we keep the questions about you instead of me."

"You're the only person who's interested in helping me figure out who I am," I told him.

"And who you're becoming." He folded his hands. "It's very important. Especially now."

"That's what it feels like! I used to be able to... kind of ignore my whole gender situation. But I can't anymore. I worry about it all the effing time! Ever since... ever since—" I choked up a little, unable to say the word "accident" aloud.

"—you hit puberty?" he finished for me instead. "Reyes, you're going through a lot of changes right now. That's normal. What in Dante's inferno are these counselors telling you?"

"They're not telling me anything because I'm afraid to talk about it with them! They'll tell Aunt Elena."

"Ah." He closed his eyes briefly. "So I really am the only one talking with you about it."

"Exactly."

When he opened his eyes it felt like he was staring right into my skull. "You say you can't remember what happened in the accident?"

"No. They say that happens sometimes with traumatic things. It gets blocked out."

He spoke carefully but precisely. "I don't want to traumatize you further. But I want you to consider the fact that your inability to find a name for yourself and your inability to remember the most crucial moment of your life just might be connected."

My turn to swallow and look away. "So I have to... un-repress my memories to figure myself out?"

"Or maybe you have to figure yourself out before you can remember," he said. "If the two things are one and the same."

My heart was in my throat again and I had to take a couple of deep breaths. In fact, I could hear his voice telling me to breathe over the sound of roaring in my ears. My vision seemed red, too. It cleared as I listened, as I breathed. They said it was normal after a traumatic event for my stress to spike suddenly, for the adrenaline rush to cause my blood pressure to soar and that kind of thing.

He was looking at me with concern.

"I'm all right," I said. "I'm okay."

"Maybe we should stop for today." He seemed afraid to move.

"No, no, I'm okay now." I didn't want him to go. I didn't want our time to be over yet. "Let's talk about names again?"

"You'll know when you find the right thing," he said. "You'll know. When Master Brandish called me Timothy for the first time, it rang like a bell in my head."

I stared for a second. He'd just admitted to me that Timothy wasn't the name he was born with. "But you prefer to be called Frost?"

"Yes."

"Why?"

He prickled frostily in my direction. "It's just... it's the way I..." He huffed and started over. "In my social circles, only those who are somewhat intimate with you call you by your given name, and then only in private. It's kind of a prep school thing. We use family names for common use."

That didn't sound like the whole story. "So your girlfriend...? boy-friend? calls you Timothy? or, Tim?"

He ignored my question. "Let's talk about your name, not mine, hm?"

"Okay, but if you go with Frost, you're really fine with the way family names erase the mother's contribution?"

Frost glared at me for a moment before continuing coolly. "I'm an orphan. I didn't know either parent. My family name is all they left me."

Well, that made me feel like crap, didn't it? And that was another effing thing he and I had in common. An orphan, too. "Um, just trying to have a feminist consciousness, you know. Didn't mean to demean your preference."

He chose to ignore my non-apology, plowing on with the lesson instead. "Remember what I said about names being like a magic word? A power word. Patrilineal power isn't more important than matrilineal, but if you want to access the hereditary power of your patrilineal line, your family name gives you that."

He said it as if accessing power was a real thing and not just symbolic.

"Isn't yours Reyes?" he asked.

"Yeah. It means 'kings.'"

"It means *royals*," he said with a cock of his head. "Which would make Reyes both plural and gender-neutral."

My mouth hung open slightly. He was right. How could it be I'd never thought of it that way before? My father had always said "kings" when I was growing up and I had never questioned it. Until now. My voice shook a little as I felt the need to argue, to explain myself and maybe defend why I thought that way. "But it's not just any royals. It's a reference to the Three Kings from the Christmas story," I said. "Aside from the sexist assumptions of male family names, though, there's a lot of Spanish colonial Catholic bullshit like that in Filipino names that I'd like to leave behi—"

Frost seized my hand, which startled the heck out of me, and so did the intensity of his voice. "Stop. I know all that. But your name is still part of who you are. The three wise men from the Christmas story. What do they call them?"

"The Magi, you mean?"

"Yes." He seemed about to hyperventilate and I wondered why he was getting so emotional about this, of all things. "Balthazar, Melchior, and Gaspar. *The Magi*." He squeezed my hand so hard it hurt and repeated. "The. Magi."

Tears sprang into my eyes as I snatched my hand back, mind reeling. "You're being weird!"

He forced himself to speak calmly. "If you want to reject your symbolic lineage, that's your choice."

What was in my heart was a churning sea of acid right then, though. "My father wouldn't even have a Spanish name if the conquistadors hadn't turned the Philippines into a colony three-hundred years ago! Eff Magellan and the ship he rode in on!"

Frost was breathing deeply in through his teeth and then slowly out through his nose. It was the opposite of calming breaths. Was he seething? His voice was low. "Throw away the gifts of your happenstance if they mean nothing to you or if you feel they're tainted. I'm just saying don't do it lightly."

I stood up. "You think I'm joking? You think this is a lark, a phase I'm going through, like wanting t-to color my hair or—?"

He stood also, but took a step backward, and kept backing away. His spine was ramrod straight, his eyes guarded. "If you believe I'm not taking you seriously, if I've said anything to make you think that, then I should leave now."

He had nearly reached the open door. I realized then that he was trying to escape. From me.

"Are you leaving?" God, I sounded like a little kid when I said that.

"If you're going to keep attacking me, yes." He glanced around nervously.

I didn't want to drive him away. That was the last thing I wanted to do. "I'm sorry. I'm just... easily upset." Which I knew was an understatement, but I had to say something.

"I know you are. But so am I." His eyes were shiny. Watery. The thought that I'd made him cry was almost too much to take. He swallowed.

I sat down quickly. "I'm sorry. I'm..." What else could I say? "I'm sorry. Sometimes I get too emotional. Sometimes I lash out. I know I should control it better but I'm trying."

He took a tentative step back in my direction. "You'll have to learn control. But not from me. Just... look. This is hard for me, too, all right? You shouldn't have to... worry about my issues. But how about recognizing that they're there."

It was possibly the most human thing an adult had ever said to me. And I had a glimpse of what feral teenage Frost must have been like. "I'm sorry," I said again, stuck on those words as the only ones that made sense.

"Excuse me," chirped a voice from the doorway. Mrs. Tettlebaum, the librarian. "Are you two done for the day? We'll be locking up in 15 minutes."

Frost cleared his throat, schooling all emotion from his face and then producing a stage smile for her. "Oh yes, thank you. We're done."

"Until tomorrow," I burst out. "Right? We'll need this room again tomorrow, Mrs. T. Is that all right?"

I was asking her, but really I was asking Frost.

"You can sign the log for it, dearie," the librarian said, but I was barely listening. I was hanging on any sign from Frost that I hadn't just driven him away.

What I got was a bare nod of acknowledgment but that was enough. *Yes!* My heart thumped in my chest in relief, as if it hadn't been beating at all until that moment and was hurrying to make up for lost time. I was almost dizzy with it.

"One last thing," he said before he left. "If you feel like you're... about to lose it. Call me or Master Brandish, all right? Or text. Write our numbers down. I'm very, very serious about this."

"Okay." I wrote down the numbers he gave me. It seemed odd. Why would he want me to call him if I was having a little flip out? Maybe he didn't realize how often that happened to me.

"Promise me," he said.

"I promise," I said, and then he fled. I sat there, recovering, for a few more minutes, trying to stay calm.

It was true what I told him. Sometimes I lost my head and yelled or screamed. More than one counselor had told me that was normal after a traumatic accident, after losing both parents.

What I didn't dare tell them is that I hadn't just started being like that since the accident. It had happened before.

* * *

That night before I sat down to dinner with Auntie I changed into whole, unripped jeans. No reason to provoke her more than necessary. We had the leftovers of the night before. All my mother's recipes fed four people so this was our usual pattern.

Neither of us spoke for a while but she eventually asked me, "So, how was your meeting with your tutor today?"

"Oh, it went great. He can do both science and math, so we did chemistry today. I have a quiz tomorrow so we'll see if it helped."

"Good, good." She put on a tight smile. "This Sunday is the church social."

"Which is what?"

"After church, a kind of picnic."

"A picnic? Where?"

191

"Right there, in the church basement. You know what I mean. Where everyone brings something."

"Oh! You mean a *potluck*." That made much more sense. "What should we bring?"

"I was going to bring a flan but after what happened yesterday, I don't know." She fingered her napkin nervously.

"Okay, how about I make the flan? I used to help Mom make it all the time. Maybe you did something different."

Her eyebrows rose in surprise. "You would do that?"

"Sure, why not?"

"You seem very against doing anything your mother did."

"Oh for Pete's sake, Auntie, I'm not against doing *everything*. Just certain things." How was I going to explain this without it turning into a big fight?

"Female things," she said, and I knew that couldn't be good. She was getting more and more direct and I was worried another ultimatum was coming. "Do you think I don't know what you're trying to do, Bebe? You're trying to deny who you are."

No, you are trying to deny who I am, I wanted to shout, but I held it in. I thought about how Frost could turn on the charm when he wanted to. I cleared my throat but I couldn't quite manage his poise. "Auntie, please. I know baking desserts is a traditional feminine pursuit. But it's not exclusively so. After all, so many of the top chefs in the world are men."

"So that makes it okay? Because men do it, too?" She examined me, her eyes flicking up and down. "I'm trying to understand it, Bebe. Is all this because your father always wanted a boy?"

My brain locked up for a second. Like, wow. She really couldn't understand that I would want to do something—be something—other than what my parents wanted? As if what they wanted was more important than what I wanted. No, not wanted. Than what I was. Who I was.

And my father might have wanted a son, but he definitely wanted me to be a daughter with a capital D. He'd made that crystal clear. The last time I ever spoke to him.

That time in the car.

"Bebe?"

My ears were full of a roaring sound, making her voice sound distant. My own voice was trapped in my throat, which was as tight as if it were being squeezed by a fist. I thought about Frost taking that breath, blowing it out through a tiny hole in his lips. I tried it. It helped.

The sound receded. I was able to focus on her again.

"Bebe, are you listening to me?" She looked worried, but pressed on. "I know you don't like to talk about the accident. But today, I have some more details. From the police and the insurance."

"Details." The sound of my own blood rushing in my ears returned. Did they know? There was no way they could know about the argument. The screaming. The fight. I was the only one who knew that and even I barely remembered it, my memory going blank at the edges whenever I thought about it...

"Bebe!" Her voice seemed very far away as redness seemed to press in all around my vision. This time the slow breath didn't help. The redness only deepened, as if I were blowing on an ember and making it glow.

I'd promised Frost I would call if this happened. I promised. As my breath grew short, I clung to that thought. I hurried away from the table and ran into the bathroom.

I splashed my face with water first, and that helped. My breath began to slow down. As I stood there with my phone, looking at his number, I felt myself calming. Okay. I hadn't actually lost my head. I had come close, but not actually blown up this time. So I didn't have to call him after all. I could wait until tomorrow to tell him.

I shut off the water and I could hear my aunt on the phone. She must not have realized how loud she was being while she was upset. She must have been right outside the bathroom door.

"I'm so worried!" she said. "What if she's possessed? That would explain everything. She's different since the accident."

"Elena. You told me yourself the doctors warned you about panic attacks and stress reactions. Everything you've described so far, the moods, the outbursts, even the occasional blackouts, could all be explained by the trauma of the accident. If anything you should be concerned about post-concussion syndrome and make sure she sees a doctor about that. Demonic possession this isn't." Oh, man. She was talking to a priest.

"If you're sure?"

"Your niece is at the age where she is going to undergo a lot of changes even without the extra strain of the accident and her bereavement. You're going to have to let her find her own way, Elena. And what about you? Isidro was your brother..." She must have gone back to the kitchen because I couldn't hear it anymore.

Exorcism. Wow. Now she was trying to explain what was "wrong" with me as demons. I didn't think highly of our priest, as I'd told Frost, but at least he'd talked some sense into my aunt.

* * *

The next day I knew the moment Frost arrived outside Mr. Glazer's classroom. I could hear him on his cell phone.

"Have you talked to Aunt Elena or the school administration? I'm concerned about leaving Reyes for the weekend. I'm no good at dancing around these issues, Callendra. I really think we should just come out with the truth."

The truth? All of a sudden all of the times I'd felt like he was hiding something from me jumped to the front of my mind. He was hiding something from me! But what? It had to be something about the scholarship. What else could they be stringing me along about? And why? It made no sense.

"None of these counselors know what they're dealing with. Did you read that assessment from the school psychologist? That the amnesia is protecting Reyes from a psychotic break? Reyes isn't psychotic. Reyes is *magical.*"

Well, that was very nice of him to say but I thought about the way he had tried to edge out of the room yesterday, like he was afraid I was going to attack him. Maybe what he wasn't telling me was what he actually thought about my mental state. Frost, are you sure you don't think I'm psychotic?

When the bell rang I sat for a minute, waiting for everyone else to file out of the classroom. Frost finally stuck his head in, looking for me.

"Ah, Mr. Frost," Mr. Glazer said from his desk. "I did some reading after our conversation yesterday. You were quite right about Rudolph the Second inviting astrologers and alchemists from all over Europe to his court in Prague. Ultimately, though, his belief in the occult didn't keep him in power. He was possibly quite insane."

"A history written by those who disbelieved in the occult. Therefore by definition they considered him of unsound mind," Frost said smoothly.

"Hm, true, my boy. True. The layperson believes history is a record of facts, when it is in fact the record of the predominant point of view. Any story looks very different from the margins."

As Frost and I made our way toward the library I muttered, "Maybe his class would be less boring if he didn't just teach the predominant point of view."

"Everything is less boring when looked at outside the predominant point of view," he said. "It's why what's considered hip or cool is almost always something co-opted from the marginalized."

"Yeah." Normally I would have been ecstatic to have a pro-social-justice conversation, but I was itching to ask him about the phone call I'd overheard. I waited until we got into our usual room in the library.

Before I could ask him about it, though, he said, "Tomorrow's Saturday. I know we didn't set up weekend tutoring sessions but I was wondering if we could convince your aunt you should come meet me at the library on campus. Do you have a big test coming up Monday we could say was crucial to your grade or something like that?"

That feeling we were in a spy thriller was back, except this time he was keeping the secret from me. "We could tell her that. It'd be more convincing coming from you or Master Brandish than me, though. I don't have the ability you do to put on such a convincing face. You're really good at hiding things."

He looked especially guarded. "It was less an innate talent than a survival skill I learned early."

"Really? You seem to have this way of knowing just what to bring up. Sometimes it feels like you know what I'm thinking." I saw the way he stiffened. I was getting warm. "Like you're psychic or something."

He held his breath, then let it out. "What would you think if I told you I was psychic?"

Omigod, was that the secret?

"Would you think I was crazy or would you believe me?"

Something clicked. Something he said days ago. About thinking he was crazy when he was younger, and then finding out he wasn't crazy, that it wasn't just his imagination or an escape. I'd thought at the time he was talking about gender transition but it seemed suddenly clear he wasn't.

"I-I'd probably ask for proof of some kind," I said. My voice was shaking and I wasn't sure why.

"I've always been honest with you, Reyes—"

I suddenly couldn't stop myself from cutting him off. "No, you haven't. You've been hiding something the whole time."

He held up his hands like he was surrendering to a bad guy with a gun. "Slow down. I'm trying to explain what it is I've been slow to explain."

"Don't tell me you're another one of these 'it's for your own good' types!"

"No, I'm not." He was doing those forced-calm breaths. "Please, give me a second to make the explanation of why I'm being so careful."

I was so angry, though. So tired of people talking about me instead of to me. "Because the school psychologist told you I'm a psycho? Is that why?"

He narrowed his eyes with one of those "I thought so" looks. "Kind of. Seriously, take a deep breath with me now, okay? One. Two. Three."

I did it to humor him, but like last night it helped me calm down.

"Now try to follow this logic, okay?" he said. "Let's say I am psychic. If you believe that can't be real, and I present you with proof that it is, if your mind's kind of fragile, you could have a break with reality. No one wants that, all right? So I'm treading carefully."

"Okay." That sounded reasonable. "Do you think my mind's fragile?"

"No, I think you're quite resilient, but I'm still going to be careful, and that was just an example."

An example of what? "So, are you psychic?"

"Only with people I am very close to," he said, like it was a total fact.

I blinked. "Really."

"Really. I usually have to be in physical contact, too." He shifted uncomfortably. "Which I know makes it hard to prove. It would be very easy to fake."

"So you're asking me to believe you're psychic?"

"I'm not asking you to believe anything, yet." He sounded as impatient as I felt. "You're the one who suspected I was psychic."

"True." My mind was whirling now, though, trying to settle all the things I thought I knew which were now all up in the air. "So you used to fantasize that you were psychic while you were in traumatic circumstances, and you worried you were nuts... but then it turned out to be true?"

His eyes searched around while he digested that thought. "Partly, yes," he said. "There's more, but can you let that thought sink in for now?"

"Don't tell me we're going to study algebra now."

"How'd you do on that chemistry test?"

"I got an A." I gritted my teeth. "But don't change the subject. I don't like people hiding things from me. Even when—maybe especially when—they're for my own good."

His mask slipped then and I saw his own anger and fear when he swallowed. "And what if it's for my good? For fuck's sake, Reyes, I thought we went over this."

I tried not to yell, so it came out a kind of vehement hiss. "I'm not going to hurt you!"

"You don't know th—!" He jumped out of his skin when the fire alarm went off. I'll be honest, I jumped too.

He quickly slung his own bag over his shoulder and said, "Come on. Let's get out of here."

"Okay. Where are we going?" I picked up my own things and we ducked into the hallway.

"Let's go to campus. It's the safest place."

"Safest? You mean, emotionally, for you?"

He didn't answer, just picked up speed toward the exit. He was halfway down the street when he finally said, "I have some things to show you which will help you understand."

"Understand what?"

"What it is I haven't told you yet." He looked back at me. "And you haven't figured out for yourself."

He led me a few blocks from my school to the edge of the Harvard campus, then through one of the brick and wrought-iron gates into Harvard Yard. We were headed toward the Widener Library, I thought, but he peeled off on a path to the left and we ducked suddenly behind another building.

"Who are we hiding from?"

"Did you see Master Brandish come out of one of the buildings across there?"

"No, but why are we hiding from her?"

"Because she doesn't think you should know what I'm about to tell you." He sat me down on a stone bench against a brick building in a slightly sheltered nook. He took my hands in his, which I thought was kind of weird, but felt okay. "She thinks we should wait. I don't think she realizes how urgent it is, and she's not listening to me when I tell her the warning signs."

"Okay."

"Tell me what you've learned from me so far. I mean, besides algebra and chemistry."

"What, you mean like, um, I should accept myself as I am or something like that?"

He held in a laugh. "I mean more specifically."

"Oh, um," I had to stop and think. He'd said a lot of things I hadn't thought of at the time as teaching me, but he'd seemed very intense about. "That the three kings were important? That they were, what, magi? Doesn't that mean wise men?"

"In some translations, maybe," he said. "Did you hear what Mr. Glazer said today?"

"About King Rudolph inviting the alchemists to Prague?"

He nodded. "Have you ever wondered why old stories, and even history, seem to be full of people doing magic, but you never see them anymore?"

"I thought they were just stories."

"History is told by those in power. There's nothing magical about the people who run this world. What else did I tell you?"

"Names are power?"

"Yes." He let go of my hands. "I'm going to show you something now that may come as a shock, but I'm hoping you'll take it in stride because you're ready to hear it. Because deep down you knew it all along. What's my name?"

"Frost? Or you mean Timothy."

"Do you know what Timothy is?"

"It's some kind of plant?"

"It's a kind of grass, yes." His hands were right in front of me. I didn't see him move. I must have blinked, and then his hands were full of stalks of grass. There were a few purple blossoms, too. Violets. He picked them out and tossed them aside like they were weeds and then put the stalks of grass into my hands, I guess to prove they were real.

"What did you just do?"

"Invoked the power of my name," he said. "And then there's this." He snapped his fingers and the stalks in my hands grew crusted with ice crystals. Frost.

I stared at them, feeling along the icy stalks. "This is... kind of... wow." I blinked. "So, is it really real? Or is this just you making me think it's real because you're psychic?"

"I told you, I'm only mildly psychic." He held up a fresh stalk, topped by a long fuzzy seed flower. "It's sometimes called the 'common cat tail' as well."

"Okay, but what did you do to make it appear?"

"It's called conjuration, and it's not as easy as I just made it look." He seemed to relax a fraction. "You seem like you're not having a psychotic break?"

"Not yet, anyway." I turned the stalks over in my hands, and I could see that they were shaking. I remembered what he'd said to Master Brandish on the phone. "You said it earlier today. I'm not psychotic. I'm magic."

"Exactly." He relaxed another fraction.

"You meant it literally."

"Yes." He looked at me curiously. "And there's no way you could have overheard that conversation."

"Sure I did. You were right outside the door."

"Did it seem like anyone else heard me?"

"Oh, probably. They just weren't paying attention. Lately I can always tell when someone's talking about me."

He raised an eyebrow. "Oh, really."

"Yeah. I can't believe how some of these counselors will go on about me as if they think I can't hear it."

"Reyes, stop and think for a second. You 'can always tell.' Doesn't that sound just a little bit psychic to you?"

My hands were shaking harder. Wasn't I supposed to be happy right now? When people find out they're magical in books, they're always happy. I was feeling mostly... stress. "Are you serious?"

"I am serious. Hearing when you are being talked about is a very specific talent. And you just developed the ability? Since puberty or since the acc—"

I threw the plants at him. "No. No, it's not true. It can't be true!

199

Because that means—" I couldn't say it. I turned and ran. I sprinted away from him as fast as I could, running past buildings and across walkways and grass, running until my lungs burned and I saw spots before my eyes. I stumbled and my knees hit damp grass and a few moments later Frost caught up.

I heard him behind me. "Reyes. Please. Take a breath."

But it was hard to breathe when I was sobbing. "It means I—"

"No, it doesn't!"

"You weren't there! You don't know!" No one alive knew what happened that day in the car.

My father had been driving, my mother in the back, me in the passenger seat. Supposedly on our way to the mall, but although it had seemed like a spur-of-the-moment trip, it quickly became clear that my parents had planned it so they could corner me for a "talk."

"You're not a child anymore, Bebe," my father began. "You could be a tomboy all you wanted as a kid, but now it's time to grow up."

"Your old clothes are getting worn out," my mother added, as if this was just about clothes. "You need some things suitable for a young lady."

Like they hadn't even heard any of the things I'd been saying over the past two years. "I don't want things 'suitable for a lady.'"

"Don't be ridiculous. You're going to wear those ratty things to the Sanchez party next week? I don't think so." My mother huffed.

"I don't mind new clothes, but you know how I feel about feminine shit."

"Language, Bebe!" Dad barked.

"Language, my ass, Dad!" I was getting more and more angry with each passing second.

"That's the attitude that is going to hurt you in life! That's what I'm talking about, Bebe! You have to clean up your act and conform to the standards—"

"Conform? Did you actually use the word conform? You've got to be kidding me."

Mom tried to be a peacemaker, but it was clear she was on his side. "We've been very tolerant of you for a long time, Bunny—"

"I told you not to call me that!"

"I told you we should have cracked down long ago," Dad said to her, ignoring me for a second. "She's out of control."

"I am not out of control!" I shouted it, though, practically beating my fists against the dashboard. "I am perfectly well in control when I'm not being shoved into a... a cage!"

"Society is a cage? Getting a good job, raising a family is a cage?" My father's face was as red as mine, as red as when he drank too much Christmas punch, sweat standing out on his forehead below his dark, black bangs. "You'd rather be a wild animal on the street? We have rules for a reason!"

"Bunny—Bebe—Bonita," my mother tried, "you don't have to change everything, just, for this one party, just try on a nice dress, you'll see how nice you look, I know you'll love it—"

"No! *You'll* love it! I'll *hate* it!" I couldn't believe they were ganging up on me like that, and over what? A stupid party where all my father's colleagues would be judging each other's wives and children? Fuck that. "Did you even read that brochure I gave you about gender—"

"Propaganda," Dad spat. "Ridiculous."

"It's not ridiculous! Trans people are—"

"It is a plot by rich deviants," Dad insisted, "who use the gay name to play victim and then lure young women such as yourself into their depraved way of life! That's what I've read."

"What!"

"You have your pamphlets, Bebe, and I have mine!"

"Mine come from my school! They're approved!"

"Mine come from the Sanchez's church. They're approved, too." He nodded like that settled it and banged on the steering wheel. "No more arguing! I am the father in this family and my word is law!"

That's when I lost it completely. He'd never invoked the "my word is law" thing before. I saw red, and then redder, and then the car had literally burst into flames.

* * *

I could feel something cold on my forehead and my cheeks. Had I passed out and was I at the school nurse? I tried to open my eyes.

"Shhh, stay still." That was Frost's voice, and the cold was coming from Frost's forehead and hands. He was holding my face, our heads pressed together. He eased back from me. I opened my eyes and saw we were covered in ash and bits of grass and flowers, and his normally perfectly white shirt was streaked with soot and one sleeve appeared to have been burned away. We were sitting in a circle of scorched grass.

My clothes weren't in much better shape than his.

He let go of me slowly, holding in that smile of his, with his teeth on his lip. "I thought that might happen." He sounded pretty cool for someone who'd just been hit by a firebomb. Cool. Of course. *Frost.* "I'm just glad we weren't in the library when it did."

"Are you okay?"

"I wasn't sure if I would be resistant to fire. I'm pleased to find out I am. Or you'd be feeling even guiltier now than you already do... Blaise."

My mouth hung open like I had to part my lips to let such a name slip inside me, but in it went. "Eff me. That fits." My vision went blurry and I had to blink away tears. "That fits." I looked at the palms of my hands. They were the same as ever. Unscathed. Unburned. The memory of the accident was fresh and vivid now. "But... but..."

He took my hands in his, like he could counteract my heat with his cold. Maybe he could. "I lived through your flashback. That happens sometimes, when something suppressed breaks loose."

Tears stuck in my throat, choking me, and I sat up quickly, coughing, a fist of grief squeezing my chest. "Then... then... you know."

He closed my hands inside his in a prayer position. "I know the accident wasn't your fault."

"Yes, it was! You just saw the proof! I'm... I'm... an effing fireball."

He shook his head. "The flames of your rage are what protected you from the fire. But the truck that slammed on its brakes in front of the car? That was not your fault."

I wanted to argue—my reflex was to fight. "But if I hadn't been distracting my father, he might've stopped in time."

Frost pressed his lips together, as if chewing on what he was about to say. "Or he might not've. He was distracting himself, if anything."

"But I could've... waited. I could've played along with them, waited until we got somewhere safer for an argument..."

"Could you have?" he asked. "Think about it, Blaise. Could you have stayed silent? Could you have pushed your true self down deep one more time, and if you had, would it just have burst out at an even worse moment? Your parents could have chosen somewhere 'safer' for the argument. I don't see that you had much choice about it."

"But they're *gone*," I cried, and I mean it, I really cried. Tears poured out of me as easily as flames had earlier.

Frost held me. Frost stayed there, not moving, holding me for as long as it took for the tears to run out.

When they did finally stop, I felt too wrung out to be embarrassed about the fact I'd been crying. "Um. Thanks."

"You're welcome." He sat back and looked around. "I can't keep us invisible from everyone else for much longer. Do you mind if we go indoors for a while? We can go into my dorm and get hot cocoa."

I was pretty sure if I was having a psychotic break there wouldn't be hot cocoa. "Okay. Give me a sec." I wasn't sure I could stand up. "Can I ask you something?"

"Sure."

"What's the deal with the violets? Is it, like, your middle name or something?"

He sighed. "Let's just say not everyone's gender transition is as complete as it might seem to be on the surface. Transition implies there's a simple line to be crossed. The reality is more complex than that."

"Definitely." Sometimes you know something is true but until you hear it out loud, or hear it from the right person, it doesn't sink in. This time it sank in. I got shakily to my feet. "So is this when you tell me the fairy-tale is true and I can stay here forever and ever and never go back?"

Frost arched an eyebrow. "You're not getting out of Mr. Glazer's history class that easily, I'm afraid."

"Okay, but if the moral of the story is I have to be true to myself... what happens if I still can't really figure out where I fit? Am I non-binary? Am I trans?"

Frost sighed. "I don't have an answer for you but I do have a warning."

"What's that?"

"Stop holding back from your counselors and using it as your excuse to hold back from yourself. They need to hear about your survivor guilt, your fear it's your fault, the argument with your folks, *and* your gender questions. Or the next fire you start really might be your fault."

I stared at the palms of my hands. Heat seemed to lurk just under the surface of my skin, my palms mottled by the Irish part of my heritage. "You'll teach me to control it? My flame power?"

He shrugged. "Me or another tutor on campus. I will say this, though. If you're going to use the power of your name, it helps to know yourself well. Very, very well."

What do you know? Frost finally did what no one else had; he gave me an incentive to want to see a counselor.

The Grimoire Girls

By E.C. Myers

As Mom drives our truck up the long winding driveway to the Doheny Preparatory Academy, I get that short-of-breath, sweaty-palms, deer-in-the-headlights feeling that is way beyond first day jitters, past cold feet, and on its way to a powerful impulse to jump out and run. If I actually did it, it would serve Mom right for teaching me how to dive from a moving car safely.

I tug the hem of my pleated skirt down to cover the fresh scabs on my knees. All right, so I still need to practice the whole tuck-and-roll thing, but in my own defense, I'd been rattled by the banshee screaming from the backseat of my car.

"Stop fidgeting, Lexi," Mom says. "Why are you so nervous? We've done this dozens of times."

"I hate prep schools," I say. "Why do they make these skirts so short?"

Mom glances over at my ensemble: grey and black tartan skirt, white blouse, black tie.

"When I was your age, we used to roll our skirts up."

I pull the skirt over my knees again and hold it in place.

"Maybe that's why you had me at my age," I say.

"Ooh, someone's hitting below the belt, so to speak."

I roll my eyes. Mom and I look alike—same curly black hair, bright blue eyes, and curves that some people had sold their souls for—but while she thrives on attracting attention, I try to avoid it.

"Really, what's gotten into you?" she asks.

"I'm just tired." I punctuate this with a heavy sigh.

"After two cups of coffee?"

"Not that kind of tired. This is my third school this year. I was starting to like the last one."

"You mean you liked someone at the last school," she says.

"Like that matters," I say. "Our lifestyle doesn't exactly invite long-term relationships."

"You're telling me, kiddo," she says.

Mom pulls into the circular driveway in front of the school. There's a stone statue of an angel in the center, hands folded in prayer. Why do people buy those creepy things? If they knew how easy they were for demons to possess, they would crush every last one into dust.

Of course, if people knew about demons, then they might not need us so much.

I stare ahead so I don't see the kids who are watching and judging us. Our dusty blue pickup truck is probably shocking to their refined sensibilities, but they'd be even more shocked by the small arsenal stashed in the back.

I grab my army camo backpack by its straps and work the door handle. Mom opens the driver-side door.

"What are you doing?" I hiss.

"I'm coming with. I should introduce you to the headmaster or announce you to the butler or whatever rich people do."

"Dressed like that? Your skirt's shorter than mine. And tighter. In fact, that is my skirt. From when I was ten!"

"I just want to make a good impression."

"We're here to hunt monsters, not dates."

"I'm good at multitasking."

"Go away. It's bad enough you had to drop me off on my first day."

"Excuse me, but who drove her car into a lake?"

"I did mention the banshee?"

I had been out of holy water and figured a lake on church grounds would be close enough.

It wasn't.

"Not only did we have to skip town in a hurry, but you wasted a perfectly good car," she says.

"That's being generous." But I do miss my rusty old Yugo.

"Oh my God!" Mom says.

"What?" I pull my nail file from my kneesock and look for danger.

"I just realized my Paul Anka CD was in your car."

"So there's the silver lining." I slide the nail file back into my sock. "Mom, I have to get to class."

She closes her car door. "You'll tell me if you have any cute teachers?"

"No. Remember what happened with Mr. Logan?"

"I knew he was an incubus," she says. "No English teacher is that hot and charming."

"Uh huh. Then why did I have to save you?"

"I had him exactly where he wanted me."

"And I can never unsee that. Good-bye."

I open my door and hop out. I sling my bag over my shoulder and walk down the cobbled path to the entrance, concentrating on not tripping while everyone is watching. The truck roars to life and gravel crunches behind me as mom drives away.

I feel naked without my Winchester rifle—and did I mention this skirt? —but they frown on students carrying that sort of thing around, even if you're trying to kill an urban wendigo that's masquerading as the high school's QB1 and eating cheerleaders.

In fact, the only weapons I can sneak into schools these days are the crucifix around my neck, which is only any good because it's made of iron; a wicked sharp nail file boiled in the blood of a dead man; a mini-crossbow, some assembly required, that fires really pointy pencils; a pencil sharpener; a water bottle filled with holy water (the good stuff, not just lake water); a steel garrote rolled into the waistband of my skirt; a lunch bag filled with salt; a bracelet with an unspecified protection spell on it, which I worry is only going to protect my wrist from harm; and the Grahame family Grimoire—which is worth more than everything else combined.

I don't carry the actual thing around of course. The tome is like, 800 pounds, and moldy and falling apart. But I had scanned it in as an eBook.

And then, of course, there's me. As long as I can speak the spells I need and I keep my eReader charged, I'm the best weapon of all. I always keep the eReader charged; Mom still won't let me forget the time it died during an incantation. Instead of being banished, the demon imploded, and my skin was green for a week. Fortunately, it was Halloween. So things worked out.

* * *

I check in at the main office and collect my class schedule and a stack of books. I glance over the courses—all honor classes, naturally. I may not stay at one school for long, but while I'm there, I kick ass, which isn't easy with my extracurricular activities. And I don't mean Yearbook. I had my hands full with missions, late night patrols, and training.

It's hard to fit in even superficial friendships with all that going on. It's just more important that I get good grades. I'm not going to be doing this forever. I'm going to Harvard or Yale in three years and leaving this life behind for one a little more ordinary.

My orientation packet includes a list of the class rankings. If I keep up my grades here, I'll be number two, right under "Costa, Bristol."

"Alexis Grahame?" a girl says.

I look up. There are two students in front of me: a slight girl with long, honey brown hair and tan skin and a taller boy with spiky black hair and the whitest teeth I've ever seen.

"Lexi," I say. "Alexis is my mom."

"Welcome to Doheny Prep," she says. "I'm Bristol Costa. Class president."

We have identical uniforms, but hers is tailored to flatter her in all the right places and mine was stolen from a thrift store and would better fit a different girl.

"I'm Rowan Frost, vice president," the boy says. "We're here to show you around." His clothes are carefully arranged to look casually unkempt while still not violating dress code: loose black tie, partially untucked shirt, rumpled blazer.

"Thanks," I say.

Bristol gathers my new books in her arms. Rowan holds the office door open for us. Classy.

"Do the president and vice president welcome all transfer students?" I ask as we step into the empty hall. The first bell rang five minutes ago. "Or should I feel special?"

"You are special. We were curious about the new competition."

"She is, anyway. I'm here because we have a buddy system. No one's allowed in the halls alone," Rowan says.

"Because of the missing kids?" I ask.

Rowan's face falls. "Yeah."

"Your locker's over here," Bristol says. "We can drop some of your books off on the way to class."

"I like keeping my books with me," I say, hefting my gigantic backpack.

She shoots me a curious look. "A girl after my own heart," she says.

I follow her down the row of lockers, while Rowan trails behind us. When she points mine out, I fumble with the combination on the slip of paper I got from the office. After going around the dial twice, I still can't get it to work. I finally read the numbers aloud while I spin the lock and it pops right open.

"So what brings you to Washington Depot?" she asks.

"We travel a lot for my mom's work," I say.

She ruffles the pages of one of my textbooks. "And you decided to transfer here even after hearing about the missing girls?"

"This is still the best school, isn't it? I thought they ran away."

"No, it was a demon," Rowan says.

"Demon? What's it look like?" I ask.

Bristol raises her eyebrows. "That's a first. Most people assume demons look like the Hollywood standard. Horns, tail, scales, that kind of thing."

"Demons can look like anything," I say. "Statues, animals, teachers... Hot girls." I blush. Did I really just say that?

She smiles. "So we can't rule you out as a demon. I'd better keep an eye on you."

Rowan shakes his head and wanders down the hallway, hands stuffed into the pockets of his blazer.

Bristol leans closer and whispers. "His girlfriend was the first girl who disappeared." Bristol smells like vanilla and incense.

I check my schedule again as an excuse to hide my burning face. I sort out the books I'll need for class today: Pre-calculus, American History, Chemistry.

I flip through the latter. When I find the formula for dichloro-benzene, I mutter it under my breath: "$C_6H_4Cl_2$." I concentrate on getting rid of the stench of old pickles in my locker. The inside instantly looks cleaner and the scent of vanilla and incense wafts out.

I quickly slam the door and catch Bristol watching me intently. She couldn't have noticed that little spell.

"So, are we in any classes together?" I offer her my course sheet.

"No, I don't think so," she says without even looking at it. "I'm in the advanced classes."

"So am I," I say.

"Not as advanced as mine," she says.

We catch up to Rowan and they lead me down another hallway.

"How do I get into those classes?" I ask.

"Forget about it," Rowan says. "Your parents had to be in those classes. I can't get in. I don't even know what they are."

I've been to some snooty schools, but never one this elitist. It sounds like a kind of secret society, and that's always the first place you look when something weird is going down.

I need to get into those advanced classes.

As we pass a classroom, the safety glass in the door suddenly cracks followed a moment later by a muffled boom.

I rush for the door, hoping I can help with my magic without making Bristol and Rowan suspicious.

"Lexi, leave it." I hear a hard edge in Bristol's voice that tells me she's used to people listening to her.

I glance back at her. "It could be the demon."

She laughed. "You fell for that? And I thought you were smart."

I glance back at the door and the glass is perfectly fine.

"Did you see that?" I ask Rowan.

"See what?" he says.

I didn't imagine it. I press a finger to the window—it's buzzing with magic. The students inside, about 20 girls, seem oblivious to anything unusual while the teacher writes on the whiteboard.

Bristol pulls me away. Either there was a glamour around that spell to divert attention from it, or magical events are completely normal around here.

I'm not sure which scenario makes me more concerned.

#

I call Mom at lunch, hiding behind a book in a corner of the courtyard where I can study everyone else without being seen.

"Something hinky's definitely going on here, Mom."

I sprinkle salt from my lunch bag on the bland mashed potatoes from the cafeteria.

"Could you be more specific?" She speaks low. She's at the local library searching for anything supernatural in this sleepy Connecticut town.

"How about demon sightings in the school?" I say.

"A demon? What's it look like?" she asks.

I grin. "I've talked to about 30 students who claim they've seen it. They all agree: cloven hooves, red skin, pointed tail, horns. The boys are emphatic about its horniness."

"Thirty kids have seen it, and survived to describe it? That can't be right."

"And it's weird to get so many identical descriptions," I say.

"Whatever it is, it isn't a demon. And it wants to be seen," Mom says. "I'll dip into the school's servers and review the security footage."

"There's something else, Mom. Loose magic. I saw glass crack then fix itself, while a boy didn't even notice."

A girl across the courtyard knocks over her cup of soda, spilling ice and Coke everywhere. A moment later, she's holding the cup in her hand and sipping from a straw, her blouse still clean and dry. It's like catching a bad continuity edit in a film.

I describe that too, and all the other things that had been happening to me throughout the day: I tripped over absolutely nothing on my way to Chemistry. In math class, I couldn't open my textbook; the pages seemed like they were glued together, but when a boy helped me, the book was perfectly fine. None of my pencils wrote, though they were all freshly sharpened.

"Trickster? Or it could be a hazing. Or maybe someone has a crush on you," Mom says.

"This school is buzzing with magic. But I can't pin down the source. It seems to be coming from everywhere."

"And you're taking precautions?"

"Yes." I sigh.

When magic users like us are exposed to a lot of power all at once, it feels... Well, I'd never tried pot before, but Mom says it's kind of like that. It makes you happy, and with more exposure, you get high. Too much, and you start doing stupid things and could cause serious harm. You should never use magic while under the influence of magic.

To manage it, you have to redirect some of that excess magic building up in your body, like letting off steam to prevent an explosion. This is the perfect excuse to use magic liberally to make people more communicative.

"The boys genuinely seem to know nothing," I say.

"Naturally."

211

"But some of the girls are hiding something. I just can't get at it yet. Have you found anything?" I ask.

"There's a town festival next week," she says. "Oh, and a sale on spring fashions on Main Street."

"Anything useful?"

"Not yet, but I have a solid lead."

"What's his name?"

"Landon," she says. "He has glasses."

"That doesn't mean he's smart."

"No, but they look damn sexy."

"I may have a lead too," I say.

Bristol walks across the courtyard, flanked by three girls who are all wearing their hair like hers and copying her walk.

"Hey, what were the names of those missing girls again?" I ask.

Her nails tap against a keyboard. "The first one was Lien Phan, back in November, followed by Marissa Bauer in February."

I pull out the list of class rankings. "What were their GPAs before they went missing?"

"Hold on." Mom types some more. "Phan had a 99.8. Bauer had 99.1." She laughs. "Sounds like a fever, doesn't it?"

According to the paper in front of me, Bristol Costa, the number one student at Doheny, only has a 98.9. She's taken the top slot by default.

It looks like I'm going to have to keep a closer eye on her.

* * *

I visit the headmaster's office the next morning before homeroom. Headmaster Spengler is heavyset and bald with a milky blue glass eye. I want to splash holy water on him to see if he's a demon, but that isn't polite.

"Ms. Grahame. I'm sorry I wasn't able to welcome you to Doheny myself yesterday. Settling in well?" he says.

"Oh yes, Headmaster."

I glance furtively around his office. There isn't the slightest whiff of magic around him, except for the paper on his desk, which he scrutinizes.

"I understand you've met our star pupil, Ms. Costa," he says.

"Yes, sir."

"What do you think of her?" he asks.

"Sir?" I ask. I feel another blush creeping up my neck to my cheeks.

"Is she the type of person to do anything to get ahead?"

The headmaster must have come to the same conclusions I have. But why is he asking me about Bristol?

I look him in the eyes and decide that's a mistake. I focus on a spot just above his head.

"I think so," I say. "But so is everyone at Doheny."

"And what about you?" he asks.

"I don't know, sir."

He glances down at his desk while his glass eye continues looking right at me. Creepy.

"Apparently your mother, also Alexis Grahame, graduated from Doheny... Seventeen years ago?" He looks me over and clucks his tongue in disappointment.

"That's right," I say. "She was in the advanced classes, sir." Whatever that means.

"Odd. I was headmaster here then, but I don't remember her at all. And I remember everyone." He holds up the blank page that Mom has spelled to show him what I want. "This is a forgery. Impressive magic, but not quite impressive enough to fool me." He taps his glass eye.

I've screwed up.

Spengler stands and pulls a book from the bookcase behind his desk. He riffles through it.

"Read to me from page 13, if you would be so kind." He hands me the book.

It's heavier than it looks, and it buzzes in my hands. Somehow the magic is bound up so tight, none of it leaks from the covers, which is why I didn't notice it before. It's a powerful grimoire, almost as powerful as the one passed down in our family. I wonder what else he has on these bookshelves.

"Just read?" I ask.

"Page 13," he repeats.

He sits back in his leather chair.

The title page of the book says it's "A History of 13th Century Masonry." But I tilt my head just so and look at the page with my peripheral vision. That's how I think of it, but Mom taught me that it's a technique of using your inner eye.

The real text is hidden, like a message written in lemon juice for grimoire girls like me.

213

I turn to page 13 and begin reading from the top:

"Lorem ipsum dolor sit amet, consectetur adipisicing elit, sed do eiusmod tempor incididunt ut labore et dolore magna aliqua."

That's not what I actually read, but that's what Headmaster Spengler probably hears. To people with no inherent magical ability, true words of power look and sound like gibberish.

The spell surges inside of me, and as I utter the final word, it releases. The air pops. I feel an immense pressure leave my chest and I'm briefly giddy and tingly all over, like taking an illicit sip of champagne.

I've just used a lot of magic. I should be exhausted, but I've already absorbed so much power from the mysterious source in the school, it's more like sprinting a short distance than running a marathon. I just don't know what the spell has done.

"Very good, Ms. Grahame. You may have a place here at Doheny after all. Ms. Costa, we have a promising new recruit."

"Sir?" Bristol says right behind me.

I jump from my chair and turn to see Bristol glaring at me. Her cheeks are flushed, her eyes are bright.

"My apologies for pulling you out of class." He smiles. "Ms. Grahame needs an escort. She has just tested into the advance classes, on a probationary basis."

"She summoned me here?" Bristol asks.

"And quite masterfully," he says. "I'll notify the office of her change in schedule. Now be off with you both."

Bristol stomps out of the office, but before I can join her, Headmaster Spengler calls me back.

"Ms. Grahame, books are never to leave this office," he says.

"Sorry." I'd forgotten I was carrying it. I put the heavy grimoire down on his desk. "Thank you. I won't let you down, sir."

"I should hope not. Now that you are enrolled in the advanced classes, I'm afraid that if you don't meet Doheny's high expectations, your magic will be stripped from you and redistributed among your classmates. Is that understood?" His dead eye seems to look through me.

I swallow. I nod. I feel the agreement bind me and my magic up in the school. Mom's going to be pissed that I agreed to this, but it's the only way—and it's not like I'm going to flunk out.

"And do be careful around Ms. Costa. I would appreciate you letting me know if you observe anything concerning about her."

"Absolutely, sir."

He nods. "Good day."

Bristol is waiting impatiently for me in the outer office. She starts off right away.

"How did you do that?" she asks. "We don't do translocation until next year."

"I just read the spell." I shrug. "What class are we heading to?"

"Nekomancy with Tanaka-sensei."

"Neko, as in the Japanese word for cat?" I ask.

"You've never heard of nekomancy?" That brightens her mood. "Harnessing the power of LOL cats?"

"You mean, those internet memes? 'Can Haz Cheeseburger' and all that? 'I'm in ur school, using ur spell'?"

She laughs. "Stop that."

Grimoires are simply collections of spells other people have come up with over the years and then written down. Any magic user can devise a spell from any unique combination of written words: books, the internet, the backs of cereal boxes. All it takes is focus, intent, and a reservoir of magical energy—either your own or an outside source.

So a spell is basically just a recipe. Someone tried it before, it worked, and they passed it on. But just like cooking, spells have varying results depending on the person following the directions and the quality of the recipe and ingredients. The equivalent of overcooking a turkey in the magical world is not pretty.

Contrary to what you see in movies, there aren't magical schools all over the world training magicians. If there were, do you think I'd be home schooled and driving around the country with my mom in a truck? In fact, it's very rare for any school to know about the mere existence of magic, let alone offer a course track in mastering it alongside regular students.

I'm also surprised they have enough students to fill those classes. Our kind of magic—and there are plenty of other ways to do magic—is typically passed down in families, from mother to daughter.

Out of 250 students, Doheny Preparatory Academy has 21 girls who can cast magic. They must be the source of the power I've been sensing.

"Here we are," Bristol says.

"Hold on. Those girls who disappeared. Were they in the advanced classes?" I ask.

She frowns. "Yeah. Lien and Marissa were in my classes."

"They were the top students, so I guess they were good at magic?"
"They were the best," she says.
And they still got caught.
Okay. Now I'm starting to worry.

* * *

"You just couldn't investigate without getting involved in a coven?" Mom asks.
"You hate the c-word." I push some stray grains of rice around on my plate with the wooden chopsticks.
Mom's summoned sushi from our favorite restaurant in Toronto again. We use magic to steal food and supplies occasionally—Mom figures the world owes us because we're helping to keep people safe, people who will never even know we exist—but meals from Blowfish are on the house. We killed an akkorokamui there, an octopus-like monster that got mixed in with the day's catch then caught the owner's daughter.
"I wouldn't call it a coven," I say.
"If this place was legit, I would have heard of it," she says.
"I'll be fine."
"How about that other c-word? Why do you get so competitive?"
"Schoolwork is who I am, Mom. I need something other than..." I wave my hand around the cheap hotel room that looks like every other hotel room I've lived in since I was eight. "Plus, if I'm right about Bristol taking out those girls, challenging her is the best way to force her hand. And if I'm wrong, I'll at least attract this supposed demon. Whatever it is, it's obviously drawn to magic."
"You'll have to do something big to get noticed if the school is as buzzy as you say it is."
"But if I do something too big, I'll be defenseless during the refractory period."
"Which is where I'll come in," Mom says.
"So I'm the bait. Again." I sigh. "Have you discovered anything that will help us?"
She sips sake from the bottle. "Actually, yes. Landon is an expert on local history, and particularly on Doheny Academy. He graduated from there last year."
Oh, Mom. "And we're sure he isn't an incubus. Or a djinn," I say.

"You keep bringing that up. He had a great pick up line."

"'Hey baby, rub my lamp, and your wish is my command'?"

"It sounded better when I was drunk."

"And what about the kappa?"

"He was a gentleman!"

"The pooka?"

"He was hung like a—"

"Never mind!" I say. "What did Landon tell you about the school?"

Mom puts down her chopsticks.

"It was founded in 1928 as a boys-only academy."

"Of course."

"At the time, Washington Depot was a hotbed of paranormal activity. The next three decades show reports of witch hunts, exorcisms, the works—especially around the local public high school. Until 1965."

"What happened then?" I ask.

"Doheny opened to girls. And those supernatural reports suddenly dropped off to almost nothing in September 1965. Just isolated incidents, the same you would find in any small town."

"So, they started training the girls to control their power, and the random magic events stop?" I say.

If I hadn't had Mom to teach me when I started conjuring characters from my favorite books at four, I probably would have ended up as a case for another hunter to clean up. We saw it all the time: Girls who had lost their mothers and didn't know they had powers, girls who didn't have anyone to show them how to read safely and not abuse their abilities.

"Then in June 1969, we have our first missing student. The class valedictorian."

"A girl?"

Mom nods.

"How do you know a disappearance more than 40 years ago is linked to this case?"

"Because it happened again in June 1973," she says. "Again the valedictorian, and again a girl."

"Four years later. Graduation!" I say. "What do you think? Ritual sacrifice? They made some devil's bargain to contain the magic?"

"Could be. But there any other missing students until June 1989: a boy, ranked 16th in his class."

"If they've been sacrificing students to demons, there wouldn't have

217

been such a gap. But that one doesn't fit the pattern. And we've just had two in the last year, both girls with the highest GPAs in the school."

"These advanced classes must be involved," Mom says. She picks up a piece of octopus and scrutinizes the severed tentacle before popping it into her mouth. "You have to question Bristol."

"Or warn her," I say.

* * *

I look for Bristol the next day, but she isn't in school. Her three minions tell me that she's never missed a day; the poor girls look completely lost without her. I get her cell phone number from them, but when I call, I only get her voice mail.

"I'm too late, Mom," I murmur into my Bluetooth earpiece, hidden under my hair. Cell phones aren't supposed to be used in the building, but that's not the only rule I plan to break today. "I'm changing the plan."

"What plan? What are you going to do?" she says.

"I'm going to look for her."

"She probably knew we were onto her and skipped town."

"Or she's in trouble." The bell rings and I duck into the women's restroom to wait for the halls to empty.

"You seem very protective of her. If she's been captured, you'll be this thing's next target."

"I'm counting on it," I say.

"I'm on my way," she says. "Don't do anything stupid."

Like cutting class and wandering the school alone, like we've all been warned not to do? This is who I am.

I walk around with my eReader, clicking through my favorite books and casting spells here and there. I'm leaving breadcrumbs, putting as much power into each spell as I can in order to draw the demon out. And I'm setting traps.

I read: "'When Charlotte's web said TERRIFIC, Wilbur had tried to look terrific.'"

A web springs up spanning the hallway behind me. The word "TERRIFIC" is written in the center of it—and I know that now I look terrific too.

In another hall, I read: "'And now that the web said RADIANT, he did everything possible to make himself glow.'"

A second web stretches across this hallway. My skin becomes luminescent, making me even more of a target.

These kinds of spells wouldn't necessarily work for other grimoire girls, because all my knowledge and passion for my favorite book is caught up in the magic. Children's classics work better for me than anything—strengthening my spells with nostalgia and the collective love they've accumulated over the decades. One caster we work with sometimes only uses the Quran. Mom once used *Fifty Shades of Grey* because there was nothing else on hand, with hilarious and unmentionable results.

I cast a finding spell and throw up more webs as I go, so the demon can't sneak up behind me, and I follow the magical buzzing to a row of lockers. There's something hidden here.

I settle on a reveal spell I've marked in The Lion, the Witch, and the Wardrobe.

"'Well, sir, if things are real, they're there all the time.' 'Are they?' said the Professor; and Peter did not quite know what to say."

Three adjacent lockers click open. I nudge the first locker door wider with a corner of my eReader.

"Oh no," I say. There's a body inside in a Doheny skirt, with a crimson scarf wrapped around her neck.

I recognize her as Lien, Rowan's girlfriend. She was the first to disappear. I open the locker next to her and find Marissa, wearing a puffy winter jacket.

They've been here for months. Somehow they're still alive, just barely. But no magic remains in the two grimoire girls, not the tiniest drop of it. And that shouldn't be, especially with all the magic coursing around us. They should be soaking it up like sponges, but instead they're just conduits for it—transferring the power elsewhere. What had done this to them?

I'm almost too afraid to look in the third locker. I catch a whiff of vanilla and incense from the cracked open door.

As I reach for it with a trembling hand, I hear a vicious bellow from behind me. I race back to my last web and see something has gotten caught in the HUMBLE web.

I laugh. I've caught a B-movie version of a demon; it has a big horned head made out of papier-mâché, a felt body suit, and a flaccid tail dragging on the floor. This couldn't fool anyone, but it was enough to hang a simple glamour on, which I've just stripped away with my revealing spell.

"Grrr... Argh!" it says. It flails its arms menacingly.

I laugh again.

"You aren't scared?" it says in a deep voice.

I read: "So, to punish it, she held it up to the Looking-glass, that it might see how sulky it was—'and if you're not good directly,' she added, 'I'll put you through into Looking-glass House. How would you like THAT?'"

A large mirror appears in front of the "demon."

"Oh," it says, when it catches its reflection.

I pull off its mask then drop it in surprise.

"Bristol?" I say.

She presses gloved hands to her chest. Her eyes widen and she grins.

"You're the demon?" I ask.

"And I would have gotten away with it, too," she says. "If not for your meddling."

"I can't believe I was worried about you." I pull my bottle from my backpack and splash her in the face with holy water. Just to be sure.

She splutters and blinks the water from her eyes. She licks her lips.

"I'm not really a demon. Except in bed." She winks. "You look terrific, by the way."

"Ignore that. It's just a side effect of a spell," I say.

"And you're humble, too." She pulls against the strands of web holding her.

"Why the goofy costume?" I kick her papier-mâché demon head down the hall. It bounces and gets stuck in SOME PIG.

"I was just having some fun. Get me free, will you?" she says.

I sigh. I hate it when humans turn out to be the monsters behind the crimes. It's more difficult to justify killing them.

I tug her out of the web and she tumbles into my arms. Her elbow bumps my eReader to the ground. Then she steps on it. It crunches under her shiny black Oxford shoe.

"Oops," she says.

I step away and narrow my eyes. I stare at her shoes. Something isn't right.

"The thing that surprises me most is that you used such a basic glamour," I say. "Beginner level stuff."

She tears off the rest of her demon disguise and tosses her hair out

220

of her eyes. Underneath, she's wearing a slightly rumpled boy's button-down shirt, slacks, and a loose tie. Even though the uniform is too big for her, she's totally working the cross-dressing.

Then I remember why I'm here. I ready myself for a fight, but without words to work with, we're both equally powerless. Just reciting a spell from memory isn't enough. You have to read it.

I casually reach up and tap a button on my earpiece to redial my Mom. She answers on the first ring.

"Lexi? Are you all right?"

Bristol starts rolling up the cuffs of her shirt and I see she has a trick up her sleeve: Her arms are tattooed with words. Not quotes from children's books, but words of real, ancient power. Lorem ipsumy words. She's got a freaking grimoire printed on her body.

That is so hot.

Two can play this game. I loosen my tie and tear my blouse open. She pauses to appreciate the view, which gives me the moment I need. See, I have a trick up my sleeve too. Well, not my sleeve.

I pull a thin scroll of paper from my bra; it has copies of some of my more powerful spells. On a hunch, I pick out another reveal spell and quickly read it.

"'That is the Princess Ozma—the child brought to me by the Wizard who stole her father's throne. That is the rightful ruler of the Emerald City!' And she pointed her long bony finger straight at the boy."

I point at Bristol and her form shimmers, revealing...

"Rowan!" I say. "But that's impossible. Boys can't use magic."

"Only because you weren't sharing. Until now." He touches his flat chest. "That was weird. Sometimes more than just magic gets transferred from the host."

"The bodies in the lockers... They're somehow relaying power to you?" I say.

"Uh oh. That's not good," Mom says in my ear. "I'm almost there, kiddo. Keep him busy."

"You've been taking their magic," I say.

"Borrowing," he says. "Not that I'm one to kiss and tell, but Lien and I accidentally discovered that it's possible to give a person like me a temporary magical charge. That gave her the idea to use my body to store some of it for her. She found the absorption spell in Spengler's office and set up a permanent link between us."

221

"Why would she do that? Love?"

He laughs. "Maybe. We were using each other. I helped her with her problem, and she helped me with mine."

"Seems like you were her only problem."

Rowan lifts his arm and mutters, "Excepteur sint occaecat cupidatat non proident!"

A mini-tornado tears through the hall and around me, clearing Charlotte's webs and tearing my crib sheet out of my hands.

Now I'm in trouble.

I grab the nail file from my sock and slide it into my sleeve; the dead man's blood won't do anything to Rowan except cause an infection maybe, but it'll hurt like hell. Bonus if I can stab him in the eyes so he can't read anymore.

The wind dies down as Rowan walks through it toward me, looking over his arms for just the right phrase. I back away, but he murmurs something—"anim id est laborum"—and my feet are firmly rooted to the checkered tiles on the floor.

"Lien was under a lot of pressure, on the verge of a nervous breakdown. She was overwhelmed with all that magic," Rowan says. "She couldn't handle any more. And if the top student in the school loses it, then we all lose."

Rowan walks around me slowly.

"How's that?" I ask.

"Bristol didn't tell you?" Rowan laughs. "No, she wouldn't. She loved being class president. See, the top spellcaster at Doheny has to draw in excess magic from the less experienced students. She stores it until they're able to use it responsibly."

"Until graduation," I say.

"So that's how they manage the magic," Mom says. I jump. I'd forgotten she's listening. "They handicap the other girls to lower the risk if something goes wrong in their training."

Rowan leans close to my face and tilts his head to listen. "It's rude to eavesdrop." He plucks the Bluetooth earpiece from my ear and disconnects the call. "Who were you talking to?"

"My mom. She's always interested in what I learn at school. So you were saying... What happens if someone loses control of the magic?"

I think I already know the answer.

"All the power releases at once and poof! Now you see her, now you don't," he says.

That could explain the missing girls from 1969 and 1973.

"So Lien linked up with you and siphoned off some of the magic," I say.

"A lot of it. And once I was able to finally cast spells, I decided to take all of her magic."

"How did you get Marissa and Bristol?" I ask.

"Lien and I are still connected, so I used her spell to link their magic to her. And through her to me."

"Like a series of batteries," I say.

I follow him with my eyes as he walks behind me. It makes me nervous when I can't see him.

"You're addicted," I say. I try to lift one foot, then the other. My shoes are stuck fast, but my feet slide a little in my too-large thrift store shoes. "This is why boys aren't supposed to have magic. Because you're idiots."

My cell phone beeps in the side pocket of my backpack. Rowan reaches for it.

Here goes.

My nail file drops into my waiting hand and I stab at him. He bellows. I slide my feet out of my shoes and run down the hall in my socks. The funny thing about these spells is they're awfully literal.

As I run down the hall, I grab my phone and check Mom's text message.

Is he still monologuing?

"Mom!"

Beep. I'm in the headmaster's office. Nice library.

I get to the end of the hall and realize I've run past the exit and am now trapped.

Rowan rounds the corner, filing his nails with my nail file. The right side of his shirt is bloody.

He mutters something and throws my nail file at me like a dart. The tiny silver missile flies toward my face. I flinch and hold up my right arm over my eyes.

And my bracelet deflects the blade like I'm freaking Wonder Woman.

Protection spell for the win! We both stare in shock for a moment as the bent nail file clatters to the tiles.

My phone beeps again. I glance at the text on its screen.

Then I smile and raise my phone as he raises his arm. And we start reading.

"*Sed ut perspiciatis unde omnis iste natus error sit voluptatem accusantium doloremque laudantium...*"

"*Sed ut perspiciatis unde omnis iste natus error sit voluptatem accusantium doloremque laudantium...*"

We're reading the same passage, I realize. Panic shows in Rowan's face. He starts to stumble over his words. Amateur.

I'm more experienced and a slightly faster reader.

His power slams into me, fills me completely, my whole body humming with the magic of 20 hormonal grimoire girls. I'm tempted to hold onto it all, but I know what the danger is. I'm glad that I've taken my shoes off, because I grit my teeth and channel most of the power back into the stones of Doheny itself, like a lightning rod.

For one, two, three beats, the walls vibrate in harmony with me—briefly alive. The power will disperse as it leaves the building, and who knows what chaos it will cause.

Rowan is right. It feels flipping amazing.

I hold back some power, so I have something to give back to the students when they graduate. Enough to maybe revive Bristol and the other girls. And there's plenty left to make sure that Rowan will never do anything like this again.

* * *

Mom pulls into the driveway in front of Doheny Prep. Things are finally settling into a new normal on campus. Fortunately, the school has excellent insurance coverage.

"You really want to stick around here for another three years?" Mom asks.

"I have to," I say. "I'm the repository for the students' magic now." Some days it's all I can do to control it on my own.

"I never imagined you as a queen bee, but you're doing a pretty good job."

"I never imagined you as a dean at my prep school, but we all have a lot to get used to."

Mom had been amazing at managing the aftermath of my little stunt. Most of the school didn't even notice the jungle that had erupted around the building. The only thing she hadn't fixed were the walls inside, which were now all bright yellow—my favorite color. We both agree it's more cheerful this way.

"I suppose there's plenty to keep us busy for a while, since someone had to go and unleash untold magical energy on the unsuspecting population of Washington Depot."

So I still can't give up the training and the late nights, because of all the demons that are being attracted to the town like a moth to flame, not to mention all the other magical things born from the combination of undirected magic and my active imagination. (Really, please don't mention them. Every time we run into one on patrol, Mom calls out, "It's one of yours!")

But I find I don't mind all that, because we have a little house now, and mom promises to jack me a new car the next time she's in New York, and for the first time in a long time, I have real friends.

"Well, see you in there," I say.

I climb out of the car and one of my minions takes my backpack. The other one takes my rifle.

I'm queen bee and the new class president. I make the rules, and no one can argue with the usefulness of a weapon when the undead sometimes show up to register for continuing education classes. We all have a lot to get used to.

Mom drives around to the faculty parking lot. Doheny finally has someone who knows what she's doing, and she isn't so embarrassing to me anymore.

"Hey, babe." Bristol sidles up and kisses me.

"B, not in front of... " I roll my eyes at the angel statue in front of the school. Today it's flashing both middle fingers. It takes the stone figure all night to change positions.

Bristol shudders. "So creepy. No offense, Rowan."

This year, Doheny has only lost one student, Rowan Frost, the boy who caused this whole mess. It's small punishment compared to Bristol, Marissa, and Lien completely losing their magic, like batteries that can no longer be recharged. But I'm working on that. And I'm going to let him out of the statue one day.

Probably.

I pull Bristol out of the angel's line of sight, and this time I kiss her. I slip a little magic into it and she shivers and sighs.

She may not be a grimoire girl anymore, but she's still brilliant and beautiful. And she's especially stunning in a boy's uniform.

Like I said, I make the rules. Doheny students can now wear boy or girl uniforms. And pants are definitely the way to go if you're serious about hunting. You can carry so many more weapons and spells when you have pockets.

I tuck my new eReader into my back pocket—now spelled to be indestructible—take Bristol's hand, and we go to class.

The Cost of Being Caelan

By Scarlett Ward

The house I stood outside was frozen in perpetual decay, the walls scorched, and its foundations shaky. It was like it was falling down but could never quite finish its descent: stuck between broken and whole. The front garden was more like a small jungle, the grass impossibly high and choked with weeds, while vines and ivy grew upwards, declaring war on the walls of the house.

I knocked on the door. I'd never done anything so brave, or so stupid, in my entire life.

I flinched as the door opened, but I wasn't faced with the monster I'd expected. Her skin was dark and wrinkled, her eyes hollow, and she looked more vulnerable than any villain had the right to appear. An old knitted jumper hung around her, too baggy by far, but sensible considering the season. She looked like someone's lonely grandma, not an immortal witch from the dawn of man.

"I don't bargain with children." She snapped. "They don't know what informed consent means. Go away."

"I know what informed consent means." I frowned, offended despite my wariness. "I'm 15."

She laughed. "And I predate the concept of adolescence. Get out."

"I don't want to bargain with you." I said quickly. "I already have magic."

"Then what?" Her eyes narrowed and the air between us burnt, her magic crackling around me. "Did you decide to seek out the Witch of the Woods for fun? To have something to brag about?"

I swallowed, ignoring my trembling knees. "I was hoping you'd teach me how to use it. The magic."

She scowled. "I don't want an apprentice."

"No one does these days." I said. "All the boarding schools have ridiculous fees and gendered dorms."

She smiled, revealing pointed teeth. "You were rejected by lesser wizards so you came to a Mother of all Magic, known for turning annoying little boys like you into toads, and thought you'd be welcome?"

I tried not to squirm under her gaze. "Well, yeah, when you put it like that it sounds stupid. But I'm not a boy."

"Doesn't make a difference to a toad." She said, but didn't make me vanish in a haze of smoke. "What do you want to be called?"

"Caelan? I use they, instead of he or she, no matter what I look like at the time." I hesitated, but she seemed to appreciate honesty, so I added, "I thought you'd be a traditionalist."

"I lived to see tradition born and my shape is more malleable than yours. You think I've always called myself a witch?" she scoffed. "Are you sure you're here to beg teaching? I can't change anyone's perception of you, you'll need my sister's magic for that, but I can change your physical form to whatever you like. It'll cost." She smiled again, something hungry in her eyes. "It always costs."

"I'm a shape-shifter; I can do that myself." I said, and instantly regretted sounding so dismissive.

Her eyes narrowed. "What kind?"

"The generic one?" I ventured. "I can change into lots of things, with practice, I was hoping you'd shed some light on the limits."

Her mouth set in a thin line. For a moment, her disguise of humanity slipped, and I caught sight of what seethed beneath it, the wolf under the grandma's skin. She stepped aside. "You'd better come in."

Fortunately, the inside of her house was nowhere near as dilapidated as the outside. The air inside was stale and dead, and the walls were a sickly shade of green, but that seemed to be a design choice, not centuries of mold. Her living room was messy but devoid of character, thrown together without much care and holding nothing of value. A house that was lived in, not loved.

"What am I meant to call you?" I asked, since she'd given me the same courtesy. "The Witch of the Woods? Mother of us all?"

"Morrigan will do."

A cage of mice caught my attention. I ran over to them, crouching to see them better, caution forgotten. "They're cute! What are they called?"

"Alan Cross, Terrence Davison and Harvey Mills."

I blinked. "Kind of weird names for mice."

"Oh, I didn't name them."

I paused, watching the little rodents scrabbling through wood shavings with muted horror. "Are they... Were they people?"

"They asked for immortality and said they'd pay anything. They didn't specify what they wanted to live forever as." She shrugged. "Never give me a blank cheque. I can't resist damning someone with their own words."

"I'll keep that in mind." I said, turning back to her, this time with all the caution and wariness she deserved.

"Why are you so desperate to have a tutor?"

"I ran away from home." I said, dreading the inevitable next question. I didn't want to talk any further about my gender or, rather, my lack of it. It didn't come.

"You might think that living with me would offer you protection. The Witch of the Dawn will take you and make you hers if she finds you. She's devoted an impressive amount of her life to ruining mine and I can't lift a hand against her."

"Um." I said. "I heard there was a rivalry, but aren't you sisters? I thought it was, like, friendly rivalry."

She laughed, the sound like rattling bones. "Once, perhaps. We were given the first magic in the world and she became a monster. Dawn must have missed the time when we did everything together, because she made me into one as well. She's why I spend my life making bargains."

"You don't actually want to be a lonely hermit buying people's souls?" I blurted out and then blanched, eyes going to the mice. There was room in the cage for a fourth. "I didn't mean that. Old ladies can live alone without being lonely—" I stopped, before I could dig myself any deeper into the hole.

"I've never asked for someone's soul." She said, raising an eyebrow. "I suggest you learn the value of tact, before someone less amused than I teaches you the lesson far more harshly. Do you think this is what I wanted my profession to be, cutting off parts of myself for every fool who finds my door and knows my name?"

"You can't stop?"

"Whatever force or twist of nature set the rules didn't leave a complaints box. I can't fucking resign."

"Oh." I said, quietly, and thought over my words more carefully. "Doesn't the Witch of the Dawn have to do the same?"

"She gets to choose who she gives her gifts to. The rules said we couldn't kill each other, that the day and night had to be balanced, but she found a loophole. She destroyed those dear to me, knowing that I would attack her for it, since she's never loved anything that couldn't be replaced. This is my punishment."

"Oh." I said, anything else I had to say seeming insignificant in comparison. "So, if she comes after me, I should just start digging my own grave?"

"She can't lie. Neither can I, it's against the rules. Ask her the right questions." She said. "There are rules you have to follow too. Don't run. Don't lie. Don't look behind you."

"Running sounds like it'd be a good idea."

"Predators chase." She shrugged. "Feel free to avoid my advice. I always need material for cautionary tales."

A pregnant silence fell between us, until Morrigan said, "You have another question for me, I can tell. Spit it out."

"Do you have to charge so highly?" I asked, carefully. "All the kids with magic that I know, they inherited it. They didn't seek you out, they didn't get a choice, but they still pay its price. It's not fair."

"I never claimed it was fair. There's always a cost, there has to be. I'm the villain, the monster at the end of the story, all because I make people pay a price for what they want? I don't think that's fair either." She shrugged again, resigned to it all. "That's the way of things."

I felt like I should say something more, after she'd shared such a personal story, one that must be secret- it wasn't in any of the books about the history of magic, though, maybe she'd just never had someone willing to listen. "My father always used my magic for his own purposes, and I always let him, no matter how petty it was. If I had to do that kind of thing on your scale, I can see how it would suck. Why you wouldn't want to have much to do with anyone."

"Yeah." She said, an odd, unreadable expression settling over her face. "You can be my apprentice. I won't charge- I'm grouchy as hell most of the time, that's cost enough. It's been a long time since I've had a child around."

"Good thing I'm not a child."

"If you ever wake me up before dusk again I reserve the right to turn you into a mouse." She continued, as if I hadn't spoken. "I'm nocturnal."

"Right." I said. "Should have guessed."

Father had never told me what he'd paid for his magic, though it was so weak I wasn't even sure what it was. From the way he counted days and feared every new year, I'd always been sure he'd paid with decades of his life, that his end was drawing near. He must have really pissed her off.

Usually, the bigger the magic, the higher the cost. The extent of my shapeshifting had terrified me since I was old enough to understand the maths. It was hard to feel like you had your whole life ahead of you, when you might not make it to adulthood. If anyone knew what the cost of my magic- her magic, really- was, it would be Morrigan.

I opened my mouth to ask, but something made me let the words die in my throat. Maybe ignorance is bliss.

* * *

I stood at the edge of the sea, four shells clutched in my hand. Morrigan had asked for five shells, one from each side of the beach, and using fairy-tale logic, the sea had to be the fifth side. When she'd asked me to run errands for her, I thought it'd be nothing more than getting the groceries from Lidl.

Resigned to getting wet, my magic rose around me, tasting of ash and smoke. I'd never tried gills before so I wouldn't know if there was a problem until I was already drowning but I pushed past my hesitation, throwing myself into the sea, a mermaid by the time I hit the water.

Mermaids were a popular choice, as far as gifts of magic went. I don't know why we call them gifts, when they always cost, even if they're not the kind you pay with currency. I guess magic predated capitalism. Morrigan barely needed to charge to make it a double-edged sword- the magic weakened with every generation and the children of mermaids could easily end up belonging to a sea that only knew how to drown them.

Fortunately, drowning didn't seem to be a problem for me. Holding my breath wasn't uncomfortable, I was getting oxygen another way, but my mind didn't have the right frame of reference to feel it, let alone describe it. My neck and ribs itched- they had to be where the gills had appeared, but scratching the things currently letting me respire registered as a bad idea.

I found a conch shell in a bed of coral and kicked my tail, propelling myself up until I broke the surface. The splash I caused hit someone I hadn't noticed. I turned to apologize, finding myself staring at a pretty Asian girl with warm skin that blended into the startling patterns of a koi. The mermaids in the illustrations I'd based myself of had been thin, fragile things, and I was beginning to wonder if the artists had ever actually seen a mermaid.

Her arms were toned and brawny and she was chubby instead of thin and ethereal. Really, it made more sense. If I had to swim to get everywhere, I'd probably have killer muscles too, and there had to be an evolutionary advantage to having extra layers of fat when half your body was covered in impractical skin.

"Are you skipping?" she asked, her tone brash, but familiar, as if I were a friend and not a stranger who'd just doused her in water. If she noticed that I was some kind of overly idealized merman, she didn't seem to care.

"Are you?"

She grinned. "Hey, a girl's got to have a day off, right? I've just finished my winter solstice exams, no idea how I'm going to survive another 20 years of this."

I wasn't sure what mermaids learnt in whatever version of school they had in the sea- were there really enough things to learn about swimming to justify a 20-year curriculum? But some things that had to be universal. "The homework's the worst."

"Tell it, brother." She said, unaware of how her casual words sent a wave of discomfort through me. Gendered words never fit right but, more than that, I'd never be even a cousin of hers, no matter how often I wore a tail and breathed through gills. "I'm Maia."

Before I could reply, a horse plunged out of the water, startling me into falling back with a splash. It had a mane of wet kelp, bulging gold eyes and legs that ended where they met the water, fur and muscle blending into seafoam.

Maia gave me an odd look. "Haven't you ever seen a kelpie before?"

The kelpie neighed, pawing the waves with hooves that existed only when it wanted them to, and bowed low in front of me. It was beautiful, it was the sea given form, and it wanted me to ride it?

Maia pulled me back before I realized I'd moved, stopping my hand from reaching its seaweed mane. "Why's it want you to ride? It's not like you'd drown."

"Maybe it's bored." I said, looking away before jumping on to it could start to look like a good idea again.

"Drowning is their solution to boredom."

I risked looking back. It had gone, leaving nothing but fog and mist in its wake, not a corpse as it had hoped to. The first rays of the sun were filtering through, dancing over the waves and making my tail feel like an uncomfortable costume stretched taut around legs I didn't currently have.

"I have to go." I said, starting to float in the direction of the shore.

"This is a cliché. A mysterious merman who I've never seen before flees from kelpies and daylight?" She giggled, the sound reminding me of the high-pitched laughter of a dolphin. "Do you transform into something terrible at dawn?"

"Something like that."

Sometime later, I pulled myself on to the sand, with my scales itching and the gills feeling like unwelcome scabs. I closed my eyes and changed, not putting much thought in what I was shifting into. Shifting is about intent, Morrigan had said. It was hard to have intent when I wasn't sure what I wanted to be.

I coughed, trying to get the taste of ash and salt-water out of my mouth as I stumbled back onto my feet. I glanced down at myself in vague curiosity, finding that the form I'd ended up in wasn't going to be mistaken for a man anytime soon.

"Seriously?" I asked the waves. "I was half-fish a second ago and this is what I'm focusing on, whether or not I have breasts?" The sea, unsurprisingly, didn't have any pearls of wisdom about puberty, magical or otherwise.

* * *

Morrigan's title was a bit of a misnomer. Forgotten woods were the place people expected to find her in, near faerie rings, ancient hills and hawthorn trees. Fewer people thought to look for her in London, especially on a street that looked so poverty-struck that gentrification would never be a problem for its inhabitants. Her home looked a bit out of place amongst all the council flats but the locals must have assumed it to be a remnant of some ancient past when houses had been affordable.

This time, when I knocked on the door, she was waiting for me. "You're late." She snapped, snatching the shells from my hand. "And wet."

233

"I went swimming with a mermaid." I said. "I didn't realize I had a curfew."

"You don't, but your dinner went cold."

I followed her inside, finding a roast dinner on the table, the kind that took ages to cook even with magic. "No one's going to believe the Witch of the Woods scolds me for being late to dinner." I grinned.

"I'm still on the fence about turning you into a toad." She said, dryly.

I sat down, immediately spearing a piece of stuffing with a fork. "Couldn't I just turn myself back?"

She smirked. "You could try."

The stuffing was surprisingly good, considering it was cold. "Does it take 1,000 years to learn how to cook the perfect roast?"

"Flattery will get you nowhere." She said but waved a hand, the burning scent of her magic rising up, choking the room, and leaving the food piping hot again.

"Cool!" I said, pouring warm gravy all over it. "There aren't any exams I should be studying for, right?"

"I don't do exams. You're going to be graded on how long you survive, how many people you turn into mice, how many firstborn children you steal, and how many bees you befriend. The classic stuff."

I blinked. "You can't befriend bees. Wait, can you? Are bees sentient?"

"I foresee a lot of Fs in your future." She shrugged, leaving me to mull over a new problem as I demolished my Yorkshires- where one was likely to find bees. "What did you think of the mermaids?"

"I only met one. And a kelpie. I almost got on its back." I said as I stabbed my last potato. "I don't think it could have drowned me but it was going to do its best. I don't recommend a holiday, there's too many opportunities to drown."

She snorted. "What makes you think the land's any safer?"

"Optimism?"

"I'll endeavor to crush that out of you." She said. "To start with, you can do some reading on the many land creatures that'll be happy to try and kill you."

"Fine." I groaned and promptly shut up before I could get myself into any more homework.

* * *

Back in my room, I reluctantly heaved one of the books I'd supposedly already read onto my lap. Had no one bothered to write a modern version with bad jokes and puns yet? If someone had just gone and written 'Shapeshifting for Dummies`, I'd be set.

I looked up to the sound of my door opening, finding a skeptical Morrigan watching me. "That's the first time you've read any of that, isn't it?"

"I looked at the pictures?" I offered. "I wouldn't have procrastinated on it if you'd warned me about needing to swim. Okay, I'd probably still have procrastinated, but I'd have been forewarned about it!"

"What would be the fun in that?" She tossed a bracelet into my lap.

I put it on, bemused. The shells I'd collected for her were woven into it. "That was all for jewelry?"

"It's more than that. I'd ask for pints of your blood for a trinket like that if you asked for it." She snapped. "Put it on every time you leave the house and it'll protect you, as much as sea-shells can."

"Protect me from what?" I asked, but she'd already left the room. "Is being vague and cryptic a contractual obligation, or do you just get a kick out of it?"

After glaring at the closed door for a moment, I examined the gift in more detail. The one I'd had to shift to find was the nicest of them, its smooth insides coloured pink that faded to pearly white around the edges.

I lifted it to my ear, pretending it was the sea I could hear and not the sound of my own room reflected back at me. A trace of Morrigan's magic had settled on it, wildfire warring with the lingering scent of sea-salt, but what really convinced me it had been made magic, into something more than reason could explain, was the faint giggle of the pretty girl I'd lied to, rising above the sound of a false sea.

* * *

Every night, the shadows became alive with cats. London's rooftops and chimneys had long ago been claimed as Cat Country, and they reclaimed it every evening. For them, reclaiming seemed to mostly consist of either sleeping or doing impressive, if dangerous, acrobatic feats. I could join in, if I was willing to lie.

This time, I'd studied cat physiology beforehand but I'd studied the eyes in such detail that it was possible I was going to end up with perfectly functioning tapetum lucidum and missing something more crucial, like fur.

Fortunately, when I padded to the mirror, I found an ordinary black cat staring back at me. Satisfied, I jumped onto my windowsill and started my ascent.

Human eyes would have barely seen anything, unless they were moving. Even I had to squint before I noticed the tabbies blending in with the brickwork or the tortoiseshells that almost sunk into the skyline.

They were almost all normal cats, intelligent, but not conversationalists, at least not in a language I could understand. Cat-wizards were common enough but most had only their grace or their ears or their claws. Only a few could shift from human to cat and back again, and they declared themselves King or Queen over all the others. I didn't particularly want to call myself either but monarch of cats just doesn't have the same ring to it.

One cat stood out from all the rest- her white pelt was bathed in moonlight and magic danced around her like a crown. Perhaps mine did the same, for she bounded to my side, recognizing me for what I appeared to be. Her magic smelled like marigold flowers, pleasant to taste, unlike the ashy scent of my magic, or the wildfire that was Morrigan's.

For cats, fighting was a dance, even when claws were unsheathed, but our dance was playful, free of blood, of everything but the urge to test our limits while we were young and free. Feline grace was new to me but as natural to her as breathing and it took no more than a minute before she had me pinned.

"I've never seen you before." She said primly, her accent as proper as the human Queen's, "I thought I knew every other Princess of Cats in London."

"Maybe I'm not a Princess." I said, as she released me. Up close, I could see she wasn't purely white- three lone black hairs stood out on her chest. "Is that like, the cat version of a tattoo?"

She licked the black hairs flat, almost self-consciously, ears flicking forward. "It's the mark of a royal cat, or so my mother says. Don't you have one?"

Well, now I did. I curled my tail forward for her to see, which was now tipped with three single white hairs. "We match."

She appraised me for a moment, a museum exhibit on how to look royal. Then, she came to life, aloofness replaced with mischief and a wildness so fierce that I wondered if cats remembered their all their lives, even the ones where they might have been lionesses or leopards or, more realistically, wild cats on Scottish moors. "Catch me if you can!" she crowed and darted away.

We were moonlight and midnight, chasing and being caught, winning and losing, all at once. We dared each other to jump further and further, from roof to roof, spurred on by the quasi-immortality promised to all cats, except pretenders like me.

Like anything wonderful, it had to end. The Princess grew weary, and so did I, both of us slowing down until our games weren't games at all, but quests for a spot to sleep in. "I'm Primrose." She said, as if the introduction wasn't at all belated. "You can call me Rose."

"I'm Caelan." I said. "No one's shortened it before, but you're free to try."

"Cay could work." She said sleepily, curling up and dozing off.

I didn't join her, the withering night setting me on edge. Soon enough, the world around us was shot through with sunlight, leaving a human girl lying next to me, the faint scent of marigold clinging to her. No other trace of her feline form remained and she'd be human again until the day died.

While my transformation hadn't been stripped away, the weight of dawn hung heavy around my magic and the body felt borrowed, the gracefulness stolen, none of it my own. I let the dawn chase me away before she woke, like Cinderella fleeing before her glass slippers melted beneath her.

* * *

I spent the rest of the day downstairs, switching between napping and sulking until dusk brought Morrigan out of her room.

"What was it, then?" she asked. "Did the little kitties not want to play?"

I stared at her. "Were you spying on me?"

"No, there's cat hair everywhere and you're predictable."

"I made a friend." I said. "But only because she thinks I'm the same as her."

"You might not be as lonely as you think," she said, sounding bored by my teenage angst, "if you told the truth."

"Yeah, look how well that worked out for you." I shot back and winced, this time because it was cruel, not because she might turn me into a mouse. "I just— I mean— I want to belong somewhere, I don't want to just exist in the spaces in-between. Is that my cost? Was belonging the cost of my magic?"

"No." She said, all the harshness gone from her voice. "You belong, even if you don't realize it yet."

"Then what? Am I going to die from pricking my finger on a needle on my next birthday? Do you think I'll hate you for it, if I know what it is?"

"Don't." She hissed. "Don't make me tell you."

The temptation of knowledge was too much to resist. It was about me, it was my life, didn't I have a right to it? "What is it? What did you charge?"

Her eyes went dark from side to side, all the humanity seeping out of her. "Your magic isn't your own," she began, every word sounding like it was being pulled out of her unwillingly. "If someone wants the tail of a fish, or the ears of a cat, or to turn their enemies into a swarm of bees, you must name your price. If someone wants your most treasured possession, your death, your child, you must name your price."

Time seemed to slow to a stop. I couldn't think about what it meant for my future, all I could do was focus on the part that had nothing to do with me. "Why don't you make that the price for everything? If there were 100 people who could give magic out, you could retire."

"That's against the rules. Who do you think you inherited it from?"

It couldn't be my father, he'd never given anything to anyone. My mother... I tried to speak but choked on the words.

"I said you belonged." She hadn't raised her voice but her words were like thunder, drowning out everything else.

"Didn't you want me?" I managed, finally, my voice small and vulnerable. "Didn't you want to keep me?"

"What I want never matters." She snarled. "Don't you listen? That's the price I pay. That's what you'll pay."

I backed away from her, gravitating towards the door without thinking.

"Are you going to run away again?" she hissed. "You're going to run out of places to run to."

I slammed the door behind me, running until I was lost.

* * *

My anger had fizzled out, leaving me with only horror, for what my father had done, and disgust, for myself, for owing my existence to his greed and entitlement.

"Are you alright, dear?"

I looked up to find a kindly looking woman staring at me, her hair honey-gold and her eyes sun-bright, the Summer incarnate. Olive leaves and roses crowned her head, but the flower crown somehow didn't make her look out of place, nor did she look like your average hipster. She was the kind of person you might wish were your mother, if your own was absent or otherwise wanting.

My sea-shell bracelet started to burn, jolting me out of my thoughts. I ripped it off and it cooled instantly, but left an angry red mark around my wrist. If Morrigan was using it to deliberately hurt me, I was going to do something dramatic, like throwing it into the sea.

"You don't want that, dear." Said the nice lady. "It's broken."

The bracelet did look scorched now, the thread frayed and twisted, but something about her words sent a chill through my spine. I put it back on, caution overtaking my petty impulse. It went hot again, this time magic rising with it, burning through the lady's illusion.

Just for a second, I saw her for what she really was- something ancient, wild and terrible, a monster from the dawn of man. She was beyond pale, her skin devoid of all pigment, with eyes that followed movement like a predator, and she was beautiful, but it was a cold, inhuman beauty.

The moment ran out and her lies returned. I clung to the memory, now that my eyes and every other sense was telling me that she was nothing but sweetness and roses. She was a rose, perhaps, but one that was more thorn than flower.

"You're the Witch of the Dawn." I said, with dreadful certainty. The illusion she'd spun around my bracelet fell away, showing it to be intact and unbroken.

"Indeed." She smiled. "You say that like it's a bad thing. Do you think you're above a Mother of Magic? Your parentage doesn't make you a Chosen One, dear, it makes you a monster."

"I know." I said, slowly backing away. She'd take me as hers, remake me into something she could tolerate, and throw me away when she got bored, all to spite her sister. For all the centuries she'd lived, it struck me that she'd never quite grown up.

"Are you looking for a teacher?"

I swallowed. Don't lie. Don't look back. Don't run. "I have one."

"Are you looking for a mother?"

"I have one of those too."

"I'd be better. My sister's all darkness and dead, ruined things. I've never understood it. You're shape-shifters, you could be anything you wanted, why do you choose to be beastly? Don't you want to walk in the light?"

The scent of her rosy magic was overpowering, like she'd emptied several bottles of terrible perfume. Wouldn't it be nice to walk on the beach at day, to have the light touch my skin without making my body feel like a lie? To live somewhere I could show Primrose without horror or judgment?

"All you have to say is yes." She said, her voice honey-sweet.

"To what?" I asked, trying to blink my sudden light-headedness away.

"Being mine."

I didn't answer. My arm started to itch, and when I looked down, the skin was crumbling away, leaving only rotted bone, like I had already been dead for centuries.

"Stop it!" I started to scratch at it, my nails sharpening enough that I tore through real skin, leaving it bloody and stinging. She didn't give people a choice, not really, she stole it from them with illusions and falsehoods. She couldn't lie, but she could make the world around me a lie, and that was worse. "Please!"

"Nothing's happening to you, darling. You're just the same underneath it all." She said, her tone completely unchanged. "I'm just showing you there's more ways to change yourself than through shifting."

She was distorting my body but that was something I'd always had control over. My eyes turned hawk-like and my hands curled into talons, making myself into something beastly, because she took beautiful things and made them her own. I smiled at her, revealing a set of bird-like teeth, sharp and small.

"Is that your choice?" she hissed, a crack in her façade.

The shells went cold around my wrist, the sensation pressing around me like fear. "Yes."

I walked past her. Something urged me to turn around, to look back at her, a thousand times stronger than the impulse to mount the kelpie had been. I couldn't feel the seashells anymore, all I had was my own resolve.

I didn't look back.

* * *

I hadn't been so lost that I couldn't find my way home, I'd just needed to try. As sheepish as I felt, slipping back into the house without a word, I didn't know what to say to mend things between us. Before I could gather up the courage to seek her out, there was a knock at the door.

Not opening the door to strangers was, strangely, not one of the many cautionary rules Morrigan had given me, presumably because talking to strangers that wanted to take pieces of me away was the only job I was destined to have.

A man crowned with golden curls of hair waited outside. "I'm here to bargain with the Witch of the Woods." He said the words like they were a ritual, one that held its power even now, which was perhaps why he was so bold.

"You people can't stay away, can you?" I said, letting the ghost of a snarl creep into my voice. "All you have to do is stop asking."

"We never stop needing magic." He said, carefully. "I know the rules, you can't hurt me."

I grinned. "Sure, but I'm not the Witch of the Woods. I'm Caelan. Are you looking for me?"

He checked his surroundings, making sure he had the right ruin of a house. "No, but everyone says she's here." He turned a smile on me, his expression puppy-dog pleading. "I'm a hero. I need your help."

"She's not just the deus ex machina for your stories!" I hissed. Morrigan didn't get to choose, just like we couldn't help inheriting our parent's gifts and burdens, their curses and costs. Why did we always blame her, never the ones who'd made the choice? "The world doesn't owe you magic. I'm the new gatekeeper. Get past me without getting eaten and you can have your bargain."

For a moment, he looked unimpressed. The bitter taste of ash and smoke filled my mouth as I shifted, my spine mutating, skin distorting into grey fur, and wolves' teeth filling my jaws. By then, his expression had completely changed. Impressed didn't begin to cover it.

He was gone before I finished howling, the sound echoing and shaking the house's flimsy foundations. I shifted again and for the first time I found something that felt like the truth.

I turned to find Morrigan staring at me, stiff with shock, like she expected some deadly consequence to instantly befall us. "I can't refuse them. You can't refuse them."

"Sure, you can't. He didn't ask for me." I smiled. The shape I'd fallen into was almost a mirror of hers, but smaller. "Fairy-tales always leave a loophole."

Quick-Change Pupa

By Vrai Kaiser

"Hold still. It's going to feel funny when I disconnect you from the veins." Harriet's hands were on my arms, or that's what my eyes told me. She was smiling like it would all be okay, when I was technically her second practice run.

"I can't." My voice croaked, and the sound of it shut me up. I'd gone under two hours ago, but it sounded like I hadn't had water in weeks.

Harriet kept smiling. "Remember not to move. If you panic, it'll know something's wrong. The field's still all wonky."

The thought of having to start over was worse than the worst of Harriet's gross surgical-sounding techniques. I closed my eyes and thought about why I was here.

Strong shoulders. I formed those in my mind first. Even if most of the spell had taken hold while I was sleeping, I didn't want to take any chances. A flat chest, and long fingers, and... *please, please let me still be able to sing.*

"Okay, you're done!" Harriet's voice was suddenly hard to hear; when I opened my eyes I saw she was across the room, facing toward the wall. The back of my neck was red.

"Be careful getting out," she added. "The herbs get kind of goopy afterward."

I went slow, expecting my legs to feel shaky. Big-time magic took a lot out of the subject as much as the caster, after all; Isabella, our mentor, had been drilling that into us since we were old enough to walk to the playground. There'd been something about not attempting transmutation magic on humans without at least a full apprenticeship and careful supervision, but these were desperate times. If I spent one more day putting on a bra I was going to claw my skin off.

"There's a towel and some clothes on the chair!" she called, sounding like she'd pulled her head down into her shirt for extra safety.

It felt like I was floating with every step. My body was heavier, not muscled but solid, and it wrapped around me like a blanket now instead of a noose. I sniffled once, loud, and then the tears started.

"What's wrong? Does something hurt?" Harriet was kneeling next to me in a flash; her teleportation work was really getting better. "I'm sorry about your hair; I should've looked for a way we could've gotten the goop out instead of just saying you had to shave it—"

I wrapped the towel around my waist before throwing myself at her, letting the ugly wails wash over both of us. They sounded strange, pitched half an octave down. "Thank you so much!"

Her hand thumped me on the back; I could feel it now, strong and warm. "Don't scare me like that. You know this stuff is dangerous when it goes bad."

"Yeah, it just," I sniffled. "I'm so happy."

When I was quiet enough for us to talk, she craned her neck to look over my head. "…We do need to figure out what to do with that thing."

It hadn't even occurred to me to look back. When I did, I saw myself— or the wrong version of myself, preserved in a flaky husk. I was bigger now, but the old, wrong copy didn't look split or warped. It was just… there. Like an afterimage in a picture, but one you could touch. Harriet squatted down in front of it, leaning forward with itchy-looking hands.

"You can have it." I shifted on my feet, uncomfortable. "I don't like how it's looking at me. It's all calm, and just… weird."

"I wish," she sighed. "I can't touch it."

"Why not?" I shuddered at the thought of putting my hands on that thing.

"It's a part of you. If I tried to decide what to do with it, I might hurt you." From her tone, it was probably something I'd missed in a lecture.

"I'm willing to take that chance," I said.

"Well I'm not!" It was like I'd slapped her. "You have to take this seriously, C—"

We both froze.

"You never told me what you decided on," she said.

Even though I'd been wearing baggy hoodies and boys' jeans to school for almost a year, none of the names I'd tried had managed to stick. "I was kind of thinking about Claude?"

She raised one eyebrow—perfect Vulcan alchemist. "That's not very different."

"Yeah. I mean, I might change it," I said, mostly to placate her. "But that's easy to remember, right?"

"Yeah…" she changed her tone to a force of cheerfulness. "Yeah, okay. Claude. I like it."

She ducked her head when I smiled. "Um," she said. "Can you put those clothes on? Sorry if they're the wrong size. I borrowed them from my sister, since she's pretty tall. I know it's not your style, but. Um."

I stepped into the skirt, made for someone taller and leaner; the fabric swished around my calves, tickling my skin. I hadn't worn anything like this in years.

"Very handsome," Harriet giggled. I made a Superman pose, hands on my hips, modeling the powder pink skirt. It looked surprisingly good with the oversized flannel I'd put on earlier; the sight of the two fabrics layered together sparked an ache in my chest. It was still there when we were done laughing, just the two of us in an abandoned locker room.

"Do I really have to take that thing?"

"I mean, it might disappear on its own. The," she went on in a rush, "book wasn't that clear actually but—I'm sure it'll be fine!"

"Tell me you at least brought gloves."

* * *

"It's been two days!" I hissed; our table was across the room from the librarian's desk and the computer terminals, but it still felt like everyone could hear us. "You said it would come to me!"

"It was supposed to!" she said. "Where are you keeping it, anyway?"

"My dad thought he was going to landscape our garden for a minute. We've still got a shed back there full of old supplies." Harriet had assured me that non-magical people wouldn't be able to see the thing, but I'd still shoved it as far back as it would go, hoping it would go away if I didn't think about it. "I can feel it out there, like it's watching me."

"You'll think of something soon." She seemed more concerned about the impending sogginess of her pizza than the mummified-me in my backyard. "Just remember not to tell anybody about the spell until it's gone."

"It better hurry," I said. "There's only so long I can avoid my mom asking about my new growth spurt."

245

Harriet believed in the "power of positive thinking," which seemed pointless to me when she could also have been learning to turn her junky inherited automobile into solid gold. At least the car wouldn't follow her around, waiting just out of the corner of her eye.

"By the way, do you still have that skirt?" she asked.

"Yeah, sorry. I was gonna bring it back today, but it needs washed." It was a lucky break I'd started doing my own laundry a year ago.

"Are you sure you're okay? You look really tired."

"Thanks," I grumbled, pushing back my chair.

"Hey." Harriet caught my sleeve. "If you're really worried, maybe you should talk to Ms. Isabella."

I tugged myself free. "It's fine. I'll bring your skirt tomorrow."

The skirt was already clean, actually. It was sitting on my bed, mocking me when I got home with its soft fabric and the stereotypically girly color—everything I'd decided I hated, because it made people think I was a girl.

I should be lifting weights or something, right? I thought as I played with the hem. The blogs I'd followed were full of guys wearing tank tops and bragging about their biceps. Some part of me had expected that once the spell was over I'd have some kind of epiphany along with the dick. But I still caught myself putting my hand to my mouth when I was thinking, or moving out of the way when someone came toward me on the sidewalk.

I'm a boy, I repeated to myself as I got ready for bed, staring into the mirror. It was supposed to be easy. Once everyone else could see me like I saw myself, that was meant to be the end of it. It felt right. Smoothing down my amateur-cut cowlicks with quick-bitten hands, I found myself thinking about the afternoons I'd spent with my mom at the nail salon. Everyone there had fussed over me, scolded me with warmth in their voices before covering the nervous habit with a glittery sheen; I'd felt happy. It was the first time I'd learned my fears could be banished with the right coat of arms.

They called you a girl. I'd stopped going at some point, when I cut away everything that might give people the wrong idea. I'd rebelled against pink. Some things were easy to give up—I'd never gotten interested in makeup or nails or dolls. I liked wearing Star Wars shirts and playing videogames and other "boy" things.

But...

It's worth it. I told myself again. *It's worth it.*

246

* * *

I woke up to a short, ominous text from Harriet. *Sorry! I was worried.*

The knock at the door came soon after. My heart dropped into my stomach as I came down the stairs—on the other side of the door was my immaculately dressed mentor, Ms. Isabella.

"Harriet already told me everything," she said when I opened the door. "Let me see it."

Marching like a marked man, I took her out to the shed. It was almost a relief. The worst part of Ms. Isabella's style was her willingness to let you squirm.

"I give up," I said preemptively. I was so tired. "Just tell me all about how I screwed up."

"I want you to look at something." She pulled a smooth orange stone from her pocket. As her thumb ran along the edges, small fragments rained down onto the carpet. "It took years to get it to this point."

My eyes widened. "Is that… you?" It was gorgeous; the sunlight coming in from the window set off ripples of color across the stone's surface, making it look infinitely deep even though it fit flat against Isabella's palm. I thought of the flaking, awful thing in the shed behind us.

"It took a long time." She'd been so much taller than me before. Now I could almost measure up. She pocketed the stone again. "I had to take it little by little, for years. Leaving pieces behind so there was room for the new parts of me that I'd discovered."

"So what do I do?" I burst out, frustrated. "I can't exactly cart a statue that's as tall as me until I'm 40!" I cringed, expecting a lecture on respect, but she was smiling.

"You're still impatient," she said. "When you were only this high, I remember you started crying because I'd taught you a light spell, but you still couldn't look right at the sun and study it. That love of learning is one of the most wonderful things about you."

She'd never paid me so many compliments at once. I felt lightheaded.

"I didn't tell you two not to try that spell because I didn't think you were talented enough, or that you were wrong about wanting to change your body," she went on. "I wanted to shield you from feeling the way you do now. You'll always carry parts of who you were. Some you'll be able to let go of with time, as you form new connections and learn new things. I don't mean to say you can't change—but it takes time, and work, and you'll always be ready faster than the world around you." We both looked at the third body in the room. "You're going to have to fight."

I gritted my teeth. "So I should've just stayed like that? Letting people think I was something I'm not?"

"No," she pinched the bridge of her nose. "I let you down. I didn't know how to prepare you for this, because I don't understand it. I suppose I thought forbidding you would put it off until some future day when one of us would be inspired with the perfect answer.

"I'm sorry for that, Claude." She looked me square in the eye as she said my name. "I'm sorry I wasn't there for you."

I shifted awkwardly. "S'okay. You couldn't—"

"It isn't," she cut me off. "I've been remiss in my own learning. It will take time, but I will make sure I become someone you can speak to."

I wasn't used to crying so much. I nodded my head hard, afraid to speak.

"For now, at least let me tell you what I know of magic." She walked to the husk. "Have you talked to it?"

"No?" Standing behind her made it easier to hide my incredulous face.

"Try."

"Okay." I took a breath. "I'm really tired of carting you around, and you freak me out, and—"

"Not like that," she said. "Be kind to yourself. You don't need to be that person anymore, but it's alright that you were."

We were both quiet. "I'll wait outside." Isabella let herself out, closing the door behind her.

I stared at the blank eyes that looked like mine, but wrong. The body that had been mine, but wasn't. "I hate you," I whispered.

The mouth sloughed, dribbling a little down the face. The flaking mush trembled on the edge of its jaw, like it might spill. I swallowed.

"I hate the way people looked at you." I balled my hands into fists. "I hate that people thought they knew me when they looked at you."

No response, but I felt something cracking.

"I miss going on spa days," I whispered to it. My hands fiddled with the hem of my shirt. "I miss my old clothes."

My knees wobbled. "Am I just lying to myself? Am I—"

Something made me look up. The statue hadn't changed at all, but it felt warmer in a way I couldn't explain. Its face was soft as it looked down at me.

"I'm not a girl," I whispered to it and myself. "I'm a boy. I'm a boy who likes wearing skirts."

I reached out to steady myself; the statue's shoulder was warm and soft, like flannel. It smelled like shampoo and old memories.

"My name is Claude." My hand moved across the collar and down, sinking into the chest like warm oatmeal. "I'm going to be okay."

Something hard and heavy pulsed inside my fingers. Slowly, cautiously, I pulled it out: a clean, violet stone as big as a grapefruit, and as heavy as the statue that was now disintegrating around my feet. Deep in the center, I could see the smallest glint of light when I ran my thumb over it.

"It's going to be okay," I repeated, holding it to my chest. A few violet flakes fell from the stone onto my shirt, like a dusting of glitter. I was going to take Harriet her skirt back—after I asked my mom about the salon.

Fishing for the Dead

By Eric Esser

You have to get three things right to catch a ghost: the lure, the pole, and the spell. Tonight Carlo was trying for a dog. Most kids use a tennis ball or dried pig's ear for the lure, but Carlo tied a stuffed squirrel with a fluffy tail to the end of his line. They'd been his dog Loki's favorite. Every night for almost a year after Loki'd died, Carlo had sat beneath the stars on nights of the waxing moon, waving his pole over the corner of the backyard where they'd buried Loki beneath the acacias. He'd spend hours hypnotizing himself by swaying his line though the moonlight before he felt it brush Loki's soul.

Four years later he was the best ghost fisher at Monte Vista High, and had dibs on the prime spot on the lowest level of the fire escape in the alley behind the SPCA. He shared it with his best friend Lyssa, their spider silk lines glistening side by side in the moonlight. Most kids preferred the strength of tarantula, but he favored the greater sensitivity of black widow; he could sense a guinea pig three months gone with that.

"Sorry about your boyfriend's dad," Carlo said to Lyssa so low no one else could hear. A half dozen other kids sat above or below in other fire escapes or on dumpsters. No one was down on the ground; elevating the line helps when you're fishing, especially if the remains haven't been buried but burned to ash and smoke like that which rose from the wide steel pipe at the back of this building. The spirits of dead dogs and cats and rabbits and most any animal you could think of suffused the air of this alley, at one time or another.

"Walter's not my boyfriend. We just hang out sometimes," Lyssa said.

"I think the phrase is 'hook up.'"

"Asshole." Lyssa swung her pig bone lure into Carlo's shin. Lyssa had an edge to her with her powder blue hair and half a dozen piercings that Carlo found irresistible, but she went for the burly types, like Walter Resnik: varsity outside linebacker and only a Junior. Carlo was fit but slender and pale and his cheeks were almost as smooth as hers.

"So how's he doing? Walter?"

"Hasn't really talked about it. Tough guy." She paused. "Fucking moron."

Carlo nodded because he agreed. "I hear they can't afford a fisher," he said, trying to sound casual.

"Yeah, no insurance."

"I wouldn't mind giving it a shot."

She raised an eyebrow. "Catch a human soul? With that little pole of yours?"

She glanced toward his crotch. Carlo tried to look uncomfortable but it pleased him. He had crafted his fishing pole from the bough of a dying ash tree, then inlaid the handle with bone he fished out of dinner scraps, mostly cow he had sawn into slivers and polished down. He'd fitted it with a Shimano high speed spinning reel engraved with an invocation to Ereshkigal in cuneiform; he'd worked all last summer bagging groceries to afford it.

"I have skills," he said.

She looked away. "I bet. Like Dukehart?"

Dukehart had been a fisher a few grades ahead of them when he'd been pulled under. He'd snuck onto the site of a double homicide in SF, thought he might turn up a clue the forensic fishers overlooked. He'd been missing three days before anyone thought to troll for him there, after the cops found dozens of links to reports of the murders in his browser history. They'd fished him out and taken him to Kaiser ER, but he'd wound up in Martinez Psychiatric, and would probably never leave.

"I could hold him," Carlo said. "And I might have a line on some pro gear, mirrors and nets and stuff."

Lyssa raised an eyebrow but didn't turn back. "No you couldn't. But I'll ask."

He let it drop, satisfied he had impressed her, and tried to relax back into fishing. He closed his eyes, emptied his mind, and let the energy his line drew off the underworld flow through him. He listened. A whimper to his right. Most kids would miss it, more an absence of silence than a sound.

He cast his line toward it and began the spell. People sell spells that include incantations and Sumerian refrains, but they're just hucksters. A real spell is a story, a story you use to persuade the dead back to life by reminding them how much better it is to be alive. A canned spell is no better than a lie. It takes imagination or experience, usually both.

He focused on one of his best memories of Loki. His mother was handing out Christmas presents. She pulled one from under the tree and said, "Oh, this one is for Loki." Loki had walked right over and taken the package delicately in his mouth, found a spot on the living room floor, laid down, held it between his paws, and torn the wrapping off in little bits, ears back the whole time, head glancing up every few seconds at Carlo with so much excitement he looked almost panicked. Only when the stuffed squirrel was completely unwrapped did he pause, appraise his gift, then set to tearing it apart, ending up so happy it left him panting. Carlo wanted Loki back just as much as Loki would have wanted to come back, if he could. Loki had been dead too long for Carlo's line to reach, but some other dog newly dead would want what Loki'd had.

Nothing tugged on the line, not at first, but the rod tingled in his hands like they were falling asleep. The air flexed, sound and light rippling through it like waves across the surface of a pond, and Carlo was there, the smell of pine and roast turkey in the air with Loki's grunts of satisfaction as he tore off another scrap of paper. Carlo's spirit had entered that place between this world and the next where the longing of the dead could give life to the stories of the living.

The stitching of the squirrel's fabric tore, white cotton innards spilling out as if pulled by an invisible hand. Carlo heard a crack like the breaking of a great sheet of ice, and suddenly there was a dog hovering at the end of his line, a medium-sized mutt with some collie and German shepherd and something black mixed in, though you could only see it if you didn't look right at it, if you peered at it from the side or turned your vision inward. The dog shook the squirrel, stretched out with it between its paws, and dismembered it with its ears back, just like Loki had.

Carlo was so good at this by now he rarely lost himself in Irkalla for more than a few seconds before the animal emerged; he would have to practice teasing it so he could spend longer in the waters below.

Lyssa whistled. "Damn smooth, Reyes." She was a jealous. He could tell.

Light applause filtered up and down the alley from the other fishers.

Carlo slowly reeled in the line, and the dog floated up with the lure. Once its head lay level with his, he reached up and scratched it behind the ears. Its fur was soft, but its flesh cold down at the skin. The dog glanced at him lovingly, the way a dog who's first met you can do only because it is a dog and not human.

"Good boy," Carlo said.

* * *

The best ghost fishing happens around midnight, which meant on nights out Carlo usually got home around two. When he got back that night, his father was still awake on the couch watching Classic Boxing: Robinson v. Moyer from 1961. He held a Miller Lite in one hand, a cone of his favorite indica in the other. Carlo had once looked up to his father but these days did his best to ignore him.

Carlo made a beeline from the front door to the kitchen. His father shot the end of his beer down his throat then called out, "Hey, Carlo, bring me another?" like Carlo knew he would.

Carlo grabbed his father a beer from the fridge and tore himself off a hunk of sweet roll. He glanced at the pile of dishes and silverware balanced in the sink and sighed but couldn't bring himself to deal with it. As he brought the beer to his father he kept his eyes on the TV screen. Moyer hugged Robinson close, pounding him in the gut with his right.

"Catch anything?" his father asked. He spoke too loudly, like he talked over a crowd in a bar.

"Nothing," Carlo said. "You know Robinson wins, right?"

"Sure. But those moves!" His father made a little jab. His eyes were red and he laughed too hard. Carlo wondered what would happen if his father were in a car accident like Mr. Resnik, about what precise amount of alcohol would get his father drunk but still willing to drive down to Safeway for more.

"I'm going to bed," Carlo said.

"You'll catch something next time, eh?" his father called after him.

Carlo closed his door, threw on The Soft Moon and cranked it up to drown out the TV and his father. He kicked off his Docs and pitch-black Levi's and stretched out on top of the covers with the lights off. Moonlight shone onto one of his posters, the one of the Green Demon, his favorite luchador. Years ago, before his father's accident, he had taken Carlo to a match down in San Jose; their seats had been up two levels, but Carlo could tell it was the Green Demon down there from the way he spiraled through the air as he leapt from the ropes to pin his opponent. He'd been up against his arch nemesis, Omega, with their masks on the line.

Carlo was certain he could craft a compelling spell for Walter's father from that memory. Walter was a jock, so father-son sports bonding should be just the ticket. Carlo'd never fished for a human soul himself, but he'd watched Ghost Fishers on National Geographic, studied vids on the web, and even spied on a couple of pro jobs from a distance at the local graveyards. They didn't look so different from what he did. He promised himself one day he would be out there himself, contracting for the glory jobs, with the military or prisons, maybe some inner-city graveyard, fishing holes where the ghosts might be afraid to come back to life, because of how they'd lived, or died. The ones that could pull you under if you weren't careful.

* * *

Lyssa told Carlo he could probably catch Walter beneath the bleachers during morning break. When he got there, he found Walter kissing Lyssa against the aluminum frame in the crisscrossing shadows. Walter was so much bigger than Lyssa that in his arms she looked like some mischievous gothic faerie.

Carlo cleared his throat. Lyssa looked up over Walter's shoulder and smiled like she'd been caught in a scandal, and liked it. Carlo played it cool, as if he was amused by her antics and not at all stabbed by a pang of jealousy through his heart to the gut. "Bad time?" he said.

Walter turned with a start. When he recognized Carlo his interest seemed to flag. "Hey, Carlo," he said. This was all they'd ever said to each other. Walter didn't hang out with them; they had different crowds, Walter with his jocks and Lyssa her goths, but social segregation had no place beneath the bleachers. "Yeah, kinda busy."

"You should listen to him, Walter," Lyssa said. She used her serious voice, one Carlo rarely heard.

"Yeah," Walter began, "about that fishing thing. I don't really need your help on that, man. Thanks though. It's cool of you to offer."

Carlo sighed. "You guys hired someone after all? Who? Petrelli? Diablo?"

"Nah. We're just gonna skip it, I think."

Carlo caught Lyssa's eye and made his "what the fuck" face. She raised her shoulders like she wasn't responsible.

"Oh. Sure," Carlo said. He knew it was a cheap shot, but said, "I just thought you guys were closer than that."

Walter rose, all 6'3", 200-plus pounds of him. "What did you just say to me?"

Lyssa reached for Walter. "He didn't mean it like that. Chill dude."

Walter let her pull him down. "Fucking freak," he mumbled.

"Ah, no," said Lyssa. She got up, brushing her hands a few times. "Really gotta get to Trig. There was a cliffhanger last class and I don't want to miss the resolve."

Walter reached toward her like he couldn't understand how he had possibly offended, like he was the good guy. "Wait, Lyssa, come on." He turned to Carlo. "Hey man, I'm sorry. It's just, he's gone, you know? I don't see the point."

Carlo had heard about this kind of reaction on the ghost fishing blogs: the desire to just move on. He'd also read how to make the hard sale, and he didn't give a fuck what Walter wanted. "But it's not over. Not for your dad."

Walter rolled his eyes. "Man, I know you believe all that stuff, but seriously, you don't even know. Not really."

Carlo cocked his head. "You think when I pull a German Shepard out of thin air it's like a trick of the light or something?"

"No, man, but like, those holy rollers, they don't think it's dead people."

Carlo had seen the Pentecostals with their picket signs outside the bait and tackle shops. They didn't believe it was ghosts being fished over, but demons pretending to be ghosts to corrupt the souls of the living. When you died you went straight to heaven to be with God, and you certainly couldn't fish a soul away from God.

Carlo shook his head because there was really nothing he could say if Walter was determined to ignore the evidence of his eyes. But the blogs had his back here too: if the head was locked down, aim for the heart. "Do you know who they're with down there?" Carlo said low, he hoped a little ominously.

Walter shook his head.

"No one," Carlo said. "They can't see the living or the dead, at least

255

not that anyone's been able to prove. They're just alone with their memories, played over and over again, at least as far down as we can reach them. Bad deaths have it worst. Your dad's probably thinking about the crash right now. Living it really. Again and again. I can't even imagine what that must be like, to die in agony over and over."

Walter started getting up again. It appeared to be his signature move. "What the fuck, man? Who says that to someone?"

"We can help him. We can help him take control."

Behind Walter, Lyssa said, "Walter, if you don't, you'll regret it."

Walter turned toward her; Carlo couldn't see Walter's face but he could see Lyssa's and he knew then that Walter was no casual pick up for her. Walter turned back and waved. "Fine. Fine. We'll do it." Carlo could see he was really doing it for Lyssa, that she was no casual hook up for him either.

"We'll need a lure," said Carlo. "I could make one, but it'd be better to use something your dad's familiar with, something he's touched from you or your brother." Carlo could have asked for an object from Walter's sister, but he wouldn't be able to play her as convincingly as one of the boys. A fisher with a practiced imagination could do it no problem, but he was going on personal experience, like he always had.

"From whichever one of you he loved most. If you want it to work, be honest."

* * *

Friday night Carlo and Lyssa went out to liberate some pro gear before fishing for Walter's father on Saturday after the funeral. What they were doing was dangerous; that's what made it exciting. Fishing for people wasn't like fishing for animals. You tell a ghost a story, it listens. Tell a human a story, you'll hear one back. Maybe it will make you glad to be alive, or maybe it will pull you under. The pros had a few tools to make it safer, but the only time they weren't under lock and key was when they used them.

Carlo and Lyssa snuck around the back of the Lafayette Park Hotel and slipped through the gap in the fence of Oakmont Cemetery they'd opened a few months back, then hid behind an obelisk. A few dozen yards away a team of pro fishers from Diablo Valley Fishing was setting up their nets. Carlo had found the listing in the obituaries.

He'd seen them all before. Arsenio Perez was the primary fisher. He'd been in the business 35 years, had once attended Monte Vista High himself. Bob Kurtowski held the moon mirror: a concave silver disc polished with beetle oil thrice blessed by the High Priestess of Ereshkigal at Kuthu. It reflected moonlight onto the grave like a spotlight, helping guide the ghost back into this world. Perez's assistant was Althea Ma. She'd been a senior when Carlo was a freshman two years ago. Now she was in a trade-program and only a few years away from fishing herself. She'd be the one watching the gear for poachers, along with anything else Pérez needed, from standing ready with a secondary pole to netting a ghost that tried to run. A woman Carlo didn't recognize in her late-forties or early fifties-in a charcoal overcoat stood with the fishers, probably paying enough to buy a nice new midsize sedan for another 10 minutes with someone she'd loved.

Safety regs required the team keep backup equipment on hand: spare harnesses, another net and mirror. Once the ghost came, the team would be distracted, and might not notice a couple of kids in the dark lifting a few choice items.

As they lay in the darkness watching the team harness up, Carlo couldn't resist whispering, "So. Walter seems nice." He raised his voice at the end, like he was asking a question, which of course he was.

"Asshole," said Lyssa not taking her eyes from the fishers. "If you hate him so much then why are you helping him?"

"I just want to catch a ghost."

"You sure that's all you want to catch, sailor?"

Carlo's heart nearly stopped. If there was one thing he wanted more than for Lyssa to understand how he felt about her, it was that she never found out. "What's that supposed to mean?"

"Nothing."

"Jeez, I just want to help the guy see his father one last time. Isn't there anything you'd want to say to your dad, if you could?"

It was another cheap shot and he knew it. Carlo didn't feel guilty complaining to Lyssa about how pathetic his father was, because he knew she hated her parents worse, wherever they were. She snorted. "I wouldn't go out of my way." Then she said, "Hey. Althea's holding the pole."

She was right. Althea stood on a platform holding the ten-foot rod, torso and pelvis in the harness, legs planted wide, eyes closed, trailing the line across the grave. Perez stood by Althea's shoulder, nodding and talking quietly. She had a look of determination, of jazzing herself up, like she was going to do this no matter what. It might have been her first time, Carlo couldn't know for sure. It looked like it was still important to her, that if she did not focus completely she might not succeed.

The line pulled taut. Carlo couldn't see the lure; it was inside the sort of undyed silk pouch they used for small, delicate objects like jewelry or photographs. The bag collapsed as if gripped by an invisible hand. Althea's eyes stayed closed, but her lips began to move.

"Now, Carlo, no one's watching," whispered Lyssa.

Carlo started toward the team's backup gear but he couldn't take his eyes off the job. The air around the grave danced like it was superheated, though Carlo knew it had actually dropped by at least 20 degrees. An expanding sphere of gaseous light rippled out from the purse; the ghost was hooked, trapped in that place between death and life where the past could be lived again.

Blue-white light flared over the grave site; Carlo had to turn away. When his eyes readjusted to the darkness, a second woman several years younger than the first flickered in and out of view on the clearing. The living woman kissed the dead one in moonlight reflected through a cloud of fine blue dust, the residue of the barrier between worlds. Vacuum suction machines by the gravesite softly hummed as they pulled it in, collecting it for processing into astral projection charms.

Lyssa shoved a bag in his hands. She was holding a mirror. "I got 'em, spacer. No harness. Let's motor." She ran over the rise and Carlo stumbled after, but couldn't help stopping before he was completely out of sight to look back. He didn't want to see the couple. He wanted to see Althea and Perez.

Althea could not tell because her eyes were on the couple, but Perez looked toward her with great pride. The Althea Carlo had seen when he was a freshman could never have caught this ghost. Her luring skills were clumsy, her spells rote, but Perez had taught her. Everything Carlo knew, he'd learned from other kids or TV or the forums online.

"Carlo!" he heard Lyssa hiss. They slipped out of the yard smooth as spider silk.

* * *

When he got home, Carlo saw the glow below the garage door from the end of the driveway. He found himself listening for the sound of a car engine running and that this made him nervous. He thought he heard the whirr of an electric drill.

He went through the gate to the backyard, and peered in through the garage window. His father bent over a workbench. Carlo opened the door at the back of the garage.

"Hey, dad. What's going on?"

His father looked up, eyes bloodshot and hair wild like Beethoven. "A project!" he said like he was five. Carlo's father had once enjoyed building things. He'd made the bookshelves in the living room, solid oak with geometric patterns in different shades of wood polished smooth, and Carlo's crib, long since passed through the hands of half a dozen relatives. He hadn't made anything since the accident, over four years ago now.

Carlo had gotten the details from the local news like everyone else. The cable company had been laying new fiber from power line poles. The guy laying the cable had been riding in the bucket of an aerial lift crane when it had accidently run into the lines, sending 10,000 volts through him and blasting him right out of the bucket to the ground.

Carlo's father hadn't been the guy in the bucket. He'd been the one who drove it into the lines.

Tonight he was polishing down a ten-foot reed. On the workbench were some off brand reel and a length of nylon fishing line. He had a half-finished Miller beside him, along with half a dozen empty ones.

"I thought maybe you could use a longer pole," he said. "Catch those dogs you been after."

Carlo shook his head. "Where'd you get the wood?"

"Down at the hardware. Bamboo. Has some flex to it."

Carlo rolled his eyes. "That's not going to work. It has to be a dying tree. That's not a tree and I doubt it was dying."

"Oh, sorry. I didn't know. Where do you buy some of that?"

"You don't. It's hard. I'm going to bed."

"Carlo," his father called to him.

Carlo turned back to his father. "Yeah?" His father's eyes looked through him and Carlo found he wished they didn't. "I'm tired, Dad," he said, though he wasn't.

"Na, that's ok. Sleep tight," his father said.

As Carlo fell asleep that night, he went over the spell he would cast tomorrow night. Every detail had to be perfect to induce the ghost. Ghosts never want to cross back over at first, because they can't believe what they're being offered is real. They have to be persuaded, like a dog who's been kicked too many times disbelieves when you offer it a treat. You have to make the ghost believe life is possible again; it has to take the bait before you can reel it in.

* * *

Carlo, Lyssa, and Walter arrived at the graveyard Saturday evening. The yard was deserted of other fishers, but sounds of the night still filled it, the pulse of crickets and small creatures rustling in long shadows cast by the low half-moon. Though Carlo had come here many times to watch the pros, he'd never had his pole with him before. Every step he took he heard whispers from those buried here, most so long ago they could no longer be fished out.

They found the site, adorned in wreaths of carnations and lilies. Lyssa hadn't said much, but when they were ready, she touched Carlo's arm and gestured for him to come aside, sending a shiver up his arm. "Remember, no harness. If you have to, just let go. Don't make me fucking save you," she said.

"And lose my pole? Not a chance."

Carlo took out the lure, a scuffed-up Wiffle ball Walter's family used to hit around their backyard, and tied it on the line. He motioned Walter focus the mirror on the grave. Lyssa stood by with a net in case the ghost broke free of the line and tried to run.

Carlo sat on top of the gravestone and dangled the line over the plot. He closed his eyes, emptied his mind, and focused. There'd be no point trying to picture something Walter had experienced with his father; the best fishers have their own techniques, but they all agree it isn't particular words or images but feelings that draw the specters over. Carlo was better off imagining something personal.

He visualized that wrestling match with the Green Demon as completely as he could. How he and his father left before dinner so they could get something to eat at the arena. On the drive over, they had relived the Green Demon's past matches, his victories and the moves that had led to them, and debated whether his opponent Omega was at the top of his game, about what would happen if the Green Demon was unmasked, whether his career could continue or he'd be finished. Omega had never been defeated.

As they walked in, his father told him how when he was a boy, luche libre hadn't been fought in the big arenas like the Pavilion; his own father had taken him across the border to Tijuana to see matches in converted gyms with clay walls and dirt floors. Carlo could see how much his father missed his own father since he'd died, but that this made him happier to be there with Carlo. They took their seats and ate beef franks with mustard and ketchup and relish and chili cheese fries, and his father had gotten a huge plastic cup of beer, but only twice. When the Green Demon walked down the red carpet to the ring, Carlo glanced away a moment, toward his father. He caught his father watching him from the corner of his eye with what Carlo could tell was pride, though he hadn't done anything to deserve it.

Carlo was no longer in the graveyard, he was in the arena, the sweet stench of beer dried on concrete, the roar of the crowd shaking through the soles of his boots, the sound of the Green Demon's back pounding onto the mat. Omega had him pinned. Carlo screamed "No!" as loud as he could, louder than he ever had, because it was okay to shout here in a way it wasn't at any other time, so loud he felt the vibration down his throat into his gut. "Get up!" he cried. "Get up!"

But the Green Demon did not get up. Omega held him, chest pressed against his, arms splayed wide and heavy, forcing the Green Demon against the mat. The Green Demon pushed upward with all his might, arms trembling under the strain, then fell back, and tried to role to his right, then fell back, then his left, then collapsed against the mat as the referee laid out the count.

There were cheers from some, stunned silence from more. Omega had won. Though Omega had never lost and the Green Demon had suffered a few defeats over the years, no one really thought the Green Demon would lose. They had no business thinking it, but most had hoped the Green Demon would win.

Omega offered his hand to the Green Demon and pulled him to his feet. They paused, and the Green Demon set his hands on his hips and tilted his head toward the ground. His mask was sparkly silver on one side and green on the other, a curving white stripe dividing them at a diagonal across his face. The audience hushed. This was the moment that would decide if his career would continue, whether the crowd was so excited about finding out who was beneath the mask that it was ultimately happy he lost. Carlo wanted to know.

The Green Demon removed his mask. Carlo saw his hero's face, and he was just a man, but somehow more than a man ever to have been considered a hero. Carlo was glad he saw it. The Green Demon took the microphone, and announced his name to the world. In the years since, he had become an even greater star, and gone on to defeat Omega in a rematch on technical grounds. Carlo hadn't been there for that rematch, but he'd been there for the unmasking, and everyone agreed that was better.

An arm reached around Carlo's shoulders. The weight of it felt good. Carlo looked over.

It was not his father's. The man had a clean face, early gray hair swept back against his scalp, and Walter's nose and chin. He wore a pressed navy-blue suit over a white shirt and black tie with thin white stripes. The man smiled at Carlo. His eyes were deep black pools. The distance between Carlo and the man narrowed like the turning of a telephoto lens.

Carlo was inside the man.

Carlo was no longer in the arena but behind the wheel of a 1970s Cadillac de Ville, driving with one hand and rustling through a Trader's bag with the other, checking to see if he'd forgotten to pick up the chia seeds Katie'd asked for again. It was dark outside, and the lights of the other car shown bright in the passenger compartment just before it hit. The driver's side door crashed in, vinyl and chrome and plastic wood finish grinding into his body like the serrated head of a mining drill, crushing his ribs into his lungs and his heart in a hot white light that burned him out of the world.

And yet despite the pain, he though mostly of Katie, whom he loved, though he wished he'd loved her more, and Benji, Walter, and Theodora. More than pain and death he feared what would happen to them without him.

The pole jerked forward, yanking Carlo off the top of the gravestone. His legs sank into the earth like it was water up to his knees. Where his legs extended beneath the surface, Carlo felt his bones shatter, just like Walter's father's had. Even though Carlo knew it was just a memory and not real he screamed and fell to his knees, submerging in the grave up to his waist. Nauseating pain racked his pelvis and sparks flew along the length of the pole, something he had never seen in real life but only on pirated snuff videos from Japan. Ripples in the ground began cycling around him like a vortex. A pro fisher would calm the ghost with a soothing memory, but Carlo saw only blood and steel.

Carlo barely heard Lyssa whisper in his ear as her hands wrapped around his on the pole, "Stop, Carlo. Just listen."

Carlo did not hear what Lyssa said next in words. With a ghost at the end of the line, they were both connected to that same space between this world and the next; he saw and felt what Lyssa created there, as would the ghost.

He found himself standing beside a little girl in a flower print dress staring out the window by her front door into the driveway. The grass on the lawn rose in tufts like it needed a good mowing. The little girl's big eyes grew wider; she heard a car engine, and Carlo somehow knew she thought it sounded like her father's Chevy. The car passed. An Audi. Not even close.

The days sped forward like flipping through a picture book. The little girl, a little bigger, sat in front of a Hello Kitty birthday cake with eight candles. Her aunt sat to one side, her mother the other.

"Blow out the candles, Lyssie. Momma's got an appointment," her mother smiled as she took a drag from her Virginia Slim. Her teeth had already begun to darken from more than cigarettes; a few years hence the crystal binges would burn them away and she'd be fitted with a false set by Inmate Dental Services.

"Take your time dear," her aunt said. "Think of something you really hope comes true."

The little girl knew what she most wished for, what she wished for every afternoon when she paused at the front window. She blew out the candles and was sad because she finally understood her father might not come back. Otherwise, she wouldn't have to wish so hard. She wouldn't have to use a birthday wish.

Carlo became aware of the man standing next to him watching the little girl too. He wore the same dark suit as before. The man stepped toward the little girl.

The scene changed. Summer sun warmed Carlo's face as he stretched out in a reclining chair by the neighborhood pool, the air thick with chlorine and the shouts of dozens of children and the sounds of their feet slapping on the smooth white concrete as they ran by. He turned and saw Lyssa wading through the kiddie pool with orange inflatable flotation devices on her arms. She was younger than before, five, maybe six.

Her father came over, though he looked too young to be a father. His hair was painted shoe polish black, and he wore a wet Fields of the Nephilim T-shirt and swim trunks that went down to his knees. He lifted her out of the water, took off her life preservers, and held her hand as they walked over to the big pool. He hopped in the pool and held her waist as she crawled over the edge. She had to tread water; there was nowhere she could touch the bottom.

"Take a deep breath," her father said.

She pulled in her breath and puffed out her cheeks. Her father took her hand. They sank into the water and swam from the shallow end to the deep end like mermaids. She could only hold her breath long enough because her father swam faster than she could, and pulled her to the other side before she had to breathe again. When they rose at the far end, she giggled and cried out, "Again!" Her father laughed and they dove back under; the water rippled against her like Jell-O they moved so fast. They went three more times before she became so light-headed she had to stop, and her father bought her an Orange Crush to help.

The man stood by Carlo again, even as they both also floated in the water next to Lyssa and her father then sped with them down the length of the pool and back again. Carlo could see on the man's face that he wanted this moment or something like it. Even after everything she'd said about her father over the years, Carlo knew if Lyssa could have this moment back again, she would, no matter how she felt about her father now.

The man turned to Carlo, "Is it really so easy?" he said.

"Sometimes," said Carlo, offering his hand. Mr. Reznik's grasped it. They rose into the bright sky, following the light to the surface.

Carlo knelt on top of the grave. Mr. Resnik flickered in front of him. Walter shone moonlight on his father, and where the beam cast through his father's specter it was solid and did not flutter like the rest of him. Mr. Resnik stared at the Wiffle ball on the end of the line. He'd probably expected to see bathing suits and flowing mermaid hair. He looked up and saw the fishing line. A horror passed over his face like everything he'd ever believed was undone.

"Dad!" Walter called out. Mr. Resnik turned his eyes toward Walter. He hesitated, but only a moment. He dropped the lure and stumbled to his son. He wrapped his arms around Walter and Walter hugged him back.

Lyssa's hands released Carlos' and the rod, and Carlo felt her body peel away. He turned toward her. She stood closer than she usually did. She seemed different; he could see the little girl in her.

"I didn't know you could be so sincere," he said.

"Fuck you." She laughed.

Carlo hesitated because he wanted to say the perfect thing. He wanted to explain to her not only what it meant to him that she had risked herself to save him, but that now he understood her in a way no one else ever would. She looked up at him like she knew what he wanted to say, and wouldn't stop him. It was a great moment. It seemed to go on forever.

And then he heard Walter say, "Dad! Wait..." They turned, and Walter stood alone, eyes red and face flushed.

"That's it? He's gone already?" Lyssa said. "Jesus, I'm sorry, Walter. I suck."

"Are you kidding me?" Walter said to her. He took her in his arms and pulled her head to his chest. "Thank you so much, Lyssa," he said. She looked surprised but something in the way she smiled reminded Carlo of how she'd laughed at the far end of the pool.

"We'll try again next week once the waters have settled down," she said. "It shouldn't be such a shit show now that he knows what's going on. For a few months, anyway." She turned to Carlo. Another moment passed between them, and in it he was certain she knew how he felt about her. Then time moved on and he wasn't. Lyssa wasn't like him. If she felt the same way about him as he did about her, she'd have acted on it. "Couldn't have done it without that pole of yours," she said. "Mind if I borrow it awhile?"

Carlo handed it to her. "Keep it. You're good with it."

"Carlo you love this pole."

He did, but it didn't matter. He had to respect that.

"I've been meaning to make another," he said.

* * *

Carlo snuck in well after three. He found his father passed out on the couch with a tequila bottle between his legs and some late-night talk show host blathering on the TV. Carlo took the bottle out to the recycling, then

265

fetched a blanket for his father from the cupboard, draped it over him, turned off the TV, and waited. His father mumbled something, grasped the blanket, then settled deeper into the couch.

Carlo slunk off to bed. He had staked out a number of ash trees, and held a reserve of the engraved copper nails used to kill them. He'd hammer them into the roots of one under a waning moon after making the offering to Ereshkigal. He also had a line on a supply of human bone, donated by old fishers who'd passed on and wanted to help kids starting out. That could really up the ante if he laid it in right with some fresh spells; those fishing industry archeologists were always turning up new ones from the digs in Iraq, and he'd engraved the ones on his old pole over a year ago. New pole could make that old pole look like nothing. Maybe he'd ask his father to help him build it.

Heart of a Fox

By Aaron Canton

Jin Rachel continued working on her amulet as the door to her dormitory room cracked open. Even as soft footsteps crept in her direction, her only reaction was a faint smile. But no sooner had the intruder moved into range than she swiveled in her chair and wrapped her sister into a big hug. "Deborah!" she chirped. "Having a good day?"

"Hey!" Jin Deborah pouted for a few moments before dissolving into giggles. She looked like a human girl of about ten, except for her pointed ears, wagging tail, and furry cheeks. "You caught me again!"

"That's what big sisters are for, kitto." Rachel swung Deborah around so she could sit on her desk. "What've you been up to?"

Deborah grinned. "Biyu showed me something really awesome today! Look at this!" She took a deep breath and shut her eyes. When nothing happened after a few moments, she scrunched up her face in concentration. A few beads of sweat formed on her brow.

And then, after a few seconds more, Deborah was a kitten.

Rachel's sister purred merrily as she scampered around on the desk and leapt over amulets and textbooks. She had a soft, reddish coat, blue eyes, and a fluffy tail that swished in the air. When she returned to her mostly-human form a few minutes later, she was beaming. "What'd you think? Isn't it the greatest ever?"

"I think..." Rachel gathered Deborah into another hug. "That I've got the most talented little sister in the world."

After a few moments, Deborah asked, "So... can we play tag later, please? I wanna use my new form! We can—"

"Depends." Rachel held up a hand. "Did you finish the homework I gave you yet?"

Deborah drew back her ears and adopted a puppy-dog expression. "Not exactly..."

267

"Sorry, kitto." Rachel lowered Deborah down. "Before Mom and Dad had to leave, I promised them I'd look after you. That means making sure you keep up with your studies."

"But none of the *other* kits have to study Hebrew and Kabbalah and the *Sefer Radish—*"

"*Sefer Raziel,*" corrected Rachel. "And none of the other kits are from Kaifeng." They were the only huli jing—fox spirits—from the city's flourishing Jewish community, the offspring of an Orthodox mother and a fox spirit who had fallen so deeply in love that he had converted and married her. It was an unusual syncretism, but Rachel fully intended to ensure that Deborah understood both halves of their heritage. "You need to know this stuff to appreciate your culture. Plus..." She nodded at the amulets on her desk. "Once you get good enough, you'll be able to make these."

Deborah's eyes widened. "What do those ones do?"

Rachel pointed to a sapphire inlaid in silver and mounted on a thin chain. "This one here can heal all kinds of injuries." Gesturing at a piece of paper covered in Seals of Solomon, Magen Davids, and Hebrew script calling on God and the angels, she added, "And this one alerts me to danger."

"Wow!"

"If you keep doing your homework, I'll keep teaching you everything I know about crafting them," said Rachel. "And, when you get a little older, I'll even ask Headmistress Yi to let you come with me when I get assigned hunts or 'practical' tests in Shanghai. Having another huli jing with me who's good with amulet magic would be a big help. How's that sound?"

Deborah's face brightened. "Okay," she said, bowing her head. "I'll study hard."

"Great." Rachel glanced out her window. "Now, I can't finish my next amulet until sunset, so I have a few minutes. If you *promise* to hit the books right when I say so, we can play until then—"

"YAY!" Deborah switched to her natural form, a brown-coated fox kit, and ran across the room. She yipped a challenge to Rachel as her tail wagged. *Catch me if you can!* she seemed to say.

Grinning, Rachel stood, stretched, and changed. The body of a Chinese teenager with brown eyes and shoulder-length dark hair became that of a reddish fox, similar to Deborah's form but larger and with a thicker coat. The only part of her that remained the same was her tail—no huli jing could shift that away in human form—but now it dangled behind her instead of remaining tucked against her legs. Wagging it merrily, she stalked towards her sister and pounced, giving Deborah just enough room to dodge. Deborah yipped as she leapt to one side, and Rachel circled around for another pass.

The door opened and Shao Ling—Class Vice-President, brilliant shifter, and the most beautiful girl around as far as Rachel was concerned—entered. "Headmistress Yi wants to see all the students..." She glanced down at Rachel and Deborah, the latter of whom was still yipping. "Am I interrupting?"

Under her fur, Rachel felt herself blushing.

* * *

"Sorry!" Rachel hurried to catch up with Ling. Though she had taken the time to shift back to human and say goodbye to Deborah, her cheeks were still a bright crimson. "I didn't realize you were stopping by. I was just helping Deborah—"

"Don't worry about it," Ling said. "Kits need attention."

Intellectually, Rachel knew that it was silly to appreciate the appearance of a fox that could look like anything she chose, but whenever she saw Ling she couldn't help but do it anyway. It wasn't just the beauty of her usual human form, that of a statuesque Chinese girl with russet-red hair and piercing green eyes, but also the perfect poise and grace with which she inhabited the body. Add in her academic brilliance and her shifting prowess—she had mastered over 40 animals, and could showcase them all in under two minutes—and Rachel could only come to one conclusion: Ling was the perfect girl for her.

Granted, Ling was also out of her league and far more interested in the class's other top students and shifters, such as Class President Tang Biyu. But Rachel knew she could dream.

"Was she why you missed the hunt yesterday?" Ling asked. "Were you helping her with something?"

It took a moment for Rachel to remember what Ling was talking about. "No, I wasn't with Deborah. Biyu said the hunt was for a boar, and I can't eat pig, so I didn't go."

"Ah, right." Ling smiled. "Never thought I'd meet a fox that kept kosher. Isn't that difficult?"

Sometimes. Maybe we could go hunting later and I could tell you all about it, Rachel imagined herself saying. What she actually said was, "Not really. But anyway, how was the hunt?"

"Excellent. The boar almost got away from the pack, but Biyu and I worked out a plan where she shifted into a hawk and swooped down to distract it while I flanked..."

Ling was still recounting the adventure when they reached the auditorium and sat with several other huli jing. Rachel opened her mouth to ask about the next group hunt, but then Biyu approached Ling and the two immediately began chatting. Turning abruptly, Rachel glared around the auditorium. *Can't this thing start already?*

A hundred huli jing students were seated in their human forms. The skill of their shifting varied; Ling and Biyu looked flawlessly human, but many of the students retained foxlike features, ranging from pointed ears to protruding muzzles. Rachel quietly took out a hand mirror and checked her own appearance for anything that might flag her as a fox. There was nothing, though, not a whisker, patch of fur, or elongated canine that might give her away. Her transformation was perfect.

She tilted her head slightly and hoped that Ling would notice.

"Attention, class!" A nondescript woman whose dress was embroidered with the words 'HEADMISTRESS YI' had walked onto the stage. Her voice was quiet, but it cut through the chatter in the crowd nonetheless. "I have a new practical mission in Shanghai for you."

The students cheered. A practical mission meant they could leave their secluded wooded campus and go into the city, usually for days at a time. Shanghai had plenty to offer a clever fox spirit, and Rachel knew that she wasn't the only one thinking of finishing the mission quickly and then taking some time to sample the city's delights.

"But first," said Yi, "Which of you know the legend of Diaochan?"

Ling's hand was the first one up. "A tyrant named Dong Zhuo was once the brutal ruler of China. Seventeen warlords allied and sent their armies to overthrow him, but they could not get past Dong's greatest general, his adopted son Lu Bu. In order to save the people, a huli jing named Diaochan went to work as Dong's singing girl and used her magic and her music to bewitch both Dong and Lu. Ultimately, she drove them apart and convinced Lu to strike Dong down. One huli jing thus succeeded where 17 of China's mightiest warlords had failed."

"Exactly," said Yi. "Note that Diaochan's success was not solely due to her shifting abilities. She played her lute well enough to bewitch Dong's and Lu's ears, just as she cast glamours and changed shape to ensnare their eyes. Diaochan's lute is thus one of the most significant treasures of the huli jing. It was lost several centuries ago when the Mongols sacked Hangzhou, but it recently turned up in the private collection of a financier named Hao Lan. It seems she showcases the lute and other treasures in order to impress potential clients. Unfortunately, Ms. Hao has refused all reasonable offers to buy back the lute even though she knows it is ours by right. And so..."

Yi nodded at the students. "Before the staff and I move to recover the lute, we will offer you the chance. Any student whose human form passes inspection," she glared at a few of the students whose appearances were particularly sloppy, "may travel to Shanghai and attempt its recovery. Successful students will, of course, be suitably rewarded." She smiled. "Does anyone wish to try?"

Every student yelled that they did, Rachel's voice among the loudest. She could see herself returning with the lute in hand, shrugging off Yi's compliments, but perhaps accepting a few from Ling. In fact, if she finished quickly enough, maybe Ling would be impressed enough to spend some of her time in Shanghai with her. They could visit a nightclub or two, and...

She cut off her thoughts. She first had to get the lute, meaning she'd have to beat not only Lan but all the other students as well. That would be tough; many of them were better shifters than her. But she was a clever fox. She'd figure something out.

Besides, she thought, visualizing the amulets on her desk. *I have a few advantages of my own.*

* * *

"Are you sure I can't come with on your mission?" asked Deborah, running in front of Rachel before she could leave their hotel room in downtown Shanghai. "Please?"

Rachel laughed. "When you're older, kitto. I promise."

"But I can help! I can be a fox, or a girl, or a kitten, or a mouse, or—"

With a brief shake of her head, Rachel became a massive tiger. She roared, bared her teeth, and swept a paw towards herself, as if to ask, 'Can you match this?'

Deborah paused for a few moments, clearly trying to shift, but nothing happened. "Aw..."

Rachel changed back to her human form and hugged her sister. "You're getting better all the time," she said. "I promise, you can come with me soon. But for now, you need to stay here—and do the homework I assigned you. If you finish before I return, I'll take you to the zoo, okay?"

Deborah nodded. "Thanks for bringing me into town with you," she said.

"Don't mention it. But study quick—I'll be back before you know it!"

Rachel left the hotel and walked the two blocks to Lan's skyscraper. She had shifted her body into the form of an older woman with a tall and wiry physique; it was identical to Lan's, except for the face. As for magic, she wore her sapphire amulet and had concealed several more charms in the pockets of her dark suit. She was, she thought, ready for anything.

Having investigated the company online, Rachel had some idea of what she would be facing. She would first have to get through the front door, which was locked with a keycard scanner as well as a facial recognition system. Next was a secured elevator constantly monitored by an armed guard. Finally, she'd have to break through the vault door itself, a state-of-the-art high-security steel portal that could withstand a bomb without cracking. And then, of course, she'd have to do it all again on the way out.

Rachel struggled to hide her grin. This was going to be *fun.*

The front door was simple enough. She waited until she saw another employee with a similar height and build as her, then 'accidentally' tripped her and slipped her keycard out of her handbag as she helped the lady back up. The front door accepted the keycard, and the facial recognition system accepted Rachel's copy of the woman's face. She was inside in minutes.

Rachel next hid her face behind a newspaper and shifted it into that of Hao Lan, then approached the guard by the secured elevator and ordered, "Vault." The echo of her voice had barely faded by the time he unlocked the elevator door and sent her on up. Rachel couldn't help but smile as the elevator began to rise. *Two down, one to go!*

She exited into a small vestibule with the vault door at the far end. Rachel drew a hand into her pocket for the door-opening amulet she had crafted, but a flicker of motion above her head stopped her. Glancing up, she saw two security cameras rotating above the steel door. A whirring noise above her head indicated that more were mounted above the elevator entrance as well.

I guess they added some new security features, she thought. *And I can't use magic while humans are watching me. Hmm...*

After a moment's thought, she walked to the vault door's keypad and pretended to press buttons. When nothing happened, she dialed the building's head of IT on her phone—she had memorized his information from the company's online directory just in case—and complained that the vault wasn't opening. A few threats, and a glance at the cameras to prove that she really was Hao Lan, did the trick. The door swung open and Rachel strolled inside, no longer able to hide the big grin on her face.

She took two steps into the vault before stopping, her body frozen in awe as she gazed at the treasure before her. There were piles of coins and ingots stretching back as far as she could see, innumerable display cases for antiques and jewelry, and dozens of famous sculptures. As for the walls, they were covered with famous paintings by the greatest classical masters. Even though Rachel had familiarized herself with Hao Lan's assets, it still took her several seconds to get moving. "Well," she murmured as she looked down multiple corridors filled with treasure. "Might take a little longer to find the lute than I expected..."

Her thoughts were interrupted by yips from deeper within the vault. She worked her way down the narrow, twisty corridors that cut through the heaps of treasure until she saw eight foxes standing hip-deep in a pile of gold coins. Sighing in mock frustration, Rachel said, "Guess I wasn't the first one up, huh? I... wait." She frowned. "Why aren't you shifted?"

She heard heavy footsteps behind her.

Rachel swiveled and saw a woman with dark hair, fiery red eyes, and a tall, wiry body stepping out from behind a stack of gold bars. Her face and form were identical to those that Rachel had adopted. "Lan, I presume."

"Yes." Lan smirked as she moved a few steps closer to Rachel. "Points for getting through the vault door instead of trying to creep in through the vents. If your stupid friends hadn't set off the alarms, you might even have broken in undetected." She chuckled. "But probably not."

You think you can outsmart a fox? Rachel let her teeth shift back slightly so that, when she bared them, she showed off her sharp canines. "The lute is ours by right, Lan. Give it back."

Lan spread her arms wide. "You're welcome to it, fox—if you can take it!" And then, moving so quickly that she was almost a blur, she leapt at Rachel. The fox couldn't dodge before Lan grabbed her shoulder with one hand and poured a foul-smelling liquid from a flask on her head with the other. Rachel's skin immediately began to crawl, and when she opened her mouth to insult Lan, she could only yip. Her suit jacket slipped off her now-furry body as she realized that she had somehow been forced back into her fox form.

"You foxes are so arrogant. You think there's no other magic besides your one gimmick." Lan lifted Rachel by the scruff of her neck with one hand and took several gold coins from the nearest pile with the other. Idly stacking the coins into a column, she continued, "For example, I'm pretty good at sympathetic magic. Do you even know what that is?"

What? thought Rachel. Sympathetic magic was a method of magically linking an object to a representation or part of that object. A classic example was bonding a doll and a person such that damaging the doll would injure the victim. It was part of Jewish mysticism, and Rachel knew a few such spells, but she had no idea how it was relevant at the moment.

"Here's an example!" said Lan, dropping Rachel onto her discarded suit as she threw down the column of coins. The nearest pile of treasure collapsed as Lan's coins scattered over the floor, and Rachel barely got to her paws before an avalanche of gold buried her up to her neck. Lan laughed as she turned away. "Hope you enjoyed the lesson, fox. When I get back, you won't enjoy what comes next."

Rachel struggled to shift, but that part of her felt tight and paralyzed. Her efforts to dig herself out of the heavy gold were similarly useless. Nonetheless, she bared her teeth and growled at Lan's back. *You might have magic too,* she thought, *and you might have somehow blocked my shifting, but I'm not done yet!*

Her sapphire amulet was lying within the pile of clothes that was under her body. Rachel wriggled a paw through the collar of her suit until she was touching the gem, then carefully visualized the geometric shapes and mystical symbols that were inscribed on its surface. With effort, she then yipped the required ritualistic words as best she could. Nothing happened for a few seconds, but then the amulet glowed softly as a warm pulse washed over her. She was able to shift into her human form moments later.

Rachel carefully knelt and grabbed her jacket and sapphire amulet in one hand before pushing herself out of the pile of gold. Lan turned as coins clattered to the ground, but Rachel had already reached into the jacket pocket and picked up a shielding charm. She raised it and chanted a few words—

But before she finished, Lan snapped her fingers. A fireball appeared from nowhere and blasted into the amulet, incinerating it. "Jewish magic?" Lan asked. "Who ever heard of a Jewish fox?"

Rachel yelped as she threw down the scraps of burning paper. *I didn't think I was this bad!* she thought. *But she's beaten everything I've thrown at her!*

"Actually, forget it." Lan snapped her fingers again and created another fireball in her hand. "I'm a descendent of Fucanglong, fox. Do you know who that is?"

"A dragon," said Rachel, backing away from Lan. "A treasure guardian."

"Exactly. That's my job too, and I won't—"

Shao Ling, in the form of a sleek and graceful fox, sprang through the air from behind a pile of sapphires and tackled Lan. Rachel moved to help, but Ling looked up at her and flicked her head towards the others. Free the others, she seemed to be saying. She could handle Lan on her own.

Burning with shame at needing to be rescued—by the girl she'd been hoping to impress, no less—Rachel grabbed a nearby staff that was covered in ornate runes and began digging out her classmates. She freed them quickly and led them to the exit just as blasts of fire began echoing throughout the entire room. The vault door had closed, so Rachel pulled down a Renoir painting, grabbed a quill and jeweled inkpot from a case, and began rewriting the door-opening amulet she had planned to use on the way in. "In Shaddai's name, He who made the heavens, seas, and earth, and in Raphael's name..."

A jet of fire scorched the ceiling.

"... by the writing of this amulet, made by I, Jin Rachel, daughter of Jin Esther... "

Ling yipped as she crashed through a display case. Rachel almost ran to help, but managed to force herself to remain at the door. She knew that the other girl didn't need her.

"... and in the name of Mefathiel as well, I order this door—"

Fire streaked over her head and creased a deep line into the wall. Glancing back, Rachel saw Ling running towards her and the other foxes, fleeing a blazing Lan. The dragon's eyes glowed as a fireball materialized in front of her.

"—be opened!" finished Rachel, feeling a brief shiver of fear as she slapped the amulet against the door. They were dead if she hadn't made the charm correctly.

But the door swung open, and everyone dashed out of the vault. As the other foxes fled into the vents, Rachel heard Lan running up behind her. "Shut off the elevators!" the dragon roared. "NOW!"

Not a chance, thought Rachel.

She gripped her sapphire amulet tightly in her mouth as she smashed through the elevator's glass door, then shifted into a bird as she fell. By the time Lan reached the elevator, Rachel was gone.

* * *

Deborah climbed onto Rachel's dormitory bed, tail wagging rapidly. "Tell me all about it!" she ordered. "How did Lan look when you kicked her butt?"

"I didn't kick anyone's butt," said Rachel, managing a faint smile. "All I did was escape. Ling did all the butt-kicking."

It was the day after the disastrous raid on Lan's skyscraper. The foxes had straggled back to campus and dispersed, Rachel in particular retreating to her room and avoiding everyone else. Though she had planned on finishing some amulets upon her return from Shanghai, she hadn't been able to make herself start. Instead, she had remained in bed all day.

"Yeah, but you helped save everyone else! That's still good!"

"I guess." Rachel leaned back with her tail splayed out behind her. She thought about tucking it under her skirt so as to maintain her human appearance, but couldn't summon the energy. "I mean, I'm happy that everyone's safe, but it still sucks to lose so badly. I'd be toast if Ling hadn't saved me." She blushed. "She probably thinks I'm a total idiot."

"You're not an idiot!" Deborah protested. "You've taught me loads of stuff!"

Looking at the half-completed amulets and charms on her desk, Rachel sighed and said, "That's the other thing. I had all kinds of magic that Lan didn't, but she still trounced me. I'm not nearly as good as I thought I was. And if I'm not good... how can I teach you?"

"You can teach me because you're awesome," said Deborah with a nod of her head. "I *know* you're great at magic. And I know you'll smash Lan next time!" She beamed. "Can I come with? Please?"

Rachel couldn't help but laugh at that.

Someone knocked at the door, and when Deborah ran to open it, Ling stepped in. "Hey," she said, waving at Rachel as she approached the bed. "What's up?"

Rachel froze. *Ling's in my room!* "Noth—nothing since yesterday. Thanks for saving me from Lan." She looked down. "I know I probably looked pretty stupid—"

"Not at all," said Ling. "You did great."

"I..." Rachel paused. "Really?"

"Sure. You got in without being noticed, you fought Lan long enough for me to sneak into position, and you opened the door that let us all out. Thanks for that, by the way." She smiled. "I had no idea you were so clever. I'm impressed."

Rachel felt her stomach jump and her cheeks heat up. Her failure forgotten for the moment, she stammered, "... so, um, anyway! How did you get into the vault?"

"I turned into a sunbird, slipped into the janitor's bag before he left for work that morning, and snuck out once he began to clean the vault. I would have found the lute if Lan hadn't shown up five minutes later to catch Biyu and her team." Ling frowned. "I was surprised that Biyu really thought Lan wouldn't have the vents watched. I thought she was smarter than that."

Rachel recalled that one of the foxes trapped in the pile of gold had looked like Biyu. *So that's where she was...*

"But anyways..." Ling sat next to Rachel on the bed. "How did you fight off Lan's potion?"

"My healing amulet," said Rachel.

"May I examine it?"

Feeling like she was in a dream, Rachel lifted the sapphire and guided it into Ling's hands. "So... what was that stuff Lan used on us, anyway?"

"Garlic, pig's blood, sheep's blood, and a few other things," murmured Ling as she examined the amulet. "Neutralizes our magic. It was popularized during Wang Ze's rebellion against the Song Dynasty, since many huli jing took Wang's side."

Rachel would have commented on her knowledge, but then Ling's tail brushed against hers and a fluttering sensation spread through her body. *Dear God,* she thought, *please don't let this ever end.*

After a few minutes, Ling looked up. "This looks like it took a lot of skill to make."

"Uh, thanks," babbled Rachel, the words almost falling out of her mouth. She wondered if this was how humans felt when a huli jing bewitched them. "I practice all the time so I can get better and, uh, teach my sister better too."

"You're teaching her?" Ling asked.

"Yep!" Deborah cheered. "I'm already making little amulets and stuff, and they really work! I've got the best teacher ever!"

"I don't doubt it," said Ling.

Rachel smiled as the last of her shame faded. "You're smart too, Deborah. You're..." But then her voice trailed off because her tail had wrapped around Ling's. "I mean, uh, you're really..."

A pillow smacked Rachel in the face. Startled, she realized that her little sister was giggling at them. "Oh, just kiss already!" she yelled as she scampered to the other side of the room.

Rachel flushed and leapt to her feet. "Hey! We—" But she stopped when she heard Ling laughing, and even she couldn't help but chuckle when she turned back. "We're not dating," she stammered. "Honest."

"We can go into that later," said Ling. "In the meantime, I did want to talk to you about Lan. We still need to get Diaochan's lute back."

Rachel took a few breaths to calm down. "Right. Maybe this time the whole class should work together as one pack. Think that would help?"

"Nope. Before you showed up, Lan plucked hairs from the tails of all the foxes she caught. If they attack her again, she can drop them with her sympathetic magic. We're the only ones that have a chance." She smiled. "Want to try raiding Lan's vault together?"

"Yes!" said Rachel before she got control of herself. "I mean, that sounds fine. We'll just need a new strategy. She'll be ready for amulet magic as well as huli jing shifting, and we can probably assume her guards know about magic too, but—"

"Do you know any sympathetic magic of your own?" asked Ling.

"Sure. It's one of the first things I learned when I began studying the *Sefer Raziel*. But I'd need something of Lan's to do it. Unless we can get her hair or nail clippings or..."

Ling took three small gold coins out of her pocket and placed them on Rachel's desk. "Almost swallowed these when I was running out of there. Will they do?"

Rachel picked up the coins, examined them, and grinned. The anticipation of the hunt had crept over her again, and looking into Ling's eyes, she knew the other huli jing felt it too. They would bring down their quarry and would do it together. Rachel couldn't think of anything she wanted more.

"Yeah," she said aloud. "That'll work."

* * *

The glass elevator door on the vault floor that Rachel had shattered had been replaced and reinforced, but that wasn't enough to stop the two tigers from crashing through it.

Rachel and Ling roared as the guards—a half dozen men and women armed with assault rifles and bottles full of the anti-shifting potion—dropped their weapons in panic. As they flattened themselves against the far wall, Rachel shifted to her human form and pointed at two of them. "You, write down the vault combination. You, use your security key to lock the elevator on this floor. The rest of you, into the bathroom, or my friend starts eating you."

The guards looked stunned for a moment, but when Ling roared again they almost trampled each other in their haste to obey.

The elevator reached the floor a few moments after the guards had been barricaded inside the restroom. Rachel grabbed the duffel bag that they had stored in the elevator car and took out a suit and some amulets, then slid it over to Ling. "I'm ready," she said once she had dressed. "You?"

Ling looked up from the duffel and growled in assent.

After loading up her pockets with magic charms, Rachel walked to the vault's keypad and began entering the code. "You'll take the flunkies, I'll deal with Lan, and then we'll get the lute, right?" She grinned as Ling growled again, then pressed the last number. "Great. Let's go!"

There were 24 heavily armed guards standing inside the vault's entrance, but it didn't matter. Ling shifted as she attacked them, tackling one man as a tiger, dodging away as a hawk, and then changing into a leopard to do it again. She became a snake that hid in the treasure piles, an elephant that kicked heavy ingots at her enemies, an ape that laid waste with heavy fists. She was whatever she needed to be, and the humans could do nothing about her.

Rachel stared in wonder at Ling for several moments before remembering the job she had to do. Stowing the duffel just inside the steel door, she ran deep into the vault.

It was only a few moments before an amulet of protection tugged against Rachel's chest and she threw herself underneath a blast of dragonfire. Rolling back to her feet, she found herself looking at Lan. "You know," said the dragon, fire running over her body and charring the edges of her suit, "Some foxes would have gotten the hint by now."

"Some dragons would have returned our lute to us by now," said Rachel. She took two paper amulets from her pocket and held them up. "Just saying."

The dragon snarled and blasted another fireball. Rachel swept one of her amulets in front of her, and the flame spattered against an invisible shield a foot away from Rachel's face, but the amulet burst into flame and crumbled to ash in her hands. Lan sent two more blasts at her, both of which destroyed the amulets Rachel deployed as shields, and the fox found herself backing up as Lan approached. "How many of those do you have?" asked Lan. "Think they'll last five minutes?"

"I have enough," said Rachel as she held up another.

Lan, having reached the spot where Rachel had begun their duel, stooped to pick up something from the ground. "You know, after the lesson I gave you on sympathetic magic the other day, it's a shame you didn't learn anything."

"What makes you say that?" asked Rachel.

"This." Lan's eyes sparkled with amusement, and she brandished the item she had picked up—a scrap from one of Rachel's burned amulets. "Shall I show you again?"

Her hands burst into flame, and the amulet scrap burned... as did the other amulets on Rachel's person. Yelping, the huli jing quickly shucked off her suit jacket before she was burned. Realizing that she had no spells to block Lan's fire, Rachel shifted into her fastest form—a falcon—and flew towards Lan's head. Her talons reached for the dragon—

But Lan grabbed her by the leg first and hurled her into the nearest pile of gold. She hit it with a heavy thump and flapped her wings for a moment, then slid down to its base. She switched to her human form a moment later.

"Fool," said Lan as she approached Rachel. "Did you think a common bird could outrace a dragon?"

"Miss Hao!" Rachel saw two of the remaining guards dragging Ling, in her fox form, towards them. "We finally got that stuff on her. What do you want us to do?"

Lan smirked. "Dump her next to the bird. I'll deal with them together." She cracked her knuckles as Ling was tossed down next to Rachel. "I've been looking forward to this."

"Want us to spray the other one?"

"No, she's resistant. I'll just fry them." Lan scattered a few coins and collapsed a mound of treasure around the foxes as she had the other day. "Pathetic. As if mere foxes had a chance." She raised a hand and extended it at the huli jing.

And then a red-coated kitten with a protection-from-fire amulet around her neck sprang down from the nearest pile of treasure and landed on Lan's face.

"GET HER OFF OF ME!" screamed Lan as the kitten's claws cut into her cheeks. Flames blazed around her head, but to no effect. "Impossible! Your amulets are ashes!"

Rachel flashed a proud grin at Lan. "Yeah," she said. "But hers aren't."

Deborah mewled in triumph.

One of the guards tried to grab the cat but couldn't get his hand through Lan's fire. The dragon stopped casting her flames, the guards both went for Deborah—and Ling turned to Rachel and spat out the three small gold coins that she had stolen the previous day, which Rachel had enchanted with sympathetic magic, and which Ling had kept tucked under her tongue through the entire fight. Rachel wrenched a hand free and caught them, then muttered a few words and yelled, "Deborah! Now!" as she scattered the coins. Deborah leapt—

And the mountain of treasure surrounding Ling and Rachel burst outwards in all directions, burying Lan and her guards in a tidal wave of gold.

Rachel high-fived Ling's paw and hugged Deborah, who purred merrily in her arms, before shifting into Lan's body and returning to the vault entrance. The two remaining conscious guards hastened to follow 'Lan's' orders to bring her the lute and the hairs of the other huli jing students, to open the door so she could move it all to a more secure location, and to fetch her a spare suit to replace the one she had burned off. Neither of them noticed Deborah slipping back into the duffel, or Ling following her.

Five minutes later, Rachel walked out of the skyscraper carrying Ling, Deborah, and Diaochan's lute.

* * *

"... you have done this Academy, and all huli jing, proud."

Rachel grinned as Yi led the student body in applauding. Her face was red, but she told herself this was just due to embarrassment at Yi's copious praise. It had nothing to do with the fact that Shao Ling was standing so close to her on the stage that they could have held hands. Nothing whatsoever.

Deborah, at least, didn't seem to have any problem with Yi's compliments. She stood at Rachel's other side and happily waved to the crowd from beneath the Mickey Mouse hat she had bought at the zoo. "Thank you!" she yelled. "Thank you lots!"

When the clapping finally died down, Yi turned to the other huli jing. "I would like you all to learn from their success and incorporate its lessons into your own strategies," she said. "Now, on that note, class is dismissed for the day... but don't forget about our celebration hunt and cookout tonight in honor of the recovery of Diaochan's lute." She smiled. "Jin Rachel, Shao Ling, Jin Deborah: thank you once again." And another roar of applause greeted them.

Ling's friends surrounded her almost as soon as the presentation ended and everyone spilled outside. Rachel took a step after her, then paused and turned back to Deborah first. "Hey, kitto. Got a second?"

"Hmm?" Deborah looked up at Rachel. "What is it?"

"I just wanted to tell you again how great you were back there." Rachel lifted Deborah up and wrapped her into a big hug. "Your amulet and your shifting were perfect. I think you're better with magic than I was at your age."

Deborah blushed a bright scarlet and, for once, seemed to be at a loss for words.

"And so," continued Rachel, "I'm not going to wait any longer to take you with me when I hunt with the class and stuff. You're more than—agh!"

Deborah had already wriggled free and let out an earsplitting cheer. "YAY! That's awesome! That's—"

"*If* you keep up your studies!" amended Rachel hastily, though she was still smiling. "Foxes like us always need to be learning new tricks. But if you stick with it, I'll make sure you can hunt with everyone else— and maybe even go on missions, if Yi says it's okay. How about it?"

Deborah nodded rapidly. "Deal! In fact, I'll start today's stuff now so we can go on the celebration hunt together!"

"Great!" called Rachel as Deborah began to run off. "Good luck!"

She watched her sister head back to the dormitories for a moment before turning away. Ling, she saw, was standing next to her, a coy smile on her face. "She's a good kit," Ling said. "Talented too."

"Yeah, she's brilliant. She'll be better than me someday."

"She has a very good teacher." Rachel blushed, and Ling's smile grew. "I need to ask you something. Can we talk?"

"Sure." Rachel looked around as Ling led her to the shade of a large tree, but didn't see any other huli jing near them. "Where's the rest of your friends?"

"I'll see them tonight at the hunt and the cookout, but I wanted to see you first," said Ling. "You've got plenty of talent as a shifter, so I was wondering if you'd like me to show you a few of my more difficult forms. Seeing as how we work so well together, I was hoping we could do more missions as a team, and I'd be happy to teach you some shifts that might be useful."

Rachel's heart leapt. "Sure," she said, desperately struggling to sound nonchalant. "And, um, if you want, I could show you some of my magic too! Teach you how amulets work, maybe make you a few. Sound good?"

"Of course," said Ling, a faint grin still on her lips. "Thank you."

Rachel hesitated. She wanted to do so much more with Ling than just talk about magic. But she couldn't just ask the smartest, prettiest girl on campus to be her girlfriend...

Of course I can! she insisted to herself. *We just beat a dragon together! There's never going to be a better time to ask her!*

"And also..." she managed, "maybe we could hang out other times too? You know, go hunting, catch movies, things like that?"

Neither of them spoke for a moment, and Rachel felt as if her stomach had knotted up—but then Ling stepped close to her and kissed her on her cheek. "I thought you'd never ask," she said as her tail wrapped around Rachel's leg. "You are one of the cleverest foxes I have ever met, Rachel, and your passion for those you care about is obvious. I would love to get to know you better."

It took all of Rachel's self-control not to wrap Ling into a big hug and cheer.

"In fact," Ling continued, "Why don't we start now? A private hunt, before the big party, could be fun." She broke away from Rachel and gestured into the woods. "Want to help me bring down a deer?"

"Sure." Rachel dropped into a crouch and flashed a smile at Ling, feeling almost euphoric with glee. "Ready when you are!"

"Then let's go." Ling shifted into her fox body, the sleekest and most graceful form that Rachel had ever seen, and took off towards the woods. She was halfway there by the time she turned her head and yipped at Rachel. *Come on!* she seemed to say. *Let's go have some fun!*

Rachel laughed and shifted, and a moment later the two foxes were chasing each other through the woods.

The Chosen One

By Katrina Nicholson

"Sulfur Hexafluoride is six times heavier than air and has been known to suffocate people who play with it by displacing the air in their lungs," René's teacher warned. "As a mage, one of the ways you could save them would be to change the molecular weight of the gas and make it lighter than air. This is the principle upon which mage-built airships work."

René stared at the tank of sulfur hexafluoride. He imagined himself strutting down the hall as classes let out for the day. Tall. Handsome. Rugged whiskers. Skin like dark chocolate. He'd toss back his corkscrew curls, cock a finger, and say 'hey baby' in the voice of James Earl Jones. The girls would swoon. Probably half the boys, too. René wasn't picky. He drew the line at teachers, though.

There was nothing he could do about his big ears, buzz cut, baby face, or the fact that he had a fair amount of milk in his chocolate, but the voice? That's what sulfur hexafluoride was for.

Monsieur Jean-Baptiste turned away from writing the chemical composition on the white board. He was trendy and dark, with a shaved head and a close-cropped goatee. He was young, but his sharp eyes zeroed in on René like he could mind read dumb ideas. René folded his hands on the lab bench and pretended to pay attention.

Monsieur Jean-Baptiste turned back to the board and began to rearrange the elements on the periodic table as he explained the unintentional havoc a mage could unleash if he failed to pay attention in chemistry class. René scanned the classroom. The other students all had their mage-built remembersheets out, dutifully taking notes with their fingernails.

René grabbed the tank of gas. He wasn't a mage yet—he still had

285

two more years before his 18th birthday—and his chemistry teacher would never be, but he wasn't worried. Magic chose people from magical families. Nobody really agreed on how. Catholics said it was angels. Muslims thought it was the will of Allah acting through prophets. Scientists argued over whether mages' different DNA made them mutants or aliens. However it happened, the rule was one mage parent, one kid chosen by magic. That's why the *ordinaires*, or regular Haitians, called mages *l'élu*—the chosen ones. Because a lot of mageborn got passed over and ended up teaching pre-mage classes or doing boring regular jobs.

René was sure that wouldn't happen to him. Both his parents were mages and he only had one brother. The magic *had* to choose him. And if he put his life in danger now, it would Break early and save him. His classmate Nicola had skipped straight from second year *prépas* to Port-au-Prince's *Grande École de Magie* after her house fell on her in the big earthquake.

One puff of sulfur hexafluoride and it'd be just like his dad described. Suddenly he would feel like anything was possible—because it was. He stuck the nozzle in his mouth and cranked the valve open.

* * *

René woke up with his fourteen-year-old brother Étienne's annoyed face upside down in front of him.

"If you're done messing around, can you drive me and Ludo to the junk heap?" Étienne asked, brushing his waist-length dreads over his scrawny shoulder.

Wait, Étienne wasn't upside down. *René* was upside down. He could feel cold tile against his scalp. He tried to sit up and realized he was draped over the lab bench with his feet hooked under the taps.

"Ah, Monsieur Toussaint. Back in the land of the living, I see," Monsieur Jean-Baptiste said.

René's classmates had all gone home, but Monsiueur Jean-Baptiste sat at his desk, feet up, sunglasses on, waiting for his least responsible student to recover from his latest misadventure. The teacher dropped his feet to the floor and went over to help Étienne unhook René.

René braced his palms on the floor and flipped over, landing on his feet with a thump. Ludo, Étienne's white boyfriend, transferred his saxophone case to his other hand and scooped René's sandals out of the sinks. Ludo and Étienne were students of the art academy down the road. Their clothes stood out like sore thumbs next to the staid prépas uniform of navy polo and khaki shorts. Étienne had on a tie-dyed shirt in shades of pink and gold and baggy tribal-patterned shorts that somehow managed not to clash. Ludo wore his usual 'uniform' of skinny jeans, tight T-shirt with ironic English slogan, and trilby hat. Ludo couldn't read English, but René had it as his elective. He decided not to mention that Ludo's shirt read 'Hello Titty.'

"You were extremely lucky, Monsieur Toussaint," Monsieur Jean-Baptist warned as René put his sandals back on. "If I wasn't so smart, you'd be dead."

"He's *always* lucky," Étienne complained.

"I'm not *lucky*, I have *magic*," René insisted.

"You can't know that yet," his teacher frowned.

"Well I do. I just need to make it come out."

"Before you accidentally kill yourself," Étienne added.

Monsieur Jean-Baptiste sighed. "I'll have to send a message home about this. Wait here."

The teacher left to use the message mirror in the office.

Étienne tugged on René's arm. "Come on, let's get out of here."

"What's the big rush? He won't reach anybody."

"He might. Mom and Dad are home, remember?"

"Oh crap, I forgot."

René's mother, a mage-architect, and his father, a mage-epidemiologist, were in such high demand that they were almost always abroad doing work for the World Mage Council. But the January earthquake had brought them both home, along with mage and ordinaire contractors from all over the French-speaking world. Like Ludo's mother, who was an ordinaire-carpenter from Quebec. René's dad was off investigating some cholera cases that had cropped up in the co-operative sugarcane farms in the Artibonite Valley, but his mom was in the city helping redesign the collapsed domes of the Presidential Palace. And when she heard about this, she'd be *pissed*.

"Let's go, let's go. No use spending this unseasonably sunny day grounded," René said.

He herded his brother and Ludo to the window and opened it. The hot, sticky air felt like a slap in the face after a full day of climate control. He boosted the boys out and dived after them.

The drop was less than a meter. They tumbled into a bed of mage-grown bromeliads in the school colors, picked themselves up, and ran for René's secondhand jeep. It was parked alone on the student side of the lot. René had the doors off, so they vaulted inside like gendarmes—René and Étienne in front, Ludo and saxophone in back. René cranked the starter handle and the mage-built perpetual motion engine clattered to life. René stomped on the clutch, put the engine in gear, and sped out of the lot, taking the turn on two wheels.

Étienne and Ludo fumbled for their seatbelts as René turned off Rue Rigaud and onto Avenue Panaméricaine, which led down the hill toward Port-au-Prince proper. They left the suburb of Petion-Ville and plunged into the jungle. A pandemonium of parrots exploded from the fronds of a coconut palm.

"Slow down! Étienne shouted as he struggled to sketch the parrots on a remembersheet.

"No way!" René hooted. "This is fantastic!"

"You're scaring Ludo!"

René glanced in the rearview. There was white-people white, which was really more of a pink, then there was white-white, then there was frightened-Ludovic-Tremblay white. He looked like one of those cave worms that never saw sunlight.

"Relax!" René yelled. "Even if we go off the road, my magic will protect us!"

René grinned as he pictured the jeep losing traction and skidding into the palms. His magic would increase the elasticity of the trunks. They would bend like rubber bands and snap the vehicle back onto the road.

Étienne reached through the seats. Ludo clung to Étienne with one hand and his sax case with the other.

"Magic didn't do anything for Nicola's mother!" Étienne reminded them.

When Nicola's house collapsed, her magic had Broken early and scattered the particles that made up the concrete wall of her house, saving her life. Her father, a mage, had been out of town at the time, but her mother, an ordinaire, was just down the hall. She was crushed to death when the roof fell in. Their classmates and teachers said it was a horrible accident. Privately, René thought Nicola had panicked. Otherwise, why didn't she save mother? When René's powers Broke, he'd used them to save everybody. His plan was to become a mage-gendarme and give himself super strength so he could take down bad guys with a single punch.

But he eased off the accelerator anyway—just a bit—and only because he didn't want to have to clean Ludo's puke out of the backseat.

The jeep rattled down the winding road, through tree-lined mage-built residential neighborhoods that were largely untouched by the quake, until the terrain leveled out and they entered the city.

Port-au-Prince was one of the most prosperous cities in the Americas. It was home of the world's most prestigious magic university, the headquarters of the World Mage Council, and one of the largest multinational mage-run technology firms. But ever since the quake, the city looked like a boxer with half its teeth knocked out. The quixotic mage-built high rises and airy, historic wooden gingerbread houses remained, but anything made of concrete, stone, or brick had collapsed. Huge construction cranes, scaffolding, and crews of mage-builders floating pieces of glass and metal into place were everywhere. The clutter didn't seem to deter the tourists, though. There were two huge mage-built airships, each with gondolas nearly as large as their gas bags, disgorging passengers at the harbor.

René wove through the chaos onto the wide boulevard splitting La Place de Heroes de l'Independence. The park was home to statues of some of Haiti's most famous historical figures. The guy in the uniform with the shoulder mops and the sword was Toussaint Loverture, the former slave who became the first president of the Republic of Haiti in 1792. The robed lady holding the mirror was René's personal hero, Josephine Clermont—the mulatto mage who invented the message mirror in 1791 and brought the world's mages to Haiti. Under her leadership, they formed the World Mage Council, forced an end to slavery, and headed off the impending revolution.

They ducked down as they drove past the half-ruined Presidential Palace, just in case René and Étienne's mom was looking out. René turned north onto Route Nationale #1 and gunned it down the busy highway until they reached the outskirts, where greenery gave way to sand and desert. Here was the towering junk heap where the cleaning crews had dumped all the rubble.

It was fenced. Two bored-looking ordinaire-gendarmes in smart navy uniforms guarded the gate. They were there to keep out kids, but artists and builders were encouraged to reuse what they could. When the gendarmes saw Étienne in the passenger seat, they waved the jeep through.

When I'm a mage-gendarme, I'll have a more exciting assignment than that, René promised himself.

He parked the jeep at the edge of the pile and flicked the interrupter. The engine ground to a halt. René and Étienne climbed out. Ludo boosted himself onto the hood and took out his sax. As Étienne looked for bits of metal to melt down for his sculptures, Ludo struck up a mellow *compas* tune, his canvas slip-ons tapping out an accompanying beat on the fender.

Ludo hardly ever talked. He was self-conscious of his accent, which made him sound like he had something stuck up his nose—but damn, the kid could play! The song reminded René of being a kid and watching his father twirl his mother around the living room. His hips swayed to the music, but he forced them to stop before he embarrassed himself and started dancing around the dump.

René examined the sketches for Étienne's latest project. Étienne's sculptures were the reason he'd turned down his place in prépas and gone to art school. René liked to think of Étienne's style as Cap-Haitien crossed with Greek mythology. He made things like coffee farmers with horse legs and water-carriers balancing the world on their heads. He welded them together out of junk, painted them bright colors, then gave them away. The newly renovated Afro-European Friendship Center on top of Mt. de L'Hôpital had asked for a whole set for their sculpture garden. This new one—a trio of dancers with snakes for dreads—must be part of that. René's parents weren't happy about it (most practical mages thought art was a waste of magic) but there didn't seem to be any doubt that Étienne would turn out a mage-artist.

If he left it alone, Étienne's magic would Break in four years—at 2:35 a.m. on January 12. Magic was weird like that. It showed up 18 years to the minute after you were born, or not at all. René only had to wait half that time—until 11:39 a.m. on September 12, but René was at least 20 times more impatient than his brother.

He picked up a piece of rebar and tossed it into the air. He watched it turn end over end and caught it when it came back down. He imagined it was a bullet fired by a bad guy. His powers would turn it into pudding before it even touched him. If he threw the rebar really high and stepped underneath it, would his magic Break and transform it?

Rene heaved the rebar skyward.

"René Toussaint!" his pocket screeched.

René jumped and fumbled for his portable message mirror. He forgot about catching the rebar and howled when it landed on his toe.

"Ow! What?" René asked as he flipped the mirror open.

A dark face with an even darker expression glared back at him. "Oh, hi Mom."

At 'Mom,' Étienne's terrified face popped from the rubble like a gopher and Ludo's song ended in a goosey honk. René had explained that their parents didn't disapprove of their sons' sexuality (just their everything else) but Ludo was still more afraid of their mom than they were.

According to Vodou, the Haitian national religion, mages got their power through being possessed by *lwa*, the sprits who acted as intermediaries between God and humans. There were a lot of lwa, obviously, since there were a lot of mages, but generally speaking they could be divided into two groups: *Rada* (cool and calm) and *Petro* (fiery and aggressive). Nobody ever had trouble guessing which one Françoise Toussaint's lwa belonged to.

Étienne and Ludo gravitated together and clasped hands as René took the brunt of Françoise's anger.

"Don't you 'hi mom' me! I just got a message from your chemistry teacher. What in the name of all the lwa in the pantheon were you thinking, inhaling sulfur hexaflouride? *After* your teacher had just finished telling you it was dangerous?"

"I—"

"Let me guess. You *weren't* thinking. *As usual.* You— where are you?"

His mother's voice dropped dangerously low on that last question, which meant she already knew where they were. No sense adding 'lying' to his list of transgressions.

"We're, um, at the junk heap."

"The junk heap. The huge, dangerous, lice-riddled pile of garbage that I specifically forbade you from visiting? *That* junk heap?"

"Um... yes?"

"Is your brother with you?"

René exchanged a helpless look with Étienne. One of their mom's biggest pet peeves was Étienne's dreadlocks. She was convinced they were like a big sign that said, 'lice please live here.'

"Yes."

"Come home. Right now," his mother growled. Her voice promised an evening of yelling, lectures, and at least a month of being grounded. She closed her mirror with a snap.

René swallowed and put his mirror back in his pocket. He tried to ignore the fact that his hands were shaking. What kind of gendarme was afraid of his own mother?

"Come on, I'll drop you off on the way," René said to Ludo as he and Étienne climbed back into the jeep.

"No thanks. I'll walk," Ludo whispered, then scurried away before they could catch him.

* * *

"You ever get the feeling Mom's trying to make up for being gone all the time by acting like a prison warden whenever we put a toe out of line?" Étienne asked.

The jeep's engine growled as it pulled them up the steep side of Mt. Des Cadetes, one of the two huge, thickly forested hills south of the city proper that separated Petion-Ville from the sea. The only things up here were the World Mage Headquarters and the homes of Haiti's most prominent mages. Ordinaires traveled up mountains in airships and mages used their magic, so no one really thought it was important to flatten out the road. Near the summit, the road curved to follow the contour of the hill and became their driveway.

The Toussaint house was a series of offset, glass-fronted mahogany boxes cantilevered out from the mountain in that gravity-defying way mage-architects liked so much.

"I don't spend a lot of time analyzing her reasons," René admitted. "I need all my brain power just to keep her from pulling my damn ears off."

René's cousins referred to his ears as 'jug handles.' The little ones used them to steer when he gave them shoulder rides. René's dad swore there had been other big-eared people on his side of the family, but his mom's tendency of grabbing them whenever he misbehaved wasn't helping them get any smaller.

René parked the jeep on the asphalt patch underneath the house.

"She wouldn't *really* hurt you," Étienne worried. "I mean, the magic wouldn't have chosen her if she was cruel. She's just... strict."

292

"Yeah, well, wait till she gets strict with *your* ears."

René and Étienne dawdled as they got their school bags out of the jeep. They trudged up a long, switchbacked staircase cut into the rock and let themselves in the front door. René stuck his head cautiously into the echoey, high-ceilinged foyer. The whole place smelled like spiced meat and pumpkin. His mom was calm enough to cook.

"Coast is cle——aaaaaah!" René yelled as a pair of iron-hard fingers clamped onto his left ear.

René was left staring at the diamond-patterned *vévé* stitched into the lapel of his mother's maroon business suit. It was the symbol of her lwa, Ogou, who represented (among other things) iron and war, neither of which were encouraging from the standpoint of René's ear.

"René Toussaint! Inhaling dangerous gases! Disobeying a teacher! *Climbing out the school window!* What do you have to say for yourself?"

"Ow! Ow! Mom! I'm sorry! I'm sorry!" René whined.

René followed his mom into the kitchen on tiptoes, trying to keep the pressure off his ear. Étienne followed meekly.

The kitchen was a spacious slate-floored room with floor-to-ceiling windows that looked out over the valley. There was a huge marble-topped island in the middle with a breakfast bar on one side and a cooktop on the other. René's father stood in front of the cooktop, stripping the peelings from a basket of vegetables with a wave of his hand.

Alain Toussaint was tall with wide shoulders and a broad face. He kept his hair in short twists and his body well-muscled for all the outdoor work his job required. The two serpents of Damballah, the creator and healer, were embroidered on the breast of his pristine white polo.

René's mother deposited him onto one the stools opposite his father. Étienne sat beside René.

"Dad! What are you doing here?" René exclaimed.

His father raised his eyebrows. "I live here."

René's mother went around the island and gave her husband a kiss. With her tight curls cut into a short bob, high heels, sharp suit, and huge hoop earrings, she was the picture of a calm, self-assured business-woman. If René didn't still have the sore ear to prove it, he would never have guessed she'd just been hopping mad.

Françoise picked up a turnip and chopped it into the big pot that simmered on the cooktop.

"Dad, I thought you were in the valley," René said.

"I was. Until your mother told me what you'd been up to. I thought we made ourselves clear last month after you went to the swamp to wrestle caimans."

"We didn't *find* any," René protested.

"I was only going to draw them," Étienne mumbled.

Françoise glared at them.

"We're sorry," René said.

"We won't do it again," Étienne promised.

"Sorry won't keep you alive," Alain told René. "And yes, you will do it again," he said to Étienne.

"Check them over, won't you Alain? I'm afraid they caught something down there," Françoise said.

Alain left the vegetables in her care and went around the island. "Up," he told the boys.

They dutifully got to their feet and stood still as their father's sharp eyes inspected their skin, hair, and clothes. As a mage-epidemiologist, Alain Toussaint used his magic to see bacteria and viruses without a microscope. They showed themselves to him in different colors, which, combined with their shape, helped him identify them. Cholera, their big worry at the moment, looked like an orange worm.

Alain ran his hands over the soles of René's sandals and the palms of his hands, inactivating the bacteria he found. He took longer with Étienne. Étienne had been digging around in the junk pile and had bacteria all over his hands, feet, clothes, and hair.

"*Vibrio Cholerae?*" Françoise asked nervously.

Alain shook his head. "Plenty of *C. perfringens*, which is to be expected, some *tenani*, and a smattering of *E. coli*."

He rejoined Françoise and dumped the chopped cabbage, carrots, celery, onion, potato, and parsley into the pot. The cooker made heat by reacting with the air when it was uncovered. As mages, either one of them could have transformed the meal from raw to cooked in an instant, but Alain claimed food tasted better if it was cooked gradually the way *ordinaire* did it.

The boys watched their father boil soup for a few minutes in silence while Françoise got out bowls and glasses. Their parents' lips moved, but the boys couldn't hear what they were saying. Ordinaire parents went to another room to talk privately. Mage parents used a frequency too low for humans to hear. René could feel the rumble of it in his chest. It made him want to cough. He watched them, wishing there was a lip-reading elective at school.

"So here's what your mother and I are thinking," Alain said after a while. "René, adults aren't always going to be around to save you from your own foolishness. Intellectually you might know that, but we don't think you really understand. So this evening you'll go to see Granmè. She will show you the future so that you can learn the possible consequences of your recklessness."

René groaned. His grandmother was a mage-*mambo*, a Vodou priestess with real magic. She'd been chosen by Papa Legba, the crossroads guardian who stood with one foot in the spirit world and one foot in the human world. One of her specialties was looking into the future. Her other specialty was poking her grandson with her crutch and telling him the lwa were never going to choose him unless he smartened up.

Alain turned to Étienne. René scowled. Nothing they could do to Étienne would be as bad as a visit to Granmè.

"Étienne, your mother and I can't stop you from making your art, though we wish you'd put as much effort into your pre-mage studies as you do into your sculptures. Likewise we can't stop you from going out into the world looking for materials and inspiration. But since doing so will certainly expose you to parasites and bacteria, we think you need to take some precautions. Therefore you'll be going to see *matant* Claudette tonight for a haircut."

Étienne's lip quivered. "You... you want me to cut off my dreads?"

"Since you can't stay away from that filthy junk heap, we think that would be best," Françoise replied.

"But... but..."

Poor Étienne. He'd had those dreads since he was eight or nine. He spent ages caring for them—twisting them, squeezing special soap into them, tying them up in a scarf before going to sleep. Cutting them off would be like putting a beloved pet to sleep.

Alain brightened. "Now. That's settled. Who wants Soup Joumou?"

* * *

"Can't we just say we went and not actually go?" Étienne asked as he and René trudged down the stairs.

"Yeah, sure. We can just tell Mom that our aunt's magic decided to go on a conveniently timed vacation. And there were no scissors in the house."

Étienne sighed. He slumped into the passenger seat of the jeep and buckled himself in.

"Relax. Hair grows back."

"Not *fast*," Étienne moaned.

"They're making you cut your *hair*?!" a voice squeaked from the backseat.

René and Étienne jumped.

"Ludo!"

"What are you doing here?!"

"My mom dropped me off. I wanted to make sure you were okay but I couldn't make myself knock on the door."

"Well you're just in time," Étienne said as René cranked the engine. "You can come meet our crazy grandmother. She's a Vodou priestess. With magic."

Ludo's eyes bulged. The pink drained from his cheeks.

René rolled his eyes. "Or you can sit in the car and wait for us while we go inside."

"The second one," Ludo decided.

"Quelle surprise," René quipped.

Étienne elbowed his brother, then turned to take Ludo's hand. "Thanks for coming."

"I wouldn't miss it," Ludo replied, gazing into Etienne's eyes.

"You *are* missing it," René complained. "You're staying in the car."

Étienne and Ludo ignored him. Their faces gravitated toward each other. Their eyes closed. Their lips puckered. Then René hit the accelerator and their foreheads clonked like two coconuts.

"Ow!" they yelled together.

René laughed. "No kissing in the car."

Étienne scowled at René as he backed them down the driveway. When that got no reaction, Étienne sighed and scrabbled for the overhead bar as René floored it up the hill.

Their grandmother lived on Mt. de L'Hôpital, so René drove to the peak of Mt. Des Cadetes and headed for the bridge that connected the bizarre bubble shapes of the World Mage Council headquarters with the Afro-European Friendship Center atop the other mountain. The official name of the bridge was L'Arch de Réconciliation but everybody called it The Rainbow. It was made of mage-built gripglass, so it had no railings, no supports, nothing. It was just a huge arcing ribbon that sparkled in the slanting rays of the evening sun. The Rainbow had been built in 1792 to commemorate the end of slavery and was considered one of the seven wonders of the magic world.

René felt his body go heavy and heard the jeep's frame groan as they drove onto the bridge. He swerved left and right around vibrantly painted *taptaps* full of tourists taking photos of themselves leaning precariously over the edge.

Étienne clutched at the roll bar. "Slow *down!*" He yelled. "Even gripglass can't save us from *your* driving."

"Ha ha," René grumbled. Everybody knew it was impossible to fall off gripglass. Its titanic gravitational field was so strong that you could drive a dump truck across upside down.

Their grandmother and aunt had a house just underneath where the Rainbow met the mountain on the L'Hôpital side. They lightened as they drove off the bridge and René spun the wheel hard right. They turned away from the sprawling friendship complex and onto a dirt road that circled under the bridge. The hair on René's arms stood up and the ends of Étienne's dreads floated in front of his face. Ludo grabbed his hat as it rose off his head. It was the first time René had ever seen Ludo's hair. It was yellow and flat.

The effect lessened as they neared the house—a huge, teal-and-pink gingerbread house covered in delicate lacy woodwork. Like his parents' house, the back was built right into the mountain. René's stomach still felt too light as he and Étienne got out of the car. They left Ludo in the back reading a well-thumbed French translation of Jack Kerouac.

"I hate it here," Étienne complained. "The gravity's weird."

"I think Granmè likes it. It makes her seem more mysterious."

Claudette and her husband Gérard were *bokor*, or hiremages. They did common household magic by request for ordinaire and mageborn. They ran their business off the front porch and as usual, the lineup snaked halfway down the driveway. It was Gérard's night. He sat on a high stool, his broad chest bare and his legs covered by a gold and green wrap-around that bore the triangle-and-ribbon vévé of Papa Loko, the lwa of the first *hougan*, or Vodou priest. He had his head shaved and his eyes solemnly fixed on the customer as she explained how the huge burn got on the curtains she was holding. Gérard gave René and Étienne a nod as they went past to the side door.

Their aunt stood in the middle of the kitchen. Her hair was in corn rows and she was holding an orange polka dotted hairdresser's cape that clashed horribly with the gold-and-white palm tree print on her sundress. The diamond-shaped *vévé* for Ayizan, the lwa of the first priestess, was wrought in gold on her necklace. Her plump lips split into a grin when she saw Étienne.

"Sit," Claudette ordered. "Granmè's waiting for you in the *peristyle*, René."

René gave Étienne a slap on the back and headed up the stairs. At the top of the house, where the bridge's gravity was the strongest, Granmè kept her Vodou temple. It was cut into the mountain and (unsurprisingly) dedicated primarily to Papa Legba. The whitewashed walls featured paintings of Legba's various aspects. On the ceiling high above, sequined *drapo* flags and drums hung unaided, held in place by the bridge's gravity.

His grandmother sat at a table covered with thick white candles and beaded bottles. She wore a tattered white wedding dress with poofy sleeves. Her milky, sightless eyes peered out at René from underneath a cloud of white hair. Next to her was the *poteau mitan*: an actual live tree carved with dots and curving symbols that grew through the roof to provide a path for lwa to enter the human world.

"Sit down," Granmè said in the deep, ethereal tone René thought of as her 'mambo voice.'

René stepped carefully over the huge vévés drawn on the floor in cornmeal and sat in the chair opposite her.

"You're impatient," she said.

It was never a good idea to argue with Granmè. René kept silent.

"Reckless," she continued. "And you don't listen. Petro lwa are like that sometimes."

René perked up. If your magic came from a fiery Petro rather than a tranquil Rada, you were sure to end up with an exciting job. Granmè burst René's bubble by jabbing him in the chest with her crutch. "But the magic doesn't choose people who are *selfish*."

"I'm not—" René began.

"What are the words, René?"

René sighed. She meant the motto of the World Mage Council. The one they decided on when they pooled their power for the first time and changed the world.

"Altruism, Progress, Responsibility," René recited.

"You're zero for three," Granmè informed him.

René started to explain that he only wanted his magic to help people, but she cut him off.

"It's no use arguing with me. The lwa see the truth. *I* see the truth. But I can also see talking does no good with you. So here, let me show you what your path will be if you continue on this way."

Before he could protest, Granmè jabbed him in the forehead with her crutch and the peristyle disappeared. Out of the gloom, a scene appeared.

It was their kitchen at home, on what looked like René's Breakday. His family stood around the island, clapping and singing in a subdued version of one of Granmè's Vodou ceremonies. Granmè was at the head of the table, Claudette and Gerard on either side of her. His mother held a baby girl—probably Claudette and Gerard's first. Dad was there, with René's aunts, cousins, and grandparents from the other side of the family. But where was Étienne?

René was looking at the back of his 18-year-old head. His older self stood at the foot of the island in front of a collection of Granmè's candles and bottles. It was a great position for admiring his buzz cut and huge ears. Apparently he had a birthmark he'd never noticed behind the left one.

When the song was over, Granmè draped a pink scarf over older René's shoulders to encourage lwa to possess him. *Pink?* René thought. *But Petro lwa like red!*

René held his breath as he waited to see what awesome feat he would perform to show that he had been chosen. Fireworks? Melt the cutlery into a sword? He was disappointed when all older René did was put out the candles. His family burst into lackluster applause.

Granmè held out a spool of white thread. Unbidden, the thread unfurled and stitched a heart-shaped vévé on older René's scarf.

The vision faded. Ezili Freda? But she was the spirit of love, beauty, and gay men! René wasn't *that* gay. What happened to being a Petro? To action? Adventure? Being a gendarme? He came to, breathing hard and feeling vaguely sick, like he'd just woken up from a nightmare he couldn't remember.

"Do you see now?" Granmè asked, her sightless eyes boring into René's.

"Yeah."

* * *

René paced the yard outside. Granmè had sent him away to 'think about his future' while Claudette finished cutting Étienne's hair. In truth, he needed the time. Though he told Granmè he understood the vision, he didn't. Why wasn't Étienne at his Breakday? Étienne wasn't the kind of brother who missed stuff like that... unless... unless he *had* to. Unless he'd been sent away. Had their parents been so upset about art school that they kicked him out of the house? Was that why everyone seemed upset?

Your plan backfired, Mom. René thought. Instead of showing him the dire consequences of his risk-taking behavior, the lwa had shown him a grim future where he remained unmagical until his 18th birthday... and lost his brother. Maybe if René Broke early, it would be enough to distract Mom and Dad from Étienne and his unmagical plans. And earn him a better lwa than Ezili Freda.

René climbed the big rock in the front yard and looked down over the cliff. The canal was below. It collected runoff from the mountains and funneled it onto Port-au-Prince for drinking. It was the rainy season, so the river was swift and swollen. It was a long drop. Certain death... if you didn't have magic. But if you did, you could just solidify the air under your feet and walk right across to the other mountain.

René took a deep breath, turned his back on the view, and spread his arms like a diver. *Don't look. Just do it.* He took a step backward... and fell.

His heart leaped into his throat. Time seemed to slow. As he dropped toward yard level, Étienne came out of the house. Claudette had shorn his dreads down to the scalp, leaving Étienne with a buzz cut. *He looks just like me*, René thought as his brother turned away to talk to Ludo. Étienne's dreads had been hiding the same huge ears René saw in the mirror every morning. René went cold when he saw the birthmark that splashed across the back of Étienne's left ear.

It wasn't me in the vision, René realized. *It was Étienne. Etienne is Ezili Freda!*

But if that was Étienne, where was René in the vision? Suddenly the pieces clicked into place. The baby in his mother's arms was his sister. She would inherit the magic. And René was...

Dead. I'm dead.

Adrenaline burned through René's limbs. He threw his weight forward and tried to catch the edge of the lawn as he fell past. His nails scratched, bled, snapped. He let out a strangled cry.

Ludo and Étienne looked up. Their faces morphed into identical expressions of horror. Étienne screamed his name and ran toward him. René lost his grip and slid over the cliff. Rocks and sky, that's all he saw. Rocks and sky and the Rainbow, the paragon of safety, glittering mockingly as he plummeted to his death.

High above, Étienne leaped thoughtlessly off the cliff like a gazelle. "*No!*" René screamed.

René thought he had doomed his brother as well, but then Étienne's magic Broke. Huge wings unfolded from Étienne's back, their metal surface made up of hundreds of delicately etched feathers. In the rainbow light from the bridge, Étienne was beautiful—like one of his sculptures.

Through the roaring wind and panic, René was glad. His brother was safe. And art would be the last thing René saw on this earth. Étienne had other ideas. He folded his wings and dove. He picked up speed, gaining on René.

I'm too close to the ground. He'll never make it.

But René couldn't help reaching out. Just as René felt the mist on his back, Étienne grabbed René and spun, taking the impact of their plunge into the canal on his wings.

René tumbled in the cold water, shocked. His survival instinct took hold and he flailed. Étienne's head broke the surface nearby. They hung onto each other as they struggled for the shore. Dimly, René heard something above them. Ludo's high, nasal voice, screaming for help from anyone who would listen.

That's one way to overcome shyness, René thought as he and Étienne flopped onto the muddy shore. He rolled over and caught his brother's eye. Étienne's wings were just now disappearing into his back.

"How did you know? How did you know it would choose you?" René asked, panting.

"I didn't," Étienne replied.

* * *

"And that's why the magic chose my brother and didn't choose me. Someday I'll have a little sister—she hasn't been born yet, despite what the vision showed me, but someday she will. And she'll be a better person than I am. She'll be patient. She'll think of others first. And most of all, she'll be responsible. She'll deserve the magic. And if you want to be a mage, you'll do the same. Don't be like me, standing in front of a crowd on your 18th birthday, telling hundreds of people how stupid you are and how you'll never be a mage. Thank you."

The 400 assembled students of Montreal's *Classe Préperatoire aux Grand Écoles de Magie* burst into applause. René had given the same speech at pre-mage school commencement ceremonies all over the French-speaking world for the past two years. It started out as a kind of self-imposed penance, but over time he grew to feel protective of his audiences. These Quebecois kids were all 13 or 14, the same age Étienne had been when he leaped off a cliff to save his brother's life.

Étienne himself, now 16, stood on the lawn at the back of the quadrangle with Mom, Dad, Granmè, and Ludo, behind the assembled students in their little white folding chairs. Étienne gave him a shy wave and tried to avoid the students' curious looks. It still made him uncomfortable to be spoken of as a hero. Étienne had once confided that in his own mind, he was just an artist who loved his brother.

René loved Étienne back with a ferocity that frightened him. If he could, he'd protect Étienne from a raging bear. From a flaming meteor. Hell, he'd build a whole house just to shield his little brother from the sprinkling droplets that had begun to fall from the overcast sky. And suddenly, René felt like these things were possible. Sure, he'd never be a mage. But maybe he didn't need magic to accomplish the things he wanted to do. There were ordinaire gendarmes and ordinaire search-and-rescue jumpers. Ordinaire firefighters and peacekeepers and bodyguards and paramedics. They saved others every day—without magic.

A surprised murmur rippled through the quad as René stared at Étienne.

"René! Look!" Étienne shouted, pointing at the sky.

René looked up and saw a stream of square paving stones peel off a nearby path and assemble themselves over the crowd. They fit together in overlapping rows like... like shingles! They were making a roof! With a rumble, the clouds opened up. Rain poured from the sky, flowed harmlessly over the stone roof, and fell in sheets at the edge of the quad.

René looked at Étienne and his parents. His parents looked bewildered. They eyed the teachers, trying to find the mage responsible. But the teachers were all mageborn. Étienne laughed. "It's you!" he shouted, pointing at René.

René looked down at his watch. It was 11:39. As he watched, the white cuffs of his red polo shirt unraveled. The thread moved over his heart and reassembled itself into a vévé. A spiky jug with a cross in the middle. Ibo lwa—the brave. Beaten but never vanquished.

Startled, he looked up at Granmè. Her sightless eyes found his unerringly. She gave him a mischievous grin. Papa Legba. Spirit of crossroads, possibilities, and divination. Who can direct or misdirect as the situation requires.

Sea of Strangers

By Michael M. Jones

There was a weird vibe in the halls before first period today. As I made my way towards homeroom, weaving between people with experienced ease, I picked up a thousand different emotions—everything you'd expect from a building packed to the gills with hormone-ridden teenagers and long-suffering adults—and something new, strange, and impossible to identify. A slippery, elusive, emotional flavor that tinted the rest without revealing itself. It poked at my subconscious, put me on edge, made me just a little careless. I bounced off a man-mountain wearing a football letter jacket, and got a snarled, "Watch it, lesbo," for my troubles. The shove he gave me wasn't gentle; I stutter-stepped away, trying to regain my balance.

It was going to be one of those days. Some people hate Mondays; this was proof that Tuesdays could be just as bad, given the opportunity.

Sometimes, it really sucks to be queer and out in high school. I blame the combination of pack and herd mentalities. Those who aren't preying on the weak and different, are shunning those who don't belong... and every group has a different idea of what's appropriate. Unfortunately, when you draw a Venn diagram of "different" and "doesn't belong," the overlap tends to include people like me. The black-clad loner types with few friends and a thing for the same sex.

For what it's worth, I hadn't planned to come out for another year or two, until I was safely away at college. My secret origin involves a best friend, several drinks, a lot of mixed signals, and one disastrously ill-advised kiss. I was everyone's new favorite dyke to pick on before we'd even sobered up, and there's been lingering fallout ever since. Puxhill may be one of the most queer-friendly cities in the country, but the tolerance found in the area encompassing Caravan Street, the Gaslight

District, and Tuesday University hasn't quite penetrated the halls of Elijah Morrison High. I swear to God, some of the cheerleaders actually make the sign of the cross when I walk by, as if I'll contaminate them with my mere presence. Ironically, they'd happily accept a vampire in their midst. Oh, *Edward*. Spare me.

I made it to homeroom with minutes to spare, slumping into my usual seat near the back. There were the usual greetings for the people with whom I was at least vaguely friendly, before we all quieted down so Mr. O'Rourke could take attendance. He went through the roster with an almost robotic monotone, barely even glancing up to see if we were actually present. That was weird; normally, he was more interactive, having a few pleasant words to spare for us. He was the kind of guy, still youngish in his mid-20's, who thought he could connect with his students if he talked sports and popular shows. Not today, apparently.

"Audrey Martinez," he said, and I allowed as how I was here. Another red flag: he knew I preferred to be called "Aud" (as in "Odd"). He went on. His aura had the same slippery undertone as everyone else's. I frowned, making a mental note before putting the thought aside to finish the physics homework I'd blown off all weekend. He ran through the morning's announcements as though working from a grocery list, his eyes glazed over when he even looked in our direction. Just another fine April day. In Zombieland.

Definitely weird. I kept my eyes open and my senses straining to pick up anything out of the ordinary as I followed my usual schedule.

By the end of the day, I was anxious, downright relieved to escape the building. I made a beeline for the nearby Blackbird Café, where I settled into a booth with a caramel latte and a head full of tangled thoughts. I'd been alternately shoved, insulted, ignored and overlooked all day long, in a drastic deviation from my usual routine of amicable neutrality. I scribbled my findings into the back pages of my English notebook, frowning all the while.

"What's wrong, sweetie?" I was yanked from my thoughts by a honey-warm voice and a soft hand running over my shoulder. Blinking my way back to the real world, I tilted my head up for a quick kiss, unable to stop the smile inspired by my girlfriend's arrival. Short and slender, with smooth light brown skin, huge dark eyes and short curly black hair, she was a welcome vision of cuteness. While a junior like me, she actually attended Alabaster Court, a private school not too far away, and she totally owned the khaki skirt and white shirt combo. I'd never had schoolgirl fantasies until I met her. It made my own jeans and black T-shirt seem uninspired, but she was the one with the fashion sense, not me.

"Just general weirdness," I replied, shrugging. "Trying to figure out if I've reason to worry or not."

Charmaine slid in across from me. One hand reached out to take mine, fingers intertwining, while her other hand stole my mostly-untouched drink for a sip. She paused. "Now I know something's wrong. You scream bloody murder when I poach your elixir of life," she teased.

My smile turned rueful. "Yeah. You know me too well, Charm." When she'd discovered that I liked being called Odd, she demanded her own nickname. Charm it was. Mock at your own peril.

Charm's brow furrowed. "It's not... us, is it?"

My eyes widened. I gripped her hand tightly. "Oh, *hell* no." Charm was beautiful, sassy, confident, and stronger than she looked, but terribly prone to fits of insecurity where our relationship was concerned. She'd been burned in the past, and my unconditional acceptance still seemed too good to be true sometimes. I could feel it in her aura even when she didn't voice her concerns. I didn't care that she only become Charmaine when she hit high school. I didn't care what other people said, or what they saw in her, whether they took her for a boyish girl or a feminine guy; I looked at Charm, and saw right down to her beautiful soul. Inside, she was all woman and she made my head spin.

She relaxed. So did I. "I'm glad you're here. Let me fill you in." Over caramel lattes and cinnamon rolls, I told her about the weird feelings I'd had all day. About the jocks acting more like a pride of lions. About the cheerleaders unable to even acknowledge anyone outside their social circle. About the teachers who treated us like names on a list. "It got stronger as the day went on. Mr. Vaughn only saw us as potential troublemakers. Miss Stein defined us by our grades, and wouldn't even speak to anyone below an A average. Coach Murphy reduced people to their respective sports and positions on the team. I even went by the guidance office, and Framingham saw college choices instead of students." I rubbed my temples, trying to banish a sudden headache. "It's like... how can I explain it?"

"Like you'd lost your individuality, and become defined by your traits?" suggested Charm.

"Exactly," I said. "Like we could no longer distinguish between one another on a personal level. By the end of the day, I couldn't even tell the cheerleaders apart."

"You mean you could before?"

"Shush. They may be a miniskirt-wearing hive mind, but I've never had trouble identifying people before. Everyone's unique to me." That was true. I had no idea where my powers came from, whether they were the result of a mutant gene or a fairy in the family tree, or even an alien ancestor. No one else in my family had ever displayed anything out of the ordinary, although a great-aunt on my father's side was supposedly a *bruja*. There have always been stories of people with extra gifts, unusual powers, weird abilities, but most of the time, that's all they are: stories. Urban legends, hoaxes, exaggerations. Most people want to disbelieve; anyone who makes too much commotion is written off as an attention-seeker, or called crazy, or ignored altogether.

Dig deep enough, listen hard enough, pay the right sort of attention, and you hear other tales. Especially in Puxhill, which seems to be a hotspot for the weird, just like New Orleans attracts ghost stories and Lily Dale harbors psychics. The Gaslight District takes on a mind of its own after dark, its streets twisting and turning in a labyrinthine fashion. No one talks about it too loudly, but everyone has an urban myth or a friend of a friend who's encountered something inexplicable once upon a time. We all believe to some degree or another, even though most of us don't want to. I guess it's a coping mechanism. People are hard enough to understand without opening yourself up to the idea of vampires, werewolves, and faeries.

With my funky empathy and extranormal senses, I felt like another one of Puxhill's odd little secrets. For obvious reason, I didn't talk about it much, for fear I'd be laughed at, made into a curiosity… or worse, taken seriously by the wrong people. Charm knew; she'd known almost from the start, when I bumped into her at Bifrost Books and looked right down into her soul to see the lovely woman inside, like a butterfly in a chrysalis. Still in her early days of transitioning, she'd been blown away by my instant acceptance. Blown away… and suspicious, as though fearing I was leading her on. At that point, she still got a lot of stink-eye from random people who couldn't see what I did, and reacted less than gracefully.

She had some pointed questions for me when she realized my interest was serious. I had some extremely complicated answers, most of which were met with healthy skepticism. It took a while for her to grow comfortable with me and accept my claims. Mainly, we just learned to accept each other for all our quirks. Even so, she sometimes gives me dubious looks, as though waiting to catch me out.

"So what do we do about this problem at your school?" she asked.

"We?"

"You don't think I'd let you tackle this alone, do you?"

"What makes you think I'd do anything about it?"

"Because it worries you. Because it's affecting you and you won't stand for it. And because you may very well be the only one who's even noticed there's a problem. Take your pick." Her eyes shone gleefully as she pointed out the things I'd already contemplated and begrudgingly accepted. "You play at being all antisocial and nonchalant, but you can't resist meddling or fixing things."

I nodded. "I guess I go back tomorrow and do more recon. Try to get a better handle on what's going on. Try to find its source."

"And I'll do research," Charm volunteered. "See if any of my contacts have any ideas." She spent a lot of time online, on dozens of boards and forums. She'd started back when she was trying to figure out her identity and how to transition towards her true self, and it had snowballed from there. She frequented places I'd never even heard of, and even talked sometimes about the Dark Web, which I gathered to be the secret Internet or something. Give her a few days and she could track down anything you'd ever wanted to know. The NSA was going to visit her someday, I just knew it. (I'm not a fan of people online. It's impossible for me to "read" them with my abilities, and I've grown too dependent on the extra layer of information. Hence, my minimalist Internet footprint.) She'd become one of my primary sources of information as well, as I tried to learn more about my quirks, maybe even find others like me.

Our plan made, we turned to lighter topics, like the junior prom. There was no question about it: I was taking her, come Hell or high water, and neither one of us was wearing a tux. My Dominican heritage had blessed me with curves and an ass, and I was going to wear a dress which rocked them. Charm had waited all her life to be a pretty princess, and even though she barely had any hips or boobs to speak of, she was determined to live her dream. We're just a pair of big queer rebels, I know.

Eventually, we cleaned up our trash and left, parting outside with more kisses, ignoring the people who gave us exasperated looks. I could feel their auras; for each one who was genuinely upset, there was someone who merely missed being young and foolish and in love again. In other words, business as usual for the neighborhood. Whatever was affecting the halls of my school hadn't escaped its confines yet.

Wednesday went much as Tuesday did, but the effect was rapidly gaining strength. Athletes, male and female alike, traveled in homogenous packs, identified by a certain confident swagger and general air of physical superiority. I strained to look past the muscles and letter jacket to *see* Justin McMannis, the quarterback who wrote surprisingly good poetry in Honors English. I squinted until I had a headache to remember that one rather tall girl wasn't *just* a basketball player, she was Alice Matheson, a devout Catholic and one of the genuinely nicest people I'd ever met, who regularly volunteered at the Orange Street shelter and who always had a smile for me.

Those weren't generic theatre geeks, band nerds, stoners, skaters, freaks or brains; they were kids I'd known for years, people I'd sat behind in class, copied homework from, had blistering arguments with, seen at parties, and yeah, even been bullied and insulted by. I walked through a school increasingly filled with anonymous strangers, drifting alone in a sea of teens that looked at me and only saw the lesbo who kissed her friend and became a laughingstock. I shivered. High school was bad enough when everyone knew your name; it became infinitely worse when you turned invisible.

At lunch, I tried an experiment. I walked right up to Sophie Olson, former best friend, surrounded by her new crowd of artsy theatre drones, and rapped on the table for attention. Conversation died away. As one, they stared in my direction, half a dozen blank faces struggling to identify me. I glared back defiantly, gaze locked on Sophie. I waited for the acid-filled response, a mixture of venom and fear, which had dominated her psyche ever since our ill-fated kiss. The emotions of her friends assaulted me as I opened myself up.

Loser.

Loner.

Freak.

Dyke.

Admiration/Envy/Desire/Attraction. This last, from a sophomore girl I barely knew, surprised me. She'd forgotten who I was, but still saw me as an idol, someone to look up to, someone… she wouldn't mind becoming? I made a note to try and befriend her when this was all over, help her like no one had helped me.

From Sophie, nothing. Just a vagueness, which suddenly crystallized into *shock/betrayal/rejection/repulsion*. I'd never realized how profoundly the incident had affected her, driving her so far into close-minded homophobia that I'd become anathema, a living symbol of misguided childhood teachings. Something I'd never known about her, never realized. Her soul was a turmoil of contradictions and confusion. A mixture of guilt and pity struck me. Silently, I urged her to remember who I was, what I'd been to her. *Come on, if you won't be my friend, be my enemy, just* know *me.*

I grew desperate, even as the silence became awkward. "Hey."

"Hey." Sophie sounded puzzled.

"How're you?"

"What do you want?" Rising hostility. I became an intruder. A trespasser. An outsider.

"Do you know who I *am*?" I blurted, the desperation in my voice exposing a momentary weakness. The group stirred restlessly.

A pause. "You're..." I could see the struggle in her features. The effort to put name to face. To make the essential connections. "You're the dyke. The one that kissed me." Her face turned ugly. "Freak. Get away from me."

"Do you know my *name*?" I pressed on, despite the anger rising from Sophie and her friends. Their postures had turned aggressive, a hair away from launching into violence.

"No. And I don't care." With that, Sophie dismissed me from her presence and her thoughts; within seconds I'd ceased to matter altogether. Their conversation started back up again, and not even my erstwhile admirer seemed interested in me anymore. I got the hell away from them, my heart pounding.

Sophie was, once upon a time, the person closest to me. If she'd been affected so strongly, there was no doubt everyone else was just as far gone. Nevertheless, I repeated the experiment a dozen more times as the day wore on, with students and faculty alike. Once or twice, I thought I'd gotten through to someone, but the best I got was from the librarian, who remembered I was quiet and well-behaved and sometimes read "the classics." She had no patience for fans of modern popular literature.

I left the library, seriously disturbed by my inability to connect with anyone. I headed for my locker to collect my stuff. Deep in thought, it took me a moment to register the scuffling of shoes, the thud and clang of flesh on metal, the sharp gasp of pain. I broke into a half-run, turning the corner to find one of my fears come true. A group of guys had cornered someone, shoved him up against a locker, crowded around like a pack of feral dogs. I had no idea who they were, who their victim was. They were a faceless mob of aggressors, united by some dominant trait— the wrestling team? The chess club? Their victim was smaller, weaker, an outsider. His eyes were wide with terror, face pale, clothes rumpled. His nose was bleeding. No one said anything.

There were six of them, and just one of me. No fighter, I turned, hauling ass to the nearest classroom Empty. I tried the next few, but when I couldn't find any help, I realized it was on me to do something. I ran back to where the pack was busy punching the other kid in the stomach. He took a blow that sent him to his knees, retching and crying.

"Back the fuck off, assholes!" I screamed, balling up my fists like I actually thought I could take them all on. Taking advantage of their momentary pause, I slipped through the pack to try and help their victim up. I grabbed his arm. "Come on!" He shakily got to his feet. "We have to get out of here!"

Instead of running, he just looked at me, with a cold, distant expression. His erstwhile tormentors gathered around. They gave me the same look. I'd come to know it well. The hard eyes, the clenched fists, the intense focus—I didn't even need to *read* them to understand. Now I was the outsider.

Worse. I was the prey.

They'd united against *me*.

I got the hell out of there, and didn't stop running until I was blocks away from the school and a pain in my side made it impossible to continue. Only then did I sink down onto a bus stop bench, and cry. They were tears of frustration, and fury, and fear.

My thoughts churned sickeningly. The entire school had fallen to whatever malevolent power had seized it. What if this spread? What if it was contagious, and it followed us into the real world?? How long before someone got seriously hurt? How long before I stopped seeing Charm as my girlfriend, my best friend, my confidante, and looked on her with the eyes of a stranger?

This couldn't go on.

Wednesday was new comics day, so Charm and I met at Jackpot Comics, *the* geek place of choice for the Caravan Street community, as well as neighboring Tuesday University, Usually, I loved the time we spent here, but the events of the day had upset me to my core; Sophie's blank stare, the uncomprehending teachers, the way the fight in the hallway had gone so terribly wrong. I filled Charm in as we browsed, desperate for at least a little semblance of normality. "It's like living with zombies. I mean, everyone goes to classes and teachers do their thing, and people hang out in their little cliques…"

"The wheel's turning but the hamster's missing?" supplied Charm.

"Exactly." I flopped down into one of the comfy chairs dotting the landscape, unable to find any joy in the new arrivals shelf or the half-off bins. "It's nearly impossible to pick one person out of the crowd. I spent most of last period trying to recall what made each person unique. Some—too many—were total blanks. I only identified Diana Malone because of the *Guys and Dolls* wardrobe malfunction of freshman year." A busty raven-haired beauty I'd briefly crushed on, she was one of the darlings of the theatre department. I'd been roped into helping with stage crew for the spring musical. A loose nail, a misstep, and she'd nearly gone on stage sans an essential part of her costume. We'd worked impossibly fast miracles with safety pins and duct tape, with almost no one the wiser.

Charm's eyebrow quirked magnificently. "Oh?" I picked up a mixture of curiosity and playful jealousy from her.

I smiled sheepishly. "I saw more than I expected. That was the moment I realized I positively, definitely, preferred girls." Before it got any more awkward, I added, "But it took a memory of that magnitude to break through the fog. I'm afraid to go back tomorrow. Whatever's happening is escalating quickly and I don't think I can resist it much longer. Today was a nightmare."

Charm took the chair next to mine, curling up with her legs tucked under. She smoothed her skirt into place, and I picked up the quiet joy she got from such a mundane action. Good. She was welcome to all the skirts. They bugged me. "It started recently. What changed at school?"

I shrugged. "Beats me. It's been quiet. No new students or teachers. Sports teams won and lost like usual. A predictable assortment of hookups and breakups. Josh Grayson and Wendy Mackelson had their monthly screaming fit in the parking lot, and got back together in the girls' locker room 10 minutes later. I can't *wait* until they graduate. The debate club won some important competition for the first time in many years and brought home a shiny… new… trophy." My eyes widened.

"You think…?"

"Well, they *were* all quite impressed with their golden chalice of the silver tongue, or whatever they called it," I allowed. "Installed it in an empty case, and I'm pretty sure they started worshipping it. Down on knees and everything. That was on Monday."

Charm's eyebrow shot up.

"Kidding," I said, feeling a little bad as her expression turned disappointed. "But they did make a huge fuss and strutted about all pleased with themselves."

"Well, this still gives us a lead. I need you to get back in there, and inspect the trophy as closely as possible. Really open yourself up to it, see what you feel," Charm said excitedly.

"That might be a bad idea."

We both jumped as a new voice inserted itself into the conversation. The owner drifted around to stand in our line of sight, looking sheepishly apologetic. "I mean, I couldn't help but hear some of what you were saying and trust me, getting up close and personal with potentially cursed, possibly magical artifacts is never good." It was Irene, Jackpot's head manager. She was a perky, curvy brunette in her mid-twenties, with big blue eyes and a perpetual smile. She was prone to hippy-esque skirts and peasant blouses, rarely wore shoes, and she was definitely in some sort of relationship with Ramona, the owner. Though she was eminently likeable and several kinds of awesome, with an encyclopedic knowledge of everything in the store, I'd never been fully comfortable around her. For some reason, I just couldn't pick up anything from her aura, as though she wasn't entirely real. No wonder she was able to sneak up on us. Finding out who—or what—Irene was, was definitely on my To Do List. Someday.

Charm, who had a geek girl crush on Irene—which I usually found cute—nodded knowingly. "Makes sense."

"So what's this all about? If I can ask?" Irene shifted her weight as she watched us. Her body language screamed curiosity barely restrained by politeness.

"It's an Alternate Reality Game," explained Charm quickly.

"I love those things!" Irene chirped, bouncing on the balls of her feet. "It doesn't sound familiar. Tell me about it? Maybe I can give you a hand. I've had a lot of experience with games and puzzles."

What else could we do? We weren't exactly making a lot of progress otherwise. Charm and I took turns telling her what we knew, though we doctored the details for increased plausibility. Irene listened intently, her entire body at rest while she processed our story. When we finished, she nodded. "I think you're on to something. And you know, I might have something which can help you." A smile flashed across her face, clever and impish. For a split second, I could have sworn there were stars and static in her eyes. A trick of the light? "A clue. Or a solution. Give me your email address," she told Charm. "Or—wait, you're in the subscriber database, aren't you? I thought so. Hold on." She wandered back to the counter; a moment later, Charm's phone bleeped to announce a new email.

Charm looked at the mail, brow furrowed, then held the phone over so I could see it as well. I read it out loud. "Use this file responsibly. It will auto-delete in two days. You won't be able to save, copy, download, forward, or print it. Seriously, this thing has DRM like you wouldn't believe. Technically I shouldn't let it out into the wild at all but I think I can trust you girls. Tell me how the game turns out. —Irene." There was one attachment, which Charm opened. "*Alderman's Rituals, Secrets, & Cunning Lore?*" I read the title dubiously. "Sounds like a role-playing book."

"Sounds perfectly legit to me!" Charm grinned. "Come on, let's go back to my place where we can read this on a proper computer."

We waved to Irene on our way out, and she gave us a faux-innocent look. As we exited, she was on the phone, telling someone, "I know lending *Alderman's* out will annoy those jerks at the Library. But what can they do? I have access to their payroll..." I lost the rest as the door shut behind us.

Alderman's Rituals turned out to be the digitized version of one of those Ye Olde Grimoires... packed full of folk remedies, curious anecdotes, charms and spells— a real hodgepodge of weird stuff. Cures for warts, antidotes for snake bites, love spells, you name it. Irene had helpfully placed electronic bookmarks in several sections to narrow down our search. As Charm paged through the document, I sprawled on her bed, marveling at the sheer amount of pink and glitter she'd packed into her personal space.

It was amazing, I thought, not for the first time. Charm's parents had reacted amazingly well to her transition, accepting her without reservation (though I could always read their concern for her under the outpouring of love.) They'd welcomed me with open arms once they realized I cared for her with all my heart as well. By comparison, my parents did everything but put their hands over their ears and chant "Watermelon rutabaga" when the subject of my sexuality came up. Not disapproving, but they seemed happier living in denial. Charm confused them. A lot. I didn't take her home much as a result. It was easier all around. Yet another reason why I couldn't wait until college.

"Here we go." Charm's words brought me out of my funk. I rolled out of bed and went to look over her shoulder. "Protective charms and suggestions on how to deal with cursed or possessed artifacts. It looks as though this bit would keep you safe while you got close to the trophy, and this would undo whatever power it has. There's some really interesting stuff in here. I wish I could keep it." She sighed dramatically.

I arched an eyebrow, draping against the back of her chair, chin resting on her shoulder. "Think it'll work? I mean… you actually believe this?"

She tilted her head back to smile at me. "Like we have so many alternatives to work with?" I arched an eyebrow. I waited. Finally, she admitted, "I've always felt like I was grasping for something just out of reach. This book makes things clearer. It's the same feeling the first time I called myself Charmaine… at last, something *right* clicked into place."

I stared at Charm. We'd shared a lot in our time together, but this was a whole new depth I'd never seen before. And yet, hadn't I recognized some of this right from the beginning? Only now, we were both starting to understand it. This was part of Charm's potential. It was beautiful. It was wonderful. It was a little frightening. Before the silence grew uncomfortable, I kissed her, telling her wordlessly that magic or no, I was still hers.

Once we'd worked that out of our systems, we put together a plan, utilizing some of the things Charm had found, items bookmarked by Irene as potentially useful and "mostly safe to use." While Charm acted as emotional anchor and support, backed up by the spells in the book, I'd use my own abilities to unravel things at the source. We both knew we'd only have one shot at this.

We met in front of Elijah Morrison High the next morning. Hands linked in a blatant display of affection and shared strength, we marched up the front steps, through the doors, and down the hallways, making a beeline for the corridor housing the debate trophy. As we passed, clumps of people gazed at us with blank expressions. Their emotions were almost completely submerged under an ocean of slippery, oil-slick alienation. I looked, but couldn't recognize any of them. A voice whispered in my head as my gaze swept the halls. *Jock. Cheerleader. Nerd. Troublemaker. Fat. Crippled. Slut. Druggie.* There was something hateful, painfully bitter, profoundly lonely in the murmured words. Teachers drifted through as faceless authority figures. I gripped Charm's hand tightly until she gasped for mercy. Her presence centered me again. I saw flickers of the people I used to know, buried deep under the individuality-crushing miasma.

Outsider.

Stranger.

Trespasser.

Not one of us.

As we approached the trophy, waves of increasingly harsh emotions battered my psyche. The members of the debate team seemed to materialize out of thin air, surrounding us, blocking us in. Something that wasn't them stared out of their eyes with desperate malevolence. They whispered as they walked, a hissing of poisonous slurs like a storm of prejudice leveled against Charm and me. I felt Charm next to me, valiantly holding steady against the taunts, the stereotypes, the ignorance.

I could see into their heads, though, and the hatred was a palpable, creeping ooze, reaching out for me along our link. I risked a glance sideways, and for a single heart-stopping moment, I no longer saw my girlfriend. I saw a boy in a dress, and he was *wrong*.

Then Charm put her foot down, uttering a single potent word of power which rippled through the air, breaking apart the onslaught, disrupting whatever they'd sent against us. She was glorious and magnificent, roaring with inner fire. She held my hand so the fire raged into me as well. The debate team broke apart, fell back. I knew them. Justin, Jenny, Edward, Marisol, Lindsay, Huan-yue, and the rest. Charm nodded to me. "Do your thing, sweetie. I've got this."

I rested my hands against the glass case, and stared at the trophy. A battered silver cup on a wooden base, something passed from school to school for decades. Such a simple thing to cause so much trouble. "Okay, you fucker," I growled. "Let's dance." With the fire inside of me, I threw caution to the wind, letting my power blaze free. And the trophy and I—we *knew* each other.

An old spirit. Lonely. Unhappy. Dead before their time. A former student? I got impressions of someone painfully shy. An outsider. Mocked. Shunned. Unappreciated. Misunderstood. Something happened. An accident? Nowhere to go, so they stayed here. Unseen, unfelt, unheard. Years passed. Then a rush of jubilation, and triumph. The trophy. The ghost without a voice found a new home in an artifact that honored clever speech and bold words.

"And you reached out," I whispered. "You wanted everyone to know how you felt. Or maybe you were just looking for friends and something went wrong." I felt sorry for the nameless spirit, twisted and warped into an elemental force by their long years in the dark. "It was an accident, but you couldn't stop once the ball got rolling." There were always those who slipped through the cracks. The ones no one heard until it was too late. A victim unrecognized for too long.

All around us, students gathered, a silent crowd watching without understanding. They mingled together, cliques interspersed, each one an island in a sea of strangers. My power, free and flowing, danced through the mass, tying them together in an intricate spider-web. Charm took my hand in hers, joining the network. Slowly, it spread to encompass the entire school, classes coming to a standstill. I never knew I had so much in me. I was operating on pure instinct and guesswork. I would have a lot to learn when all of this was over.

Together, Charm and I spoke the second word of power we'd memorized. It tolled like a bell, ponderous and ominous, sinking into the wood and stone and glass of the building. It resonated along the spider-web of emotional connections, plucking it taut. It echoed again and again, increasing in speed and pitch. And then… it was gone, taking with it an immense weight from the air. The spirit in the trophy shattered into a million pieces, leaving behind sorrow and gratitude.

I felt it sweep throughout the school, like a bright light burning away the shadows. It was beautiful… and it was surprising.

The jocks shrank before my eyes, much diminished. Without the alpha confidence, they seemed smaller, more human. The cheerleaders faded, no longer the plastic doll paragons of beauty and bitchery. Stripped of the traits that had so defined them, they were… individuals again. The same was for everyone else. They looked around them, expressions full of shock and wonder, as though truly *seeing* their classmates for the first time in ages. Charm and I took the opportunity to escape.

I wish I could say that we'd somehow ushered in a new age of peace, harmony, understanding, tolerance, and love. It lasted maybe five minutes, before things went back to normal… mostly. Things were a little more relaxed, as if the moment of empathy had rekindled some inner fire. There was a general unspoken agreement not to discuss whatever madness had gripped the school—and for that I was thankful. My plan remained the same: keep my head down until graduation, and let college determine who I'd ultimately become. True to her word, the text Irene "loaned" us deleted itself with no trace of its existence; without it, the words of power we'd used slipped right out of our heads, their job done. We told her what had happened, and she just nodded. We didn't speak of it again. Charm plans to ask Irene if she knows anyone she can talk to about magic, now that the door's been unlocked. I'm still not sure I'm ready to delve into my own depths quite yet.

I passed Sophie in the hall a few days later. When she met my eyes, she held the gaze for a second or two longer than necessary. I saw no hate or malice there, just regret and a little sadness. She still won't talk to me if she doesn't have to, but it's a start. I've started chatting with that sophomore friend of hers, Martha. I'd like to be there for her, a held-out hand if she needs one.

Oh, and Charm and I are totally going to junior prom together. I'm going to rock my curves, and she's going to be a pretty pretty princess. And if anyone gives us grief for it, I'll hit them over the head with peace and tolerance and understanding.

Sometimes high school doesn't suck after all.

About the Authors

Seanan McGuire writes things. It can be difficult to make her stop. Since time is linear, you should check her website, at www.seananmcguire.com, to see what she's written most recently. Seanan lives in the Pacific Northwest with several Maine Coons, far too many books, and a horrifying number of comics. She enjoys Disney Parks, Diet Dr Pepper, and swamps. She's not a big fan of writing bios.

Emily Horner is the author of the young adult novel *A Love Story Starring My Dead Best Friend*. She has worked as a bookbinder, translator, and librarian; she now lives in Ames, Iowa, where she is on the brink of finishing an MFA degree in Creative Writing and Environment.

Elizabeth Shack lives in central Illinois. A member of the Science Fiction & Fantasy Writers of America (SFWA), she has worked as a software copywriter, a newspaper reporter, a physics graduate student, and a tour guide at a NASA visitor center, all of which she's composted to feed her stories.

Kelly Swails is an author, editor, and all-around geek. Her work has appeared in numerous anthologies and her young adult novels are available on Amazon. She also writes comics for Kymera Press. She lives in Chicago with her husband and three cats.

Evelyn Deshane's creative and nonfiction work has appeared in *Plenitude Magazine*, *Briarpatch Magazine*, *Strange Horizons*, *Lackington's*, and *Bitch Magazine*, among other publications. Evelyn (pron. Eve-a-lyn) received an MA from Trent University and is currently completing a PhD at the University of Waterloo. Evelyn's most recent project *#Trans* is an edited collection about transgender and nonbinary identity online. Visit evedeshane.wordpress.com for more info.

When **C.M. Smith** was a child, she drove her family crazy with her nonstop stories. Lucky for them, she eventually learned to write and gave their ears a rest. This love of stories led her to college where she pursued history (semi-nonfictional storytelling), anthropology (where stories come from) and theater (attention-seeking storytelling). When she isn't writing, she's painting, crocheting, gardening, baking, and teaching the next generation to love stories as much as she does.

Cheryl Rainfield is the award-winning author of *Scars*, *Stained*, and *Hunted*, and appeared in *Parallel Visions*. "I write the books I needed as a teen and couldn't find." She can be found at www.CherylRainfield.com, and on Twitter @CherylRainfield.

Rajan Khanna is an author, reviewer, podcaster, musician, and narrator. His three novels, *Falling Sky, Rising Tide,* and *Raining Fire,* take place in a post-apocalyptic world of airships and floating cities. His short fiction has appeared in *Lightspeed Magazine, Beneath Ceaseless Skies,* and multiple anthologies. His articles and reviews have appeared at Tor.com and LitReactor.com and his podcast narrations can be heard at Podcastle, Escape Pod, PseudoPod, Beneath Ceaseless Skies and Lightspeed Magazine. Rajan cohosts the Spirited Discourse podcast (with co-host Devin Poore). He lives in Brooklyn where he's a member of the Altered Fluid writing group. His personal website is www.rajankhanna.com and his Twitter is @rajanyk.

David Sklar never learned to drink coffee until he had kids. A Rhysling nominee and past winner of the Julia Moore Award for Bad Verse, he has more than 100 published works, including fiction in *Nightmare* and *Strange Horizons,* poetry in *Ladybug* and *Stone Telling,* and humor in *Knights of The Dinner Table* and *McSweeney's Internet Tendency*. David lives with his wife, their two barbarians, and a secondhand familiar in a cliffside cottage in Northern New Jersey, where he almost supports his family as a freelance writer and editor. He's also the creator of the *Poetry Crisis Line*, which features new material every Monday and Thursday at poetrycrisis.org

Sara Fox is an information specialist and a ne'er-do-well often found wandering in airports both local and abroad. A fan of continuously recreating themselves, they've been a researcher, elementary through college teacher, and a techie. Their stories generally dabble around fantasy coming of age and emotive scifi with LGBT+ characters. To learn more please go to mxsfox.com.

Rain Fletcher is a lifetime amateur storyteller, a near-lifetime choir singer, and has even dabbled in light opera, which may explain a few things. Rain lives in Southern California, which likely explains the rest. Rain is happily married, and is navigating the perils of getting two daughters through the public school system. "Awaken" is Rain's first professionally published work, and a special place on the shelf is already reserved for this anthology.

Over the past 30-odd years, **Nina Kiriki Hoffman** has sold adult and YA novels and more than 300 short stories. Her works have been finalists for many major awards, and she has won a Stoker and a Nebula Award. Nina's novels have been published by Avon, Atheneum, Ace, Pocket, Scholastic, Tachyon, and Viking. Her short stories have appeared in many magazines and anthologies. Nina does production work for *The Magazine of Fantasy & Science Fiction* and teaches writing. She lives in Eugene, Oregon. For a list of Nina's publications: http://ofearna.us/books/hoffman.html.

Cecilia Tan knows that writing is magic, but it takes readers to make it manifest. She is the award-winning author of the Magic University series of books (in which Frost appears as a character) as well as *Daron's Guitar Chronicles, The Prince's Boy*, *Slow Surrender*, and over a dozen other books and novels. Her urban fantasy series, *The Vanished Chronicles*, will be published soon by Tor Books.

E.C. Myers was assembled in the U.S. from Korean and German parts and raised by a single mother and the public library in Yonkers, New York. He is the author of numerous short stories young adult books, including the Andre Norton Award–winning *Fair Coin, The Silence of Six*, and *RWBY: After the Fall*. E.C. currently lives with his wife, son, and three doofy pets in Pennsylvania. You can find traces of him all over the internet, but especially at http://ecmyers.net and on Twitter: @ecmyers.

Scarlett Ward is a 19-year-old currently wearing many hats- writer, actor, playwright, filmmaker, and parent to a demanding cat. They live in London and have short stories and a novella in various upcoming anthologies from 18th Wall Productions. Acting-wise, they've performed at the Royal Court, the Queen's Theatre, and in various short films, charity ads, and audio plays, but they're mostly known for still being able to play 12-year-olds.

Vrai is a freelance media critic, writer, and lover of trash—think Herbert West by way of John Waters. Find more of their writing at vraikaiser.com or on Twitter @writervrai.

Eric Esser lives in San Francisco with his wife Courtney. When he was small he used to wander the perimeter of his elementary school soccer field every recess imagining stories set in other worlds, and for some reason no one ever made fun of him for it. He suspects they discussed him secretly. His fiction has appeared or is forthcoming in *Pseudopod* and *Chilling Horror Short Stories*, among others. Visit him at ericesser.net or follow him on Twitter (@ericdesser).

Aaron Canton is a Jewish-American writer. His short fantasy fiction has been acquired by *Phobos Magazine*, *Mothership Zeta*, and other venues. When he isn't writing, Aaron can often be found reading fantasy and science fiction literature of all kinds and searching local bookstores for new additions to his library. He also enjoys listening to music and plays the piano as a hobby. He blogs at aaroncanton.wordpress.com.

Katrina Nicholson has a degree in history, a diploma in writing for film and television, and works at a library. Several of her film scripts are in varying stages of production in Toronto and 14 of her short stories have been published in anthologies such as *Tesseracts Fifteen*, *Futuredaze*, *The Future Embodied*, and *Enter the Apocalypse*. She lives in Nova Scotia, but you can visit her online at www.katrinanicholson.com.

Michael M. Jones lives in southwest Virginia with too many books, just enough cats, and a wife who has an appalling amount of confidence in him. His stories have appeared in anthologies such as *F is for Faerie*, *Robot Dinosaurs*, and *Clockwork Phoenix 3*, and in magazines such as *Constellary Tales*, *Broadswords & Blasters*, and *Metaphorosis*. He also edited *Scheherazade's Façade*. For more, visit him at www.michael mjones.com.

Honor Roll
(Thanks and Acknowledgements)

School of Cantrips:
eSpec Books. Juli Baumler.

School of Spirits and Shadows
Danielle Ackley-McPhail. Dreaming Robot Press.

School of Elemental Manipulation
Anonymous Reader. Shannon Luchies. Jenett Silver. H. Rasmussen. Kristy Kearney.

Forestofglory. Joseph Carriker. Kerri Regan. Kelly Kleiser. Michael Bentley. Stephanie Cranford

Andrea Horbinski. Chuck and Rebecca Rozakis. Joseph Hoopman. H. Cykana.

David Eggerschwiler. Vae. Tanni. Merav Hoffman. Smoot. Alex Bacon. Dr. Jobo. Ty Barbary.

K. Urquiza. Linda Frankel. KVC. James Lucas. S.M. Mack. Jonathan Fortin. Ann Lemay.

Jenny Barber. Shannon Everyday. Tasha Turner. Cobie Forshaw. Amanda C. Lee.

Cheryl Morgan. Brid. Jackson October. Max Kaehn. Maria Lima. starrcat. Russell Ventimeglia.

Nathan Turner. Kay Kempers. Tory Shade. Nellie Batz. Lisa Kruse. Svend Andersen.

Carmen Maria Marin. Chayde. Mel & Arthur Goldsipe. Lorin Venniro. Sola Balisane.

Ink Lowrey. Piper. Matt Bright. shadowmaat. JBender. BSD. Jim Kosmicki. Jim Moriarty.

Rhonda Parrish. Dame Bodacious. mskkid. Benjamin J. TheVikingBunny. PJ Deyo.

Bonnie Potter. Gavran. Rachel McNulty. Lisa "Dr. Cthulhupunk" Padol.

Gina M. Gallo, Former Dragon & Current Queen. Andy McAllister. Sharyna Tran.

Amy Dryman. Sheryl R. Hayes. Mad McDaniel. Kate Kligman. S. Brackett Robertson.

Strixbrevis. Arin Murphy-Hiscock. Lauren Hoffman. Erin Kowalski. Michael Rasmussen.

Alisa Krasnostein. Spencer Hubbard. Misha Dainiak. Nicole Wilkinson. Chad Bowden.

Sharang Biswas. Olwen Lachowicz. Trip Space-Parasite. Michael Brewer. Paul S. Enns

Jean-Christophe Cubertafon. Erin Subramanian. Alan D. Scar Ward. Dan Brewer.

Stephanie Gunn. Jen1701D. G Fitzsimmons. Zaiamrah Morgnac. Sorcyress. Gabriella Crivilare.

School of Enchantment

Kathleen M. Merja. Kyrielle. Sian Dart. kytyn. Maya Sapiurka. Megan E. Daggett.

Carolyn Petersen. Thomas Bull. Han Marshall. Ginger. Alexandra J. Clifton. Laurie Sefton.

Ruth P. Narrelle M Harris. David Mortman. Jeremy Reppy. Kate Mergener. Charles de Lint.

Tim in True Blue Virginia. Nicole Dutton. Lisa Crow. Dev Singer. slycreations.

Rachel Pennington. Charlotte. Simon Munro. Celestemaisel. Emily Williams.

Stephanie Cheshire. Iliana Nieves. Eva. Mark Carter. Sven Janssen & Robert Saunders. Strang1.

Scott Schaper. E. PIck. Felix. Robert Claney. Kit McGuren. Sarah Raines. Benjamin G Turner.

RJ Hopkinson. Alex Keen. Marguerite Kenner. Amy Brennan. "Michael and Karen Pence".

Stephen Ballentine. Rue. Jami Nord. Chelsea Cooper. Erica. Warcabbit. Jen Woods.

Krystal Windsor. Sarah Kremen-Hicks. Christina Roberts. Kimberly Lloyd. A Davis.

Jon Robertson. Christina. K Lovinger. Ellen Michelson. Marzie Kaifer. Patricia Arce.

Kayliealien. Julie A. Grant. Sueshep Shepherd. Jane Austen. zvi LikesTV. John Frewin.

Katharine (thiefofcamorr). Z. Leigh Hellman. E. Zanno. Woodrow Hill.Tibs. Kat Terban.

Kate Malloy. Regis M. Donovan. Kirsten Madden. Becky Morrissey. Mary-Michelle Moore.

Gail M. Barbara and Carl Kesner. Carolyn Livingston. C. Joshua Villines. Tristan Gohring.

Nathan Rockwood. Mike Smith. Daniel Lin. Trace Hagemann. Michelle Pope.

Melissa Shumake. Rachel Schwartz. GriffinFire. Cadellin. Marian Koschwitz.

School of Divination

Essie Bee. Sacchi Green. Chris Mangum. Mela Eckenfels. Julio Capa. Charlotte Grubbs.

Casey Sharpe. Lauren E. Mitchell. Tibicina. Colleen R. Dave Bush. Charlie Seelig.

Kelly J. Cooper. Freddy MacKay. Cathy Green. B&D Comic Shop (Roanoke, VA).

lauowolf. Jaime M Garmendia III. Kirrell. Xap Esler. Yes. Annclaire Livoti. Jeffrey James.

Cindy Naval. Andreja River. Stephen Boucher. Nancy M. Tice. Darrel Melvin. Meghan Shearer.

Sara Glassman. Briana Gray. V Hartman DiSanto. Chris Volcheck. Bolivia Red. Lee McBride. Dizneeee. Tris Lawrence. Joan Shack. BriAnne Searles. Freiya. Dani Daly. Cheryl Preyer.

Kaitlin W. "Megapixie" Veronica Lacquement. Emilia Agrafojo. Kristi Weyland. Jessica Olin.

Lilian Young. Rhiannon Raphael. Elaine d'Ete. Eli and Nadine Ramey. The Digges Family. Nivair H. Gabriel. Liz Denys. Debbie Block-Schwenk. Melissa Klocke. Tiril Pollard.

Amber Bell. Kat R. Bequi Loves James. Bethany. Emily R. Dawn M. Fancher. Jeliza Patterson.

Hannah Carter-Taylor. Ash C. Amie Rose Rotruck. Dr. Mary C. Crowell. Kristina Wright.

Bobbi Boyd. Lena Kent. Emily Poole.

325

School of Alchemy and Transmutation
> Michael Bukraba. RHK. Awesomesauce. Bex. Tom Zurkan. D. M. Patterson. Dino Hicks. Timothy J Meng. Risa Scranton. Katie Hynes. Mike and Anita Allen. Rachel 'Rae' Hagen. Andrew Hatchell. Bodge Inglee-Richards. Kerry aka Trouble. House of fuzz. Allison Walters. Jamie Perrault. David. J. Truman. Kimberly M. Lowe. Erica "Vulpinfox" Schmitt.
>
> Darren Lipman. Julia Starkey. Jacinta Sarpkaya. Sean Werner. Melanie Rose.
>
> Samuel and Kit Aronoff. Anna Mier. R. Eyermann.

School of Summoning
> Lily Connors. Mike Barnes. Cassie Gustafson.

School of Illusion
> Jeremy Bottroff. ninemil. Miranda Floyd. Doridario. Rachel Ward. Michelle Dubie Mitchell. Adelai M. Terri Oda. Rod Holdsworth. Ashley Valencia. Kathy Bond. Fred Paffhausen.
>
> Setec Astronomy. Meaghan Horner. Carl Rigney. Rory and Rowan. Lark Cunningham. Lee Morey. Phillip Duggan. Heather M. Hostetler.

School of Conjuration
> Henrik Lerdahl. Rel. Marshall F. Lager. Olotie Lothwen.

School of Mending
> Helen J. Hogge. D Taylor-Rodriguez.

If You Liked This Title, You Might Also Like:

The Circlet Treasury of Erotic Wonderland
Edited by J. Blackmore

The Circlet Treasury of Erotic Steampunk
Edited by J. Blackmore & Cecilia Tan

The Circlet Treasury of Lesbian Erotic Science Fiction and Fantasy
Edited By Cecilia Tan

The Siren and the Sword:
Book One of the Magic University Series
By Cecilia Tan

The Tower and the Tears:
Book Two of the Magic University Series
By Cecilia Tan

The Incubus and the Angel:
Book Three of the Magic University Series

Spellbinding: Tales from Magic University
Edited by Cecilia Tan

The Poet and The Prophecy
Book Four of the Magic University Series
By Cecilia Tan

The Eidolon Initiative
by Vinnie Tesla